Elizabeth
front tow
life. She beg

ent. More than ies went on
be pub d or broadcast; in 1976 she won a national
short story competition and her success led her onto write
full-length novels for both adults and children.

Also by Elizabeth Jeffrey:

Elizabeth JEFFREY

Cast a Long Shadow

piatkus

PIATKUS

First published in Great Britain in 2001 by Judy Piatkus Publishers Ltd
This paperback edition published in 2012 by Piatkus

The location of Kenton's Scythe and Edge Tool Company is based on the
Abbeydale Industrial Museum, Abbeydale Road, Sheffield, although all the
characters and events in the book are entirely fictious.

A CIP catalogue record for this book
is available from the British Library.

ISBN 978-0-7499-5794-0

Printed and bound by Clays Ltd, St Ives plc

Papers used by Piatkus are from well-managed forests
and other responsible sources.

MIX
Paper from
responsible sources
FSC
www.fsc.org FSC® C104740

Piatkus
An imprint of
Little, Brown Book Group
100 Victoria Embankment
London EC4Y 0DY

An Hachette UK Company
www.hachette.co.uk

www.piatkus.co.uk

To Lynn and Stephen
And their children, my grandchildren
Benjamin and Jessica
With my love

Chapter One

It was late afternoon and the daylight was beginning to fade. Poppy waited until the tram had rattled off up the road, then she tucked a stray strand of hair up under the black straw hat that was perched squarely on her dark curls and straightened the jacket of her one and only costume. The coat and skirt were of good quality, dark wine-coloured wool, bought for her by her father in happier and more prosperous days, but now there was added a wide black band round the sleeve above the elbow. To an onlooker on that cold, damp February day in the year 1916 the only sign that Poppy was nervous was the way she was anxiously chewing her lip.

Taking a deep breath, she picked up her two suitcases, straightened her shoulders and crossed the road to begin her search. She was looking for Dale House, Whirlowdale Road, Sheffield. The address had burned itself into her brain.

'Just up t'hill yonder, then tek t'road on t'left. That'll be where Dale House is,' the tram conductor had said when she alighted. The hill was quite steep, wooded on one side and with her heavy suitcases she was glad when she came to the turning. The houses, what few there were, appeared to be mostly set back from the road and separated by tall trees and hedges. She was beginning to wonder if she had come to the wrong place after all when she saw the name DALE

1

HOUSE engraved on a stone pillar beside a tall and rather shaggy laurel hedge.

Relieved, she hurried through the gateway and then stopped, catching her breath. The house behind the hedge was so big! Much bigger than anything she had expected, although in truth what had she expected? She'd had nothing to go on. Nothing, that is, except an old faded sepia photograph she had found tucked behind a drawer when clearing out her father's desk after his death six weeks ago.

The photograph was a group of three people: a young man and two girls, one wearing a dark floor-length dress with the suspicion of a bustle, her hair piled up in an effort to make her look older and the other, much younger, in a white dress, flounced, with a sash, white stockings and black pumps. The young girl had an impish look about her, an air of suppressed excitement, and her hair fell in loose ringlets with a floppy bow over one ear. On the back of the photograph was written *Josiah's children, Arthur 21, Kate 19, Meg 13* and the date, *March 1882*. Underneath, in her father's neat copperplate handwriting, was an address. Poppy had spent a long time studying the photograph. There was no doubt that the young man was her father, his features had changed little over the years, and the two girls were clearly his sisters. His sisters ... her aunts ... Her aunts. Poppy had repeated the phrase over and over, mystified as to why he had never spoken of them. Never even spoken of Josiah, his father.

Why had he hidden the photograph? Why, until that moment, had she never known he had a family at all? Why had he never told her?

She realised that the only way to find out about his – and her family – was to write to the address on the back of the photograph. It was a long shot and she didn't really expect a reply. After all, it was thirty-four years since the photograph was taken. The two sisters, Kate and Meg, had probably married and gone away, their parents no doubt long dead.

But to Poppy's surprise there had been an answer to her letter almost by return post. Even more surprising, both her aunts were still living at Dale House. Their reply had been warm and welcoming and it was at their invitation that she was standing here now. Of course they couldn't know she had nowhere else to go.

She stood by the gatepost, staring at the imposing bulk of grey stone, with its squat portico and symmetrically placed windows, the longest on the ground floor and then decreasing in size till the ones under the eaves looked as if they had been jammed in as an afterthought. The house was enormous! And so grand! Yet her father had never, ever spoken about it. Even when his printing business was on the rocks and they were reduced to a diet of bread and jam he had never so much as hinted that he had come from a wealthy Sheffield family. Because wealthy they must be, to live in a house this size.

It began to rain, a soft, penetrating drizzle. With a slight shiver, she picked up her suitcases again and mounting the four steps to the huge front door she rang the bell. It jangled away into the distance with a faintly hollow sound, then there was silence. She took a step back and looked up at the windows. In spite of the gathering gloom there was no glimmer of light anywhere that she could see. Her heart sank and she turned away, tears of disappointment threatening.

Then she heard a shuffling sound and the door opened a few inches. A face, above which a white cap was perched incongruously, scowled round it.

'What's tha want? Tradesmen's entrance is round at t'back.'

Poppy was somewhat taken aback. 'I'm not a tradesman. I believe my aunts are expecting me. My name is Poppy. Poppy Barlow. They've invited me to stay.' She spoke quickly, firmly, anxious to state her case before the door closed in her face.

The scowl cleared slightly. 'Oh, aye. T'missis did say

3

summat. You'd best come in.' The door was opened just far enough for Poppy to sidle through with her cases. 'Be sharp now, we don't want to let t'cold in.' The door slammed behind her, reverberating through the house. 'Come on, this way. You can leave your cases there. Rivers'll tek 'em up in a bit.'

She followed the woman – parlourmaid? housekeeper? – as she shuffled across the black-and-white-tiled hall. As for not letting the cold in, the atmosphere struck chill, if anything less warm inside the house than it had been outside. Poppy gave an involuntary shiver and in the dim light from the long stained-glass window above the front door gained a fleeting impression of heavy, dark furniture and a carved stairway before they turned left into a wide passage, also tiled in black and white, with a glass-panelled door at the end. The woman walked with evident discomfort and Poppy noticed that under her long black dress she was wearing old carpet slippers with holes cut out to accommodate large, painful-looking bunions.

Halfway down the passage she flung open a door on her right. 'She's here,' she announced without ceremony. 'I'll fetch t'tea. It's muffins and seed cake.'

Poppy blinked as she found herself in a room, lit by a single oil lamp, that seemed to be crammed with furniture. Plush-covered chairs and settees, a writing desk, two matching work-boxes on spindly legs, a whatnot in the corner and numerous little tables all laden with china ornaments, photographs and stuffed birds under glass domes. A chiffonier with mirrored doors held photographs of Queen Victoria, King Edward the Seventh and various other minor members of the royal family plus two more oil lamps, unlit, with extravagant tasselled shades. The mantelpiece was draped in red plush and held two pairs of Staffordshire china dogs and a pair of china Scottish pipers separated by a large marble clock with a gilt face. A round table with a red plush cover and four spoonback chairs placed round it stood in the centre. It was a room that had every appearance of being stuffy. In fact, to Poppy's surprise it was barely warm.

A tall, thin, elegant, slightly masculine-looking woman in a long, dark grey skirt and white high-necked blouse, a jet brooch at the throat, her iron grey hair piled into a thick bun with a tiny lace cap perched on top, got up from her armchair by the somewhat meagre fire and held out her hands.

'Poppy!' she said warmly, taking both her hands. 'How very nice to see you.' As she leaned forward and kissed her Poppy got the impression of a cool, papery-dry cheek and a waft of lavender water.

She turned her head, smiling, still holding Poppy's hands. 'Look, Meg. Poppy has arrived. Arthur's daughter. You remember, I told you she would be here this afternoon?' She led Poppy between the furniture to where her sister sat on a small couch by the window, surrounded by multicoloured scraps of material and embroidery silks. Meg was the exact opposite of her sister, small and dumpy, very feminine, with curly white hair escaping from under her cap and an unlined, pink and white complexion.

'Don't get up, Aunt Meg,' Poppy said, bending over and kissing her smooth pink cheek as Meg, flustered, tried to gather her belongings into some semblance of order so that she could get to her feet. Again there was the waft of lavender water.

Meg looked up at her and then quickly looked away. 'Arthur's daughter,' she repeated, touching the spot where Poppy had kissed her. 'How nice. Yes. Kate said Arthur's daughter would be coming.' She looked a little bewildered. 'But where is Arthur? Isn't he coming, too?'

'No, dear. Don't you remember? I did tell you,' Kate said patiently. 'Arthur has died. That's why Poppy wrote to us. To tell us he had died.'

'Oh.' Meg returned to sorting out her silks.

Kate turned back to Poppy. 'I'm sorry about that, Poppy.' She glanced at Meg and lowered her voice. 'She doesn't always understand . . .' Her voice rose again. 'It was good of you to write to us, my dear. Naturally, we'd often wondered about Arthur. But of course, there was no question . . .' She broke off as the woman who'd let her in returned with the tea tray and put it down on the table beside her chair.

'Thank you, Mrs Rivers,' Kate said, seating herself. She looked up. 'Ask Rivers to take Miss Poppy's cases up to her room, will you? The room next to Miss Meg's. That's the one you've prepared, isn't it?'

'Aye. He's already done it,' Mrs Rivers said shortly.

'And is the bed well aired?'

'I dunno about that. It's not been slept in for years. I've put a hot brick in it. Can't do more than that.'

'Thank you, Mrs Rivers. That will be all.'

Mrs Rivers shuffled from the room. When she had gone Kate said apologetically, 'I'm afraid Mrs Rivers is rather inclined to take liberties. But she's been with us a long time and good servants are so hard to find, these days, so we put up with her little idiosyncrasies, don't we, Meg?' She smiled across at her sister and Poppy noticed that her lips were thin and bloodless and that her smile didn't reach her eyes.

Meg fluttered her hands. 'Yes, we put up with her little . . .' The sentence trailed off.

'You mustn't take any notice of her,' Kate said and Poppy wasn't altogether sure whether she meant Mrs Rivers or her own sister.

Poppy said nothing. The behaviour of servants was not something she was at all familiar with. She glanced at the tea tray, laid with delicate porcelain patterned with buttercups and daisies, beside a heavily chased silver tea set and chafing dish, and her mouth began to water. She hadn't eaten since breakfast and she was hungry. But to her disappointment all the chafing dish held were two muffins and there were three small slices of seed cake on the cake stand. Carefully, Kate took one muffin, cut it in two and buttered

6

it. Then she handed Meg half, keeping the other for herself. She buttered the other one and gave it to Poppy.

'Meg and I have small appetites,' she explained, 'don't we, Meg? But I'm sure you can manage a whole muffin, Poppy, even though they are quite large.'

I could quite easily have managed two, Poppy thought, biting into it gratefully, but she said nothing. After all, it was wartime. These days everyone had to make sacrifices. In the event the muffin wasn't very appetising. It was slightly stale and the butter appeared to have been scraped on and then scraped off again. But the sisters didn't appear to notice and fortunately there was plenty of tea to wash the food down, because the seed cake was heavy. Even so, Poppy was glad to eat two slices, her own and the slice that Kate declined. She noticed that Meg ate every last crumb on her plate.

When Mrs Rivers had removed the tea tray Kate said, 'Now, you must tell us all about yourself, my dear. To think you are, what? Eighteen . . .?'

'Twenty,' Poppy corrected.

'Twenty, then, and we had no idea you even existed! Think of that, Meg, we have a niece of twenty years old! What do you think of that?'

Meg frowned. 'Arthur's niece?'

'No, dear. Arthur's *daughter*. He really should have told us. But there . . .' Kate shrugged eloquently.

'He never spoke about you, either,' Poppy said. 'Why was that? Why did he never tell me that he had two sisters?' She glanced round the room. It looked more cosy than it felt in the firelight and the light from the oil lamp on the table. 'Was this where he lived before he married my mother?'

'Yes, of course.' Kate nodded, her tone clipped.

'We used to play together. All the time. When we . . .' Meg's voice trailed off. 'Were children,' she added, looking almost apologetically at Kate.

'Then why did he never say?' Poppy looked from one to the other, frowning. 'I don't understand.'

'Did he never tell you anything about us?' Kate asked. She gave a sniff. 'No. Of course he didn't. It's hardly likely that he would.' She frowned. 'How long is it since he died?'

'Six weeks.'

Kate looked pointedly at Poppy's wine-coloured costume. 'You've quickly discarded your mourning,' she said disapprovingly.

'This is my best suit. Father bought it for me. He always liked me in it.' She couldn't bring herself to tell her aunt she couldn't afford to buy new clothes, even for her own father's funeral.

Kate ignored her words. 'And had he been ill for long?' she asked.

'Not really.' Poppy said briefly. Remembering the scandal in her home town when it was revealed that Arthur Barlow the printer had committed suicide she felt it prudent not to dwell on his manner of death.

'But he left you,' Kate was watching her closely, 'provided for?'

'No, I'm afraid he didn't,' Poppy said bluntly.

'Oh, dear.' Kate's face fell. She was clearly disappointed in her brother's neglect of his duty.

Poppy was stung to defend him. 'It wasn't his fault. He used to have a thriving printing business. He'd built it up over the years with my mother's help. They always worked together. But then Mother became ill so when I left school I went to work for him in her place. That's how, with her help, I learned shorthand and typing and some book-keeping. But then she died and after that my father lost the will to live. You see, they'd been very close all their married lives.'

'Your mother? The daughter of that *nailmaker*?' Kate's lips curled distastefully as she laid a slight but unmistakable emphasis on the last word.

Poppy looked at her in surprise. 'Was she? Yes, I believe she was, now you come to mention it. Her parents both

8

died some years ago when I was quite small. As far as I know I have no relatives left on that side of the family.'

'I should hope not!' Kate almost spat the words out.

'I don't know why you should say that, Aunt Kate,' Poppy said, her voice sharp. 'As I told you, my parents were very happily married.'

'Hmph. I suppose it was your mother who chose that ridiculous name for you,' Kate said scathingly. 'Poppy, what kind of a Christian name is that!'

'As a matter of fact my father chose my name,' Poppy said quietly. 'He always said that with my dark hair and little red face I was like a poppy uncurling when I was born.'

'I think it's a pretty name,' Meg said, her voice so quiet that it was almost inaudible.

'Thank you, Aunt Meg.' Poppy smiled at her. Her voice softened. 'As I was saying, my mother was a wonderful woman and my father couldn't live without her. They were in love right up until the day she died. In fact, you could almost say he died with her because after her death he lost interest in everything. Even his business. Orders were late or not fulfilled at all, mistakes were made, oh, it was awful. I tried to keep things together but it wasn't any use, especially when he started drinking.' She looked down at her hands. 'He became a changed man.'

Kate raised her eyebrows in disbelief. 'You mean to tell me that Arthur went to pieces when that wo— your mother died?'

'Yes. That's right.' Poppy nodded.

'I can hardly believe that,' Kate said firmly.

'I'm afraid it's true, whether you believe it or not,' Poppy said with a shrug. She went on, 'As I said, he became a changed man. So much so that when I tried to take the whisky bottle away from him one night he hit me with it. Of course he was full of remorse the next morning when he saw what he had done to me and he vowed he would never touch another drop. He was full of plans, how we would start a new life, the things he was going to do to pull the business round.' She gave a crooked smile and went on in a flat, unemotional voice, 'But it was too late. Even as he was making his plans the fish-and-chip shop underneath his printing rooms had caught fire and the whole building, including the shop next door, was burnt to the ground.'

'But no doubt he was well insured?' Kate was watching Poppy intently.

She shrugged. 'My father didn't believe in insurance. Said it was a waste of money.'

'And the house? Where you lived?'

'It was rented. I had no money to keep it on after –' she swallowed – 'after he died.' She was silent for several minutes, then she lifted her chin and said in a rush, 'You may as well know the whole story. The truth is, I came home from seeing if there was anything to be salvaged from the fire – there wasn't, of course – and found him hanging from the banister.' She gave an involuntary shudder at the memory, then went on, her voice barely above a whisper, 'I called the man next door and he managed to cut him down, but it was too late.' She turned her head away, aware of the sudden hostility in the atmosphere.

'He committed suicide? Arthur committed suicide?' Kate clutched the arms of her chair, her eyes standing out like organ stops.

'Yes.'

Kate swallowed two or three times. 'But that's disgraceful,' she said at last. 'I simply can't believe that a member of our family would stoop to do such a wicked thing!'

'He must have been very unhappy,' Meg whispered without lifting her head.

'He was,' Poppy said quietly.

'That's absolutely no excuse. It's unforgivable. Quite unforgivable,' Kate said. She drummed her fingers on the arms of her chair, glaring at Poppy as if that was where the blame rested.

10

Poppy screwed up her face, puzzled at her aunt's attitude. 'I'm sorry, Aunt Kate. I didn't mean to upset you. Maybe I shouldn't have told you. I wish I hadn't, now. I nearly didn't, but I felt it would be deceitful to keep it from you.' She stared down at the plush tablecloth. 'I'm sorry,' she said again. 'I do understand how shocked you feel. It was a terrible shock to me, too.'

'Understand? *Understand?* You can have no idea!' Kate shook her head savagely. 'To think that the name of Russell, the name Papa made so honoured in the city, should be besmirched with a *suicide*! Oh,' she took out a lace handkerchief and dabbed her eyes, 'it's beyond bearing.'

Poppy looked up, puzzled. 'Russell? But my father's name wasn't Russell, it was Barlow. The same as mine.'

'Barlow?' Kate's head shot up. Then her shoulders relaxed. 'Oh, thank God for that. At least the family name is safe.'

'I don't understand.' Poppy was still puzzled. 'Has there been some mistake? Have I come to the wrong place?' For a moment she almost hoped she had.

'No. No.' Kate waved her hand impatiently. 'My brother's name was Arthur Barlow Russell. Barlow was Mother's maiden name. He obviously dropped the Russell when he . . . when he left.' She pursed her lips. 'And quite rightly, too.'

'I shouldn't have come here,' Poppy said dully, watching her hands twisting themselves together in her lap. 'I realised that now. When I found the photograph I wrote to you on impulse – I was so pleased to think I might have living relatives. It was clearly not the right thing to do. I apologise.' She lifted her head. 'But as I've very little money and nowhere to live I'd be grateful if you would let me stay here with you for just a few days until I decide what to do with my life. Then I'll go away and I promise you'll never need to see me again.'

There was a long silence in which the only sound was the

11

rhythmic ticking of the marble clock on the mantelpiece. Then Meg spoke, her voice so unexpected that both Kate and Poppy turned to look at her.

'No. Don't go away. Please, stay with us, Poppy,' she said plaintively, then embarrassed at her own temerity she bowed her head and busied herself sorting through the tangle of silks on her lap.

'Yes, of course. Meg is right. You must stay with us for as long as you like,' Kate agreed, pulling herself together with an obvious effort, although her tone was a good deal less warm than her sister's.

'Thank you,' Poppy said dully. But she realised she was not really welcome, so she was determined to make her stay as short as possible.

Chapter Two

As soon as the clock struck nine Kate got to her feet and picked up a cashmere shawl and draped it round her shoulders. 'I think perhaps I should show you to your room now –' she hesitated for the merest fraction of a second, '– Poppy. You must be very tired. In any case, my sister and I never keep late hours, do we, Meg?'

'No, we don't keep late hours,' Meg repeated obediently. She too stood up and wrapped herself in a shawl.

Kate took a candle from a shelf just inside the door and lit it, then shielding it from the draught she led the way along to the entrance hall and up the wide staircase. At the head of the stairs a corridor stretched in both directions as far as Poppy could see by the light of the candle, with doors leading off on each side. Kate indicated the one nearest to the stairhead.

'That's the bathroom,' she said, 'and this next one will be your room, Poppy. Meg's room is the next one along and mine is opposite. Mrs Rivers will bring you tea and hot water in the morning.' She held the candle high. 'I think you'll find everything you need here. Ah, yes, Rivers has brought up your cases I see.' She went over and lit the candle by the bed from the one in her hand. 'Goodnight, my dear. Sleep well.' She kissed Poppy's cheek coolly and left the room as if she couldn't get out fast enough.

Meg waited until her sister had left, then she grasped

Poppy's hand. 'Please don't leave. Please stay with us,' she whispered urgently.

'Come along, Meg. Don't stand all night chattering,' Kate's voice called from the landing.

Meg squeezed the hand she still held. 'I'm glad you've come. Whatever she says, I'm glad you've come. Goodnight, Poppy.'

Poppy bent and kissed her. 'Goodnight, Aunt Meg.'

The door closed and Poppy took stock of the room. It was difficult to see very much by the light of one candle and she wondered why the gas hadn't been lit since there were gas mantles on the chimney breast, but she could see that the room was large and furnished with heavy furniture that looked to be of very good quality. It was icy cold.

She yawned and shivered. She was very tired. The day had been emotionally draining: leaving the little house in Rotherham for the last time and coming to Sheffield uncertain as to how she would be received, fearful of the future. And then Aunt Kate's decided change of mood when she had spoken of her father's death. Of course, a suicide in the family was a terrible disgrace yet, unlike her aunt, Poppy couldn't find it in her heart to blame her father for what he had done, knowing how unhappy he had been.

Poppy shivered again and her teeth began to chatter. A fire in the grate would have been more welcoming than the decorative fan of paper that graced it. And in a prosperous house like this it shouldn't have been too much to ask of one of the maids. Hurriedly, she opened her suitcase and found a nightgown. The rest of the unpacking could wait until morning. She quickly undressed, careful to hang her coat and skirt over the back of a chair so that they didn't crease, and got into bed. It was still warm where Mrs Rivers had put the hot brick, but when she pushed an experimental toe down to the foot of the bed it struck so cold that it felt damp.

She curled herself into a ball and hugged the brick to keep warm while she took stock of the situation and tried to ignore the fact that she was hungry. A stale muffin and two slices of heavy cake were hardly enough to take her through the night.

Almost as if she had spoken aloud there was a tap on the door and Mrs Rivers shuffled in wearing a shapeless dressing gown.

'I've brought you a bit of bread and dripping,' she whispered. 'Them two don't eat enough to keep a sparrow alive but I guess a young lass like you is still clemmed.'

Poppy sat up in bed and took the plate gratefully. On it were two doorsteps of bread and dripping. 'Oh, thank you, Mrs Rivers. I was just thinking I was never going to be able to sleep for hunger.'

Mrs Rivers nodded. 'No need for that, lass. Any time you're hungry just come to the kitchen. I can allus find you a bit o' bread and jam or summat.' She tapped the side of her nose. 'Just don't let on to them.' She jerked her head in the direction of the other bedrooms.

Poppy ate the bread and dripping with relish. When she had finished she snuggled back between the sheets – they definitely did strike lightly damp – and hugged the brick again. She recalled with affection the tiny cottage she had left earlier in the day, the cottage in which she had spent her life until now. It was so small it would have fitted into the big entrance hall of Dale House and left room to spare. Dale House, the home – the mansion! – her father had rejected, along with his family name, years ago before she was even born. Why had he done that? Why had he never mentioned his family's wealth? Why had he never spoken about his two sisters? Why had he never, ever mentioned his past?

And what about his two sisters, her aunts? Kate was obviously in charge and made the decisions. But what of Meg, who was so clearly intimidated by her sister? Gentle little Meg, who had begged her to stay on at Dale House, whilst Kate, it seemed, couldn't wait to be rid of her. What would be the right thing to do? Should she stay? Or should she leave? And if she left, where should she go? The questions circled round and round in her brain until at last she fell into an exhausted sleep.

She woke as Mrs Rivers tapped on the door and shuffled in with a cup of tea and an enamel jug of hot water. She was wearing an enormous shapeless grey cardigan over a faded overall, and the same old carpet slippers.

'You'll not want to use t'bathroom for washing. It's like a morgue in there, and there's no hot water,' she said, putting the jug down beside the marble-topped washstand. She gave a shiver. 'Not that it's much better in here, it's that cold the whole house is like a perishin' ice house. You'll need to wrap up warm if you're to stay here, lass, I'll tell you that for nowt.' She went over and pulled back the heavy brocade curtains. A shower of dust motes floated down as she let in the pale February morning. 'Breakfast is at eight thirty. She likes it prompt, an' all.' She shuffled towards the door.

Poppy sat up in bed and hugged her knees. 'Thank you, Mrs Rivers. I'll try not to be late.' She glanced at her wrist watch, a present from her father in happier days. 'Three quarters of an hour.' She glanced up as Mrs Rivers reached the door. 'Oh, Mrs Rivers, where do my aunts take breakfast?' She had visions of scuttling about the house, opening doors and closing them again as she tried to find them, and upsetting Aunt Kate by being late.

Mrs Rivers turned back, her eyebrows raised. 'Why, in t'parlour. Where they were last night. That's the room they allus use. You'll not find a fire anywhere else in this house. 'Cept in t'kitchen, o' course.'

'I see. No, I suppose not. Everybody has to make economies with this wretched war. Oh, what shall I do about my bed? Shall I make it myself or will the servants . . .?'

'Servants?' Mrs Rivers eyebrows went up even further. 'There's no servants here, lass. Only me and Rivers.'

'Oh, I beg your pardon.' Poppy realised she had made a grave mistake in thinking that there might be. 'Well, thank you, Mrs Rivers.' She gave a little laugh. 'I'll make sure and leave my room tidy then.'

Mrs Rivers nodded and gave a ghost of a smile. 'It'd be a help, miss.'

Realising she had redeemed herself a little, Poppy climbed out of bed and threw back the covers. The sheets were very good quality linen but to her amazement they were patched, and not just patched, there were patches over the patches. No wonder the bed had felt so uncomfortable! What with that and the lack of servants she was beginning to wonder if perhaps her aunts were not quite so wealthy as she had first thought.

Shivering in the cold morning air she washed and dressed quickly, glad of the hot water Mrs Rivers had brought. As she brushed her dark curls and fastened them at the nape of her neck with a tortoiseshell comb she surveyed herself in the slightly pitted mirror of the dressing table. A rather pale, serious face looked back at her, the nose slightly too long, the mouth slightly too wide. It was her eyes, warm and brown, dancing with golden lights and fringed by long dark lashes, that redeemed her features and made her beautiful, a fact of which she was quite unaware.

She turned away from the mirror to unpack her suitcase and hang up her clothes in the wardrobe, fortunately empty apart from the smell of mothballs. The rest of her belongings she put in the chest of drawers. After that she made her bed and covered it with a bedspread that she found folded on the ottoman at the foot of the bed. To her amazement, when she threw it over the bed she was greeted with an extraordinary burst of colour from the most exquisite patchwork quilt. Examining it, she discovered that it was made up of small hexagonal pieces of material in all the colours of the rainbow, carefully hand-stitched together. And as if that were not complicated enough, into each separate hexagon a recognisable flower was embroidered, a

17

bluebell, a primrose, a wallflower – every flower Poppy could think of was there somewhere. Even her own namesake, a poppy. The quilt was a work of art and it was obvious from its bright fresh look that it had not long been finished. She stood for a long time simply admiring it and the intricate workmanship that had gone into the making of it.

Yet somehow it seemed out of place lying there on the bed, because in daylight the room itself looked dowdy and neglected. Cobwebs adorned the ceiling and although the furniture was obviously of the best quality it was dull for want of polish, and thick with dust. She noticed too that of the delicate china on the washstand and dressing table – all matching – several pieces were cracked and the soap dish had no lid. The carpet too was faded and worn, and on closer inspection she could see that the heavy red brocade curtains had faded in the sun and rotted into dirty pink folds. Poppy was perplexed. The aunts had had nearly a week to prepare for her coming, yet they had put her into this shabby, faintly grubby room. Was this further evidence that she was not welcome?

Thoughtfully she left the room and poked her head into the bathroom. A bathroom was a luxury she had never in her life known but this one was univiting. It was big and freezing, the white tiles halfway up the walls and peeling dark blue paint above them doing nothing to give even the illusion of warmth to the atmosphere. Dominating the room was a huge enamelled iron bath with ugly claw feet and a complicated system of pipes behind it. An orange stain marked years of a dripping tap. Above the bath was an evil-looking cylinder that Poppy could only suppose was some kind of gas water heater. Beside the bath stood a porcelain washbasin lavishly patterned in blue and white with a huckaback towel hanging beside it and on the far side of the room, which meant that you had to skirt the bath to reach it, was a throne-like edifice in matching blue and white porcelain, with a mahogany seat, standing on a kind of dais. High above this was a rusty blue-painted cistern with a chain hanging from it.

Poppy shuddered and closed the door.

Downstairs Kate and Meg were already sitting at the breakfast table. Although a small fire burned in the grate they were both wrapped in their shawls.

Kate greeted her warmly and indicated a chair on the far side of the table, away from the fire. Poppy was glad she had put on her warmest clothing.

Meg smiled happily but said nothing as Poppy took her seat.

'I trust you slept well, my dear,' Kate said, the coldness of the previous evening apparently forgotten.

'Thank you. Yes.' It would hardly have been polite to point out that the bed was damp.

'Pass Poppy the toast, Meg,' Kate ordered, as she poured tea from a china teapot. Poppy noticed that the table this morning was laid with china which, although very pretty and with everything, including the teapot, matching, was not quite as fine as the exquisite Chelsea porcelain used the previous day.

'Butter, or marmalade, my dear?' Kate asked, handing Poppy her tea.

But obviously not both, Poppy registered with some surprise. The aunts clearly took to heart the newspapers' repeated instructions for wartime economy. 'Butter, please, Aunt Kate.' At least there was no shortage of toast.

'I owe you an apology, my dear,' Kate said, dabbing at the corners of her mouth with her napkin after eating her one slice of toast. 'Please forgive me for seeming so unwelcoming last night. I can only say it was the shock of hearing about Arthur's ... about your father. It was so ... unexpected. I hope you can understand.' She looked anxiously at Poppy.

'Yes, of course, Aunt. I know exactly how you felt. I can hardly believe it myself – even now.' Poppy bit her lip against the tears that still threatened when she thought of her father.

Kate patted her hand. 'Well, you've got us now, dear. It must be a relief to know you're not alone in the world.'

Silently, Meg handed Poppy a lace-trimmed handkerchief and she blew her nose.

Kate nodded approvingly. 'There, that's better. Now, would you like more toast?' She handed Poppy the toast rack. Her voice changed. 'You don't wish for any more, do you Meg? You do? Oh, very well.' The toast rack was passed on and Kate turned her attention back to Poppy. 'I don't sleep well,' she went on, 'and I thought over what you had told us many times during the night.' She leaned over and laid a hand on Poppy's arm. 'Dear child, you must have suffered so much ... the last thing we would want is to add to your troubles. After all, the blame for what Arthur did could hardly be laid at your door.' She smiled. 'Suffice it to say that your Aunt Meg and I will be more than happy for you to make your home here with us. Permanently. In fact, we insist on it. Isn't that so, Meg?' She leaned back in her chair and picked up her cup and saucer, watching for Poppy's reaction.

'Indeed it is,' Meg picked up her own cup, nodding happily.

'You're very kind, Aunts, both of you,' Poppy murmured uncertainly. 'But I ...'

'That's settled, then.' Kate reached for the toast rack, the subject closed. 'Do finish up the toast, dear, we don't want it to go to waste. We don't like waste, do we, Meg? Not when there are so many hungry people about. And so many shortages with this dreadful war.'

'Dreadful war,' Meg repeated dutifully.

After a few moments Kate turned back to Poppy. 'You're very quiet, dear. Are you not happy with our suggestion that you make your home with us?'

Poppy finished spreading butter on her toast. Then she looked up at her aunt. 'It's not that, Aunt Kate. It's just that, well, ever since I've been here you've hinted at something my father did in the past that caused a rift in the family and if I'm to stay here I think I ought to be told what it was. Why did he never tell me? Why did he never mention that he had two sisters? We lived a very simple – I could say frugal – life, my parents and I. Why did he never say that he had come from ...' she hesitated, 'such a wealthy family?' She paused and picked up her toast but before she bit into it she finished quietly, 'I think I've a right to know, don't you?'

'Yes, I think you have.' It was Meg who spoke.

'Be quiet, Meg. Nobody asked you,' Kate said sharply. 'And look, you haven't taken your pill.' She indicated a small white tablet beside Meg's plate.

'Oh, no. I'd forgotten it.' Immediately Meg swallowed the pill with a sip of tea.

'Meg gets funny turns. The pills help,' Kate explained briefly and Meg gave a small, almost guilty smile.

'My father?' Poppy persisted. 'You haven't said ...' She had an uncomfortable feeling that the interruption over the pills had been intended to divert her attention. Kate drained the last of her tea, threw down her napkin and got to her feet.

'Very well,' she said with a trace of irritation. 'Come with me.' She turned to Meg. 'You'll be all right here, won't you, dear? You've got your silks to sort.'

Meg had already half risen. 'I thought I might come too,' she said diffidently.

'No, dear, there's no need. You stay here where it's warm. It's a very cold day and I wouldn't want you to catch one of your colds.'

'Very well, Kate.' Meg's shoulders sagged but she moved obediently to the settee under the window.

'We'll be back soon, Aunt Meg,' Poppy said, smiling at her, before she followed Kate out into the passage and closed the door. Their footsteps echoed on the black and white tiles and their breath was misty on the freezing air as they went along to the big square entrance hall. Kate stopped under an impressive portrait that hung on the wall opposite the stairs.

21

The portrait, which in daylight dominated the hall, was of a big man in grey striped trousers and a black frock coat. His hair was grey and thinning, brushed flat across his head and his face was coarse-featured and slightly florid, with shaggy mutton-chop whiskers. His eyes, under bushy brows, were steely grey and appeared to miss nothing as they looked out from the portrait through gold-rimmed spectacles that were perched precariously on the end of his long, fleshy nose. He was posed with one hand resting on a table, the hand carefully placed so that the eye was drawn towards a large ornate pair of scissors lying beside it. The thumb of the other hand was tucked into the pocket of his grey waistcoat so that the chain of his gold hunter was clearly visible. It was a portrait of an autocratic, dominant man; a man who was fully aware of his worth. And his power.

Poppy shivered as she stared up at it, and pulled her thick woollen jacket more closely round her and tucked her hands into the sleeves, unsure whether it was the portrait or the temperature of the house that had suddenly made her feel so cold.

Chapter Three

Aunt Kate was gazing adoringly up at the portrait, unaware of Poppy's involuntary shudder. 'That's Papa,' she said proudly. 'Your grandfather, of course,' she added over her shoulder. 'An identical portrait to this one hangs in the Cutlers' Hall, down in the city.'

'He looks very ...' Poppy put her head on one side and searched for a suitable word. It was difficult since she instinctively disliked the man. '... important,' she finished lamely.

'Indeed, he was.' Kate's chin lifted as she gazed at the portrait. 'He was one of the most important men in Sheffield.' She turned to Poppy. 'You've heard of Russell's, of course.' Poppy shook her head. 'No? Goodness me, I *am* surprised. The name of Russell is known far and wide in the manufacture of scissors. Papa was the biggest scissor manufacturer in the whole of Sheffield. Of course,' she added hurriedly, 'Papa didn't make the scissors himself, he employed men to do all that, mostly craftsmen known as Little Mesters, working in their own workshops dotted about the city. I believe that's how his father started, years ago, as a Little Mester. But Papa was a businessman and when he inherited his father's business he expanded it to what it became, Russell's of Sheffield.' She turned back to the portrait with something akin to reverence. 'Such a shrewd businessman, he was.

And *very* highly thought of. Do you know, he was Master Cutler no less than *three* times.'

'Indeed?' In her ignorance Poppy was unimpressed. 'What happened to the firm?' she asked. 'Is it . . .?'

'No.' Kate's smile faded and her thin mouth became pinched, her tone clipped. 'It's no longer in the family. When Papa died it had to be sold. We had no choice. There was nobody to carry it on, since Arthur, the only son, the heir to the Russell estate, hadn't seen fit to do his duty.'

'Ah, I see,' Poppy breathed.

Kate turned on her. 'No, you don't. You don't see at all.'

'Then, please . . .' Poppy took her hands out from the warmth of her sleeves and spread them. 'I've asked you to tell me.'

Her eyes still on the portrait, Kate backed and sat down on the stairs, her serge skirt spreading round her like a leaden grey sea and her purple cashmere shawl clutched round her. Once again Poppy noticed that her square-jawed face had a stern, almost masculine look as she began to speak.

'It broke poor Papa's heart,' she said, 'the way Arthur behaved. He was such a clever boy, handsome, too. There was no doubt he was Mama's favourite and, of course, being the only boy Papa had great plans for him.' She glanced up at Poppy, standing beside her, her hand on the newel post. 'I wouldn't want you to think we were jealous, Meg and I,' she said quickly. 'We were not. Not in the least. We were just as proud of Arthur as Mama and Papa were. He was our golden boy, the golden boy of the family.'

'So what happened?' Poppy prompted quietly.

'When he was old enough Papa took him into the business. Naturally, he was made to start at the bottom and work his way up so that he would know every part of the business by the time Papa was ready to hand over to him in the fullness of time.' She sighed. 'Such a wonderful opportunity. My goodness, if I'd been a man ...' She shook her head impatiently. 'But the stupid boy threw it all away. He said he hated scissor-making and everything to do with it and simply refused to learn about it. Worse, he announced that he wanted to be a journalist! Can you imagine? A member of the Russell family a *journalist*!' Her lip curled derisively. 'But he was headstrong! As soon as he was old enough he left Russell's and went to work for the local newspaper, the *Sheffield Daily Telegraph* I believe it was. Of course, Papa was very angry but he was a reasonable man and he decided to let him have his head, thinking that he would soon tire of working all hours for a pittance and come crawling back.'

'But he didn't,' Poppy said, already full of admiration for her rebellious father.

Kate shook her head, her mouth pressed into a tight line. 'No. He didn't. Mind you, he probably would have done if he hadn't met up with this chit of a lass who was also working on the newspaper – the daughter of a *nailmaker*, if you please. He even suggested that he should bring her home and introduce her to the family.' She gave a disapproving sniff. 'As you can imagine, Mama quickly put her foot down and said she was having no common nailmaker's daughter in her house.' Kate nodded. 'And quite rightly so. There was the most fearful row. It was such a pity. If only Arthur had seen sense ...' She paused, staring up at her father's portrait. 'He knew perfectly well that Papa had these great plans for him, yet the stupid boy threw his future away. It was all so unnecessary. All he had to do was to give up the wretched girl. But he refused. He said he was determined to marry her and if we wouldn't accept her he wanted nothing more to do with us.' She shrugged and turned her head away, suddenly embarrassed. 'Of course, Papa told him there was no need for such extreme measures. If the girl was – in trouble – he would pay her off. These girls can always be ...'

Outraged, Poppy crouched down so that her face was on

a level with Kate's. 'If you're insinuating that my father only married my mother because she was to have a child ...' She saw Kate wince at her indelicacy but she went on, 'Then you couldn't be more wrong. They had been married for over eleven years and had given up hope of ever having children when I was born.' Her voice dropped. 'My birth nearly killed my mother and she never properly regained her health after it, although she never complained.' She stood up again and stared down at her aunt. 'I refuse to hear a word against my mother. She was a wonderful woman and my father worshipped her.'

Kate gave another, disinterested shrug. 'That's as may be. But there's no gainsaying that it was she who caused the rift in the family because when our parents, quite rightly, refused to have anything to do with her Arthur walked out of the house and we never saw him again.'

'Didn't you even know he had left Sheffield and started up his own printing business in Rotherham?'

Kate waved a hand. 'I believe there was a rumour to the effect that he was running some paltry local newspaper or other but we took no notice. It was of no interest to us.'

'How sad.' Poppy shook her head. There was no point in trying to explain.

Kate got to her feet, her eyes blazing. 'Sad! It was nothing short of a tragedy! My father was one of the most important men in Sheffield and Arthur would have followed in his footsteps if he had shown a modicum of sense and responsibility. Instead of that, he left Papa to shoulder everything. And it killed my mother. She went into a decline and was dead within two years.'

'I'm sure ...' Poppy began.

Kate took no notice. She pulled back her shoulders and went on, 'Fortunately, Papa had me to rely on. I was the eldest – Meg is six years my junior so she was still a child – and I took over Mama's place in the running of the house.' She gave a smug smile. 'Papa often used to say he didn't know how he would manage without me.' She

26

glanced at Poppy. 'As I told you, he was Master Cutler no less than three times and on two of those occasions he chose me to be the Mistress Cutler.' She smoothed her skirt. 'It was a great honour, I can tell you, because the Master Cutler of Sheffield is second only in importance to the Lord Mayor of London. Of course, there is always a great deal of entertaining to be done – all at the Master Cutler's own expense, too. Only the very richest men in the city aspire to be the Master Cutler.' She gave Poppy a patronising smile. 'So you see now what your father gave up to marry your mother.'

Poppy looked round the lofty hall. The crystal chandelier, hanging from a chain anchored high up in the roof, was festooned with cobwebs but it still managed to reflect the coloured lights from the long stained-glass window above the front door onto the dirt-ingrained black and white tiles below. Her gaze rested on the grandfather clock standing at the bend of the stairs. There should have been a gold ball in the centre of the pediment but it was missing and the pendulum hung steady in the bull's eye. The hands stood at three fifteen.

'The clock needs winding,' she said automatically.

'It doesn't go,' Kate answered, a note of pride in her tone. 'It stopped when Papa died and has never gone since.'

Over the following days, as Poppy explored the rest of the house, she kept going over and over in her mind the things Aunt Kate had told her concerning her father. Whilst she could fully sympathise with his reasons for leaving home, she simply couldn't understand why he had never, ever mentioned the beautiful house where he had lived in his early years, nor his sisters, of whom he must surely have been very fond or he would never have kept their photograph.

She found her answer when she went into the library. It was situated on the left of the front door, opposite the portrait of her grandfather, Josiah Russell. The room was absolutely immaculate, with row upon row of matching leather-bound books that looked as if they had never been disturbed since the day they were placed there. Likewise, there were huge books of maps on the map table under the window that appeared never to have been opened, the library steps looked like new and had obviously never been climbed, the two globes, one astral, one terrestrial, sat on either side of the map table like sentinels, purely for ornament, the deep leather armchairs looked as new as the day they were bought, as did the big round pedestal table in the centre of the room. It was as if it had been furnished from a catalogue in the way a library should when the house was first built, then never touched except to keep it in its pristine condition. Poppy stared round her, trying to imagine what her big, ebullient, untidy father – a man who couldn't bear pretension in any form – would have made of such an artificial sop to convention; or of the study beyond, equally pristine and unused and dominated by a huge mahogany leather-topped desk with a shining silver inkstand and a silver paper knife laid neatly beside the blotter. As she closed the door on it she recalled her father's study, comfortably furnished with a saggy old armchair, a bulging cupboard bought at a jumble sale and his desk, an old deal table with barely room for his typewriter among the piles of papers strewn over it. As she closed the door on the library she felt she was beginning to understand a little of why he had never spoken of his old home. He must have hated his father's ostentatious sop to convention and been glad to escape from it.

In contrast, Poppy discovered that the rest of the house seemed uncared for and in some parts not even very clean. The thick turkey stair carpet was badly stained, the red flocking on the wallpaper had rubbed quite bare in places and the beautiful carving on the oak staircase was ingrained with dirt and dull for want of polish. Upstairs, the same musty air of neglect pervaded each room she inspected, yet there was no doubt the furniture and hangings were all of an equal quality to those in the library. But trays of apples had been laid out on the floor in one of the bedrooms and then forgotten, with the result that most of them were rotten, and in another a large damp patch stained the wallpaper, presumably from a long-standing leaking gutter. A narrow door at the far end of the corridor revealed uncarpeted back stairs presumably leading down to the kitchens and up to the attics.

It was very odd. Dale House was the most beautiful house she had ever seen, but yet it had an all-pervading air of genteel decay. Of course, the war and the lack of an army of servants were bound to take their toll, but Poppy had the feeling that it was more than that.

She paused at the head of the stairs and looked up at the crystal chandelier suspended from the roof. Even though it was encrusted with dust and festooned with cobwebs it was still beautiful. Suddenly, as she stared at it, an overwhelming feeling of desolation and sadness swept over her. It only lasted a few seconds and was gone but it had been so strong, so real that Poppy found tears of despair running down her cheeks. Was it just her over-vivid imagination or had she become momentarily caught up in some awful thing that had happened in this house in the past . . .?

She brushed the tears away and continued down the stairs. Her mother always said she was inclined to let her imagination run away with her. Of course there was nothing sinister about the house, all it needed was a good spring clean and some fires lit to warm it up and make it more welcoming. She must try to think of a tactful way of suggesting this to Aunt Kate without hurting her feelings or appearing critical. And that gutter really needed seeing to. Maybe Aunt Kate never went into the bedroom with the damp patch so she had never noticed the state it was in.

She reached the foot of the stairs and stopped. If her imagination wasn't up to its tricks again somebody was playing the piano in the drawing room. She hurried to the door and listened outside. The music was sad and wistful and Poppy recognised it immediately. It was a Chopin waltz she was particularly fond of. A love of music was something she had inherited from her father: in happier days they had often attended concerts together. Half fearful of what she might see after her experience at the head of the stairs, she pushed open the door. But to her amazement it was Aunt Meg sitting at a grand piano at the far end of the room, her eyes closed as she poured her heart into the music.

Poppy stood in the doorway, surveying the room as she listened. It was a large room, with three long windows hung with gold velvet curtains. Opposite the windows was the fireplace, grey marble with a large gilt overmantel. The wallpaper was badly faded, except for where two large pictures had been removed, and here the gold regency stripe was still visible. Even though the carpet and all the furniture were shrouded in dust sheets it was a beautiful room, light and airy.

Suddenly, as if she sensed she was being watched, Meg's eyes flew open and she saw Poppy standing in the doorway. Immediately, before Poppy could speak, she stood up and closed the lid of the piano and slipped silently out of a door at the far end of the room. For a second Poppy was too surprised to move, then she hurried down the room after her, noticing absently as she edged her way between the calico-shrouded furniture that the carpet under its protective drugget felt thick and springy. Untrodden was the word that sprang to mind.

By the time she reached the door through which Meg had disappeared, her aunt was nowhere to be seen.

She hesitated. To her left a passage led back to the hall and the other rooms, to her right was the baize door which led to the kitchens. Perhaps this was the way Meg had gone. In her explorations Poppy had not yet ventured beyond this door, so it was with some hesitation that she pushed it open. She found herself in a dim, narrow passage covered in worn brown linoleum with three steps down at the end. She pushed open the door at the foot of the three steps and a rush of comparatively warm air greeted her.

Mrs Rivers was standing at one end of the table, hacking away at rather tough-looking meat. At the other end sat an elderly man in an ancient tweed suit and leather buskins, a greasy old bowler hat perched firmly on his head, drinking a large mug of cocoa. When she saw Poppy Mrs Rivers cleared her throat loudly and he immediately got to his feet and snatched off the bowler, revealing a lined and weather-beaten face under the pale bald dome where the hat had been.

'I'll be off then,' he said to nobody in particular, putting down the half-empty mug and wiping his whiskers with the back of his hand.

'No, please don't go because I've come, Mr Rivers,' Poppy said quickly. 'It is Mr Rivers, isn't it?'

'Rivers, miss. Just Rivers,' he replied, putting up his hand to doff the bowler he had already removed.

'Well, sit down and finish your cocoa, Rivers. I'm sure you can do with it. It must be freezing outside.' She gave him a warm smile.

'Aye, 'tis a bit nesh,' he agreed, seating himself again.

'Would you like some cocoa, Miss Poppy?' Mrs Rivers asked. 'There's a drop left in t'saucepan.'

'Oh, I would, please, I'm frozen,' Poppy said. 'No, don't stop what you're doing, I'll get it.' She reached down another mug from the dresser and helped herself, then she sat down at the table rubbing her arms to warm them. 'I heard Aunt Meg playing the piano but she hurried away before I could speak to her. I thought she might have come here,' she said, to explain her presence.

'Oh, Miss Meg wouldn't come here,' Mrs Rivers said, shaking her head. 'She wouldn't dare.'

'Wouldn't dare? Why ever not?' Poppy asked, surprised.

'Miss Kate.' Mrs Rivers threw the meat into a dish on the table. 'Miss Meg's delicate, you see. Miss Kate looks after her, won't let her do too much, that kind of thing.

31

Very good to her, Miss Kate is, specially when she gets into one of her ... tantrums.'

'Aunt Meg doesn't look the kind of person to have tantrums,' Poppy said with a little laugh. 'She's the most gentle person I've ever met.' She sipped her cocoa, cupping her hands round the mug for warmth.

'Aye. Most of the time,' Mrs Rivers said enigmatically.

Poppy waited for her to say more but when she didn't she said, 'I've been exploring the house. Aunt Kate said I could. Of course I didn't go into her bedroom, nor Aunt Meg's. But I couldn't help noticing that there's a big damp patch in one of the other bedrooms. I think it must be caused by a leaky gutter outside. Do you think Aunt Kate knows about it?'

'Oh, aye,' Mrs Rivers said again. 'She knows about it, all right.'

'Then why isn't something done about it? The wall-paper's ruined.'

'I'll have to get the ladder ...' Rivers began.

'You'll do no such thing, Alf,' Mrs Rivers rounded on him. 'I've told you before, I'll not have you climbing up there. It's a job for a younger man.'

'Aye, I know. But all t'young men have gone to t'front,' Alf said, slurping the dregs of his cocoa.

'Then it'll not get done unless she pays for someone to do it and she'll not do that.' Mrs Rivers reached for an onion and slammed it down on the chopping board as if to make her point. She chopped in silence for several minutes, then she looked up at Poppy. 'I hope you like scrag-end stew,' she said, 'because that's what we live on here, most of t'time.'

'Your stews are delicious, Mrs Rivers.' Poppy smiled. 'I've never been used to fancy food. My father was not a rich man. Not like my grandfather,' she added with a laugh.

'Hmph,' Mrs Rivers said, turning her mouth down at the corners.

'Them's ought to be worth a pretty penny. After all, Russell's sold for a goodly amount when t'old chap died,' Rivers remarked, chewing the last of the cocoa out of his whiskers.

'That's nowt to do wi' us, Alf,' Mrs Rivers said sharply. 'Any road, t'master's been dead these ten years and more.' She turned to Poppy. 'We've no call to complain, me an' Alf. Miss Kate has told us there's a job here for as long as we want it, with a roof over our heads and all found. We're well placed and grateful for it.' She began chopping carrots.

'Hah!' Rivers got to his feet and rammed his bowler back on his head. 'Tell her t'truth. Tell her we've had no wages long since.'

'We don't need wages. What do we need wages for? We get our keep. And you get your beer and baccy money from selling what vegetables and fruit's not needed here,' she snapped. 'Tek no notice of him, Miss Poppy. He allus was a moaner. Get you back out into t'pottin' shed, man, and give over complainin'.'

Rivers went out of the back door and Poppy left the kitchen and made her way slowly back to the parlour, which was what Aunt Kate seemed to call the room she and her sister lived in. Now she had the answer to her questions about the state of the house. It was quite plain that her aunts had fallen on hard times: servants dismissed, the house falling into decay, frugal meals, the faithful Rivers's wages not paid.

Now, too, she had discovered the reason for the prompt reply to her letter. Clearly, the sisters had hoped for financial assistance from their brother's estate. She allowed herself a wry smile. Surely, they must realise by now that there was faint chance of that!

33

Chapter Four

When Poppy reached the parlour Aunt Meg was busy with her embroidery, sewing a tiny bluebell into a scrap of yellow fabric.

Poppy went and sat beside her, moving the pile of material scraps that surrounded her. 'That's really beautiful, Aunt Meg,' she said, leaning over to look at it.

'Oh, I've several more here.' Meg rummaged in a bag at her feet and pulled out a bundle of pieces, all embroidered with flowers. 'I sew them all into hexagons and fit them together.'

'Did you make the beautiful quilt in my bedroom?' Poppy asked.

'Oh, yes. I've made several.'

'You're very clever, Aunt Meg.'

Aunt Meg blushed. 'Oh, no, I'm not clever. It's just something I like doing. I'm glad you like it.' She bent her head over the task.

Aunt Kate looked up from the account book she was poring over. 'It keeps her mind occupied, gives her something to do, doesn't it, love?' she said, smiling fondly at her sister.

Poppy got up and went over and sat down at the table opposite Kate. Glancing briefly at the account book she could see, even though it was upside down, that there were quite large amounts of money entered on the debit side. A piece of blotting paper obscured the credit side so it was impossible to see how much money was coming in to support these amounts. Since Kate was obviously working on her accounts this seemed a good time to broach a subject that had been worrying Poppy for some time and was even more urgent in the light of what the Rivers had just told her.

'Aunt Kate,' she began, 'I've no wish to be a drain on you and Aunt Meg. I had no idea when I came that you ...'

'Of course you're not a drain on us, dear. Whatever gave you that idea?' Kate said brightly, smiling at her.

'Well ...' It was difficult to know what to say without giving away the fact that she had been talking to the Rivers. 'Well, I've been here nearly a month now. I think it's time I found myself a job. After all, I've always worked for my living,' she finished lamely.

Kate's back straightened and she looked down her pince-nez with an expression reminiscent of the portrait in the hall. 'We'll have no talk of that, dear,' she said firmly. 'You're living in your grandfather's family now. In our family ladies don't work for a living.'

'But if you're hard up ...'

Kate's long neck seemed to become even longer. 'Who said anything about being hard up?'

Poppy swallowed. 'Well, nobody.' She hesitated. 'But I've noticed an awful damp patch on the wall in one of the bedrooms that ought to be seen to,' she said on an inspiration. 'I thought perhaps you couldn't afford to have it done.'

'Oh, that!' Kate dismissed it with a wave of her hand. 'It's not important. It's not a bedroom that's ever used.' She went back to her accounts.

'But I must do *something*,' Poppy insisted, leaning forward and unsuccessfully trying to read upside down the figures Kate was working on. 'I'm not used to doing nothing all day.'

'Have you no embroidery? Or knitting?' Kate asked without looking up.

'Yes. But I can't simply sit and knit all day.'

Kate looked up now. 'Why not, dear? It's what ladies are supposed to do.'

'Well, I'm sorry, but I'm not a lady.' Poppy was getting exasperated. 'Apart from anything else I need to earn some money.'

'What for, dear?'

'Because I haven't got any.' Poppy spoke more forcefully than she intended.

Kate frowned. 'How much do you need, dear? Would five shillings help?'

'I don't want you to give me money, Aunt Kate,' she said, trying to keep her patience. 'I need to earn my own living.' Tired of arguing she got to her feet. 'I'll go and get some things from Mrs Rivers. My bedroom could do with a good clean and polish.'

'Mrs Rivers will do that if you ask her, dear. That's what she's paid for.'

Only she isn't being paid, Poppy thought savagely, which you seem to have conveniently forgotten. Aloud, she said, 'Poor Mrs Rivers. Her feet are very painful. I'm sure she would be glad of a little help.' She smiled winningly although inside she was gritting her teeth. 'And I really don't mind lending a hand, Aunt Kate.'

'Oh, very well,' Kate said with a sigh. 'But you must stop when you get tired. There are plenty of books in the library if you want to take a rest.'

'Thank you, Aunt Kate. I'll remember that.'

Poppy spent the rest of the day venting her frustration on her bedroom. When she had finished the walls and ceiling had all been swept, cobwebs removed, the carpet brushed so that the pattern – or in places the lack of it – was revealed, the windows cleaned, the curtains very gently brushed so as not to aggravate the rot and the furniture polished to its original warm honey colour. Then she carefully washed all the china and replaced it. When she had finished, stopping only for some of Mrs Rivers's delicious scrag-end stew, she went down to the parlour again.

'Come and see, Aunt Kate. And you, Aunt Meg,' she said excitedly. 'Come and see what I've done.'

Eagerly, Aunt Meg got to her feet and followed her, Kate coming behind more slowly.

'Oh, you *have* worked hard,' Meg said, flitting from one thing to another like a little sparrow, running her hand along the smooth wood, picking up a candlestick, looking out of the window, then smoothing the patchwork quilt.

'Yes, it's very nice,' Kate said from just inside the door, her expression wooden.

'I could do the same to the dining room tomorrow, if you would like, Aunt Kate,' Poppy said hopefully, thinking of the long mahogany table and the heavily carved chairs that would benefit from a dose of elbow grease.

'No, dear, I think not,' Kate said firmly. 'You may do as you think fit in your own room, but the rest of the house – apart from the library and Papa's study, which I myself dust each morning – should be left to the servants to attend to.'

'But poor Mrs Rivers ...' Poppy began but stopped when she saw Kate's mouth set. 'Very well, Aunt,' she finished.

'Good lass.' Kate led the way back down the grubby stairway.

Poppy slept well that night after her busy day, and when she woke the next morning she lay for several minutes savouring the fruits of her labours and imagining what the rest of the house could look like if only Aunt Kate would allow her to touch it. She yawned and stretched, feeling the patches in the sheets with her feet. She simply couldn't understand Aunt Kate. Obviously, the two sisters were as poor as church mice, yet Kate refused to admit it. Why? And why, if Russell's scissor-making company had been such a thriving business when it was sold, was there so little money left? Surely the invested capital from such a sale should have brought in a reasonable monthly income? But if, as it seemed, there was no money why was Aunt Kate so adamant that Poppy shouldn't work? After all, if they were in such dire straits even a few pounds a week would help. It was a ridiculous situation and one that must be remedied.

Her mind made up, Poppy got up and dressed and went downstairs.

'The sun is shining today so I think I'll go for a walk,' she announced over breakfast.

'Very well, dear, but do wrap up, I'm sure the wind is cold,' Kate said anxiously.

'Yes, Aunt Kate.' Privately, Poppy thought that it was probably less cold out of doors than inside the house.

It was indeed a beautiful day and Poppy admitted guiltily to herself that it was good to be away from the claustrophobic atmosphere of the big old house for a while.

She walked down the hill towards the city. She had a definite purpose in mind and that was to find a news seller and buy a newspaper. Whatever Aunt Kate said to the contrary it was important to her own self-esteem that she should find employment. She was a competent typist and bookkeeper, and with so many young men away at the war more and more women were being employed. She was determined to become one of them.

She had walked for ten minutes when she found a newsagents and general store on the corner of a small road leading off Whirlowdale Road. She went inside and with almost her last penny bought a *Sheffield Telegraph*. Then she found a bench and sat down in the late March sunshine, eager to read of any jobs that might be advertised.

There were several advertisements for workers in the munitions factories but she didn't fancy long hours on her feet filling shells with substances that were rumoured to be poisonous and that very definitely turned the skin yellow. She looked further.

To her delight there were two that might be suitable and a third that was exactly what she was looking for, work that would help the war effort. The only trouble was that it specifically asked for a man. Nevertheless, she marked it with a pencil along with the other two, then folded the newspaper carefully. She would have a battle on her hands when Aunt Kate realised her intention to find herself employment, Poppy thought grimly. The truth was, Kate couldn't bear the thought of the twentieth century encroaching on her life. Sometimes, Poppy even wondered if the two sisters were aware that the country was at war, because they didn't appear to go out at all and there was never a newspaper to be seen in the house. They were content to live in a little old-fashioned world of their own, it seemed.

It's all very well for them, Poppy decided, but they really can't go on living in a house that's crumbling round their ears, with barely enough to eat, depending for unpaid domestic help on Mr and Mrs Rivers, and expect me to add to the financial burden by doing as Aunt Kate suggested and frittering away my days arranging flowers and suchlike. Not that I was ever any good at arranging flowers in the first place.

Realising she was getting more and more annoyed at the mere thought, Poppy got to her feet and hurried back to Dale House, preparing to face Aunt Kate's wrath.

She went straight to the parlour when she arrived home, stopping only to hang her hat and coat in the cloakroom on her way. Kate and Meg were in their usual places, Meg on the settee by the window, surrounded by her embroidery silks and bits of material, Kate in the armchair by the fire. There was a book on her lap but she was dozing and when she heard the door open she came to with a start.

'Dear me. I must have dropped off,' she said, quickly retrieving her pince-nez and squeezing them back onto her nose. 'It must be the heat. It's quite hot in here.' She was obviously annoyed at being caught napping.

'*I* don't think it's at all hot in here,' Meg said with a lift of her chin. She put her head down and rummaged among her silks. 'But then, *I'm* not sitting on top of the fire,' she whispered fiercely.

'What did you say, dear?' Kate asked sternly.

'I said I didn't think it was hot, Kate. Look, the fire's nearly out and I daresay Poppy is cold.'

Kate gave Meg a withering look, then turned to Poppy. 'Are you cold, Poppy? Your cheeks are nice and rosy. Your walk must have warmed you.' Her words were accompanied by a somewhat thin smile.

Poppy gave a little shiver. 'The sun's nice but it's really quite raw outside,' she said tactfully, hiding her disappointment at the sight of the meagre embers in the grate.

'Oh, very well, if you think it's necessary.' Kate leaned forward and carefully placed three pieces of coal on the cinders, then sat back to watch the flames begin to flicker. 'There, is that better? Draw up a chair, Poppy.'

Poppy did as she was told, making sure she didn't mask what fire there was from Meg, then took the newspaper out of her handbag. 'I bought this whilst I was out,' she said, handing it to Kate. 'I thought you might be interested to know how the war is going. The battle of Verdun ...'

'Oh, don't speak of such things.' Kate waved the newspaper away. Then she changed her mind and took a closer look. 'What's all this?' she asked with a frown, pointing to the places Poppy had marked with her pencil.

Poppy leaned over. 'Oh, they're advertisements for jobs,' she said casually. 'I've marked the ones that I think might be worth trying for.'

Kate reared up – in Poppy's mind there was no other word for it – and looked at her niece over her pince-nez. 'Surely you're not still pursuing that ridiculous idea of going out to *work*!' she said, aghast.

Poppy was ready to do battle. 'Yes, Aunt Kate, that's exactly what I am doing. As I told you earlier I have always worked for my living, ever since I left school when I was fourteen. I couldn't possibly impose on your hospitality any longer without at least paying for my board and lodging . . .'

'You make it sound as if you're a *lodger*, child! Remember, you're our niece. Pay for your board and lodging, indeed. I won't hear of it.' Kate pursed her lips and gave a disapproving shrug.

'Then I'm afraid I shall have to find somewhere else to live,' Poppy said simply. 'Because I refuse to remain here without paying my way. In any case,' she added, past caring whether or not she sounded rude, 'I should find it very dull living here with nothing to do all day.'

'You could find yourself some ladylike occupation, I'm sure,' Kate insisted. She waved her hand in her sister's direction. 'I'm sure Meg would appreciate help with sorting her bits of rag, they always seem to be strewn about the place.'

'They're not bits of rag, Kate,' Meg protested, near to tears.

'No, they're not. And if they were, Aunt Meg is extremely clever in turning them into such lovely quilts,' Poppy said, defending Meg. 'She blends the colours beautifully and her embroidery is exquisite.'

'Yes, you're quite right. The quilts are wonderful,' Kate said impatiently. She returned to her theme. 'You could visit the poor, Poppy . . .'

'Oh, Aunt Kate!' Poppy was beginning to lose patience now. 'Don't you realise that times are changing? We are at war. Women are needed in industry to replace the men who have gone to the trenches. They're crying out for women to work in the munitions factories, there are women bus conductors . . .'

Kate held up her hand. 'Oh, stop! You sound like one of those dreadful suffragettes,' she said disapprovingly.

'I should like to have been a suffragette,' Meg said in a small voice.

41

'Oh, be quiet, Meg. You don't know what you're talking about,' Kate snapped.

'Yes, I do. I remember Emily Davison throwing herself under the King's horse at the Derby.' There was a trace of truculence in Meg's voice.

'That was years ago. Before the war.'

'I know. But I still remember it, Kate. I thought she was very brave.'

Kate peered at her over her pince-nez. 'Are you feeling all right, Meg? Not working up to one of your turns, are you?'

'No, I'm *not* working up to one of my turns!' Near to tears, Meg put down her sewing and got up and left the room. Minutes later there was the sound of crashing chords from the piano in the drawing room.

'She always does that when she's upset,' Kate said without much interest. 'Takes it out on the piano. Now,' she tapped the newspaper, 'you can forget all this nonsense . . .'

Poppy got to her feet and began pacing about the crowded room. 'I'm sorry, Aunt, but it isn't nonsense and I shan't forget it. Apart from anything else you can't afford to keep me here for nothing. It's as much as you can do to keep yourselves and the house is in a terrible state of repair.'

'Oh, that's not important,' Kate said, waving her hand. She changed her tactics, wagging her finger and saying with a smile, 'Now, now, come and sit down, lass. You've only been here a month, there's plenty of time to think about going out to work.' She patted the chair Poppy had vacated. 'I'm sure we can come up with some kind of occupation that befits a lady.'

Poppy obediently sat down but she picked up the newspaper again. 'Anyone would think I was planning to go down a coal mine, Aunt,' she said, 'when all I'm looking for is work in an office, which is a perfectly respectable job for a young lady. Don't you realise that ladies who can type are very highly regarded these days?'

Kate sniffed but said nothing.

'There's a vacancy in the accounts department at Coles department store. I shall apply for that, and a typist is needed at Anglo Works ...' she looked up. 'Do you know what that is, Aunt?'

'It's Walter Tricket and Company, Cutlers and Silversmiths,' Kate said grudgingly.

'That sounds perfectly respectable,' Poppy ticked it.

Kate leaned over and pointed to the advertisement from Kentons Scythe and Edge Tool Company.

'Oh, not there! You couldn't possibly go there,' she said, becoming quite agitated. 'I couldn't countenance it under *any* circumstances.'

Poppy frowned. 'Why not?'

Kate shook her head. 'No. No. It wouldn't be at all suitable. It's ... it's *industry*.' She glanced up as Meg came back into the room and took up her sewing again. 'They make *scythes*,' she mouthed, trying to appear calm.

Poppy frowned, puzzled. 'I know they do, but I don't suppose they'd want me to make ...'

'Shh.' Kate put her finger to her lips and shook her head in Meg's direction.

Poppy shrugged and raised her eyebrows and turned back to read the advertisement again. 'Anyway, they particularly want a man, although I can't think why. It's exactly the kind of work I'm used to.'

Kate took a deep breath. 'If you're quite determined on this outrageous idea of getting a job I suggest you apply to Coles,' she said with obvious distaste. 'At least it's a respectable department store and not some dreadful industrial factory.'

'I'll write to all three.' Realising she had scored something of a victory, Poppy smiled at her aunt. 'Not that there's anything wrong with working in industry,' she added.

'No. I forbid you to write to all three,' Kate said furiously. 'I will not have a niece of mine working in that place where ...' She gave a glance in Meg's direction, then

43

added, 'You know where I'm talking about.' She closed her eyes, her expression long-suffering. 'Oh, write to Coles if you must,' she said with a sigh. 'All I would ask is that you give your address as number twenty-seven Whirlowdale Road and not Dale House. That way, since your name is Barlow and not Russell, nobody will associate you – as a common working person – with us, the Russells of Dale House, should you be in the hapless position of finding employment there. Which is highly unlikely,' she added smugly.

'Oh, I hope you do, Poppy,' Meg said softly.

'Be quiet, Meg. This is no concern of yours,' Kate snapped, once again taking out her vengeance on her sister. She peered at her. 'Have you been forgetting your pills again?'

Meg looked up, bewildered. 'No, I don't think so.'

'Well, you'd better have another one, just in case.' Kate got up and went to the cupboard beside the fireplace.

'No. No, I don't want another one. Don't make me have another one. I didn't forget. Truly I didn't, Kate.' Meg was on the point of tears.

Kate sat down. 'Very well. But you must be careful. We don't want you running the risk of ending up at Lodge Moor, do we, dear?' She smiled at her sister.

'Lodge Moor?' Poppy said, frowning.

Kate turned her thin smile on Poppy. 'The local lunatic asylum.'

'But Aunt Meg isn't . . .' Poppy couldn't bring herself to utter the word 'mad'.

'No, of course she isn't,' Kate said quickly. 'Just as long as she keeps taking her pills. Isn't that right, Meg dear?'

Meg gave a shrug. 'If you say so, Kate,' she said with a deep sigh.

Poppy went up to her room to write to Coles department store, musing on this strange household of which she had become a part, where the two sisters, one of them seemingly slightly unhinged – although Poppy had seen no real evidence of this – the other obsessed with her dead father, lived in this huge house in genteel poverty and quite out of touch with what was going on in the real world.

Chapter Five

Ignoring her aunt's orders Poppy wrote for all three situations and was perversely pleased when a letter came back from Coles department store saying the position had already been filled. A similar letter came back from Anglo Works but to her delight the third application, to Kentons, resulted in the offer of an interview.

When she told her aunt about the interview Kate assumed it was at Coles, and Poppy decided it would provoke less argument to let her go on thinking this.

'I'm sure you're wasting your time. But if you're too headstrong to see it there's nothing I can do to stop you, I suppose.' Kate eyed her up and down. 'You're very like your father,' she remarked. 'He was headstrong, too, and look where it landed him.' Poppy realised it was not meant as a compliment.

She brushed her wine-coloured costume and wore it with her best cream high-necked blouse. With black shoes and her black straw hat she felt suitably smart, although Kate remarked, not for the first time, that she should have been totally in black. A black band round her arm was hardly sufficient to show she was in mourning for her deceased father. Poppy pointed out, yet again, that she hadn't been able to afford full mourning but that didn't mean any lack of respect. Or love for him.

Meg's attitude was quite different from her sister's. She

was excited and fussed round Poppy when she presented herself for inspection.

'Where did you say you were going for this interview?' she asked, wondering if she had already been told and forgotten.

'To a big department store on the corner of Fargate,' Kate said briefly. 'Nowhere you would know.'

'Yes, I do. You mean Coles, don't you? I remember shopping there ... a long time ago ...' Meg screwed up her face, trying to remember. Then suddenly her expression cleared and she turned to her niece. 'Would you like to wear my brooch, Poppy?' She unpinned the pretty amethyst brooch that she always wore at the neck of her blouse and pinned it onto Poppy. 'It might bring you luck.'

'Superstitious nonsense,' Kate said with a sniff.

Poppy felt guilty at deceiving her aunt as she set off for the interview but she consoled herself with the thought that if she didn't get the job, not telling Kate would have saved a great deal of trouble.

When she arrived at Kentons Scythe and Edge Tools Company in Abbeydale Road she found that it was almost like a small village. The grey stone industrial buildings formed a rough horseshoe round a central cobbled yard, behind which was the dam that provided the water power for the machinery. A row of workmen's cottages stood just inside the gates and opposite these but set well back was a somewhat larger house, all in the same grey stone.

Poppy asked directions from a woman standing at the door of one of the cottages and was directed to the offices, across the yard and up a flight of stone steps. The noise from the tilt hammer and grindstones was deafening as she crossed the cobbles and she could see sparks flying through the open doors of the grimy-looking workshops. She had to admit that she could understand a little of Aunt Kate's narrow-minded prejudice against her niece working in industry, insisting that it was 'no place for a lady', but for her own part she found the prospect quite exciting.

Nevertheless her heart was thumping nervously as she went up the steps and knocked at the door. It was opened by a tall, rather pale man with inkstained fingers, stooped from working at his desk.

She smiled at him with a good deal more confidence than she felt. 'My name is Miss Barlow. I've come ...'

'Ah, yes.' He gave her a slightly nervous smile in return. 'Coom in, Miss. I'll tell Sir Frederick and Mr Templeton you've arrived.'

In the time it took him to cross the room and knock on the door of the inner office, which was slightly ajar, she heard the words, spoken in a loud, truculent voice, 'Well, I'm sorry, sir, but I still think it's a mistake. It'll never work. This is a job for a man, not for some chit of a lass who can't spell and has to count up on her fingers.'

The reply came in milder tones. 'Maybe you're right, Templeton. We shall see, shan't we? She should be here any minute. Ah, Soames, the lady's arrived? Good, ask her to come in, will you?'

It was not a good beginning. Obviously, somebody didn't want her here. Poppy straightened her jacket and marched determinedly across the room.

The two men stood up as she entered. The older one, obviously Sir Frederick Kenton, the owner of the place, was slightly above average height and only marginally overweight. His hair was grey, still thick and springy, and his complexion had a healthy glow. But the two things that struck Poppy most forcibly were the determined, stubborn set of his jaw and the twinkle in his blue eyes.

The other, younger man was shorter, thickset and bull-necked, with grey, hostile eyes and a black drooping moustache which he preened constantly. In spite of herself Poppy had to concede that he was handsome, albeit in a rather vulgar way. But she disliked him on sight and she knew from what she had already overheard that he was not even prepared to tolerate, let alone like her.

They all sat down. Sir Frederick did the talking,

explaining that Kentons was normally concerned with the making of scythes and other agricultural edge tools but that due to the war they now also had a contract to make cutlasses for the navy. This and the fact that the country depended on its farmers for food meant that the men who made these articles were exempt from being conscripted into the army. Then he questioned her on her abilities and Poppy had no difficulty in answering all his questions without hesitation and to his satisfaction. She could see out of the corner of her eye that the man who had been introduced to her as George Templeton, the works manager, was becoming redder and redder with frustration and when, at the end of the interview, she asked if there was a typewriter in the office, he looked as if he might explode.

Sir Frederick merely raised his eyebrows a fraction and replied mildly, 'A typewriter? Why do you ask?'

Poppy spread her hands. 'It's just that since I am a competent typist and letters look so much better when they're typed it seemed a reasonable question.'

Sir Frederick nodded thoughtfully. 'Ye-es, I should think a typewriter would be a definite asset to the office. What do you think, Templeton?'

'Can't see the use for one meself, sir,' Templeton said, his face wooden. 'Soames writes a good hand so the new clerk, whoever he is, wouldn't have much use for it in *his* work.' He laid an insolent emphasis on the word.

Sir Frederick got to his feet and went over and opened the door. 'Would you mind waiting in the next room, Miss Barlow?' he said politely. 'We shan't keep you waiting long.'

Poppy went back to the outer office. Soames was sitting at a desk where he got very little light, she noticed absently. He coughed. 'Are you to be the new clerk, miss?' he asked.

She smiled. 'I think that's what I'm waiting to find out,' she answered. She put her head on one side. 'Would you mind, Mr Soames? Would it bother you working with a woman? I get the feeling Mr Templeton wouldn't be very happy about it.' She cocked her ear as voices were raised in the next room. 'You see what I mean?'

Soames put down his pen and steepled his fingers. 'Begging your pardon, miss, but I think it might take a little getting used to,' he said, weighing his words carefully. 'But as long as you—' he corrected himself, ''t'lass was up to t'work and did it properly I don't see there'd be any call to object.' He smiled up at her, a slightly horsy smile, showing brown stained teeth. 'Better a lass who does the job well than a lad who slacks, that's what I'd say. Not that we've had any lads after it, so far,' he added lugubriously. 'They've all gone and enlisted.'

The door opened and Poppy was called back in. Her heart lifted. She knew by the murderous look George Templeton shot her that she had got the job.

'I would have liked to go out to work,' Meg said plaintively when Poppy arrived home with her news. 'It must be nice to go out and ... meet people.' She rested her sewing in her lap and stared into the fire.

'Don't be silly, dear. You know it was out of the question with your delicate health.' Kate's tone held a mixture of impatience and affection. 'Meg was always delicate,' she explained to Poppy.

Meg frowned. 'No, I wasn't. I used to climb trees when I was little.'

'I don't think so, dear,' Kate said firmly. 'You read about it in books.'

'Did I?' Meg's frown deepened. Then her face cleared. 'No, I remember. I *did* climb trees.'

'Well, never mind. Just get on with your sewing and don't bother your head about things that don't concern you. You'll bring on one of your turns. Really, Meg!'

'I don't have *turns*.' Meg put down her sewing and left the room. A moment later there were sounds of the piano being played.

'Oh, dear, she's at it again,' Kate said with a sigh as thunderous music reached their ears. 'I suppose it's better than throwing things about.'

'Does she do that?' Poppy asked, her eyes widening. She couldn't imagine little Meg becoming violent.

'No. At least, not often.' Kate gave Poppy her thin, rather patronising smile. 'Of course, you realise you're to blame for this little outburst, Poppy.'

'Me? What do you mean?'

'Well, it was the way you came in and blurted out "I've got the job" in such a – well, I can only say, in such an unladylike manner, dear.' She studied her hands, on which she wore several rings. 'You see, Meg and I are not used to such behaviour. Ladies in our walk of life don't have "jobs".'

'I'm sorry, Aunt Kate. But I was excited about it.' Excitement that was quickly quelled, she could have added.

'No doubt. Although what there is to be excited about working in a shop I simply cannot imagine.' Kate gave a sniff.

'I shall be working in an office, Aunt,' Poppy said with perfect truth.

'I suppose that's all right,' Kate said uncertainly. She stared at Poppy for several minutes. 'I suppose you think I'm very strange and old-fashioned, Poppy.'

'A bit behind the times, yes,' Poppy agreed cheerfully.

'Yes. Well, I'm sure it will be all right.' She nodded. 'But I must confess it was rather a shock when you suggested working at Kentons Scythe Company. You see, that would never have done. I could never have allowed that. Never.' She shook her head.

Poppy frowned. 'Why not?' Her face cleared. 'Ah, I suppose Sir Frederick Kenton knew your father and you imagine it would be letting the family down to admit that your niece was a working girl.'

Kate's head shot up and her eyes bored into Poppy like gimlets. 'What do you know about Sir Frederick Kenton?'

'Me? Oh, nothing. Except that he owns Kentons. It's on a big notice outside the place. I've seen it when I've been out for a walk.' Poppy crossed her fingers under the table. That was a near thing. She would have to be more careful in future.

'I see.' Kate nodded uncertainly. 'Please don't say anything about this conversation to Meg. She wouldn't understand and as you've just seen she gets upset. I don't like to see her upset.'

'Neither do I, Aunt Kate. In fact, I'll try not to mention my work at all if you think it might upset her.' She stared into the fire for several minutes. Then she said, 'Perhaps it would be better if I found lodgings . . .'

'Certainly not,' Kate said firmly, giving Poppy what almost amounted to a glare. 'That's a preposterous idea and I won't hear of it. This is your home now.' She rapped on the table to make her point. Her voice softened slightly. 'You must remember, you're all the family we've got, dear. Now we've found you it's hardly likely that we shall let you go.' She waved her arm expansively. 'One day, dear, all this will be yours.' She leaned back, watching for Poppy's reaction to her momentous words.

But if she had expected astonished gratitude she was disappointed. All Poppy could manage at the thought of inheriting Dale House was a sickly grin.

Chapter Six

Poppy couldn't help feeling apprehensive as she climbed the steps to the office on her first day at work. She would be the only woman employed at Kentons and although she was glad to be some way involved in war work she was afraid that George Templeton might not be the only one who resented her presence there.

Well, the best thing to do is to prove that you can do the job efficiently, she told herself firmly as she pushed open the door.

To her delight, the first sight that greeted her was a brand new Remington typewriter waiting on her desk. To Poppy it was as good as a sign saying WELCOME. She smiled with pleasure.

'It arrived at the end of last week, on Sir Frederick's orders, miss,' Soames said, watching her from his corner. He coughed. 'I'm afraid Mr Templeton was a bit put out when he lugged it in. He said he couldn't see what it was needed for sin' I'd allus managed wi'out one.'

'Oh, dear,' Poppy said, the smile disappearing. She had no wish to antagonise George Templeton even further than she had already. And she certainly didn't want to start off on the wrong side of Mr Soames. 'I'm sorry, Mr Soames. I hope you don't think . . .'

Soames gave a toothy grin. 'Don't you worry, miss. I soon put him in his place. I said to him, "If the little lady can type the letters and bills faster than I can write them then it'll be a godsend to this office, and so will she." I told him there's more than enough to do here now both Pilkington and Rouse have joined up.' He gave a satisfied nod. 'I'm afraid he didn't much like that. He doesn't like being reminded that other folk have volunteered for the army because he knows he hasn't got the guts to do the same.' He coughed again. 'I'd have gone meself, but they won't take me, not with my chest.'

'I should think that's just as well, Mr Soames,' Poppy said, taking off her coat and hanging it on the peg behind the door. 'After all, somebody has to look after the order books and pay the wages. My father always used to say that it was the way the office was run that determined how smoothly the rest of the works functioned.'

'Aye. And there's a lot in that, miss,' Soames said, obviously gratified that somebody appreciated his worth.

She smiled at him. He was a nice man. They would work well together. 'Well, Mr Soames, where shall I start?'

He cleared his throat and said apologetically, 'Well, there's a whole heap of invoices over there that I've not had time to file. Would you mind starting with them, miss?'

'I'll do whatever you say, Mr Soames.' Poppy set to work in her usual efficient manner. As she worked she hummed to herself under her breath, happy to be once again earning her living at something she knew she was good at and undismayed at being given the most menial tasks to begin with.

Throughout the day Albert Soames watched her. He liked what he saw. She was neat, methodical, not afraid to ask questions and, above all, cheerful. A pretty lass, too, with those big brown eyes and those dark curls to escape from the slide that was meant to hold them in place. If he'd been twenty years younger and not married with four children . . . He checked the direction his thoughts were taking. Any road, he reckoned they'd get along famously together.

Sir Frederick Kenton came in three days a week to deal with the mail, sign cheques and iron out any problems that might have arisen. He, too, was impressed by the quiet efficiency of the new lass in the office and said as much to George Templeton.

'Aye. Well, new brooms, Sir Frederick. New brooms. I daresay if the truth be told Soames is "carrying" her, sin' he's managed on his own for the past six months. It'll be interesting to see how she shapes up when we get a rush on.' George Templeton clamped his lips together disapprovingly, determined to be proved right in his opposition to Poppy's appointment.

'You may be right, Templeton,' Sir Frederick said mildly. 'We shall see.' Templeton was a good, efficient works manager, even though he was not popular with some of the men, and Sir Frederick was anxious not to upset him. 'All I can say is, she's taken down six letters in this – what do they call it? – shorthand and typed them ready for me to sign. All in one morning. It would have taken Soames – by his own admission – nearly all day to get them done. And I would have had to write them out for him first. It's saved a great deal of time all round.' Sir Frederick nodded thoughtfully. 'I think Miss Barlow will be a great asset to us, Templeton.' He pulled out his gold hunter and gave a satisfied nod. 'I might even have time for a round of golf before dinner.'

'Just as you say, Sir Frederick,' Templeton replied, his face wooden. 'Will there be anything else, now, or can I get back to the pot shop? There's a bit of a problem there.'

'Problem?'

'Nothing I can't deal with, sir.'

'Good man.'

Seething, George Templeton left Sir Frederick's office. As he went through the outer office he shot Poppy a look that would have blistered paint. Poppy smiled at him.

On Fridays the wages had to be worked out from the time sheets filled in by the men, so that they could be paid at the end of Saturday morning. Soames always did this but he suggested that Poppy should watch him and learn how it was done. At first it all looked very complicated: some of the men who had difficulty with figures used a tally system whilst others filled in proper time sheets. Gradually it became clearer and she was able to help by filling the wage packets from the money Sir Frederick had delivered in a large leather holdall and that had been laid out in piles on the desk. Carefully she wrote on each one the name of the recipient, his trade and how the money was made up. She wondered if she would ever manage to put the right faces to the names she was writing down: Jones, Benson, Earnshaw, Beckwith, Braithwaite ... the list seemed endless. Then she came to her own name and with a great sense of achievement put fifteen shillings into the buff envelope. Perhaps that would mollify Aunt Kate a little, she thought happily as she sealed it down.

It didn't.

In fact, when Poppy put the envelope on the table Kate waved it away as if it was a nasty smell under her nose. 'No, my dear. Take it away. It's your money to spend as you wish. We want none of it,' she said. She gave a little mirthless laugh. 'Goodness me, I could hardly be so hypocritical as to take it from you when you know how vehemently I am opposed to you going out to earn it.'

'But Aunt Kate, can't you regard it as rent?' Poppy begged. 'Don't you realise I need to feel independent?'

'Independent of what, may I ask? Independent of our hospitality? That would be most ungracious, don't you think, dear?' Kate smiled her thin smile and adjusted her pince-nez.

Poppy picked up the envelope. 'Very well, Aunt Kate. You are very kind to me and I do appreciate it,' she said humbly. But inside she was seething with fury. All the things that needed doing in the house, the meagre fare they were forced to live on, and worst of all, the wages owed to the Rivers, yet Kate refused any assistance. It was un-believable.

After the inevitable scrag-end stew, saved for her from the midday meal because she took sandwiches to eat at work, Poppy went down to the kitchen.

'Well, love, has it been a good week?' Mrs Rivers asked, beaming at her.

'Yes. And look, I've earned fifteen shillings.' Poppy emptied it onto the kitchen table.

'Aye, that's gradely,' Mrs Rivers said, obviously delighted and with not the slightest tinge of envy.

Poppy pushed ten shillings across the table. 'That's for you, Mrs Rivers. And I shall give you ten shillings every week until I've paid off what's owed to you in wages.'

'Ee, love, there's no need for that.' Nevertheless, Mrs Rivers flushed with pleasure to think that Poppy had given her this much consideration. 'But I couldn't tek it. Not all that much.' The ten shillings was pushed back across the table.

Poppy pushed it back again. 'Well, use it however you wish, Mrs Rivers. Aunt Kate refused to take anything from me, although it's quite obvious she could do with it, so take what you need for yourself and use the rest to . . .'

'Pay off what's owed to the butcher?' Mrs Rivers said with a faint smile.

'Oh, no! Is that why we live on scrag-end?'

'Aye. Reckon it is.'

Poppy shook her head in disbelief. 'And yet Aunt Kate . . . Heavens, what kind of a world does she think she's living in?' She turned back to Mrs Rivers. 'Well, I shall give you this much week every week and you can spend it as you think fit. Five shillings will be quite enough for my needs.' She got up to go. 'You needn't tell my aunts what I'm doing, Mrs Rivers. It's just between you and me.' She tapped the side of her nose.

'Ee, you're a good lass, Miss Poppy,' Mrs Rivers said.

*

57

It was like living in two separate worlds, Poppy mused, as she cycled to work on the bicycle that Rivers had somehow 'come by' and renovated for her. It was a warm day in late April, the sun was shining and the trees were beginning to shake out their new leaves in a burst of fresh green. Sunshine like this hardly seemed to reach Dale House, with its heavy curtains – often kept closed so that the sun shouldn't fade the furnishings – and dark and peeling paint, so it was a real joy to be out in the fresh air, to cycle down the hill and feel the breeze on her cheeks. She lifted her feet from the pedals and holding her hat on with one hand let the bicycle freewheel till it reached the bottom. Then she pedalled on happily until she arrived at work.

Several women were standing outside the workmen's cottages, some with little children round their feet, talking together as they enjoyed the morning sun.

'Morning, Miss Barlow,' they called as she went past, her cheeks glowing from the ride.

'Good morning,' she replied, giving them a cheery wave. After working at Kentons for a month she was able to recognise some of the wives. There was Charity, a young lass, surely not much older than Poppy herself, who was the wife of Mordecai Jones, who worked the big tilt hammer. Mordecai was a large man, with arm and shoulder muscles on him that wouldn't have shamed the village blacksmith, but he had a club foot, which meant that however often Lord Kitchener pointed at him from the posters that graced every wall, saying Your Country Needs YOU, the people at the recruiting offices where he hopefully presented himself declined his services. Albert Soames, a mine of information, had told Poppy that Mordecai and his wife could be seen on Sunday mornings setting forth in their Sunday best with their bibles in their hands to walk several miles to the church they attended. Albert Soames considered that it was a rather strange church they went to but, as he was wont to say, they were God-fearing people so it must be harmless.

58

Poppy also recognised Daisy Frampton. She was an enormously fat woman who, again according to Albert, had come to Kentons after her husband died to look after her father, Sam Beckwith. Nobody quite knew how old Sam was – not even Albert – but it was reckoned he was over sixty. Nevertheless, he was still a good worker and could put as fine an edge on a blade as anyone there. It was rumoured that Daisy had been 'a bit of a lass' in her day, a rumour that had probably spread because of her peroxided, carefully frizzed hair.

Up in the office Poppy went to her desk and began work. Albert had not yet arrived, which was unusual, but she had plenty to do, including some letters for Sir Frederick which he would be in to sign later in the day. By half past ten, when she had finished the letters, there was still no sign of Albert. Concerned, she reluctantly went to find George Templeton to see if he knew what had happened to him.

The works manager was in the charge room, across the yard from the office, where the charge of raw materials for making the crucible steel for the scythes and cutlasses was prepared.

'What do you want?' he asked brusquely when he saw her. 'You shouldn't be here. This is no place for a woman. Serve you right if you get a bit of steel in your eye from that.' He nodded towards where a man she recognised as Jack Earnshaw was breaking up blister steel over an anvil.

'I came to find you, Mr Templeton,' she replied, raising her voice above the noise and refusing to be rattled by his rude tone. 'Mr Soames hasn't arrived this morning and I wondered if you knew where he was.'

'Waiting for him to tell you what to do?' he sneered. 'Took you long enough.'

'I've been typing Sir Frederick's letters and I've plenty of other work to do,' she answered coolly, 'but it's not like Mr Soames to be late like this and I wondered if you knew what had held him up.'

'Aye. I know where he is.' George Templeton turned his back on her. 'Is that ready to be weighed, Jack?'

She raised her voice. 'Then do you mind telling me, Mr Templeton?'

Slowly, he turned back to her. 'I don't see it's got owt to do with you, missy, where Albert Soames is.'

'Aw, come on, George. T'lass asked a civil question. She's a right to know where Albert is, sin' she works alongside him,' Jack Earnshaw said. He turned to Poppy. 'I reckon his chest is bad. I saw one of his little ones here not so long since. Reckon she brought a message. Is that right, George? Did she bring you a message?'

'If you say so.' George Templeton turned to a lad standing by. 'Well, come on, lad, get the lime measured,' he snapped.

'Thank you very much. That's all I wanted to know,' Poppy said. 'Because if Mr Soames won't be coming in today I must do the time sheets myself or there won't be any money for the men on pay day.' She smiled through gritted teeth at George Templeton's back. 'Unless, of course, you want to do them, Mr Templeton.'

'It's not my job,' he growled. He turned round with a sneer. 'You do them, Miss High and Mighty. Let's see what a bugger-up you make of them.'

Poppy left the charge room, seething with fury. As she went she heard Jack Earnshaw say, 'There was no call to treat the lass like that, George. She's a bonny little thing and only doing her job.' She didn't hear what George Templeton's reply was.

She hurried back across the yard and up the outside steps to the office. With Albert away there was a lot to be done, calculating each man's money from his time sheet, and she knew she must double-check everything to make sure there were no mistakes because that was just what George Templeton was waiting for.

There were voices coming from Sir Frederick's office as she took her seat at Albert's desk. This was where the time

60

sheets were kept after they had been collected, on a spike. Carefully, with a silent prayer of gratitude to her father for all he had taught her, she began her calculations. But some of the figures were difficult to read because Albert's desk was against the light, so she got up and tried to drag it nearer to the window.

At the sound of furniture being moved the door opened from Sir Frederick's office. 'What the deuce is going on here?' he asked, when he saw the wraithlike lass struggling with the big wooden desk.

'I'm trying ... to get this ... nearer to the ... window,' she panted.

'Maybe I can help.' From behind Sir Frederick a young man in army officer's uniform stepped forward, smiling at her. 'Where do you want it? Just here?' He pushed it until it was under the window.

'Yes. That's much better. Thank you. I don't know how Albert has managed, working in that dark corner.' She pushed a wayward strand of hair back behind her ear, unaware that there was a streak of dust down one side of her face.

Sir Frederick stepped forward. 'Alec, this is the new clerk I've told you about. Miss Barlow.'

'Ah, yes. I've heard a great deal about you, Miss Barlow. My father sings your praises night and day but he didn't tell me your duties included shifting furniture!' Alec Kenton smiled at her disarmingly and held out his hand. He was very tall and slim, with dark hair and a small moustache. His eyes were deep-set, grey and crinkled at the corners when he smiled. His uniform suited him very well. 'Indeed, you look as if a strong puff of wind would blow you away.'

Poppy took his proffered hand. It was warm and strong in hers.

'I – I was just working out the wage bill, Sir Frederick,' she said, embarrassed at the young man's words. 'Mr Soames is not here, you see.'

'No. I understand he's unwell.' Sir Frederick turned to his son. 'Poor chap still suffers a great deal with his chest.' He turned back to Poppy. 'It's lucky we have you here, my dear. I'm sure you'll manage admirably.'

'I'll do my best, Sir Frederick.' Her lip twisted. 'I'm sure Mr Templeton will be only too glad to inform you if I make too many mistakes.' She picked up the letters from her desk. 'I've finished these, if you wouldn't mind signing them I can get them in the post.'

'A model of efficiency,' Alec murmured, watching her with admiration. Suddenly he smiled, his head on one side. 'Miss Barlow, were you the young lady I saw freewheeling down the hill into Abbeydale Road on a bicycle this morning, holding onto your hat, with your feet off the pedals?'

She blushed. 'It was a lovely morning,' she said, bending over the desk.

'Indeed it was. I was walking the dog when I saw you and I wondered who the pretty girl enjoying the sunshine in such an unusual manner could be. It quite made my day, I can tell you.' He took a step towards her. 'I never imagined I would find you here, in my father's office. What a stroke of luck!'

'Why don't you go and have a word with the men while I do these, Alec?' Sir Frederick interrupted, his voice a trifle sharp. 'After all, you need to keep abreast of what's going on here, since it'll all be yours one day.'

'Oh, Pa. Not for a long time yet,' Alec said over his shoulder, his eyes still on Poppy. He was obviously reluctant to leave. He began to prowl around the office, picking things up and putting them down. 'Miss Barlow . . .?'

'Oh, go on, lad. Go and talk to the men,' Sir Frederick growled, shaking the letters in his hand at him.

'I don't know what to say to them,' Alec protested with a shrug. 'Anyway, why should they want to talk to me?'

'Because it's your duty to show an interest. Ask them how the work is going. Find out what they're doing. That's all you have to do.' Sir Frederick waved him away impatiently.

Reluctantly, Alec left and Poppy saw him stride across to the pot shop. A minute later he was making his way to the grinding hull and a few minutes after that he was talking to Mordecai Jones. Then he came back to the office. He hadn't been away ten minutes.

'I suppose I'd better be trotting along, Pa,' he said. 'I've several things to do before I go back off leave tomorrow. Miss Barlow . . .'

'Are you seeing Claire tonight, Alec?' Sir Frederick cut across his words as he handed the letters back to Poppy.

Alec nodded unenthusiastically. 'Oh, yes. I believe her mother has something arranged.'

'I should think it would have been more tactful to let the two of you make your own arrangements, as it's the last night of your leave,' Sir Frederick chuckled. He turned to Poppy. 'My son and Miss Claire Freeman are engaged to be married.'

'Oh, I see.' Poppy raised her eyebrows, trying not to sound surprised. To her mind Alec Kenton had not really acted as she would have expected an engaged man to behave. Or perhaps it had been her imagination that had led her to think he had shown more than a passing interest in her.

'I'm coming now.' Sir Frederick picked up his cane. 'We'll go back together.'

Alex let his father go first. At the door he turned back. 'I'm not sure that you do see, Miss Barlow,' he said softly. 'But one day perhaps you'll let me explain . . .'

'Oh, come on, lad. Don't keep me hanging about all day,' Sir Frederick's voice came from the yard.

After Sir Frederick and his son had gone Poppy tried to settle back into calculating the men's wages. It took some time because she kept thinking of Alec Kenton. It was embarrassing that he had seen her foolish display on the bicycle, the more so since she hadn't even noticed him walking his dog. She resolved never to do such a stupid and unladylike thing again.

And what had he been trying to tell her about his engagement to Claire whatever-her-name-was? Was he hinting that there was something strange about it? And why should he think she might be interested, anyway?

Chapter Seven

In spite of the fact that her mind kept wandering, to Poppy's great relief the figures all worked out correctly. With a sigh of satisfaction she closed the ledger with a slam and prepared to go home. It was only then that she realised that it was over an hour past her usual time and that the works below were silent, everything closed for the night.

She looked round the office to make sure that everything was left neat and tidy, and with a final glance into Sir Frederick's office shrugged into her coat and went to the little mirror over her desk to put on her hat.

It was then that she noticed the newspaper that Sir Frederick had left behind.

She went over and picked it up. Scanning it, she saw that there were several items about the war, including one that recorded the number of Sheffield men that had enlisted in the last month and another that listed those killed or wounded. She noticed that the numbers were chillingly similar.

But it was an item near the foot of the front page that really caught her attention.

ONCE AGAIN THE RUSSELL SISTERS SHOW THEIR BOUNDLESS GENEROSITY

The Misses K. and M. Russell, of Dale House, daughters of the city's illustrious benefactor, Sir Josiah Russell, have once again followed in the steps of their most generous father with another magnificent gift, this time of £50 to the organ restoration fund at St Paul's Church.

Poppy could hardly believe her eyes. She read the passage three times, then folded the newspaper and put it in her handbag. Thoughtfully, she locked the door to the office and went down the steps to her bicycle. What on earth did all that mean? Could it be that there was some mistake? Or were Aunt Kate and Aunt Meg not quite so poverty-stricken as they appeared? But if that was the case and there really was no shortage of money, why was the house in such a state of disrepair? Why did they exist on such a meagre diet? And, more to the point, why weren't the Rivers being paid their wages?

Puzzled, Poppy got on her bicycle and made her way back to Dale House.

When she arrived, tired and hungry, she found that Mrs Rivers had made her a shepherd's pie, which, she whispered conspiratorially, contained best quality minced beef. Kate and Meg had eaten theirs – apparently made with mince of a slightly inferior quality – in the middle of the day. Mrs Rivers bore no grudges towards her employers but she considered Poppy was entitled to the best she could give her. She was a good lass, Mrs Rivers and Alf agreed as they, too, ate the best quality mince.

'My, that smells good,' Meg remarked when Mrs Rivers brought Poppy's meal into the parlour on a tray. It was steaming hot, with carrots and parsnips and Brussels sprouts surrounding it.

'Get on with your sewing. You've already had your tea,' Kate said sharply. She turned to Poppy. 'You're very late tonight, dear,' she said with her thin smile.

'Yes.' Poppy yawned widely. 'Mr Soames is ill so I had all the wages to work out, as well as doing my other work.' She shook out her napkin and began to tuck into her meal.

Kate frowned. 'Mr Soames? Is there a *man* working in your office at Coles, Poppy?'

66

Poppy's heart sank. She really would have to be more careful. 'I . . .' She began, but Kate was not listening.

'I've said so before and I'll say it again, young ladies are not meant to soil their hands by working for their living. And as for working in the same office as a man . . .'

'I think it's wonderful,' Meg said, looking up eagerly. 'I should have liked . . .'

'Do be quiet, Meg. You don't know what you're talking about.' Kate stared at her fixedly. 'If you start rambling on about things that you know nothing about you know where you'll end up, don't you?'

Meg seemed to shrink visibly into herself. 'Yes, Kate.' She bent over her sewing and said no more.

Poppy watched, frowning. Kate seemed to have some strange hold over her sister and it was clear that Meg was more than half afraid of her. Poppy wondered what it could be.

When she had finished her meal Poppy fished in her handbag and brought out the newspaper.

Meg looked up. 'Oh, you've bought the *Sheffield Daily Telegraph*,' she said, her face lighting up with interest.

'Tch, tch. Wasting money on newspapers. Whatever next, I should like to know,' Kate said, shaking her head. 'They only print a lot of lies, most of the time.'

'I didn't buy it, Aunt. Sir F— It was left in the office,' she said, nearly slipping up again. 'I saw your names in it and thought you might be interested. Look.' She handed the newspaper to Kate.

'Oh? Where? Let me see.' Kate's mood changed immediately. She took the newspaper eagerly and read the article. When she had finished she beamed with satisfaction. 'Look, Meg. Our names are on the front page. Isn't that nice? "Another magnificent gift", it says. "Following in the steps of their most generous father". Oh, yes, that's very nice.' She patted the newspaper with a little smile of satisfaction and then passed it over to her sister.

Meg barely glanced at it before handing it back, but Kate

67

was too excited to notice. 'Papa would be *so* pleased to know we are carrying on his good works,' she said smugly. 'Not that we would ever have dreamt of doing otherwise, of course. After all, it's expected of us, being the daughters of one of the most prominent men in the city.'

'But fifty pounds seems an awful lot of money to give away, Aunt Kate,' Poppy ventured. 'Are you quite sure it wasn't more than you could afford?'

Kate sat up straight in her chair and gave Poppy a puzzled look. 'Of course we can afford it, dear. We're not paupers. What makes you ask?'

Poppy shrugged. She knew she must be careful. 'It's just that I've noticed things that need doing in the house,' she said vaguely. 'I thought perhaps you were short . . .'

'What things, dear?' Kate interrupted.

'Well, there's that damp patch in the bedroom next to the bathroom, for instance. The one I told you about the other day. As I said, I think the gutter needs mending. It looks as if it's leaking badly.'

Kate waved her hand. 'It only leaks when it rains, dear. It's nothing to worry about. It's been like that for a long time.'

'And when I tried to open the window in my room . . .'

'Oh, you mustn't do that, Poppy, you'll jam your fingers. All the sash cords are broken. In any case, this is not the time of year to open windows. It's not healthy.' Kate turned her attention back to the article in the newspaper. 'Oh, I think that's very nice,' she said, putting her head on one side. 'But we usually get a mention in the local paper for our good works, don't we, Meg?'

'Oh, yes. We always get a mention,' Meg said flatly.

'Do you often give money away then, Aunt Kate?' Poppy asked, edging her chair nearer to the fire because even though it was nearly into May the room struck chill.

Kate arched her eyebrows. 'Why yes, of course, dear. We always respond generously when we're asked for help.' She seemed surprised that Poppy didn't realise this. 'We feel that we have a duty to carry on Papa's good works. As I told you, he was always very generous to good causes in the city and very highly thought of, so it's only right that we should follow his example.'

'But surely not if . . .' Poppy began.

Kate wasn't listening. 'I'll tell you what happens, since you seem so interested in our affairs, dear,' she said, her tone deceptively sweet. 'We receive a cheque each month from our investments, from which we first give to whatever good causes need our support.'

'I didn't mean to pry, Aunt,' Poppy said quickly.

Kate ignored her and went on. 'In deference to dear Papa's memory that always has to be our first priority. Then we live on what's left. It works perfectly well, doesn't it, Meg?' She gave Meg a look that dared her to contradict.

Meg shrugged but said nothing.

Kate continued. 'You see, Poppy, after the business was sold and the money invested, we insisted that our finances should be carefully ordered to enable us to continue in Papa's tradition. This is very important to us. Papa was, after all, one of the city's biggest benefactors, so it would look very ill on our part not to continue with his good works. We couldn't have people thinking we were mean – or even worse, that we couldn't afford the same level of generosity. We must keep up the standards Josiah Russell set at all costs. We, his daughters, owe it to his memory. I'm sure you would agree with that, Poppy?'

Poppy didn't agree. It was clearly not right that so much money should be given away while these two elderly ladies were living in what almost amounted to penury, not even paying their servants. But she couldn't say this to her aunt without breaking the Rivers's confidence. It was a difficult situation and Aunt Kate was watching her, expectantly. 'Well . . .' she began.

'Of course you do, dear. There's no question of it.' Kate turned her attention to the rest of the newspaper.

'I still think the gutter should be attended to,' Poppy said stubbornly.

Kate didn't answer. She was busily reading the obituaries.

With a sigh Poppy picked up the tray and took it back to the kitchen, glad that Kate was too immersed in the newspaper to object to this small gesture of assistance to their elderly servant.

Mrs Rivers was sitting in an old rocking chair by the kitchen stove, darning. Rivers was reading the newspaper at the table. Unlike the parlour upstairs, the room struck warm and cosy.

Poppy put the tray down on the draining board. 'Would you like me to wash these up, Mrs Rivers?' she asked.

'Lor' bless you, no, love,' Mrs Rivers said. 'It'll not tek me a second to do them when I mek Alf his cocoa, last thing.'

Poppy sat down at the table and pointed to the newspaper Alf was holding. 'Have you seen the front page?' she asked. 'The bit about the Russell sisters' boundless generosity?'

Mrs Rivers nodded. 'Oh, aye. There's a bit in like that most months.'

'But doesn't it annoy you that they give money away when you're not even being paid your rightful dues?' Poppy asked, looking from one to the other.

'Nay, lass, why should it? We're comfortable enough here and our wants are little enough.' Mrs Rivers smiled at her.

Poppy shook her head. 'I know it's none of my business . . . and if you and Alf are content with the way things are . . . but it just seems so *unfair*.'

'It's better than ending up in t'Union,' Mrs Rivers said complacently.

'But . . .' Poppy looked from one to the other, amazed.

Alf looked up. 'You didn't know t'owd chap, did you, lass?'

'My grandfather? No. But Aunt Kate pointed out his portrait in the hall.'

'He were a reet owd bugger ...'

'*Alf!*' Mrs Rivers shook her head at him, shocked.

'Well, he were, weren't he?' Alf was unrepentant.

'Yes, I know. But there's no need for such language in front of the young lady.'

'Sorry, miss.' He automatically touched his forelock.

'It's quite all right, Alf, I wasn't brought up in a nunnery,' Poppy giggled. 'But tell me about my grandfather, please.' She leaned her elbows on the table. 'As far as Aunt Kate seems concerned he's next in command to God.'

'We only came here a year or so before he died,' Alf said.

'And if he hadn't died we probably wouldn't have stayed,' Mrs Rivers added.

Poppy raised her eyebrows. 'Was he that bad, then?'

'I reckon he was no worse than most,' Alf said mildly. 'Once I got the measure of him I got on all right with him.' He chuckled. 'He used to come and throw his orders about, tell me what to do, how to grow this and that, and I used to say, "Yes, sir, yes, sir, three bags full, sir," and then get on and do it my way. Then he used to say, "See, I told you that was the best way to do it, Rivers," and I'd say, "So you did, sir." That way we was both happy.'

Poppy burst out laughing. 'You're a devious old man, Alf Rivers,' she said affectionately.

He grinned, obviously pleased. 'Well, it saved a lot o' trouble on all sides, didn't it.'

'I didn't like him,' Mrs Rivers said definitely. 'I didn't like the way he treated them two lasses. Miss Meg was always the apple of his eye, she couldn't do no wrong in his eyes. He used to treat her like she was a bit of delicate china, although she were a bit of a tomboy when she was young, by all accounts.'

'Aunt Meg?' Poppy said, thinking of the demure little dumpling who sat in the parlour at her patchwork all day.

Mrs Rivers nodded. 'So they used to say. I don't know what happened to mek her like she is now. They never said.'

'What about Kate? She's the older of the two, isn't she?'

'Aye, that's reet.' Mrs Rivers shook her head. 'Ee, that lass was ready to work her fingers to the bone for that man. She idolised him. The other servants – there were three other servants living in when we first came here – used to say how she took over the purse strings and the running of the house after her mother died, and her only seventeen at the time. But it was no more than he expected of her, as far as I can make out. By the time we got here she was dancing to his tune good and proper. He only had to snap his fingers and she'd jump. He could wipe the floor with her, could that man, and she'd be grateful for his notice.'

'Yes, from what Aunt Kate has told me she was really proud that her father relied on her so much,' Poppy remarked.

Mrs Rivers nodded. 'Oh, aye. Well, she would be, wouldn't she? T'sun shone out of his b— eyes, as far as she were concerned. She thought the world of the old man. They both did. Well, they didn't know no different, did they? After all, he was a big name in the city.'

'Neither of them ever married. I suppose Papa wouldn't let them,' Poppy said wryly.

'Oh, I believe Miss Kate was engaged to be wed at one time. I don't know who to, and I don't know what happened to break it off,' Mrs Rivers said vaguely. She sighed. 'She might have been different if she'd been wed and had a family.'

'What do you mean?' Poppy asked.

'Well, she might have been – well, she's a bit sort of *manly*, don't you think?' Mrs Rivers leaned forward. 'I believe she smokes, in her room! I've smelled it, when I've gone in to clean.'

'That's not necessarily manly. I've known several women who've smoked,' Poppy said with a laugh.

72

Mrs Rivers shrugged. 'Well, you know what I mean,' she said, offended.

Poppy nodded. She knew what Mrs Rivers meant. She was also beginning to understand a little of why it was so important to Kate to continue her father's 'good works'. It seemed that Josiah Russell's influence on his daughters was such that it stretched even beyond the grave.

The next morning Poppy went into work early. She hadn't been there long before George Templeton came upstairs to the office.

'Where is he?' he asked, looking round.

Poppy glanced up from the letter she was typing for Sir Frederick. 'Good morning, Mr Templeton,' she said mildly. 'If it's Mr Soames you're looking for, I believe he's still not well. Can I help you?'

'I shouldn't think so. Don't you realise Sir Frederick'll be in shortly with the money for the men? Who's going to do the pay packets, if he's not here?'

'I'll do them, Mr Templeton. That's why I've come in early this morning, so that I can get my other work done first.'

'Oh, you know all about it, do you? Getting a bit above yourself, I'd say,' he sneered. 'T'men are on piecework, y'know. It all has to be worked out proper. It teks Soames a long time.'

'I've helped Mr Soames with the wages every week since I've worked here, so I think I know what has to be done, Mr Templeton,' she said patiently. 'In any case, I used to do the wages at my father's printing works before I came here. What happens here is not that different.' She smiled sweetly at him. 'Unless you'd like to do it yourself, Mr Templeton? The time sheets are all there. I've already worked out how much each man has earned this week. I stayed late last night to finish them.'

'It's not my job. I'm not a bloody pen-pusher,' he retorted. He wagged his finger at her. 'Just you remember

73

they'll expect to be paid when they knock off at dinner time. And you'd better watch your step because they'll not expect to get their money from a chit of a lass. What a man earns is his private affair, between him and t'works paymaster. That's Albert Soames, not you.' He jerked his finger in her direction.

'Well, since Albert Soames isn't here they'll either have to put up with being paid by me or go without their money,' she said.

'I'm just warning you. They'll not like it. They'll not want their business spread all over t'town.'

Up to now she hadn't let George Templeton's rudeness get to her but this was the last straw. She stood up, her face white with fury. 'Are you suggesting I shall go about telling people what the men here earn, Mr Templeton?' she said, her voice dripping icicles. 'Just what do you take me for? Do you imagine I've nothing better to do than spread gossip around?'

'All women are gossips,' he said shortly.

'Well, I'm not. But if you're so concerned you can come up and hand out the money yourself. It will all be ready by twelve o'clock, provided Sir Frederick brings it. Ah, I imagine it's him I can hear coming up the steps now. I'll bid you good morning, Mr Templeton. And I shall be glad if you'll stay away from this office for the rest of the morning because I shall be *very* busy.' She opened a drawer and slammed it shut again as she spoke.

He stamped off, muttering, 'Bloody bits o' lasses think they can do a man's work ...' Then his voice changed. 'Ah, Mr Alec. Didn't expect to see you here today.'

Poppy froze in the act of winding paper into her typewriter. Alec Kenton here again! What on earth could he want?

Chapter Eight

'Pa's laid up with gout this morning so he asked me to go to the bank and then come along here with the money.' Alec rattled the leather Gladstone bag he was holding.

'Good thing you're still at home, Major Kenton, sir.'

'Good thing my train doesn't go till twelve thirty, Templeton! Well, I'd better get this up to the office for Soames to sort out.'

George Templeton cleared his throat. 'Soames isn't here today, sir. His chest is bad again.'

'Oh, dear. Then who's going to pay the men?'

'I'll do it, sir. Just leave it with me. I'll sort everything ...'

Furious at what she couldn't help but overhear, Poppy went across and opened the door. The two men at the foot of the steps looked up and saw her. George Templeton flushed dark red.

She ignored him and spoke to Alec Kenton. 'Ah, Major Kenton, did I hear you say you've brought the wages for the men? Good, I've been waiting for them.'

Alec Kenton looked from Poppy to George Templeton and back to Poppy again. George Templeton scowled at Poppy. 'Bits o' lasses, think they own t'bloody place,' he muttered. Aloud, he said, 'If you'll let me have them, sir ...' He held out his hand.

'It's all right, Templeton. I'll take them up.' Alec

bounded up the steps two at a time. 'There we are,' he said, putting the leather bag on the desk. 'That should keep you busy, Miss Barlow.' He grinned. 'You and Templeton.'

She set her mouth. 'He'd better not come near,' she said, through gritted teeth.

'You and he don't see eye to eye, I take it.' Alec was clearly enjoying the situation.

'No. We don't.' Poppy's eyes flashed but she didn't elaborate.

'My, my!' He sat on the edge of the desk, swinging one leg and smiling. 'I do believe the little kitten has claws.'

Poppy said nothing but she noticed in spite of herself how well his uniform suited him. His boots and his Sam Browne gleamed with polish and his brass buttons and the pips on his epaulettes winked in the sunshine. She dragged her attention back to what he was saying.

'Pa's gout isn't all that bad,' he confided, 'but I offered to come in his place this morning because I hoped I might see you.'

'Yes?' She caught her breath, unsure whether to be flattered or suspicious.

'You see, I wanted to ask you something.'

She watched as he took out a cigarette and tapped it on his silver cigarette case. Then he lit it and blew a column of smoke straight up to the ceiling. After that, he fished a scrap of paper out of his top pocket and laid it on the desk.

'That's my address,' he said. He put his head on one side and gave her a boyish grin. 'I'd be awfully glad if you'd write to me while I'm away, Miss Barlow.'

She frowned. 'Oh, I couldn't possibly do that, Major Kenton,' she said quickly. 'It wouldn't be right. What would your fiancée think?'

'In the first place she needn't know and in the second place lots of people write to soldiers at the front. News from home is always welcome.'

'Oh, I didn't know you were going to France,' she said in some surprise.

'I'm not. At least, not yet. But that's where I'll end up before long, no doubt.' He smiled again, his eyes warm.

Still she hesitated. After all, what could she tell him if she wrote? That she made her home with a couple of batty old aunts who lived in penury and gave all their money away? Anyway, she could never have letters from him delivered to Dale House.

She shook her head. 'No, Major Kenton, I don't think it would be a very good idea at all,' she said.

But he was not to be put off. 'Well, think of it this way, Miss Barlow,' he said. 'As you know, the guv'nor is anxious that I should get to know the work force, ready for when I take this place over. He says it's important that I should know the men by name, their families, etc. I don't really see why, he's going to last for years yet, but there it is.'

'I suppose it all makes for good working relationships,' Poppy said carefully.

'Yes, I suppose it does.' He drew on his cigarette again. 'So it would make sense for you to drop me a line from time to time to let me know what's going on here, hatches, matches and despatches ...' He noticed her look of bewilderment and laughed. 'Births, marriages and deaths in the families, things like that. Then when I come home on leave I'll have more of an idea of how to converse with the men. What do you say to that? It's harmless enough, isn't it? Oh, come on,' seeing she was still unconvinced. 'Even Claire couldn't object to that, now could she?'

She looked down at her hands. 'I've not been here long so I don't know many of the men, or their families,' she said at last. 'And I know very little about what happens here, except that farm implements, scythes, things like that, are made. And cutlasses.' She shrugged. 'But you know all that so I don't really see how a letter from me would help you much. Surely it's your father who can best keep you up to date.'

'Oh, come now, you're not going to refuse to write to one of His Majesty's serving officers, are you, Miss Barlow?' he said teasingly.

She wasn't sure she liked the turn the conversation was taking. Alec Kenton was engaged to be married so it was hardly right that he should be asking another woman – almost a complete stranger – to write to him. On the other hand it seemed churlish to refuse. After all, what he was asking for would be little more than a business letter.

'I'll write if I think there's anything worth writing about,' she said at last, convinced that there wouldn't be.

'That's better.' He slid off the desk and rammed his cap on at a jaunty angle. 'I shall look forward to hearing from you, Miss Barlow. Soon.' With a smile and a brief salute he was gone.

Poppy stared at the door for some time after he had left. She was not at all sure she had done the right thing in agreeing to his strange request. She busied herself counting out the wages, determined that George Templeton should have no cause to complain. Or gloat.

Time sped by as the days lengthened and the sun grew warmer. Although Aunt Kate disapproved of the bicycle, saying it was not seemly for a lady to display her ankles, Poppy insisted on using it because she enjoyed cycling to work. Often she would forsake the road, noisy and crowded with trams and horse buses, and take a short cut through the wood where she could ride along the narrow, grass-edged paths, watching day by day as the trees burst into leaf and then blossom, and listening to the birds singing happily as they went about their business of nest-building. It was hard to believe she was less than ten minutes by tram from the centre of a big industrial city.

Albert Soames returned to work but his chest was not much improved. Poppy did all she could to spare his failing strength, making sure the heavy ledgers were to his hand so that he didn't have to lift them down, carrying messages or queries to the workshops, keeping the office tidy and dust-free because that seemed to help his cough.

Even though his desk had remained under the window

78

where Alec had pushed it to get more light, Albert still hunched over his books, entering figures in the ledgers in his immaculate copperplate handwriting, his nose almost touching the paper. He had an old-fashioned method of bookkeeping and although privately Poppy considered the method her father had taught her much quicker and easier, she kept her opinion to herself and helped Albert as and where she could, always deferring to him because she was sensible enough to realise that there was a great deal to be learned from him.

Albert was quick to appreciate this.

'You're a gradely lass,' he said when she arrived at work one day. 'I never thought to say this but you've caught on to all I've learned you quicker than any lad I've ever trained.' He looked round. 'And I've never seen this office as neat and tidy in all the years I've been here.'

She took off her coat and hat and hung them behind the door. 'You forget, Albert, I'm not totally green when it comes to office work,' she said with a smile. 'I started with my mother in my father's office when I was fourteen, so I've already had six years of experience.' She sat down on her chair and flexed her shoulders, ready to begin.

'There's another letter come for you, lass. I've put it on your desk there.' He watched as she picked it up, glanced at it and put it unopened into her pocket. It was the third letter in as many weeks. He wondered who it could be from. He hoped it wasn't an admirer. He didn't want to lose the lass. He bent over his work again, frowning.

'What's the matter, Albert? Is there something wrong?' Poppy asked, trying not to think about the letter burning a hole in her pocket.

He nodded. 'Aye. I'm sure we've been invoiced for more steel than George ordered. And there seems to be a discrepancy here, too.' He pored over the figures again. 'I'll just check them again before I go to George. I'll not hear the last of it from him if it turns out to be my mistake.'

Poppy watched him for a minute. When he looked up,

shaking his head, she said, 'Would you like me to take them down to Mr Templeton? I've just seen him go across the yard.'

'Aye. Would you mind, lass? I'm a bit short of breath today.' Albert handed them to her gratefully.

'No, of course I don't mind, Albert.'

'Right, well, you can see I've marked where the problem seems to be.'

She took the invoices and went down the steps and across the yard to the workshop where the crucible steel was made. She was used now to the constant sound of hammering and grinding from the workshops all around the yard, with the booming of the big tilt hammer and the noise of the steam engine as accompaniment, and she often wondered what Aunt Kate would have to say if she knew the kind of atmosphere she worked in. But Aunt Kate didn't know. Aunt Kate still thought she worked in the genteel environment of Coles department store and Poppy was becoming adept at keeping what happened at work quite separate from her home life. It made for a more peaceful existence.

When she reached Jack Earnshaw's workshop he was putting the charges made from blister steel and lime into clay pots that had been made in the pot shop below. These fitted into melting holes in the furnace. He was wearing a long leather apron covered in wet sacking to protect him against the intense heat of the furnace into which the pots had to be set, two pots to each of the five melting holes. George Templeton, dressed, as befitted his position, in a worn and shiny black suit and bowler hat, was standing to one side, leaning on the doorpost, watching Jack's every movement until he had dropped the covers on the furnace holes, forcing the draught up to create the temperature needed to melt the steel.

'Finished that lot?' George said, straightening up, as Jack took off his gauntlets and wiped his face with a grimy cloth.

'Aye, it's all done, George.' He pulled off the wet sacking and put it to one side.

'Well, I've a message from Connie. She says she's meking bacon dumpling for dinner tonight and she'll fetch yours over to you about seven. That all right?'

'Aye. That's fine. I'm fond of bacon dumpling. She's a good lass, your Connie.'

'When she watches her lip. She's a sight too fond of . . .' Suddenly, he noticed Poppy. 'What do you want?' he asked rudely.

'I've come with a message from Mr Soames. He'd like you to check these figures, please. I think you'll find they don't quite tally,' she said, lifting her chin as she handed them to him.

'Oh, you think I'll find they don't quite tally, do you?' he mimicked. 'Well, we'll see about that!' He gave a cursory glance over them. 'Oh, it looks as if I left a nought off there. Them should have been costed at ten shillings each, not one. That's all.' He marked it in with the stub of his pencil and turned away.

'It may be all as far as you're concerned but it's caused Al— Mr Soames a good deal of extra work, as well as wasting his time,' Poppy said hotly, stung by his casual manner. 'And what about this?' she pointed. 'They've charged us for twice the steel we ordered.'

'Oh, I doubled the order before I sent it off. I knew we hadn't ordered enough,' he said with a shrug. 'It was done at the last minute.'

'Maybe it was. But you could have let Mr Soames know, couldn't you?' she said. 'How can he be expected to make the books balance if you alter the order forms without telling him? He's not a mind-reader, you know.' She almost snatched the sheaf of invoices from him.

'Don't you try telling me what I can and can't do, Miss Hoity-Toity,' he said, flushing angrily. 'Coming here and chucking your weight about . . .'

'It's all right, George, I'm sure the lass meant no harm,'

81

Jack said peaceably. 'She's only trying to stick up for Albert.' He smiled at Poppy as George left the workshop. 'Don't tek any notice of my brother-in-law, lass. He's not used to working wi' lasses about t'place. Specially when they put him in t'wrong. But you'll find his bark's worse than his bite.' He stared after George's retreating back. 'Well, most o' time, any road,' he added quietly.

Seething with fury at George Templeton's offhand manner Poppy went back to the office and explained things to Albert, who shook his head in exasperation. 'I might have known. George never gives a thought to owt but his own concerns. Leave it with me, lass, and get on wi' your own work.'

At one o'clock Poppy left Albert to eat his 'snap', as he called it, in the office and went across the yard to the wall behind the cottages so that she could sit in the warm sunshine to eat the sandwiches Mrs Rivers had made for her.

But first she took the letter out of her pocket and read it. It was from Alec, as she had known it would be, wanting to know why he hadn't heard from her lately. She had written to him once, a short, stiff little note because she hadn't really known what to say. In truth, she was not happy about writing to another woman's fiancé, especially as his letters seemed to be getting warmer and more personal. Thoughtfully, she put his letter back in her pocket – this one had begun Dear Poppy instead of Dear Miss Barlow – and got out her sandwiches.

She had hardly begun to eat them before several of the smaller children came out, all clamouring to be the ones to sit next to her. They were each clutching a doorstep of bread and jam or dripping and she feared for her nearly new grey skirt. But before they could do any lasting damage one of the mothers came out, soon followed by two more. They gave their respective offspring an affectionate cuff and sent them off to play on the doorstep, and took their places on the wall with Poppy to settle down for a few minutes' gossip.

As the days had become warmer it had become quite a habit for the women to come out of their cottages to join her on the wall for a 'bit of a breather' and Poppy was more than happy to listen to their conversation as she ate her sandwiches. Her thoughts went back to Alec Kenton. It was all very well to ask her to write about the families at Kentons but so far she had found nothing to write that didn't, to her mind, smack of 'carrying tales'. And she was not prepared to do that, even for him.

'... I keep telling her she should go and see somebody about it,' Maud Benson was saying. Maud, a neat woman with black hair drawn back into a bun, was married to Jake Benson, a quietly spoken man who worked in the teeming bay.

'Yes, it's not reet, is it? An' her with her man off fighting at the front,' Lily Ferris, a stout woman whose husband Ted worked in the pot shop, agreed. 'What do you think, Miss Barlow? Mary oughta go and see somebody, didn't she?'

'About what?' Poppy said carefully, taking another bite of her cheese sandwich.

'About not getting her money from the government,' they both said together. Lily took up the story. 'Harry Smithers – that's Mary's husband – joined up last year. He didn't need to, Sir Frederick said he was needed here and he'd speak for him, but Harry was mad keen to go and do his bit even though it meant leaving Mary on her own to look after three kids and another on the way. I thought he was being a bit selfish, meself, but she was proud to think he was keen to go and fight so it weren't for me to say anything.'

'No, it were nowt to do with us,' Maud said. 'But the thing is, Mary's not getting any money from Harry. She says the money is being stopped from Harry's pay, he's written and told her so, but she's never had it. Not a penny. Jake wrote to the authorities for her because she said she wasn't up to writing a proper official letter. It wasn't any trouble to Jake because he's been to night school,' she couldn't resist adding, with a little wriggle of pride at her husband's achievement. She paused a minute and then went on, 'But all she got was a reply saying the matter was being looked into. That's no help, is it, when you've no bread to feed your children? Poor lass, she'd starve if the rest of us didn't rally round and help her out.'

'Yes. She's just lucky that Sir Frederick didn't turn her out. He said she could still stay in her cottage while Harry's away,' Lily added. 'Mind you, he would. He's a good master, is Sir Frederick.'

'You mean to tell me she's getting no money at all?' Poppy said, appalled at what she was hearing.

'Well, she gets enough to pay the rent by doing a bit of cleaning for Mrs Templeton, but she's not getting owt else,' Lily said.

'That's right,' Maud nodded in agreement. 'She's not getting a penny of Harry's army pay, yet it's being stopped all the time at Harry's end. Poor man, he's away fighting in the trenches, doing his best and allowing her as much as ever he can, only keeping enough back for himself for a few Woodbines and a sup o' beer and it's not getting through to her. T'bloody Government's keeping it all.'

'She's not the only one, neither, from what I've heard,' Lily said. 'I've heard there's hundreds in the same boat. Poor critturs wi' never so much as a crust o' bread to put in their children's mouths.'

'That doesn't make her case any better,' Maud said. 'Poor lass, she's at her wits' end now she's got the baby an' all.'

'Daisy's very good, mind. Sam Beckwith's daughter,' Lily said. 'She looks after the baby and the little ones while Mary works at Mrs Templeton's.' Her voice dropped. 'And that reminds me, Mary said Mrs Templeton had another black eye when she was over there yesterday. Mary told me she made light of it, said she walked into the door.'

'The number of times Mrs Templeton's supposed to have

walked into that door you'd think she'd know where it was by now,' Maud said grimly.

Lily lowered her voice even further. 'Do you think he knocks her about?'

'I'd never be surprised. He's got a vicious temper. I'd never want to cross him.' Maud looked at Poppy. 'You'll do well to keep on t'right side of him, Miss Barlow.'

Poppy finished the last of her sandwiches and folded up her napkin. 'I'm afraid it's too late for that, Mrs Benson. Mr Templeton never wanted me to be given the job here in the first place so I started off on the wrong side of him and nothing's happened to change that.'

'Oh, dear,' both women said together, shaking their heads.

'Oh, don't worry about it,' Poppy said cheerfully. 'I'm not.' She slid off the wall. 'I'll see what I can do about getting Mary's money through to her. Surely there must be something that can be done. I'll ask Sir Frederick about it.'

'Talk to Sir Frederick? Oh, could you? Really?' Both women looked at her with as much awe as if she had suggested petitioning the Almighty.

Later that afternoon when Sir Frederick came in to sign his letters Poppy told him of her conversation with the two women and he was equally appalled and agreed to look into the matter. A month later Mary began to receive the money that was owed to her.

For some reason the wives of the Kenton workers were convinced that it was Poppy who had achieved this, even though she insisted that all she had done was to tell Sir Frederick. After this they brought all their troubles and worries to Poppy, convinced that she would be able to help.

Chapter Nine

Alec Kenton was back home on leave before Poppy had found any good reason to write to him again.

She found him sitting at his father's desk when she took a batch of letters in for Sir Frederick to sign.

'Oh,' she said, surprised. 'I hadn't realised you were home, Major Kenton.'

He made a face. 'Do you have to be so formal, Poppy? Can't you call me Alec?'

'Very well ... Alec,' she said, as it seemed the easiest thing to do. 'I came in to see Sir Frederick. Do you know where he is? These letters need his signature before they're posted tonight.'

He waved his hand. 'He's downstairs in the teeming bay or the grinding shop, I believe. I expect he'll be back soon.' He stood up and took a step towards her. She registered with half her mind that he was even taller than she remembered. 'I looked for another letter from you, Poppy, but it never came. I wrote to you nearly every week. Why didn't you reply?' he asked, a trifle petulantly.

'I hadn't anything much to write about,' she said with a shrug. 'At least, nothing that I thought would be of any interest to you. You see, I have very little to do with the men, and the things their wives talk about ...' She gave another shrug and left the sentence hanging in the air.

'Nevertheless, a letter from you would have cheered me

up no end,' he said, smiling down at her in a way she found rather disconcerting. 'And you could have told me about yourself. I've thought about you a lot, Poppy.' He paused, then added under his breath, 'More, perhaps, than I should have done.' His voice rose again. 'My father speaks very highly of you, you know.'

'He's very kind.' She laid the letters on the blotter on Sir Frederick's desk, embarrassed at the turn the conversation had taken. 'Perhaps you'll be good enough to ask him to sign these when he comes back,' she said, deliberately making her voice businesslike. 'Then I can post them on my way home.' She turned to leave the room.

He took a step and barred her way. 'Aren't you going to stay and talk to me for a few minutes, Poppy? Aren't you going to take pity on a poor soldier back from the war?' He put on a hangdog air.

'I wasn't aware that you'd actually been to the war, Major Kenton,' she said, raising her eyebrows. 'I thought your father said you were based at Aldershot.'

He sighed and gave a sheepish grin. 'Yes, that's quite true. I was just trying to gain your sympathy.' He became serious. 'To tell the truth, at the moment I'm involved in training the raw recruits. They arrive all enthusiastic and eager, most of them excited because it's their first time away from home, full of grandiose ideas of getting to France and having a go at the Boche. The trouble is, most of them don't know one end of a rifle from the other.' He shook his head. 'God, they've absolutely no idea what they're letting themselves in for.'

'But you have?'

'Not at first hand. Yet. But I've been there when the hospital trains come in.' He shook his head again. 'War's not something out of *Boy's Own Paper*, Poppy. It's real and it's horrible.' He turned and looked out of the window, deep in his own thoughts. After a bit he said, 'There's talk of a big push coming on the Western Front before long. It's been talked about for some time but I think it's pretty near now. I guess I'll be sent over there for that.' His mood changed and he turned away from the window and smiled at her. 'But I shouldn't think it'll come before Pa's annual garden party next month. So I'll probably manage to wangle a bit of leave for that. And so, no doubt, will my brother.'

'Your brother? I didn't know you had a brother,' she said, surprised.

'You didn't know about Josh? Well, you'll meet him on the twenty-eighth at the party. He's a pilot in the Royal Flying Corps. Lives and breathes aeroplanes.' He looked at his watch. 'Heavens, I must go. I'm supposed to be meeting Claire for tea. I almost forgot.' He gave her a sly look. 'See what you do to me, Miss Poppy Barlow?'

After he had gone Poppy straightened the letters on Sir Frederick's desk and stood looking down at them unseeingly for several minutes. What was Alec Kenton up to? Was he simply a born flirt or was he hinting at a deeper attraction? He was not the first man who had tried to flirt with her, it was something she had learned to handle over the years of working in her father's office, and it was flattering that he found her attractive. But he was engaged to another woman and that put him quite beyond the pale as far as Poppy was concerned. This was something she must make very plain to him when they next met, and there would be no further correspondence, even under the pretext of getting to know the workforce. She gave a grim smile. He must have thought her naive to fall for that one!

She straightened up, then another thought struck her. But supposing that was exactly what he had in mind? Perhaps his request was based on nothing more than a desire to do as his father asked and become familiar with the people who worked here. In that case, what a fool she would appear, assuming that he found her attractive and thus reading far more into his request than he ever intended. She found herself blushing bright scarlet at the mere idea.

Frowning, she went back to her own office, the problem unresolved.

Albert looked up from his desk. 'Major Kenton went off in a bit of a hurry, didn't he?' he said with a smile.

'Yes. He suddenly remembered he had to meet his fiancée,' Poppy said. She gave a nervous little laugh. 'Fancy nearly forgetting to go and see your future wife!'

'Oh, I don't think there's overmuch – what shall I say? – romance between Miss Claire and Major Kenton,' Albert remarked. 'It'll be more a marriage of industries, if you ask me, sin' her father is a big steel manufacturer down in t'town.'

'That's a very cynical thing to say, Albert. I'm surprised at you.' Poppy said, shocked.

He picked up his pen and examined the tip of the nib. 'Oh, she's a nice enough lass, I daresay, but you'll see what I mean when you meet her at t'garden party.' He plucked a hair from the nib and rubbed it with his pen wiper.

'Yes, Alec— Major Kenton talked about a garden party, Albert. What is it?'

'Oh, aye, t'garden party.' Albert leaned back in his chair as expansively as his lean frame would allow. 'Always a reet good do, is that. Every year Sir Frederick holds a garden party in the grounds of his house, Kenton Hall, for all the men in his employment. And their families.' He nodded encouragingly. 'There's allus plenty to eat and everyone's allowed to walk round the gardens and the kids play on the lawns. You must come. You'll enjoy it, lass.'

'Will Lady Kenton be there?' Poppy asked, interested.

Albert shook his head. 'Oh, no. Sir Frederick's a widower. Lady Kenton passed over some ten years ago.'

'I see.' Poppy bent over her work but her mind was elsewhere, already beginning to plan what she would wear at the garden party. It would be interesting to see Kenton Hall. It would also be interesting to meet Alec Kenton's fiancée, Claire, daughter of the steel magnate. And his brother. What did he call him? Josh.

There was, however, one very large problem with regard

to Sir Frederick's garden party. She realised this as she cycled home a few weeks later with the invitation in her pocket.

Her aunts were still under the impression that she worked at Coles department store.

Not that she had deliberately lied to them, she would never have done that, but in the beginning, when Kate assumed that the position she had been offered was at Coles, Poppy had thought it easier – kinder, even – to let her go on thinking this was so. As for Meg, some days she was too fuddled to realise Poppy went out to work at all, and on the days when she did seem aware she was liable to become so upset at her own lost opportunities that she would spend hours weeping and playing haunting music on the piano, much to Kate's impatient annoyance.

Several wild explanations for the invitation passed through Poppy's mind as she pedalled through the wood in the warm late June air, each more unlikely than the one before. In the end she decided that the best solution would be to tell her aunts the truth; for one thing she hated the deception and for another, sooner or later it was bound to come out – she had nearly slipped up several times already in the two months she had worked at Kentons.

Her mind made up, she hummed to herself as she reached Dale House and pushed her bicycle round to the shed at the back and went in through the kitchen door.

Mrs Rivers's face broke into smiles when she saw her. 'Ee, lass, you're looking a bit weary. Just go and wash your face and hands and I'll bring your dinner through. The butcher let me have a nice bit of gammon and I've made some Cumberland sauce to go with it.'

Poppy looked uncertain. 'What about the aunts? Did they have some, too, Mrs Rivers?' She had always been unhappy at being given better food than her aunts, even though she was the one who paid for it.

'Don't worrit yourself, love. They had their share earlier so they'll not complain.'

By the time Poppy reached the parlour her meal was there, on a tray.

Kate eyed it thoughtfully over her pince-nez. 'The butcher seems to be looking after us better these days,' she remarked. 'There was a time when his meat cuts were very poor. I considered changing to the Co-op butcher but Papa would have been horrified that I should even think about that. He used to say that only common people went to the Co-op.'

'This gammon is very nice,' Poppy said, amazed that her aunt could be so wilfully ignorant of the real state of affairs.

'Did you have a good day at work?' Meg asked wistfully. 'I should have liked . . .'

'Oh, don't be ridiculous, Meg,' Kate said irritably, knowing exactly what she had been going to say because she said it most nights. 'You know you've never been strong enough to work.'

'I've been invited to a garden party,' Poppy said to prevent further argument.

'A garden party? Who's invited you?' Kate demanded, immediately suspicious.

Poppy took a deep breath. 'It's for the people where I work. Apparently Sir Frederick Kenton holds it every year in the grounds of his house.'

The effect on the two sisters was electric. Meg threw down her sewing and rushed from the room as fast as her little legs would carry her. A moment later chords could be heard crashing from the piano. Kate gripped the arms of her chair, her face ashen. 'What's *he* got to do with Coles department store?' she said, her voice a vicious whisper.

'I don't work at Coles. I've never worked at Coles,' Poppy said wretchedly, pushing her plate away. 'You assumed that was where I had found work although it wasn't, the position had already been filled by the time I got there. But it seemed easier to let you go on thinking that because you were so adamant that I shouldn't work at Kentons.'

91

'You deceived us! You wicked, wicked girl! You deceived us.' Kate scrabbled in the large carpet bag by her side till she found her smelling bottle. 'Oh! The very thought that you should do a thing like that when my sister and I had given you a home out of the goodness of our hearts makes me feel quite faint.' She waved the smelling salts back and forth under her nose like an angry metronome.

'I had to deceive you. You gave me little choice.' Poppy's voice rose. 'What would my life have been if I'd told you I worked at Kentons for Sir Frederick Kenton?'

'You wicked, wicked girl.' The metronome waved faster. 'That you should have gone behind my back to work for *that man* . . .!'

Poppy stared at her aunt. 'Look at you, the very thought of him seems to bring on a fit of the vapours. I can't think why. He's a charming man.'

'You don't understand . . .' Kate lay back in her chair, still fanning herself with the smelling bottle.

'No, you're quite right, I don't understand!' Poppy said angrily. She pushed back her chair and left the room.

Kate made a rapid recovery and followed her into the hall. 'You're your father's daughter, stubborn and wilful to a degree.' She had to shout above the crashing sounds of the piano still coming from the drawing room. 'Why can't you behave like a lady instead of a common working person?'

Poppy paused halfway up the stairs and leaned over the banister. 'Because I *am* a common working person,' she shouted back. 'I need money to live and be independent. You and Aunt Meg are still living in the past. This is the twentieth century, Aunt Kate. The country's at war.'

Kate waved her arm. 'That's nothing to us.'

'No, and I daresay it's nothing to you that it's my wages that have paid the butcher's bill and ensured that we have better meat now because you give more than half your money away.'

'I've told you before, it's important that we keep up appearances. For Papa's sake.'

'To the point of starving yourselves and not paying the Rivers their rightful dues?'

'We have quite enough to eat, thank you. And the Rivers have a roof over their heads. What more do they want?' Kate's tone was icy.

'They are entitled to be paid. They're servants, not slaves! Oh, you make me tired.' Poppy turned away and continued up the stairs.

'Where are you going?' Kate still had to shout over the sound of the piano.

'Upstairs. To pack,' Poppy yelled back at her. 'You won't want me here after what I've just said and I don't want to stay. I've had enough.' As she spoke the piano fell suddenly silent and her words echoed round the hall.

She turned and ran up to her room and dragged out her suitcase. She didn't know where she was going, but now she had a little money in her pocket she felt sure that she would find lodgings somewhere without too much trouble. Perhaps Albert Soames would know of something. She began throwing clothes into the suitcase. Anything would be better than staying in this mausoleum with these two crazy old women, she thought savagely, although she was sorry that she would be abandoning the Rivers.

A noise on the stairs stopped her as she began dragging things out of the wardrobe and flinging them on the bed.

'It's all right, dear, don't get upset.' Kate's voice was soothing.

'Don't let Poppy go away, Kate. Please Kate, don't let her go.' It was Meg and she was sobbing as if her heart would break.

'Of course she won't go, dear.'

'But I heard her say she was leaving . . .'

'She didn't mean it, dear. Now, come along. I'll give you a nice powder to make you sleep. You're upset, dear. You know you mustn't get upset.'

'I don't want Poppy to go away, Kate,' Meg pleaded desperately. 'You mustn't let her go. She's all we've got.'

The voices faded as Kate led Meg to her room and closed the door.

Poppy stood looking down at her half-packed suitcase. She was very fond of Aunt Meg and didn't want to leave her but she had no choice now that Kate knew the truth. The mere mention of Sir Frederick Kenton's name was like a red rag to a bull as far as Kate was concerned. Poppy wondered why. Probably something to do with her father; some business deal or other that went wrong. Everything Kate did seemed to be under the influence of old Josiah Russell. It would have been interesting to find out what the trouble was but it was too late now. With her outburst on the stairs she had burned her boats, so to speak. Not that she wanted to stay. Not now. She resumed her packing.

She had nearly finished when there was a tap at the door and Kate put her head in. 'May I come in, Poppy?' she asked almost diffidently, a far cry from the bundle of fury Poppy had left less than half an hour ago.

'Of course, Aunt Kate.' Poppy kept her voice cool.

Kate came in and sat down on the edge of the bed. 'I think we should talk, dear,' she said.

Poppy paused in the act of folding up a jersey. 'I really don't think there's much left to say, Aunt Kate,' she said.

'Yes. Yes, there is, dear.' Kate nodded two or three times. 'You see, Meg ... I ... we don't want you to leave Dale House. You're all we've got and we want you to stay. I think we should forgive and forget all that's been said and start again.' Kate spoke calmly, her hands folded in her lap. 'We don't mind you working, really we don't. That's the way of the world now and I'm sure you'll be able to find employment elsewhere ...'

Although she was seething inside Poppy tried to match Kate's calm words.

'But I have no intention of seeking employment elsewhere, Aunt Kate. I enjoy my work at Kentons for Sir

Frederick. I'm happy there. If you can't accept that then I can't stay here.'

'But can't you see . . .?' Kate shook her head. 'Can't you see how much it upsets me to know you're working for *that man*?'

Poppy shrugged. 'Yes, but I can't see why. Sir Frederick's a charming man.'

'Oh, dear.' Kate looked down at her hands. 'I can see I shall have to tell you . . .' She twisted the lace handkerchief she was holding. 'But it's all so long ago . . .'

Poppy fastened the suitcase. 'It might help,' she said.

Kate got up and went over to the window. 'A long time ago Freddie Kenton and I were to be married,' she said in a muffled voice.

Poppy stared at Kate's back, her eyebrows raised in surprise. 'Ah, so that's it.'

'No. Wait. That's not all. You see, the night our engagement was to be announced . . .' She hung her head. 'Something happened . . .' She fell silent.

'What happened?'

Kate shook her head. 'I can't speak about it . . . Suffice it to say he married someone else.'

Poppy nodded. 'Oh, I see.' No wonder Aunt Kate couldn't bear the mention of his name if he jilted her all those years ago.

Kate turned back from the window, her face ravaged. 'Yes. Now perhaps you can understand why his name is never mentioned in this house.'

'Yes, and I'm sorry, Aunt Kate. But I don't see why it should upset Aunt Meg so much. After all . . .'

Kate waved her hand. 'No, of course you wouldn't. You have no sisters. What you must understand is that Meg and I have always been very close. And of course . . .'

'Meg has always been delicate,' Poppy finished the sentence for her, nodding again.

'So now you know why it is not possible for you to remain working for that man,' Kate said firmly.

Poppy sat down on the bed and began to trace her initials, stamped on the top of the suitcase. She was silent for a long time, then she said, speaking slowly and thoughtfully, 'I don't want to give up my job, Aunt Kate. In fact, even after what you've just said I refuse to give it up. After all, although I realise that what happened to you was very painful, it was also a very long time ago and nothing whatever to do with me. But if you can accept this then I won't leave Dale House. I heard Aunt Meg begging you to persuade me to stay and in truth I don't really want to go.' She looked up at her aunt and said honestly, 'Even in these enlightened days the world is a difficult place for a woman on her own.' She shrugged. 'But if it's a case of staying here or keeping my job then I'm afraid the job will win. Every time.'

Now it was Kate's turn to be silent. At last she said, speaking slowly, reluctantly. 'I suppose, since I've only just discovered that you've worked at that place for the past two months I can't really object to your continuing there. Just as long as that man's name is never mentioned in this house. You can, I'm sure, understand how painful that would be.'

'Yes, of course, Aunt Kate. And now that I know the reason I shall be even more careful . . .'

'More importantly, he must never know that you are my niece.' She glared at Poppy. 'He doesn't know, does he?' she snapped.

'No. No. How should he? I am Miss Barlow to him.'

Kate's shoulders relaxed. 'That's all right, then.' She closed her eyes. 'I . . . we have never clapped eyes on him since that dreadful night. And we never shall. Never.' She shook her head and shuddered. Suddenly, she opened her eyes and smiled at Poppy. 'So you may as well take your things out of the case, dear, and come and finish your meal. Although I expect it's cold by this time. Never mind, Mrs Rivers will warm it for you.' She went over and opened the door.

'But what about Aunt Meg?' Poppy asked, surprised at the sudden change in Kate.

'What about her? She's asleep. I've given her a draught. She won't remember any of this in the morning.' Kate spoke in quite a matter-of-fact tone. Then she smiled, a sad little smile. 'Her mind is quite delicately balanced, you must understand. I have to keep a very careful eye on her.' She came over and kissed Poppy's cheek. 'Now, let's hear no more talk of you leaving us, dear. Not now. Not ever.'

As she went out and closed the door firmly behind her Poppy couldn't help feeling that it was a little like a prison door closing. A very gentle prison door but a prison door nonetheless.

Chapter Ten

There was a further argument, carefully conducted out of Meg's earshot, over the wisdom of Poppy's attending Sir Frederick's garden party.

'Working for that man is one thing, although the fact that you insist on staying there against my express wishes I find disappointing in the extreme, particularly as there must be much more suitable places in Sheffield where I'm sure you could find employment if you are so determined to work for a living. But attending a private social function at his house is quite another matter and something I cannot condone under any circumstances.' Kate pursed her lips disapprovingly. 'Of course, I can't forbid you to go to this garden party but I will say that I don't think it would be at all a suitable thing for you to do.'

'But it isn't exactly a "private social function" as you call it, Aunt Kate,' Poppy explained. 'This is an annual party for all the workers from Kentons. I'll only be one of the crowd. And it's to be held in the garden of Kenton Hall, not in the house.'

Kate moved her shoulders uncomfortably. 'Nevertheless ...'

Poppy smiled conspiratorially at her aunt. 'You really don't need to worry, Aunt Kate. I promise your secret is quite safe with me,' she whispered wickedly.

Kate turned a dull red. She didn't return her smile. 'On

your own head be it, then,' she said coldly.

The day of the garden party at Kenton Hall dawned with the kind of misty light that heralded a really hot day. Kate made a great performance of taking Meg, complete with all her bits of material and sewing baskets, to a secluded spot in the garden known as the arbour, saying it would do them both good to sit outside and get a little fresh air. Poppy helped to transport chairs and tables for them, knowing full well that this was only Kate's way of making sure Meg was out of the way so that she wouldn't begin to ask questions when she saw Poppy getting ready for the garden party. It seemed rather an elaborate subterfuge to Poppy, but seeing Meg flitting excitedly about at the prospect of doing something a little different made her realise just how cloistered and dull life must be for both her aunts.

When she had seen them comfortably settled Poppy went upstairs and put on the new dress that she had bought for the occasion, a blue flowered cotton with a deeper blue ribbon sash that showed a good deal more ankle than Aunt Kate would have approved. With it she wore a wide straw hat trimmed with white flowers and more blue ribbon, white gloves and black patent-leather shoes and handbag.

'My word, you look a real treat, lass,' Mrs Rivers said admiringly when Poppy presented herself in the kitchen for inspection.

'I don't feel it,' Poppy said, turning the corners of her mouth down as she peered into the mirror on the over-mantel and brushed a speck of powder off her nose. 'I've never been to anything like this before. I'm so nervous . . .' She adjusted the angle of her hat for the twentieth time.

'Well, you don't look it, lass. Now, be off with you before her ladyship comes in from the garden and starts criticising.' Mrs Rivers chuckled and gave her a push towards the hall. 'And I'll want to hear all about it when you get back, so mind you have a good time.'

Kenton Hall was a beautiful L-shaped house in rose-coloured brick, with a gable at each end. The party was being held on the extensive lawns, which were gaily decorated with flags and bunting and already full of tumbling, squealing children playing leapfrog and 'last touch' whilst their mothers, dressed in their Sunday best, sat decorously in groups on the grass and tried, with much head-shaking and frowning and no success at all, to encourage them to sit quietly. The men, in dark suits, stiff-collared shirts and either their best caps or bowler hats according to their status, stood around in twos and threes, hands in pockets, talking awkwardly. Sir Frederick was moving from group to group, obviously trying to put everyone at their ease. At the far end of the lawn, in front of the house, stood a long table with cups and saucers and plates on it. On another, a snowy white cloth covered the food.

She felt a hand at her elbow. 'They're like a lot of stuffed dummies, aren't they?' a voice beside her said. 'But they'll start to let their hair down once they've had something to eat and a cup of tea.'

She turned and saw Alec Kenton smiling down at her.

'You're looking very charming this afternoon, Miss Barlow,' he went on before she could speak.

'I've only just arrived,' she said unnecessarily.

'I know. I've been watching out for you.' As he spoke he was guiding her across to a cluster of empty chairs under a large oak tree. 'I'll tell Pa you're here. As you can see, he's doing his patriarchal bit, talking to his workers. I'm sure he'd much rather talk to you, though.'

'No. Please don't disturb him,' Poppy said quickly. She sat down and looked up at Alec. 'Is your fiancée here? I'd very much like to meet her.'

He sat down with her and glanced round without much interest. 'Oh, she's here somewhere. I can't see her at the moment, though. She's probably doing her Lady Bountiful act, getting in the way of the maids under pretext of "helping".'

'Oughtn't you to go and find her?' Poppy asked, thinking

that was rather an unkind thing to say.

'Good gracious no. She wouldn't thank me. Claire can look after herself.' He stretched his long legs, out of uniform today and clad in pale grey worsted trousers, out in front of him. 'In any case, I'd far rather talk to you, Poppy.'

'You mustn't say that,' Poppy said, frowning uncomfortably.

'Why not? It's true.'

'But you're engaged to be married.'

'I know that. But it doesn't stop me from appreciating a conversation with a pretty girl, does it?' He smiled at her disarmingly.

'Ah, there you are, Al.' A tall, black-haired, rather large-boned girl, dressed strikingly in yellow, came up and sat herself down with them. 'Go and fetch me a cup of tea, will you, darling? I'm absolutely gasping. God, it's awful, having to be polite to all these plebs. They've absolutely no conversation.'

'I expect it's only that they're a bit shy,' Poppy said.

The girl, about Poppy's own age, turned cool grey eyes on her. 'And who might you be?' she asked, raising her eyebrows.

'Ah, Claire, I'm sorry. I should introduce you.' Alec leapt to his feet. 'Claire is my father's secretary, Miss Barlow. Miss Barlow, this is Miss Claire Freeman, my fiancée.'

Poppy smiled and held out her hand but Claire ignored it, instead looking her up and down. 'So you're the new broom that's swept the office clean, are you?' she remarked.

Poppy's hackles rose and she kept her temper with difficulty. 'I think you misheard. I'm a secretary, not a cleaner. Sweeping the office isn't one of my tasks,' she answered, wilfully misinterpreting Claire's words.

Claire ignored her and turned to Alec. 'Go on, darling. Chop, chop. Get the tea. And a cream bun before the hoi polloi get to the food and mangle it.'

'Would you like some tea, Miss Barlow?' Alec asked. He looked very uncomfortable.

'No, I don't think so, thank you, Major Kenton. Not yet. Perhaps I should wait and have mine with the rest of the employees.' With a deliberately pleasant smile at Claire – which wasn't returned – Poppy got up and walked away across the lawn.

Mordecai Jones and his wife were standing together admiring the roses, Mordecai in a stiff collar and his Sunday suit, Charity in a navy blue serge dress with a white collar that was far too thick for such a hot day, and a straw boater.

Poppy went across to them.

'This is a beautiful garden, isn't it?' she said conversationally.

'Aye, it is, that,' Mordecai answered, nodding. 'And have you been round to t'back and seen the vegetable garden, miss? It's a picture. Everything in rows as straight as a die.'

'It must keep Sir Frederick's gardeners very busy,' Poppy nodded. 'Are they here today?'

'Oh, aye. They allus come to these dos.' He smiled. 'Look, there's one of 'em over there, watchin' t'kiddies laikin' about on t'lawn. I reckon he's frettin' about what they're doin' to his precious grass, don't you?'

'They're not hurtin' anythin'. They're just enjoyin' theirselves,' Charity said shyly.

'Yes, they're a happy bunch, aren't they,' Poppy agreed, turning to watch them running and tumbling about. 'And really enjoying their afternoon out.'

Mordecai sighed. 'I'd allus thought as I'd like a garden. Not as big as this, o' course, but a little patch where I could grow a few vegetables and flowers.'

'We do manage to grow a few roses round t'back door, Mord, don't we, love?' Charity said. 'Pink ones. They're pretty ... Oh ... I don't feel ... I think I'm going to ...' Her voice tailed off as she suddenly staggered and clutched

Mordecai's arm before slipping to the ground in a dead faint.

For a moment Mordecai stared down at her in horror. Then he said, 'Oh, Charity, love,' and quickly bent down and scooped her up in his arms as if she were a rag doll. Then he stood looking round, uncertain what to do next.

'Take her over there. Look, there are some chairs in the shade of that tree,' Poppy said, pointing. 'I'll go and fetch some water for her.' She ran across the lawn to where the teas were being dispensed and asked for a glass of water. 'Mrs Jones has just fainted,' she explained.

Maud Benson, standing nearby waiting her turn for tea, heard. 'I'll come over,' she said. 'Charity's not been well for several days and this sun won't have helped.' She hurried off.

A young man in blue trousers and a white open-necked shirt with the sleeves rolled up, who seemed to be helping with the teas, said, 'I'll fetch the water and bring it across. And would you like some tea, Miss Barlow? It is Miss Barlow, isn't it?'

'Er ... yes, yes, please. But later. The water's the important thing at the moment.' She registered with half her mind that the young man's face looked vaguely familiar but she couldn't think where she had seen him before. He wasn't dressed as formally as the men from Kentons so she supposed he must be one of Sir Frederick's servants, since he was helping to dispense the teas.

She went back across the lawn to where Maud Benson was just putting away her smelling bottle and Mordecai was fanning his wife with her hat. She had come round now but was still looking deathly pale. 'Someone's bringing you some water, Charity,' Poppy said. 'Are you feeling better now?'

'Yes, I don't know what in t'world made me act so daft,' she said, plucking nervously at the skirt of her dress. 'Fancy me makin' an exhibition of myself like that. I hope no-one saw.' She turned to Mordecai. 'I'm ever so sorry, love, showin' you up like that.'

'I expect it's the heat. It's a very hot day,' Poppy remarked, taking off her own hat and fanning herself.

'Tea for four and one glass of water.' The young man in the white shirt put the tray down on the lawn between them. 'I thought the lady might like some tea now that she seems to have recovered a little.' He smiled at them all as he spoke. 'Would you like me to bring you some food?'

Mordecai had scrambled to his feet. 'Oh, no, thank you all the same, sir. We can't have you waitin' on the likes of us. No, we'll fetch ourselves summat in a while.'

'Nonsense, Jones. This is your afternoon out and it's my pleasure to wait on you. I shan't be a tick.' He went off, whistling.

'That's Mr Josh all over,' Maud remarked, watching him go. 'He's a nice man. A real chip off the old block. Not like the other one.' She nodded in the direction of Alec, still sitting under the tree with his fiancée and looking bored.

'Oh, was that Sir Frederick's other son?' Poppy asked. 'I thought I must have seen him before, somewhere. It must be a family likeness.'

'Aye, that's right. He's a captain in the Royal Flying Corps,' she said proudly, adding, 'He's very like his pa.' They both watched as Mordecai gave his wife a drink of water and then dipped a spotless white handkerchief in the glass and gently wiped her face with it.

'There, love, is that better?' he asked lovingly as the colour began to return to her cheeks.

She nodded. 'I'm ever so sorry, Mord. I didn't mean to let you down like that,' she repeated anxiously.

'Don't be daft. You couldn't help bein' ill, love.' He put his arm round her and gave her a squeeze.

Josh Kenton came back across the lawn with a tray laden with sandwiches and yet another cup of tea. 'I thought I might join you all, if you have no objections,' he said, putting down the tray and pulling up another chair. 'Come on, everyone, dig in. I don't know about the rest of you but

I'm absolutely famished and I've talked so much to so many people that I could drink a well dry.' He picked up his cup and took a draught. 'Ah, it's a good cup of tea, anyway.' He handed the sandwiches round. 'These are cucumber and these are cheese, I think. Oh, and those are fish paste, bloater paste to be exact. Come on, there's plenty more where they came from. Do you think you could manage a cucumber sandwich, Mrs Jones?' he asked. 'You're looking better, anyway.'

Shyly, Charity took a sandwich. 'Thank you, sir,' she said. 'Yes, I'm feeling much better now.'

'I expect it was the heat,' Josh said with a smile.

'Very likely,' Maud said dryly.

Josh surveyed the table. 'Ah, I forgot to bring any cake. There were some delicious-looking chocolate eclairs, too. I'll go and bag some before they all disappear. Shan't be a tick.'

'Such a nice man,' Maud repeated as they watched Josh cross the lawn, laughingly extricating himself with some difficulty from the children that crowded round him and stopping here and there for a word with their parents, who were becoming much more relaxed and easy now. Some of the younger men even had their jackets and ties off and were playing cricket at the far end of the lawn where there was no possible danger to life, limb or windows.

Suddenly, Maud got up. 'Oh, will you just look at them rascals of mine. What will they be up to next!' She hurried across to where her two sons were trying to climb on each other's shoulders to reach the branches of the big beech tree.

Mordecai was studying his wife. 'Do you think it would be very rude if I was take Charry home?' he asked Poppy. 'She's still lookin' a bit peaky.'

'I'll be all right, Mord. Don't fuss. I'm hot, that's all,' Charity insisted, fanning herself.

'I think it would be nice if you could stay a bit longer. I'm sure Mr Josh will be back soon with the eclairs,' Poppy said with a smile.

Charity clapped her hand over her mouth. 'Eclairs! Oh, I couldn't.' She turned pale and swallowed hard, twice. 'I think you're right. I think p'raps I should go home, Mord,' she said weakly.

'Coom on then, love.' Mordecai helped her to her feet and put his arm round her. 'Will you make our excuses, Miss Barlow?' he asked over his shoulder as he led her away.

'Yes, of course. I'm sure Mr Josh will understand,' she said.

Poppy watched them go, Charity leaning heavily on her husband's arm, then she turned away and sat waiting uncomfortably among the remains of the sandwiches. She didn't quite know what to do. On the one hand she felt it would be rude to leave before Josh arrived with the eclairs he had gone to fetch, but on the other it didn't seem quite right that she should be sitting and waiting for him alone. She kept looking round anxiously, hoping that Maud would come back, but neither she nor her two boys were anywhere in sight.

Groups of women were sitting on the grass wherever there was shade to be found, drinking tea, gossiping and fanning themselves with their best straw hats, quite relaxed now. Men were in other groups, drinking the beer Sir Frederick had thoughtfully provided, the cricket match abandoned because of the heat, their talk and laughter becoming ever more raucous as the beer took effect. She could see Sir Frederick sitting with one of the groups, a mug of beer in his hand, his panama hat pushed to the back of his head. On the far side of the lawn she saw Alec walk across to a knot of men who were lying on the grass, collars and hats abandoned, sharing a joke. As he approached, they scrambled to their feet, brushing themselves down and fastening their collars. She noticed that unlike his father his bearing was stiff and that he laughed rather too heartily as he spoke to them. They were clearly glad when he moved on. Claire was nowhere to be seen.

Then she saw Josh coming towards her across the lawn, the plate of eclairs held high out of the way of the children who were clamouring round his legs. He was not quite as tall as his brother, not quite as handsome, definitely less suave. But there was something about him, an openness and energy, a readiness to smile, that made him very much more attractive.

'No,' she heard him say, 'these are not for you, you ragamuffins. You've already had your share and more.'

Laughingly he shook them off and came over to where she was sitting.

'Oh,' he said, looking round, disappointment in his eyes, which on closer inspection she could see were a very dark blue. 'Where has everybody gone?'

'Mr Jones had to take his wife home because she felt ill again and Mrs Benson had to go and attend to her boys. I'm sorry, I'm afraid there's only me left.' Seeing the crestfallen look on his face, she wished the ground would open and swallow her up.

Chapter Eleven

To Poppy's relief, suddenly Josh's face cleared and he smiled at her. 'Oh, please don't apologise, Miss Barlow. I was only thinking that I'd wheedled extra cakes out of Cook and now there are only the two of us left here to eat them. But no doubt we'll manage between us. I can vouch for the fact that they're delicious.' He put them down on the table. 'Nothing too serious with Mrs Jones, I hope?' he added, raising his eyebrows.

'No. I think she found the sun a bit too hot, that's all. Well, that and the thought of eating chocolate eclairs . . .'

'Oh, dear.' He sat down and pointed to the plate of cakes on the table between them. 'You don't find the thought of all these eclairs daunting, do you, Miss Barlow? I'm afraid our cook will be most offended if I take any of them back to the kitchen.' He offered her one, then took another himself and bit into it. 'Mm. Delicious. Poor old Mord and his wife don't know what they're missing.'

'Indeed, they don't.' Poppy ate her eclair and wiped her fingers on the napkin he had thoughtfully provided, all the time watching the children, who were now playing a form of hoop-la in the middle of the lawn. She smiled. They had all started the afternoon with their clothes, even those that were threadbare and shabby, spotlessly clean. But now the girls' starched white pinafores and the boys knee-length breeches all bore grubby stains and grass marks, and boots that had been highly polished for the occasion were scuffed and dirty.

'Those children are having a wonderful day,' she said with a smile. 'It's something they won't forget.'

'Yes. They really look forward to it every year.' He handed her the plate. 'Have another, Miss Barlow.'

Poppy hesitated. 'Perhaps we should save some for your brother. He seems to be making his way in this direction.'

'Oh, there'll be plenty left for him. Anyway, he's busy being the dutiful son. Go on, have another. I dare you.' He grinned at her and helped himself to another one.

She followed suit and as they ate they both watched Alec. Carefully skirting the children he was approaching a group of women who were sitting or half-lying on the grass, talking and laughing among themselves, completely relaxed. As with the men, as soon as he got near they fell silent and scrambled to their feet, smoothing their skirts and ramming their hats back on their heads. After a few minutes of clearly uncomfortable conversation with them he moved on, at which they flopped down onto the grass again, obviously relieved.

Josh, watching, shook his head. 'Oh, dear. My big brother really hasn't got the right idea at all, has he?'

'What do you mean?' Poppy wiped the corner of her mouth with her napkin.

'Well, just look at him. Pa is always telling him he should talk to the men and their wives so that he gets to know them a bit as people and not just cogs in the money-making machine, so Alec dutifully does just that. Or at least, he tries. But he simply doesn't know what to say to them, mainly because he isn't really the least bit interested and feels he's wasting his time. Of course they realise this, they're not daft. The result is that they feel uncomfortable and he barks at them so they get tongue-tied and that makes him impatient. He needs to relax a bit. The trouble is, poor old Al's far too anxious to do the right thing. It doesn't always pay.'

109

She turned and looked at him with interest. 'Does that mean that you *don't* try to do what's right, Captain Kenton?' she asked with something of a twinkle in her eye.

'Ah, you won't catch me out like that, Miss Barlow,' he said with a laugh. 'There's quite a difference between "doing the right thing" and doing what's right, you know. To my mind, doing the right thing is purely mechanical, acting in the way that's expected, to make a good impression, whereas doing what's right is rather more complicated. A question of conscience, if you like. And not always calculated to gain popularity. So not the same thing at all, wouldn't you agree?'

'No, I suppose not,' she said thoughtfully. Suddenly, she smiled. 'I've noticed you've spent most of the afternoon talking to the people here, Captain Kenton. Why, look, you're even spending time talking to your father's secretary! So you're "doing the right thing", aren't you?'

He threw back his head and laughed. 'Touché, Miss Barlow. And the answer to that is, not at all. I'm having a very enjoyable afternoon. I like talking to people and I've done a lot of that and I had a very pleasant game of cricket with the chaps down at the end of the lawn a little while ago. Now I'm enjoying sharing these eclairs with you.' He took another and offered her one, which she declined. 'I suppose it's partly because I've no axe to grind. I can talk to these people as friends in a way that Alec finds difficult because he knows that one day he'll be their master.' He stroked his chin thoughtfully. 'Not that that should make any difference, of course, now I come to think of it. My father has never had any problems in that direction. He has always talked man-to-man with his employees.'

'I take it you've no interest in Kentons then, Captain Kenton?' she asked.

'Oh, I wouldn't say that. I wouldn't like to see the old firm go down the pan,' he said quickly. 'No, of course I wouldn't. Not that there's any danger of that, of course. But you see, I've got my flying. Aeroplanes have always been my passion. I've always wanted to fly and that's what I love more than anything else.' He was quiet for a minute, then he said, 'Although I could have wished it had been in different circumstances. I'm not terribly keen on hunting other planes and shooting them down.' He grinned suddenly. 'Particularly as those other planes are doing the same to me. All the same,' he crumpled his napkin, 'I'd hate to have to give it all up in order to keep the family firm running. But fortunately that's not something I have to worry about because it'll all fall on Alec's shoulders when the guv'nor gives up – and quite rightly so, since he's the eldest son.' He gave her a boyish smile. 'I don't know why I'm telling you all this, Miss Barlow. I don't usually run on like this.'

'You're not "running on," Captain Kenton. And anyway, I'm interested,' she said, smiling back at him. 'Tell me some more about your flying.'

'Have another cake, then. You'll need it if I'm going to talk about that. It could take some time . . .'

'What could take some time, Josh?' Alec came up, mopping his face with a large white handkerchief, and threw himself into an empty chair between Josh and Poppy. 'No, don't tell me. Talking about flying.' He leaned over and helped himself to the last eclair. 'God, I need this. I'm so bored! I never know what to say to all these people.' He bit into his cake, then turned and smiled at Poppy. 'But I've done my duty and said a few words to practically everyone here so now I can legitimately enjoy myself in your company, Miss Barlow.'

Poppy coloured but said nothing.

'And what have you been doing with yourself all afternoon?' he asked, moving his chair a little closer. 'Have you been bored, too?'

'No, I haven't been bored at all, Major Kenton,' Poppy said. 'This is such a beautiful garden that I could happily sit here all day and not be bored, even without watching all the children playing. They are having such a wonderful time

111

that it's a tonic to watch them, isn't it?'

'If you say so, Miss Barlow. Myself, I can think of better things to watch.' His eyes were on her and she knew it but she carefully avoided his gaze.

Josh raised his eyebrows slightly. 'Where's the redoubtable Claire, then, Al? Isn't she around to gladden your heart?' he asked a trifle sharply.

Alec dragged his attention to his brother. 'No. I think she's taken herself off to the conservatory with a book and not to blame her, either.' He looked at his watch and nodded to the crowd that had gathered on the lawn. 'How long before these people go home, Josh?'

'Not until Pa's made his speech,' Josh said cheerfully.

'Oh, Lord,' Alec groaned.

'Well, it doesn't look as if it'll be long now. They're all gathered ready for it.'

'Thank goodness for that. I've had enough for one afternoon. I could do with a stiff whisky.' He turned to Poppy. 'How about you, Miss Barlow? I'm sure you could do with one, too. Shall we go inside where it's cool and . . .'

'Ah, so there you are, darling.' From behind them Claire's voice dripped tinkling ice. 'I might have known I'd find you somewhere near the little secretary.'

Both men leapt to their feet. 'Sorry, darling. I thought you were reading in the conservatory,' Alec said guiltily, pulling up a chair for her. 'Where have you sprung from? I didn't see you cross the lawn.'

She ignored the chair. 'I've finished my book and I came through the shrubbery, if you must know,' she said briefly. She gazed down at him. 'Well, have you finished doing your duty here? Because if you have I'd very much like to go home now. I think we've both suffered enough for one afternoon, don't you?'

'Yes, of course, darling. But wouldn't you like a drink first? I'd just suggested to Josh and Miss Barlow that we should go inside for a whisky.'

'No, thank you, darling. You know I don't drink.' She

waited, tapping her foot impatiently.

'No, of course not. Stupid of me. I'd forgotten.' He smiled brightly at her. 'I'll go and fetch the car. Shan't be a tick.'

'Don't bother. I'll come with you.' She tucked her hand proprietorially through his arm. 'Good afternoon, Josh,' she called over her shoulder as they went off together.

Josh watched them go, shaking his head.

'What's wrong?' Poppy asked. 'Or shouldn't I ask?'

'Oh, nothing. Nothing at all,' he said, adding thoughtfully, 'I just hope my brother will find enough strength of character to stand up to his future wife. As you can see, she's a very forceful and determined young lady.'

'How long have they been engaged?' Poppy asked.

'Since last Christmas. And they're intending to marry this Christmas. Or at least, that's Claire's idea, which of course Alec will go along with. I believe plans are already well under way in the Freeman household under the redoubtable Mrs Freeman's eagle eye.'

'You don't sound very impressed,' Poppy remarked, trying not to giggle.

He stretched his legs out in front of him and clasped his hands at the back of his head. 'Well, put it like this. I'm glad I'm not in my brother's shoes. Mind you, he's about to make a very expedient marriage, which will please the Freemans and won't entirely displease my father because it will unite the two engineering firms. Eventually, of course, Alec will be head of the whole shebang, which he will enjoy as long as he isn't forced to have too much to do with the poor chaps who make his money for him, money which, incidentally, Claire will have no trouble in spending. So everyone will live happily ever after, as they say in the best storybooks.'

'Now you're sounding cynical,' Poppy said.

'Am I? I don't mean to.' He sat up straight. 'Don't get me wrong, Miss Barlow. I wish my brother all the luck in the world. He's ambitious, which I have to confess I am not, so I really do hope he gets what he wants and that it brings him joy. All I'm saying is that I'm not sure that mutual ambition is the best basis for a happy marriage. It wouldn't do for me, anyway. Not that I'm anticipating getting married,' he added, studying his hands. 'At least, not for years and years.'

'You're wedded to your flying?' she said lightly.

He nodded. 'Mm. Something like that.'

As he spoke, Poppy experienced a shaft of something which she couldn't quite put a name to, but which felt a little like disappointment.

Aunt Kate was hovering in the hall when she arrived home from the garden party and from the way she was straightening her skirt as she emerged out of the gloom Poppy had the distinct impression that she had been sitting on the stairs, waiting for her.

'Oh, you're back,' she said, with studied nonchalance. 'I didn't expect you quite so early. I was just on my way upstairs to see if Meg wanted anything.'

Poppy blinked to accustom herself to the light – or rather the lack of it, after coming in from bright sunlight. 'Oh, dear. Is Aunt Meg ill, then?'

'No, dear, not really. Just a touch of the sun, I think. I sent her up to lie down.' Kate sat down on the stairs and motioned to the step below her. 'Well, come along, sit down and tell me all about it,' she said, with a touch of asperity. 'Was Fred— Sir Frederick there? I expect he's quite grey now. Or bald. Bald and bewhiskered and stout.' She sounded quite vindictive.

'He's none of those things, Aunt,' Poppy said quietly, without sitting down. 'He's clean-shaven and his hair is thick and white. And he's by no means stout.' She started up the stairs. 'I'll go and see if Aunt Meg wants anything, if you like, Aunt.'

But Kate hadn't finished with her. 'But you haven't told me ... Did you have a pleasant time? Were there many people there? Who did you speak to?'

Poppy shrugged. 'Nobody you would know, Aunt Kate. I talked mostly to the people who work at Kentons. And I spoke to Sir Frederick's sons. Or, rather, they spoke to me.'

'Ah, yes. His sons,' Kate said thoughtfully. 'Are they . . .?'

Poppy cut her short. 'The older one is a major in the army and the younger one is a captain in the Royal Flying Corps. They both managed to get leave so that they could be there today. There, I don't think there's anything else I can tell you. Shall I go up to Aunt Meg now?'

'Yes, if you wish,' Kate said a trifle impatiently. 'Although she's probably asleep and won't want to be disturbed.' She moved so that Poppy could pass her, clearly forgetting what she had said earlier about being on her way up to Meg.

Poppy left her still sitting on the stairs. It was plain that Kate's romance with Freddie Kenton had left more scars than she was prepared to admit, Poppy realised with some surprise. She continued up and along to Meg's room and knocked on the door. 'It's me, Aunt Meg. Poppy. May I come in?'

'Oh, yes. Please do,' Meg's voice sounded welcoming. 'Has Kate sent you to tell me I can get up now?' she asked eagerly as soon as Poppy opened the door.

'I'm sure you can get up if you want to, as long as you're feeling better,' Poppy said.

'Better? I'm not ill. Oh, pull back the curtains, dear, will you, I hate this dim light. But Kate will insist . . .' Meg had been lying on her bed covered with one of her patchwork quilts, but now she swung her legs over the side and sat on the edge of the bed. She put her head on one side and looked at Poppy. 'Have you been out, dear?'

'Yes, I've been to a garden party,' Poppy answered.

'Oh, that's nice, dear.' Meg was not at all curious. 'That's a pretty dress you're wearing. I use material like that for my quilts sometimes. Have you got any to spare?'

'I didn't make it, Aunt Meg. I bought it,' Poppy said. 'So I'm afraid there aren't any scraps.'

'Oh. That's a pity.' Meg sat quietly, her hands in her lap, her feet not quite touching the ground. Poppy sat down in a wicker chair beside the empty fireplace and glanced round the room. It was a very feminine room, furnished totally in bamboo and cluttered with all manner of frilly, embroidered bits and pieces that had obviously been made by Meg, lampshades, covers for jars and bottles, runners for the chests of drawers and duchesse sets for the dressing table. Even the upholstered footstools had petit-point embroidered tops. The usual drift of eau de cologne scented the air.

'Would you like a cup of tea, Aunt Meg?' Poppy said at last.

Meg looked up. 'Can I come downstairs for it? I've had my rest,' she pleaded, for all the world like a small child.

'Yes, Aunt Meg. Of course you can, if you're feeling better now.'

Meg frowned. 'I told you. I'm not ill.' Her face cleared and she smiled. 'We sat in the garden. All the afternoon. It was lovely. I could see the birds and hear them sing. Did Kate say I could get up now?'

'Yes. Come along, we'll go down together and have a nice cup of tea.' Poppy pulled herself up short. She mustn't treat Aunt Meg as a child even if she did act like one at times.

Much later that night, at Kenton Hall Josh and Alec went up the stairs together after a nightcap with their father.

'Well, thank God that's over for another year,' Alec said heavily. 'If there's one thing I hate it's the works' garden party.'

'Pa seemed very pleased with the way things went,' Josh remarked. 'And there were no hitches. Not like that year when Ted Ferris's son got stuck up the chestnut tree and we couldn't get him down.'

116

'As I remember you went up for him in the end,' Alec nodded.

'Yes, I lured him down with a doughnut, cheeky little beggar. He's in the infantry now, I believe. Over in France.'

'Is he?' Alec yawned. 'Oh, yes, now I come to think of it, old Ferris asked me to keep an eye out for him when I go over. Fat chance of that!'

'I hope you didn't tell him that,' Josh said.

'No, I mumbled something suitable.'

They reached the head of the stairs and Josh turned to go to his room.

'Have you got a minute, Josh?' Alec said, his expression suddenly serious. 'There's something I'd like to talk over with you.'

It was Josh's turn to yawn. 'Can't it wait till morning, Al? I'm a bit fagged out tonight.'

'Not really. I've got to make an early start back to camp and I'd like your advice before I go.'

'Well, make it snappy, then. I have to go back tomorrow too, you know.'

Alec followed Josh into his room and sat on his bed watching Josh take off his tie and shoes. 'I'm in a bit of a quandary, to tell you the truth, Josh,' he said.

'Over what?' Josh's voice was muffled because he had his shirt half over his head.

'I'm in love,' Alec said.

Josh pulled his shirt back on and stood gaping at his brother. 'What do you mean, in love? I should hope you are, man! You're to be married in less than six months.'

'That's just it, Josh. It's not Claire I'm in love with,' Alec said wretchedly.

'Then who, for God's sake?'

'Can't you guess?'

Josh stared at him, shaking his head, mystified. Then, 'Oh, no, Al! Not ...'

Alec nodded miserably. 'Yes, Poppy Barlow. Pa's

117

secretary.' He shrugged. 'I suppose you could say it was love at first sight. I admit she's really bowled me over.' He held up his hand. 'Oh, I know what you're going to say, Josh, that it's the sort of thing that only happens in penny romances. And I would have agreed with you, till it happened to me.' He looked up at his brother, his face full of anguish. 'What am I going to do, Josh?'

'What does the lady in question have to say about it?' Josh asked, his tone clipped.

'Who, Poppy? Or Claire?'

'Both, I suppose.'

'The answer's the same in both cases. I haven't said anything to either of them.' He spread his hands. 'How can I break it to Claire? Her wedding dress is half made, the guest list is almost complete ... God, she'll sue me for breach of promise.' He shook his head. 'But how can I marry her when all I can think about is Poppy?'

'But does Poppy feel the same way?' For some reason that he couldn't quite fathom Josh found he was totally unsympathetic towards his brother.

'I haven't told her how I feel yet, but I think ... well, I asked her if she would write to me and she did. She wouldn't have done that if she wasn't interested, would she?' He was almost pathetic in his eagerness for Josh to agree with him.

Josh shrugged but said nothing.

'I've written to her every week.' Alec watched for Josh's reaction.

'And has she replied?'

'Oh, yes. Well, not every time.' He wasn't going to admit that Poppy had only written once, a stilted little note, at that.

Josh sat down in the armchair at the foot of his bed, elbows on his knees, his hands hanging loosely between them. 'You go back tomorrow?' he asked, looking up at Alec.

'Yes. I'm being drafted to France.'

'Not much time to do anything before you go, then.'

Alec shook his head. 'Perhaps I should write to Claire when I get over there, break it to her gently, just tell her I can't marry her, not that there's another woman involved. That wouldn't be fair to Poppy, would it?'

Josh frowned. 'Would you be happy to go ahead with marriage to Claire if it weren't for Poppy?' he asked.

'Oh, yes,' Alec said. 'If it weren't for Poppy . . . Claire's a good sort, really.'

'Then don't you think you should make sure of Poppy's feelings in the matter before your burn your boats, so to speak?'

Alec smiled. 'I reckon she feels the same as I do.'

'But have you asked her?' Josh insisted.

'Oh, come on, man. I'm not such a cad that I'll go making love to one woman while I'm engaged to another. What do you take me for? No, I think the right thing to do will be to write to Claire and tell her the truth. Then, when I've done the honourable thing I'll be free to speak to Poppy.'

Josh got to his feet. 'I don't know why you bothered to ask my advice, Al. You seem to have made your mind up already,' he said.

Alec got off the bed and went to the door. 'Yes, but it's nice to talk it over with someone sympathetic. Helps clarify the mind.' He came back and shook his brother's hand. 'Don't know when we'll see each other again, Josh, but I wish you all the best, fighting the Boche in the sky. It's an awful long way to fall, pal.'

Josh clapped him on the shoulder. 'Likewise, Al. But you'll be fighting him in thick, stinking mud. I know where I'd rather be!'

'I'll let you know how things go when I've written to Claire.'

'As long as you don't expect me to pick up the pieces. Claire really isn't my type, you know,' Josh said grimly.

After Alec had gone Josh flung himself down on his bed

without undressing. It was true. Claire wasn't his type. But he rather suspected that Poppy Barlow might be when he got to know her better. Which he undoubtedly would when she was married to his brother. The thought gave him no pleasure.

Chapter Twelve

'I didn't see you at the garden party last Saturday, Albert,' Poppy said when Albert arrived at work the following Monday morning.

He smiled as he went over to his desk and began sorting through the post. 'Oh, I was there, all right. Wouldn't miss it for worlds. Neither would t'missis and kiddies. They had a great time.'

'Where were you, then?' she asked. 'Mind you, there were so many people about I'm not surprised I didn't see you. Who were all those people, Albert? I'm sure they can't all work here. Still, I never see the families of the men who don't live here so I wouldn't recognise them, would I?'

He laughed. 'That's true. But a lot of 'em were friends and relations o' t'staff at Kenton Hall as well as folk from here. Sir Frederick Kenton's garden party is a reet big do, these days. But me, I spent nearly all t'time down wi' t'cricketers. My lad were playing and he scored twenty-four runs. Well, it were thirty, really, but Mr Templeton were umpire and he disallowed the six Archie hit. It were a bad decision but folk know better than to argue wi' Mr Templeton if they want to keep their jobs.' He was sorting the post into heaps as he spoke. 'He's a good bat, is Archie,' he added. 'And mad on cricket, just like his dad.'

'Do you play, Albert?'

'Nay, not wi' my chest. I used to, mind. I were a fast bowler in me time. I still like to watch though, and it's nice my lad's keen. He'll go far, will Archie.' He got up, a wad of letters in his hand. 'These'll keep Sir Frederick busy when he arrives,' he said, waving them as he went over to Sir Frederick's office. 'And you, too, lass, I don't doubt, when he gets to answer them.' He stopped for a moment, watching her type. 'That typewriter's worth its weight in gold, in't it. Ee, I wouldn't have wanted to write that long report you're doin' there out by hand. Have you nearly finished it?'

She looked up. 'Yes. I'll have it done this morning. It won't take long.' She gave him a brief smile and went back to her typing. Soon the only sounds to be heard were the scratch of Albert's pen and the tapping of the typewriter.

Poppy was so engrossed in what she was doing that the sound of the door opening made her start.

'Make you jump, did I, lass?' It was George Templeton. He came across and perched on the end of her desk.

'Yes, you did, rather,' she replied briefly, carrying on with her work. Just recently he seemed to have abandoned his unpleasant treatment of her and instead would go out of his way to seek her out and be nice to her. She didn't understand his change in attitude; it made her uneasy, she didn't know why.

He leaned over to look at what she was doing. 'By, that's clever,' he said admiringly. 'Have you seen this, Soames? The way she types the words go on the page quicker than you can speak them.'

'I seem to remember that you considered a typewriter a waste of money when I first came here,' she reminded him, her voice cool.

'Ah, yes, but I hadn't seen what you could do with it then, had I?' He smiled at her and preened his moustache.

'If you've come to see Sir Frederick he isn't in yet,' she said without smiling back.

'Oh, I'm in no hurry.' He crossed one leg over the other,

making himself quite at home on her desk.

She went on working, trying to ignore the fact that he was watching her.

'You enjoyed the garden party, then?' he said after a while.

'Yes, thank you.' She didn't look up.

'Yes, I could see you were having a good time with Mr Alec and Mr Josh.' He leaned towards her. 'You need to watch your step, my lass. The likes of them aren't for the likes of you, so don't go getting ideas into that pretty little head of yours. Remember, Mr Alec is already spoken for and Mr Josh's not the sort . . .'

Poppy looked up. 'I don't think it's any concern of yours who I speak to, Mr Templeton,' she said, her voice icy. 'And I'm not *your lass*. Now, please get off my desk. You're sitting on my work.' She managed to keep her voice low, although inwardly she was seething.

'Why didn't you say so, my dear?' he said expansively, moving the papers he was sitting on out of the way. 'As I was saying . . .'

'I'm not interested in what you were saying, Mr Templeton.'

'As I was saying, you need to look to your own class if you're looking for a young man.' He preened his moustache again. 'There's plenty who wouldn't say no . . .'

She stood up. 'When I need your advice I'll ask for it, Mr Templeton,' she said, her voice shaking with fury. 'But now, I'd be glad if you would get on with your own work and let me get on with mine.' She picked up a pile of invoices and took them over to the filing cabinet on the other side of the office, where she turned her back on him and busied herself filing, a task she usually found quite tedious.

After a while George Templeton took himself off and she went back to her desk. 'Thank goodness he's gone,' she said as she resumed work.

'I think he's taken a bit of a shine to you, lass,' Albert said with a chuckle.

123

Poppy groaned. 'Heavens, I hope not. I can't stand the man,' she said. 'And he couldn't stand me, either, when I first came here! I think I liked it better that way.'

Albert nodded, suddenly serious. 'You'll need to watch out, lass. He's a dangerous man to cross.'

'Don't worry, Albert. I've met his type before,' she said confidently. 'I think I can handle him. He'll soon get fed up when he finds he's not making any impression on me.'

Nevertheless, she was careful to listen to what was said about George Templeton by 'the wives', as she thought of them, when they joined her for a gossip as she ate her sandwiches each day.

It was obvious that nobody liked him and Mary Smithers, who enjoyed a good audience and had first-hand knowledge because she cleaned for her, told vivid tales of Connie Templeton's sufferings at her husband's hand.

'You need to tek what Mary says wi' a pinch of salt,' Maud Benson whispered after one of Mary's more lurid stories, 'although I'm sure she's right about him knocking Connie about. I've seen her with a black eye more than once.'

'It's a good thing she's got Jack to run to,' Lily Ferris remarked. 'He looks after her.'

'In more ways than one!' Daisy Frampton said with a sly wink.

'Don't be daft. Jack's her brother-in-law,' Maud said sharply.

'Only by marriage. Jack was married to Connie's sister, if you remember,' Daisy said. She gave a knowing nod. 'I live next door to Jack, so I see the comings and goings. I can tell you, she's always in and out of his house.'

'Well, she does his cleaning for him, doesn't she?' Lily Ferris asked.

'Yes, and that's a laugh. She cleans for Jack and then pays Mary to clean for her,' Daisy chuckled.

'All the same, I'm quite sure there's no hanky-panky,' Maud persisted. 'Jack's a decent chap. He'd never do anything ... well, you know ...'

'No. I daresay you're right,' Daisy agreed. 'But I do know she cries on his shoulder because I've heard her.'

'Well, all I can say is it's a good thing she's got somebody to turn to, after what she goes through with that man,' Mary said. She looked down at her hands. 'He tried it on with me once,' she said quietly. 'You know, the old story, trying to tell me a slice off a cut loaf is never missed, that kind of thing. I told him he ought to be ashamed of himself, trying to make up to me while my Harry was off fighting for his king and country.'

'Good for you, Mary,' the others said.

Mary grinned. 'I told him it'd be more to his credit if he did the same, instead of making out he'd got a bad leg whenever joining up was mentioned.' She gave a satisfied nod. 'He didn't like that. But it shut him up and he keeps out of my way now, I can tell you.'

'Poor man.' It was Charity Jones who spoke. 'Doesn't anybody love him? We all need someone to love us and Jesus says we should love our neighbour.'

'Well, just don't let George Templeton hear you say that or you might get more than you bargain for, Charity love,' Daisy warned with a wink. Then her expression softened as she saw the expression on Charity's face. 'Oh, don't mind me, lass, I'm only kidding.'

'Aye, tek no notice of Daisy, love,' Maud said with a smile. She turned to Daisy. 'You shouldn't tease the lass. Not in her condition.' She smiled proudly at Poppy. 'She's up for one, you know.' She nodded meaningfully when she saw Poppy's blank expression. 'You know. A baby. I guessed that's what it was when she was took queer at t'garden party, but of course it wasn't for me to say at t'time. But I was right, wasn't I, Charity love?'

Charity nodded. 'I hadn't realised. I thought it was the hot weather,' she said blushing. 'Mord's ever so pleased. But he's a bit worried. You know ... his foot ... he wouldn't want the baby ...'

'Bless you, he's no need to worry on that score. Things

125

like that aren't passed on,' Daisy said comfortingly.

Poppy gathered up her things and got to her feet. 'I must get back.' She stopped by Charity's chair and gave her shoulders a squeeze. 'Congratulations, Charity. I'm very pleased for you,' she said.

But as she walked back across the yard it was not Charity and her coming baby that occupied her thoughts, it was George Templeton. Even allowing for the wives' exaggerations it was clear that he could be a dangerous man.

Poppy never discussed these matters, or anything else concerned with her work, back at Dale House. Life there went on quietly and uneventfully, the only excitement provided by Kate's inability to make up her mind whether to send her monthly charity cheque to the workhouse or for comforts for the troops in France.

'You could divide it between the two,' Poppy suggested helpfully, glad to see that at last Kate had unwrapped herself sufficiently from the safe cocoon of Dale House to acknowledge the fact of the war.

Meg clapped her hands. 'Oh, yes, what a good idea.'

'No. We couldn't do that.' Kate pursed her lips. 'Because neither party would know we had subscribed to the other, so it would give the impression that we had halved our giving. Dear Papa wouldn't like people to think we were less generous than in his day.'

Poppy got up from the table and piled the breakfast things onto a tray, biting her lip against pointing out that dear Papa was hardly in a position to like or dislike what his daughters chose to do. And had he been, a lick of paint on the rotting windows of the mansion he had built to show off his wealth might have pleased him more than knowing they were giving away money they could ill spare in order to get their names in the newspapers.

Kate looked at her over the top of her pince-nez. 'There's no need for you to do that, dear. I've told you before, that's what Mrs Rivers is employed to do.'

'It's perfectly all right, Aunt Kate, I don't mind lending a hand,' Poppy replied, anxious to leave the room before she said something she might regret later. 'In any case, I've promised Mrs Rivers I'll help her give the dining room a really good clean today.'

'That's quite unnecessary. It's never used.' Kate was quite snappish.

'Oh, but it used to be. We used to have wonderful dinner parties, didn't we, Kate?' Meg's little round face lit up and she clutched both hands to her breast. 'The ladies' dresses were beautiful, and their jewels sparkled in the candlelight. I remember I had a dress that was ...' she rummaged excitedly in her bag of scraps, '... this colour. No, it was a bit darker, I think ...'

'Oh, do stop running on, Meg. You don't know what you're talking about,' Kate said impatiently.

'Yes, I do.' Meg sat up straight. 'Papa used to have important people to dinner. And I used to play for them afterwards. Papa was proud of my piano-playing. And my singing.' Her chin lifted truculently. 'That was something I could do that you couldn't, and you didn't like it, Kate. Especially when Papa praised me in front of other people.'

'Don't be ridiculous,' Kate said, flushing with annoyance. 'And look, you haven't taken your pill this morning.'

'I don't want it. I feel quite well, thank you.'

With an obvious effort Kate smiled at her and said gently, 'That's because you take your pills, dear. You wouldn't feel so well if you didn't take them. We've had this argument before. Now, come along, swallow it with a sip of water or you'll be having one of your turns.' Her tone was soft but her expression was steely.

Meg hesitated, then Kate's will prevailed and she snatched up the pill. 'Oh, very well,' she said and swallowed it with the water placed there every morning for the purpose. Then she got up from the table and left the room. Shortly afterwards the strains of a Chopin waltz filtered through the house.

'Do you remember big dinner parties being held in this room, Mrs Rivers?' Poppy asked, as she and Mrs Rivers gazed round the vast dining room and wondered where to begin.

'Oh, yes.' Mrs Rivers stood with her hands on her hips, surveying the long mahogany table, dull for want of polish, and the twelve heavily carved Chippendale chairs. 'The master used to sit in the elbow chair at this end and Miss Kate in the one down at the other end. Oh, she was in her element, that one, playing the lady of the house.'

'What about Miss Meg, then?' Poppy went over and flung open the big window at the end of the room.

'Oh, she was allus made to stay in her room in case she got too excited and it brought on one of her turns.'

Poppy came back up the room, frowning. 'What *are* these turns, Mrs Rivers? Have you ever seen her in one?'

'No. Can't say I have. But that's what the pills are for, to stop her having them.' Mrs Rivers was busily taking the silver and glass out of the cabinets round the wall.

Poppy began to help her. After a few minutes she said, 'Aunt Meg really does need to keep taking those pills, then?'

'Oh, yes. She's been on them ever since her illness. And I must say Miss Kate is very good with her. She watches over her like a hen with a chick. I'm sure Miss Meg wouldn't be as well as she is if it wasn't for her sister. There, that's the cabinets emptied. Will you wash the shelves while I go and wash the glass? Then we can clean the silver between us.'

'Yes, of course.' Poppy fetched water and cleaned out the cabinets, then sat down with Mrs Rivers to clean the silver. 'It was before you came here, Aunt Meg's illness, wasn't it?' she said, carrying on with the conversation where they had left off.

'Aye, that's right. I've often wondered if it might have been something to do with her mother dying, but nobody ever said. She was bedridden for quite a long time, as I

128

understand it, and from what I've been told it was her sister who looked after her, nursing her day and night, so you can't wonder Miss Kate watches over her the way she does. Mind you, she's a lot better than she was. When I first came here she'd go days on end without speaking to a soul.'

'And what about my grandfather, "dear Papa" as Aunt Kate calls him?'

Mrs Rivers pulled a heavy salt cellar towards her and began to rub it with silver polish. 'We should really have taken all this to the kitchen to clean,' she said absentmindedly, 'but never mind, we've put a cloth on the table so it'll not do any harm. And it's saved us carrying it all through.' She looked up. 'What were we talking about? Oh, yes. The master. He looked exactly like the picture in the hall,' she said. 'He allus dressed that way and his glasses allus slipped down the way they are in the picture. He used to look over the top of them.' She gave a sniff. 'I didn't like him. He had cold eyes.' She paused for a minute, then went on, 'Sometimes he used to treat Miss Kate like so much dirt, but she never seemed to mind. I've seen that lass run where a dog wouldn't, for that man. Funny, that.' She shook her head. 'He treated Kate like that, yet he was allus kind to Miss Meg. I expect it was because she'd been so ill.'

'And of course, Meg was the baby of the family, wasn't she? She was several years younger than Kate and my father. Perhaps that had something to do with it.'

Mrs Rivers nodded. 'Aye, happen it did.'

'You don't remember my father, Mrs Rivers?'

'No. I never met him. In fact, to tell the truth I never knew he existed till you came here. His name were never mentioned. Funny, that. Him being the only son and all.'

It seemed there was a great deal of the Russell family history of which Mrs Rivers was in total ignorance.

They worked on companionably together and by the end of the day the room was transformed, the crystal all washed and sparkling and returned to its cabinets, the silver bright, the cobwebs all gone, the carpet brushed and the furniture polished.

Mrs Rivers brushed her arm across her forehead, weary now but smiling with satisfaction. 'Thanks for your help, lass. This is how this room allus looked when the master were alive. We used to polish it every week. Of course, there were more of us to do the work then. There were six indoor staff and four outdoor. Now there's only me and Rivers. It's no wonder the place is going to rack and ruin.' She went out of the room and began to hobble back towards the kitchen. Poppy followed her.

'Are your feet sore, Mrs Rivers?' she asked.

'Aye, they are a bit,' she admitted. 'I've had these shoes on all day and they're beginning to pinch. I'd put my old spaddicks on now we've finished, but I've left them upstairs in the bedroom. Rivers'll fetch them for me later. I can't haul myself up all them stairs to fetch them.'

'I'll fetch them for you,' Poppy said. 'That is, if you don't mind . . .'

'Bless you, no, lass. I'd be grateful, my bunions are playing up summat cruel now. You can go up the back stairs. Our room is the one right at the top nearest the stair-head.'

Poppy opened the door in the corner of the kitchen and went up the winding staircase. There was a landing and a door at first-floor level and then the stairs wound up to the attics, where another door opened onto a long corridor with rooms opening off. Poppy took the opportunity to have a quick look round. The rooms were small and contained very little, the odd bedstead, a chest of drawers, a broken chair or two. Clearly they had been servants' quarters in the past. One room was locked and as there was no key she looked through the keyhole to see what treasures it contained. But she was disappointed – all she could see was rubbish, old discarded furniture, rolled-up carpets, suit-cases and trunks, an old rocking horse. Obviously this was the family junk room, where things had been put out of the way and forgotten. She promised herself that one day she would find the key and come exploring. She might find clues to her father's early years here.

She went back along the corridor to the bedroom at the head of the stairs. This was slightly larger than the rest and was furnished comfortably, with a double bed, a wardrobe and dressing table. It was immaculately tidy and Mrs Rivers's slippers were neatly side by side on the rug by the bed, a large ragged hole cut into each one to accommodate the painful bunions.

Poppy picked them up and carried them down to the kitchen, smiling gently to herself. She had grown very fond of Mr and Mrs Rivers in the few months she had lived at Dale House and she knew that affection was returned. It seemed the ties that held her to Dale House were drawing ever tighter.

Chapter Thirteen

The summer wore on. Sir Frederick came into the office most days, always with a copy of *The Times* under his arm, which he read before doing anything else.

'I don't like the way things are going with this war, Miss Barlow,' he confided, folding the newspaper as she went in to sort out the day's work with him. 'This Somme business seems to be dragging on, even with these new tank things they've got. Terrible loss of life, too. Terrible.' He shook his head and sighed. 'I suppose I should be thankful that all my workforce are exempt or I don't know what we'd do.' He looked up and gave her a ghost of a smile. 'I suppose it would mean young ladies like you working in the pot shop and wielding the tilt hammer.' He shuddered. 'Heaven forbid *that* day should ever come!'

Poppy smiled back at him. 'A lot of women are on war work, Sir Frederick. Haven't you seen the women who work in the munitions factory? Most of them have a definite yellow colour to their skin. It can't be healthy. And there must always be the danger of explosion, working with TNT and the like. I think I'd rather wield the tilt hammer, myself. Mind you, women already drive ambulances and there are a lot of women bus conductors – bus conductresses, I suppose you'd call them.' She put her head on one side. 'I wouldn't mind doing that. In fact, I've often wondered if I should volunteer . . .'

He looked up, and the expression on his face was almost fearful. 'Oh, you couldn't do that, Miss Barlow. You couldn't leave us. We couldn't do without you.' He paused and stared out of the window, his jaw working. 'It's bad enough, God knows, with my boys both away.' He made an attempt at a smile and Poppy noticed that he was looking much older, these days. 'For God's sake don't you desert the ship as well, lass.'

'Are they well, your boys?' she asked. 'You hear from them?'

'I believe so, thank God. I get the odd letter. Nothing regular of course. Alec is in France – I don't know exactly where although I fear he's in the thick of it – and Josh ... well, he's over there too. I believe the Flying Corps is mostly concerned with reconnaissance, which entails flying over enemy territory to see what's going on behind the lines, as far as I can make out.' He passed his hand over his face. 'I don't know which is worse. Planes in the air get shot down, men on the ground get shot up. It's all such a damnable waste of life ...' He lapsed into silence, shaking his head.

Poppy turned to a clean page in her notebook. While she waited for Sir Frederick to begin dictating she stared at the page and thought about Josh, recalling her conversation with him at the garden party, words obviously not repeated to his father. He had said, 'I'm not terribly keen on hunting other planes and shooting them down, particularly as those other planes are doing the same to me.' She remembered the warmth in his dark blue eyes and his wry smile as he had spoken the words and she felt a sudden, unexpected lump in her throat and sent up a swift prayer for his safety. Her thoughts turned to Alec. With his highly polished boots and carefully pressed uniform she couldn't even begin to imagine him in the mud and filth of the trenches. She had had another letter from him this week, the second in less than four days. It was beginning to worry her that he wrote so often and also that the tone of his letters was becoming rather too familiar and affectionate.

Not that she had ever encouraged this. True, she wrote back to him, but not often, and then only out of politeness, because she had heard how important mail from home was to the men in the trenches. She tried to make her letters friendly yet at the same time quite impersonal and inconsequential, speaking often about his forthcoming marriage to Claire because she was anxious not to give him the wrong impression of her own feelings towards him.

Josh, of course, never wrote to her at all. She often wished he would.

Sir Frederick was speaking again. '... so goodness knows when he'll get leave,' he was saying. 'Claire is going ahead with the wedding preparations in her usual headstrong manner, convinced that all he'll have to do is go to his commanding officer and demand Christmas leave on compassionate grounds.' He sighed. 'Maybe she's right. She's used to getting her own way so I'm sure she won't allow a small matter like a world war to put a stop to her plans.' He gave a somewhat cynical smile and Poppy gained the impression that he was not particularly fond of his future daughter-in-law.

He pulled himself together. 'But never mind all that. We've got work to do. Have you got your pencil and pad ready, Miss Barlow?'

She smiled. 'I have them right here, Sir Frederick.'

'Good. Then let's begin.'

She took dictation for well over an hour, by which time the back of her neck and shoulders ached. She moved in her chair and flexed them briefly, then bent her head again.

Sir Frederick noticed. 'Oh, I'm sorry, my dear. I've kept you writing for much too long without a break.' He took out his pocket watch. 'Good gracious, it's past lunch time. Why on earth didn't you say?'

'It's hardly my place, Sir Frederick,' she said with a smile.

'What?' He looked at her with something akin to

surprise. 'No, I suppose not. Somehow I never think of you as ... well, anyway, run along now. You can type the letters up later. Tell Soames ...'

'Soames isn't in today, sir. His chest, you know. The hot, dusty weather affects him as much as the cold winters.'

Sir Frederick frowned. 'Good grief. He's off *again*? I know the poor chap's not well, but things can't go on like this. What about his work?'

'He's very well organised and he's taught me to do most things. It just means I have to stay a little later to finish, sometimes.'

'Does Templeton give you a hand?'

'I can manage quite well without his help, thank you,' she said firmly.

'Good.' He nodded thoughtfully. 'You should be recompensed. I'll see to it that you are.' He ran his fingers through his thick white hair and smiled at her. 'I must admit I was slightly apprehensive when you first came here to work, Miss Barlow, a woman in a man's world, but now I really don't know how we should manage without you.'

She flushed with pleasure. 'Thank you, sir.'

'Well now, you'd better run along. You're a busy woman and I've taken up rather a lot of your time.' He frowned. 'Most of those letters are quite important ...'

'It's all right, Sir Frederick, they'll be on your desk in the morning.'

Poppy took her sandwiches and went outside to eat them. The sun was almost too hot to sit on the wall outside the cottages and for once nobody came to join her, although this was partly because she was late. She was quite relieved at this because it meant that she could get back to work as soon as she had eaten without offending anybody. But as she began to unwrap the lunch Mrs Rivers had packed for her she saw Connie Templeton, George Templeton's wife, coming across from her house opposite.

'You're very welcome to come and sit in my garden to eat your lunch, Miss Barlow, she said a trifle stiffly, twisting her hands together as she spoke. 'It's quite private.'

'Thank you, Mrs Templeton but ...' Poppy was on the point of refusing, then she saw the look in Connie Templeton's eye and saw that she expected rejection, expected her to refuse, so instead she gave a wide smile. 'Oh, that's very kind of you, Mrs Templeton. I'd love to.' She began to gather up her lunch. 'Have you got a big garden?'

'Oh, no. Just a small plot at the back.' Connie shrugged deprecatingly. 'It's nowt special, but it's shady on a day like this. You must be baked, sitting on that wall.' She led the way across to the manager's house and round to the back where a rather dilapidated garden seat stood in the shade against the back wall of the house overlooking a patch of grass no bigger than a tablecloth. The grass was surrounded by a riot of bright flowers.

'Oh, what a pretty garden,' Poppy said in surprise.

'Yes. Jack – that's my brother-in-law – gave me the plants and I put them in.' Connie was obviously pleased at Poppy's remark. 'George, my husband, hasn't the interest in gardening. Well, he wouldn't have the time, would he, he's a very busy man.' She led Poppy to the seat. 'Please sit down and eat your lunch, Miss Barlow. I'll go and mash some tea. I daresay you can drink a cup.' She smiled nervously.

'Yes, indeed. Thank you.' Once again Poppy unwrapped her sandwiches and had nearly finished eating when Connie came back with a tray of tea and two cups.

'This is nice,' Connie said, sitting down beside her and pouring the tea.

'Yes, it is. Thank you for inviting me over, Mrs Templeton.' Poppy smiled at her.

'Oh, no. Thank you for coming. And please call me Connie.' She handed Poppy her tea, darting a glance at her and giving another nervous smile. 'I'm sure George wouldn't mind you calling me by my name although he thinks it wouldn't be right for the workers' wives to do that. He says we must remember our position here.' She spoke rather jerkily and her movements reminded Poppy of a little fluttering bird. 'It can be a bit lonely, sometimes.'

'Yes, I'm sure it must be,' Poppy said, recalling the pleasant times she often shared with the women from the cottages.

'I expect they think I'm stand-offish,' Connie said sadly. 'I don't mean to be. But George . . .'

'I'm sure they understand,' Poppy said quickly.

Connie sipped her tea. As she did so her sleeve rode up, revealing an angry blue bruise on her forearm. She quickly covered it up, glancing across to see if Poppy had noticed. 'I'm always banging into things,' she said apologetically. 'George says I must be the clumsiest woman in the world.'

Poppy made no comment. 'Does he come back for his lunch?' she asked instead.

'Oh yes. He's been and gone again. He's had to go into Sheffield this afternoon to see about some blister steel or something,' Connie said vaguely. She gave her nervous smile. 'It's because you were late taking your lunch hour that I could ask you over.' Then lest Poppy should get the wrong impression she added quickly, 'George is very good to me. He pays for Mary Smithers to clean the house.' She looked down at her hands. 'Not that I really need her, but George thinks it's the right thing to do, since he's manager here.' She gave a shrug. 'Any road, it helps Mary a bit so I don't mind. But I do get a bit bored with nowt to do and nobody to talk to and I really like housework so I go over and do a bit for Jack most days. George doesn't like me doing it but he doesn't say much because he knows I do it for my sister – she died two years ago and I promised her on her deathbed that I would look after Jack. Not that he's not capable,' she added quickly. 'But it's no trouble to me to cook a bit extra at meal times and take it over to him and to do a bit of washing for him. Jack's a good man. I expect them over there . . .' she jerked her head in the direction of the cottages, 'I expect they all say there's summat going on between Jack and me, but there's not. He respects me too much for there to be any hanky-panky.' Her voice softened. 'He's a lovely man, is Jack.' All the time she had been speaking she had been staring out at the garden. Now she turned to Poppy. 'Oh, hark at me, will you? I've done nowt but chatter ever since you came. You must think I'm a regular old gossip.'

'No, of course I don't.' Poppy put her teacup down and stood up. 'I've enjoyed talking to you, Connie, and I hope I'll be able to come and see you again.'

'Yes. So do I,' Connie said warmly. 'But I have to be careful ...' Even as she spoke she glanced over her shoulder.

'I understand.' Poppy smiled at her. 'But I must be getting back now. I've about twenty letters to type as well as all my other work before I go home tonight.'

She went back to the office, glancing at her watch as she went. To her dismay it was nearly half past two. She quickened her steps. She had intended to take only a short lunch break because she was late and had so much work to do, instead of which she had spent well over an hour with Connie Templeton. She sighed. It was obvious Connie was lonely and needed someone to talk to, so the time hadn't been wasted. It was also quite obvious that Connie was more than a little fond of her brother-in-law, although Poppy believed her when she said their friendship was quite innocent. It was a good thing she had a friend in Jack since she was not allowed to make friends with the other women at Kentons, especially in view of the bruises she seemed to pick up so frequently ...

Poppy hurried up the steps to the office. She was going to be very late leaving tonight if she as going to get all Sir Frederick's letters typed. The heat hit her like a wall as she opened the door, and she went over and opened every window to let in what little air there was. Looking down into the yard she could see the men at work, some of them stripped to the waist in the heat of the workshops.

At least she wasn't having to work in the added heat of a furnace, she thought with gratitude as she sat down at her typewriter, although the office itself resembled something like an oven even with the door and windows open. She began to work, the banging and clanging from men working in the yard providing a noisy accompaniment to the clatter of the typewriter keys.

She was so engrossed in what she was doing that it wasn't until she finished the last of Sir Frederick's letters that she realised that everywhere was quiet. She looked at her watch. It was gone half past six. She should have left work over an hour ago.

She gathered up the letters and took them through and laid them on Sir Frederick's desk. Then she stood for a moment, rubbing the back of her neck where it ached from an afternoon at the typewriter. She was hot and sticky and very tired. What she needed was a long cool bath. Even the thought of the vast ugly bathroom at Dale House was appealing.

She stretched her arms above her head to ease the tension in her back. As she did so she suddenly felt two hands snake round from behind and cover her breasts.

For a split second she froze, too surprised even to cry out. Then she tried to push them away, at the same time straining to twist round and see who it was behind her.

'No need to struggle, my beauty. We've got the place to ourselves.' It was George Templeton's voice and in one deft movement he spun her round to face him, holding her hands behind her back in one of his. She registered with half her mind that he was looking very smart in a dark suit and stiff collar and tie. His hair was sleeked back with some kind of pungent oil and he was sweating slightly. He grinned at her. 'They've all gone home so there's only you and me. It's what we've been waiting for, isn't it?' His knee was already busily trying to work its way between her legs. 'Not that we need to be in any hurry. We can take our time.'

Suddenly, she found her voice and screamed, but he cut her off, his mouth crushing hers, his moustache scratching her face as she turned her head this way and that to free herself from his foul embrace.

'Leave me alone. Get off me.' She wriggled one hand free and brought it up to give him a stinging blow on the head. Then she pulled his hair and scratched his cheek, all the time trying to twist away.

'Aw, come on, don't pretend with me. You want it as much as I do. I've seen the way you look at me.' He was trying to nuzzle her neck as he spoke, still holding one hand behind her back.

She did what she could with her free hand, scratching and hitting him as hard as she could, but he had her pinned against the desk and there was no way to escape.

'That's it, my lovely, fight me,' he laughed and she could see a dangerous glint in his eye 'I like a bit of spirit in my women. Don't you know a bit of a fight adds to the pleasure? Come on, my beauty, hit me as hard as you like. I love it.' She felt his foul mouth on hers again.

She closed her eyes, trying to think what to do as she felt his hand tearing at her blouse. He was quite right, everybody had gone home, so there was no point in trying to scream. She was alone to fight this man. This animal. God, how she hated him.

He had her blouse open now and was nuzzling her breast, and she could tell he was getting more and more excited as she struggled to free herself. She tried to twist away from him but he held her in a vice-like grip. All she could do was to rain blows down on his head with her free hand but it had not the slightest effect.

Then, suddenly, with an enormous effort of will, she relaxed and let herself fall against him like a rag doll.

He lifted his head and took a step back, his mouth wide open in surprise. 'What the hell? Christ, she's not fainted on me . . .?'

'No, she's not fainted on you.' As she spoke through

gritted teeth Poppy brought her knee up between his legs, hard, all her pent-up hatred in that one movement. Caught by total surprise he released his hold on her, yelping with pain as he began to dance round the room, doubled up and clutching his wounded manhood, swearing at her and calling her all the names under the sun.

Poppy didn't care. Her only thought was to escape. She fled from the room, grabbing her handbag from her desk as she rushed through her office and half ran, half fell down the steps to the yard, straight into the arms of Mordecai Jones.

'Miss Barlow! What's up? We thought we heard a scream but we weren't sure. Charity said I should come and see . . .' The poor man looked quite bewildered.

Poppy clung to him. 'Oh, Mord. Thank God you did. It's him . . .' She jerked her head back towards the office, at the same time pulling her tattered blouse together. 'He tried . . . Oh, God, here he comes.'

Mordecai put his arm protectively round her. 'It's all right, Miss Barlow, he'll not hurt you again.' He stood with her at the foot of the steps as George Templeton came down, looking white-faced and walking rather stiffly but smilingly trying to look as if nothing unusual had happened.

'Still here, Miss Barlow?' he said genially. 'I would have thought it was long past your knocking-off time. And what about you, Jones? Does your pretty little wife know you're carrying on with Sir Frederick's secretary?' He made to walk past them and Poppy could only marvel at his cool, self-assured manner.

But Mordecai stepped into his path, with one arm still round Poppy. 'There's no need for you to make remarks like that, Mr Templeton,' he said without raising his voice. 'You know there's no truth in what you're saying. You're only trying to cover up your own sins. I tell you here and now, if it were not against my religion to strike a fellow man I'd knock you down for what you've been trying to do to this young lady. You should be ashamed of yourself, Mr

Templeton. And you a married man, too.'

'Rubbish. I don't know what she's been telling you but she's made it all up. I never touched her.' George Templeton tried to brush past them both.

'She's told me nowt. She didn't need to. I've got eyes in my head. Look at her, scared half to death and her blouse all torn.' He turned to Poppy. 'If he ever tries to lay a finger on you again, Miss Barlow, just let me know and I'll report it to Sir Frederick. He'll not take kindly to such goings-on.'

George Templeton stepped up and wagged a finger in Mordecai's face. 'You need to watch your step, Jones, or you'll find yourself looking for work. And a house to live in. Your little wife won't take kindly to *that*, will she, and her with a bun in the oven,' he sneered.

'I'll thank you not to speak of my wife that road, Mr Templeton,' Mordecai said, his voice level. He turned to Poppy. 'Come along, Miss Barlow, I'll tek you home with me for a cup of tea. I guess you could do wi' it.'

'No, thank you all the same, Mord, I'd rather go home, if you don't mind,' Poppy said. 'My aunts will be wondering where I've got to.' She could have bitten her tongue out the moment she had spoken. It was the first time she had mentioned her home. But neither man seemed to have registered what she had said.

'Very well, miss, I'll tek you to where you keep your bicycle. Or would you like me to walk you back?'

'That's it, walk her back through the wood so you can tumble her in the grass,' George Templeton sneered.

They both ignored him.

'Oh, no, thank you, Mord. I'll be home in five minutes.'

They walked across to where she left her bicycle every day. 'Are you sure you'll be all right, lass?' Mordecai asked, forgetting to be formal in his concern for her. 'You're still trembling.'

She looked over her shoulder. George Templeton was still watching, a look of absolute hatred on his face. If he hadn't been her enemy before, he most certainly was now. 'Yes, thank you, Mord. I'll be fine. Thank you for rescuing me.' In full view of George Templeton she reached up and kissed him on the cheek. Then she got on her bike and pedalled off up the road as fast as she could go.

Chapter Fourteen

Poppy wheeled her bicycle round to the back of the house when she got home and went in through the kitchen door, anxious to avoid any chance of encountering either of her aunts in her present state. Mrs Rivers was standing at the table ironing. She looked up as Poppy entered, her jaw dropping, the iron forgotten.

'Mercy me, lass, whatever have you been up to? You look as if you've been pulled through a hedge backwards and seen a ghost, all at once!' she said.

Poppy slumped down in a chair by the table. 'It's a long story, Mrs Rivers. Albert wasn't well so I had extra to do. I was working late to catch up ... George Templeton, the manager at Kentons ... just lately he seems to have taken a fancy to me, goodness knows why, he always used to hate the sight of me ... well, he came up to the office ...' She shook her head, unable to go on. 'What I need right now is a nice cool bath and some clean clothes, Mrs Rivers.'

'Oh, lass, he didn't ... I mean, he didn't ...?' The old woman's face was a mask of horror.

Poppy shook her head wearily. 'No, Mrs Rivers, he didn't.' She gave a ghost of a smile. 'But it wasn't for want of trying. He would have done if he'd had the chance.' She looked down at her blouse, torn where two buttons had been pulled off, and shuddered. 'He's an animal, that man. I've heard tales about him, now I know they're not

144

exaggerated.' She stood up. 'But I mustn't sit here like this. If Aunt Kate sees me she'll never stop saying "I told you so! I said you should never have gone to work at *that place*."' She gave a fair imitation of Kate's prim voice. 'How can I get up the bathroom without running into her?'

'Nip up the back stairs, love. I'll tell them you've come home all hot and sticky so you've gone to have a bath before you have your meal. It's true enough, when all's said and done. But like I'm always telling you, do mind that old geyser up there. It tends to flare a bit when you put a match to it.' She glanced down at the iron. 'Oh, will you look at this, now I've gone and scorched Alf's shirt. Never mind, it's only the tail so nobody'll see it.' She gave Poppy a smile that was practically toothless. 'Go on, now, love. I'll have your meal all ready by the time you come down.'

Ten minutes later Poppy was lying in a cool bath in the ugly old bathroom, listening to the water struggling noisily through the pipes and staring up at the flaking whitewash on the ceiling. Never had she been so glad to be there. As she scrubbed her flesh to rid it of any trace of George Templeton's touch – not that he had managed to get very far in that direction – she was thankful that her father had not been shy to warn her of the dangers to a woman in a man's world and had taught her the best way to defend herself should the need arise. She smiled to herself. How it would shock the aunts if they knew what he had told her! But it had saved the day, although she knew she would never get a whiff of Parma violet hair oil again without remembering George Templeton's lecherous leer. And to think he had expected her to welcome his advances! The arrogance of the man. Well, he wouldn't try anything like that again, of that she was certain.

She climbed out of the bath and towelled herself dry. By the time she went down to the parlour, in a clean print dress, her hair neatly brushed and a green floppy bow holding it back at the neck, she was feeling more like her old self again.

'That's a pretty dress, Poppy dear,' Meg said, giving her a welcoming smile as she always did. 'Is it new?'

'Of course it isn't new,' Kate snapped. 'Don't be silly, Meg. Poppy's worn it before, several times.' She turned to Poppy, her tone hardly less snappish. 'You're very late, Poppy.'

Poppy sat down and began the meal Mrs Rivers had just brought in. 'Yes, I worked late because I wanted to finish what I was doing. I was so hot when I came in that I went up and had a bath.'

'That's two baths this week. Goodness knows what the gas bill will be. Did you bring a newspaper home with you?' Kate glared at her over her pince-nez.

'No, I'm afraid not. I didn't think of it.' Poppy didn't admit she had had other things on her mind.

'Hm. That's a pity.' Kate gave a little self-satisfied smile. 'Our names are probably in it tonight.'

Poppy helped herself to more potato. 'Been giving your hard-earned wealth away again, Aunt?' she asked, doing her best not to sound sarcastic. 'What is it this time? Comforts for the troops or in aid of the Waifs and Strays?'

'Neither,' Kate said shortly. She suspected her niece was mocking her although she couldn't imagine why this should be and she couldn't be sure because Poppy's expression was serene. She battled with herself against saying anything more but in the end couldn't resist announcing, 'We have bought a silver salver in memory of dear Papa. I've asked for it to be placed in the Cutler's Hall.' She simpered a little. 'I expect there will be a small dedication ceremony which Meg and I will be asked to attend.'

'Oh, that will be nice for you both.' Poppy paused with her fork halfway to her mouth. 'Just a minute. I believe I saw a local newspaper in the kitchen. I don't know whether it was today's. I'll go and see.' She got up from her chair.

'What were you doing in the kitchen? No, eat your dinner before it gets cold. I'll ring for Mrs Rivers. That's what servants are for ...' Poppy could hear Kate's voice following her down the passage as she hurried to the kitchen. Her aunt was still calling directions to her when she got back, the evening paper in her hand.

She handed it to Kate, who looked through it avidly, searching for her name.

'Oh!' she said after several minutes, disappointment in her voice. 'Here it is, on the back page. We usually get a mention on the front page, don't we, Meg?' She didn't wait for Meg's reply, but when on, 'Listen to this. "The Misses Russell have with their usual generosity donated yet another gift to the Cutler's Hall in memory of their illustrious father, Josiah Russell, this time in the shape of a large silver salver. Would it be asking too much of them to donate a display case next to house the many gifts dedicated to him over the years?"' She folded the newspaper carefully, again and again, her lips tight.

'Do you think they might be implying we've given too many gifts in Papa's memory, Kate?' Meg asked nervously.

Kate glared at her. 'Indeed, no. Whatever gives you that idea? I think it's a very good idea that we should donate a display case. It would be very fitting. I don't know why I hadn't thought of it before. I shall order it immediately. Oak, of course.'

'Do you think that would be wise, Aunt?' Poppy said carefully. 'If you have money to spare I'm sure a donation towards comforts for the troops in France, or help for their families at home would be very much appreciated.' The fact that in truth the sisters didn't have money to spare was an argument Poppy realised she had lost long ago.

Kate turned a glacial stare on her. 'I like to control where our money is spent, Poppy. It's the Government's business to look after the men who are fighting this war and their families, not ours. War is not something I approve of.'

Poppy opened her mouth to point out that of course nobody in their right mind wanted war but then closed it again. It would be useless trying to discuss the matter with

Kate any further. She lived in a world quite isolated from reality and kept her sister equally cocooned. She had noticed how her aunt had passed over the pages containing reports from the front, showing no interest in them at all, unlike Alf Rivers, who sometimes bought a paper because he had a nephew in France and read the reports out to his wife, slowly, laboriously pointing to every word as he read. If a Zeppelin came over and dropped a bomb on the Cutler's Hall Kate would soon show an interest, Poppy thought grimly, if only because the portrait of her precious father might be damaged. She put her knife and fork together with more than usual firmness and picked up her tray.

'I'll take these back to Mrs Rivers and then I'm going to my room. I'm very tired.'

'Don't take it yourself. Ring the bell. How many times have I to tell you that's what servants are for ...' Kate's droning voice followed her out of the room.

Albert Soames was back at work the next day. Poppy didn't tell him what had happened with George Templeton, feeling confident that the manager had learned his lesson and would leave her alone from now on. But she reckoned without Albert's shrewd eye.

'What's got into George?' he asked one morning several days later, his gaze following George as he walked through the office looking neither to right nor left, on his way to see Sir Frederick. 'He goes through the office like a dose of salts these days wi' a face like thunder and never so much as a "good morning" to anybody. It's not like him. He allus used to stop for a word on his way through, specially wi' you, lass, lately. I was beginning to think he'd teken a bit of a shine to you, to tell the truth.'

'Well, if so the shine has very quickly worn off,' she answered without looking up from her desk. 'Thank goodness.'

'You've never been keen on our George have you, lass?'

Albert persisted, trying unsuccessfully to read her expression.

'No,' she said shortly. 'And I liked it better when he wasn't keen on me.'

'Well, he's good at his job, I'll say that for him.' Albert went back to his work. Obviously, something had happened between the two of them and he was rather afraid he could guess what it was. George Templeton had the reputation of being a randy sod. He smiled into his ledger. If he was right he'd wager a week's wages George had picked the wrong one if he'd tried it on with Poppy. That lass could stand up for herself, he was in no doubt.

But Poppy had other things to think about, things that had pushed the business with George Templeton to the back of her mind.

There had been another letter from Alec Kenton this morning. Lately they had been arriving at the rate of at least two a week. He always sent them to her at work since she had been careful not to let him know her home address, and so far she had managed to get to the office in time to intercept the post before Albert could begin to recognise the envelopes and ask questions.

The letter was in her pocket now, burning a hole by its presence. She wracked her brain to try and think what she had ever put in her letters to Alec – not that she had written many – that he could possibly have misconstrued. She had always been so careful to make her letters light and chatty and quite impersonal, beginning *Dear Major Kenton*, and ending *Yours sincerely, Poppy Barlow*. She could hardly have been more formal without appearing rude.

Yet today she had received a letter clearly written by a man almost at the end of his tether.

My dearest, dearest Poppy,

I have come to realise, living in this hellhole, that life is too short for pretence. You must, by now, know how I feel about you. I've scarcely veiled my feelings in my letters to you although you have – quite rightly – been too much of a lady to respond in like manner. I respect you for this but watching men suffer and die before my eyes and not knowing whether I shall be the next victim, I feel the time has come for total honesty between us.

They say there is no such thing as love at first sight but this isn't true. The moment I saw you I knew you were the only girl in the world for me. My first waking thought each morning is of you and your face is before my eyes when I close them at night. It is only the thought of you that sustains me in this hellish nightmare we are living through.

But, of course, there's Claire. Naturally, I have agonised over my engagement to her, the last thing I want to do is to hurt her, but I am sure that in the long run it would hurt her far more if I were to marry her, knowing my heart wasn't in our marriage.

As soon as I hear from you, my darling, and know that you share my feelings I shall write to Claire and break off our engagement – in all honesty it was never to be more than a marriage of convenience so I fear her pride will suffer more than her heart.

Please write back soon. If there is one thing I have learnt in this dreadful place it is that what little happiness there is to be had in this life must be grasped with both hands.

I love you, my darling.

Alec.

She didn't need to take the letter out and read it again, the contents were burned into her brain. And the feelings it aroused in her were so mixed that she didn't know which was uppermost. At first she had been appalled. How could Alec Kenton imagine he was in love with her? He knew hardly anything about her. And worse, whatever had given him the idea that she might return his affections? Then she felt guilty, and raked through her mind to recall what she might inadvertently have said or done to give him that impression. But she could think of nothing. Oh, he was a pleasant young man and she liked him well enough, but he was just not the sort of man she would ever fall in love with.

But how could she write and tell someone who was risking his life in the trenches every day, who had poured his heart out so intimately to her, that she didn't and never could love him? How could she destroy the thing he seemed to be pinning all his hopes on?

On the other hand, how could she allow him to go on thinking that she returned his love? What had she ever said or done to give him such an idea? And what about Claire, up to her eyes in wedding preparations? What about her feelings? At the very least she would sue him for breach of promise if he broke off the engagement, never mind if he broke her heart.

The thoughts went round and round in her head as she tried to find a solution to the problem, sending her hot and cold in turn. Even after she got to bed that night she was still no nearer deciding what she should do. And there was nobody she could to talk it over with.

She closed her eyes, trying to court sleep, and suddenly Josh's face appeared before her. He was Alec's brother. If only she could talk to him, perhaps he would be able to suggest a way of dealing with this. She let her mind travel over the conversations she had had with Josh. He was nice, he made her laugh. She recalled his twinkling eyes and mischievous smile. He was a man it would be all too easy to fall in love with ... Now if the letter had come from him ...

Suddenly, it all fell into place, almost as if Josh had spoken to her. Of course, she must write to Alec and explain her feelings towards him, letting him down as lightly as possible and at the same time thanking him for the great compliment he had paid her. She wouldn't mention Claire, that was a problem for him to resolve. After all, he had made her a promise so he must have had some regard for her and would have married her quite happily if she, Poppy, had not come on the scene.

It would be a difficult letter to write because the last thing she wanted was to hurt him. She lay staring up into the darkness for a long time, trying to compose it in her mind. She fell asleep just before dawn.

Three days later the letter still hadn't been written although her waste-paper basket was full of unfinished attempts. She waited until Sunday, then went up to her room after lunch, determined to stay there until it was done. Then, without reading it through, she put it in the envelope, sealed it, stamped it and took it to the post, praying silently that Alec wouldn't be too upset, trying to convince herself that what he felt for her was nothing more than infatuation heightened by the conditions of war.

She walked back feeling totally drained. It had been another very hot day but it was a little cooler now, and the shadows were lengthening. She glanced at her watch. It was almost seven o'clock. She had been working on the letter for nearly five hours.

She let herself into the cool hall. The hours she had spent scrubbing the black and white tiles while Mrs Rivers swept the walls and polished the carved staircase made it look a good deal more welcoming than when she had first arrived at Dale House. She glanced up at the huge chandelier. That had posed a bit of a problem, and it had taken the strength of Alf Rivers to let it down by its system of pulleys so that they could clean it. But now it sparkled in the myriad lights from the long stained-glass window above the front door. The grandfather clock at the bend of the stairs also gleamed with polish.

Poppy smiled. She herself had polished the clock and out of idle curiosity had taken the key from its hook inside the door and wound it up. It immediately began to tick and had been keeping perfect time ever since.

She recalled Aunt Kate's face when she saw it.

152

'But the clock stopped when dear Papa died and has never gone since!' she had said, an expression of horror on her face. 'It must be some kind of omen. When did it start to tick?'

Poppy had bitten her tongue against saying she'd simply wound it up and said instead, 'I must have moved it a little when I polished it. That's all it would take to set the pendulum swinging again, so all I had to do was to wind it up.'

Kate had given a satisfied smile. 'I shall do what Papa always did and wind it up on my way to bed every Saturday night.' She had gazed up at the ceiling. 'I think it must be a sign that Papa is looking down with approval on the way we live.'

Remembering all this, Poppy smiled and made her way to the parlour. Sometimes she was sure her aunts were completely batty. But she had grown to love them, all the same.

Meg was playing hymns on the harmonium in the corner and Kate was singing, 'I will cling to the old rugged cross,' with her eyes closed, slightly off-key, when Poppy entered the room. They both stopped when Poppy walked in.

'Where have you been, my dear?' Kate said, her voice a mixture of annoyance and concern. 'Tea was hours ago.'

'I was in my room, writing letters,' Poppy said. 'I didn't realise the time.' She sat down at the table and passed her hand across her eyes.

'You must be hungry,' Meg said. 'I'll ring for Mrs Rivers to bring you some tea.' She got up from the harmonium.

'No, you carry on playing. I'll do it,' Kate said, getting up from her chair. As she passed Poppy she laid a hand on her shoulder. 'Is something troubling you, dear?' she asked kindly.

Poppy waited until she had rung the bell, then looked up at her. 'Were you very upset when your engagement was broken off, Aunt Kate?' she said.

Kate shot her sister a sharp look but Meg was happily

153

playing 'Love Divine All Loves Excelling', at the same time cleverly weaving in the strains of another hymn that Poppy couldn't quite recognise. She turned back to Poppy, her mouth primly set, all traces of concern gone. 'It's not something I ever discuss,' she said shortly. 'Ah, Mrs Rivers. Some tea and crumpets for Miss Poppy, if you please.'

'I couldn't eat . . .' Poppy began.

'Nonsense. Of course you can.' Kate's tone brooked no argument.

Poppy gratefully drank the tea that Mrs Rivers brought and managed to eat the crumpets, even though they tasted like nothing so much as wet blotting paper. But all the time her thoughts were with the letter that even now lay in the postbox on the corner, the letter that she still wondered if she had been right to send to a man facing death every day in the trenches.

Chapter Fifteen

Over the next days Poppy immersed herself in her work, trying not to imagine how Alec Kenton would react when he received her letter, taking a strange kind of comfort from knowing that post to the front often took some time to reach its destination. She was still not sure she had done the right thing, yet in all conscience what else could she have done? It would have been even more of a tangle if she had pretended that she returned Alec's feelings, because he would have broken off his engagement to Claire with no hesitation at all. Poor Claire. Whatever happened Poppy could only feel sorry for her, even though she hadn't liked her very much the one time she had met her.

Her own feelings were mixed. At one and the same time she felt guilty, wondering if she might unknowingly have encouraged Alec, yet furious with him for putting her in such a difficult position. Added to that, in the deepest recesses of her mind she couldn't help feeling flattered that he should hold her in such high esteem.

But mainly she felt that it was all a horrible mess that would never have happened if it had not been for this dreadful war, and she wished she need have had no part in it.

And she couldn't even get away from thinking about the war during her lunch breaks. 'The wives' were full of the news that their husbands had received their call-up papers.

'It used to be only men under twenty-six that got called up, but now it's all between eighteen and forty-one,' Maud Benson said. 'So they all got 'em.'

'Aye, even me dad!' Daisy Frampton roared with laughter, tossing her peroxide-blonde head. 'An' him over sixty, too.'

'What did he do?' Charity Jones asked, her innocent eyes wide.

'Sent 'em back, o' course, wi' his birth certificate. Sir Frederick said that was what he'd to do. He never heard no more about it.'

'Mord failed his medical,' Charity said, putting her hands protectively over her swelling belly. 'We knew he would, because of his foot, but I thanked the good Lord, all t'same.'

'He'd not have had to go, any road,' Florrie Braithwaite said comfortably. 'None of the men here can be spared. Their work's too skilled an' important. Sir Frederick said so.'

'George Templeton's work's not skilled. Any fool could strut about t'works throwin' their weight about like he does,' Maud Benson said, her voice disparaging. 'My Jake's educated. He could do what George Templeton does, a damn sight better, an' all.' Maud never let an opportunity slip to remind people that Jake had been to night school.

'I heard he failed his medical, any road,' Lily Ferris said. She was quiet for a minute, then her face clouded over and she said, 'It'd do him good to be where our Henry is, right now.'

'Where is your son?' Poppy asked.

Lily shrugged her massive shoulders. 'They're not allowed to say, but somewhere in France. I just pray God he's safe,' she murmured, closing her eyes.

Charity bowed her head. 'Amen to that,' she said.

'My Harry's over there, too, but he's in the stores so I hope he's somewhere safe. I tell myself he is or I'd never sleep,' Mary Smithers said with a sigh. She brightened up.

'Any road, I asked Mr Alec to keep an eye out for him so he'll see he's all right. And you're right, George Templeton did fail his medical. Mrs Templeton told me when I was over there the other day.' She gave a little smile. 'I reckon she wished he hadn't. He gave her a cruel beating when he got back from it. Not that he wanted to be called up, the lily-livered so-and-so, but he didn't like to think he was less than perfect.'

'What was his trouble?' Daisy asked.

'Summat wrong with his back, I think. He had rickets as a child.'

'Didn't we all!' Lily said, with a mirthless laugh. 'But it didn't stop most o' t'lads going. My nephew's nearly blind in one eye so what did he do? He waited till ten o'clock at night when t'recruiting officers were tired, and held the paper over t'same eye twice. They passed him A1.' She shook her head. 'He joined up wi' my lad, Henry. They was both mad keen to go an' do their bit. I'm proud of 'em, but I wish to God they was out of it and back home.' Her eyes filled with tears but she bit them back. 'Well, I must get on,' she said briskly. 'I'm all behind today. I've still got t'wash house to scrub out an' t'back yard to swill.'

Poppy slid off the wall. 'And I must be getting back to work,' she said, brushing the crumbs off her skirt.

'Have you heard how Sir Frederick's boys are?' Maud asked. 'They're both in France, I've heard.'

'As far as I know they're both well,' Poppy said. 'Sir Frederick doesn't say much about them.'

'No, but he's their pa. I've no doubt he worries,' Daisy said sagely.

'Aye, when it comes to family he's no different from the rest of us,' Mary agreed.

Poppy walked back across the cobbles to the office deep in thought. She lived what almost amounted to a double life. Here, the reality of war was ever present, there was constant hammering and banging from the grimy workshops as gleaming scythes and cutlasses were turned out, miraculously in Poppy's eyes, from lumps of raw metal. And the language, when the men didn't realise she was within earshot, was often ripe.

Quite different was the atmosphere at home, where her aunts continued to live in their lavender-scented cocoon of genteel poverty, barricaded by Kate's wilful ignorance against what was going on in the real world. Poppy smiled to herself. She realised now what a shock it must have been to them when she had turned up, bringing her twentieth-century ideas and fashions with her. It was to their credit that they had allowed her to stay. Allowed. Poppy pondered the word. It was not a case of allowing her to stay. Rather, it would break their hearts if she were even to suggest leaving them now, after all these months. As for the aunts, she had grown to love them, in spite of their idiosyncrasies, and they had wound themselves round her conscience, binding her to them with their very frailty and unworldliness.

Unworldliness that reached even to the books Kate read. Each Saturday now Poppy took the tram down into the city. She enjoyed the hustle and bustle, the clanking trams, the clip-clop of the horse buses and wagons, the clatter of clogs on the pavements. And she loved to browse in the brightly gas-lit department stores or stop by the smaller shops, where almost everything for sale, from tin kettles and cooking stoves at the ironmongers to great sides of beef and long strings of sausages at the butchers, was displayed outside the front, displays sometimes reaching up to the second and third floor so that she had to step into the street and hold her hat on to take it all in.

In contrast, it was quiet at the library, where she changed Kate's book each week and everyone talked in a hushed whisper, if at all. It had been Poppy's idea to bring home library books although Kate had been doubtful at first, finding the idea of reading books other people had handled distasteful, especially as she would have to pay twopence a book for the privilege. But now she looked forward to her weekly book and read Dickens and Sir Walter Scott avidly, Thomas Hardy with less enthusiasm, remarking that 'of course people didn't really behave like that'. She refused to have books by Hall Caine in the house, Poppy was at a loss to understand why since to her knowledge her aunt had never read one. Sometimes Meg looked longingly at the books Poppy brought home but Kate somehow managed to prevent her from actually picking them up, saying she must read them first to make sure they were suitable. They never were.

Poppy smiled to herself as she climbed the stone steps and went into the office. If she tried to tell people how her aunts behaved they would never believe her.

Albert had finished his sandwiches and was reading the newspaper. He looked up as she walked in.

'Glad you've got summat to smile about, lass. There's precious little in the paper, here. Bread's gone up to tenpence a loaf.' He shook his head. 'I don't know what the world's coming to. The Government says it's due to the price of imported wheat but I thought we grew most of our own now.' He shook the paper irritably. 'Bah! They'll use any excuse.'

Poppy put her hat down and fluffed up her hair at the piece of mirror on top of the filing cabinet. 'I'm afraid it'll cause a lot of hardship among the poorer folk,' she said.

'Aye, it will, that. Folks'll starve even worse than they do now. My wife allus makes her own bread. It's better than that bought muck. But I doubt she'll gain much in price because I expect flour'll go up as well.'

She sat down and wound paper into the typewriter. 'Yes. I expect it will,' she replied, her mind on the work ahead.

'Casualty list is longer than ever. Look.' He held up the newspaper so that she could see the long column of names. 'Dreadful business on the Somme. Dreadful business.' He shook his head, folding the newspaper at the same time. Then he put it down on his desk and went back to his figures.

Poppy began typing the letters Sir Frederick had dictated earlier. She felt vaguely troubled, vaguely flat. It was probably all this talk of the war dragging on with its deprivations at home and its horror stories from the front. She gave herself a mental shake and tried to concentrate on what she was doing. Sir Frederick would be back later to sign the letters; he had gone off to a luncheon appointment at the Cutler's Hall. She gave a slight smile. The war wasn't allowed to interfere with some things.

It was four o'clock before Sir Frederick arrived back, his nose a little red, his expression genial.

'There's no hurry for the letters, my dear,' he said, patting Poppy's shoulder as he passed her desk. 'I've several important things to see to in my office so I shan't be leaving yet. See that I'm not disturbed, will you?' He went into his office and shut the door.

Ten minutes later the sound of gentle snoring came through the wall.

Poppy looked over at Albert, who raised one eyebrow. 'It must have been a good lunch,' he murmured.

She giggled. 'I wonder what the other important things are that he has to do,' she whispered.

Half an hour later the telegraph boy arrived, his pillbox hat perched jauntily on the side of his head.

'Hullo, Billy, what have you got for us today?' Albert asked. Quite often orders were telegraphed to Kentons if they were urgent, so they knew the telegraph boy quite well.

Billy looked at the envelope in his hand. 'It's for Sir Frederick Kenton at his home address. The maid at Kenton Hall said to bring it here. He usually gives me sixpence,' he added cheekily.

'Well, he left orders he wasn't to be disturbed so you'd better leave it with me,' Albert said. 'But you won't get your sixpence, I'm afraid.'

'Never mind. I'll get it next time.' Billy went off whistling.

Poppy glanced at the buff envelope. It was no different from dozens of others she had seen delivered to the office with orders, delivery dates, cancellations, so why did it send a shiver down her spine? But Albert didn't appear worried.

'Didn't Sir Frederick say his sister was coming to stay?' he said, picking it up and getting to his feet. 'I expect she's telegraphed to say what time her train's arriving.' He listened at the door. 'I can hear papers being shuffled so he's finished his nap. I'll tek it in to him. Knowing his sister she'll not be pleased if she arrives and there's no-one there to meet her.'

A moment later he came back. 'Mark my words, he'll be out of that office like a streak of lightning in a minute if he finds her train's due,' he chuckled.

Ten minutes later, Poppy wound the last letter out of her typewriter and rubbed the back of her neck, yawning. 'Obviously she's not arriving yet,' she said. 'So I can take these letters in and get them signed.' She gathered them up, knocked at the door and walked in.

Sir Frederick was sitting at his desk and staring out of the window. His face was paper white. He didn't move as Poppy entered.

'Sir Frederick?' She hurried over to him. 'Sir Frederick? What is it? What's wrong? What's the matter?' Then she saw the telegram in his hand. 'Oh, no!' she breathed, closing her eyes.

He still didn't move except to put up his hand, holding the telegram.

She took it and scanned it. It was from the War Office, regretting to inform Sir Frederick that his son, Major Alec Kenton, had been killed in battle on the River Somme on 28 September 1916.

She laid her hand on his shoulder and he put up his own to cover it. Neither of them spoke for several minutes, then she said quietly, 'Can I get you anything? A glass of whisky?' She knew he kept a bottle in the cupboard of his desk.

He nodded, shutting his eyes tightly against the tears that threatened, and she busied herself with pouring the whisky to give him time to pull out a white handkerchief and blow his nose.

He took a draught of whisky and sat staring down into the glass.

'Sit down,' he commanded in a voice that made her jump.

She obeyed, pulling up a chair on the other side of the desk. Then she sat quietly waiting, but the thoughts that ran and jumbled through her mind were anything but quiet.

Alec was dead. Alec, who had poured his heart out to her those few short weeks ago. Had he realised, with some sixth sense, that he was about to die and wanted her to know how he felt? Had he been waiting, full of hope, for her reply when the bullet or whatever it was that killed him came? Or had he received her letter . . .? Had she sent him to his death? She screwed up her face against the unbearable thought, then forced herself to think rationally. When had he been killed? The twenty-eighth. She had posted her letter on the twenty-ninth. Her whole body sagged with relief. At least he never knew what she had written. She sent up a silent prayer of thankfulness for that small mercy.

Suddenly, Sir Frederick began to speak. 'I knew it would come,' he said, as much to himself as to her. 'I knew I should lose one of my boys. It was inevitable. All that carnage. Why should I be spared? But Alec. My firstborn.' He pressed his knuckle to his mouth. 'I can only thank God his mother is not alive to see this day. He was her boy. The apple of her eye.' He took another draught of whisky and continued, the words coming jerkily. 'Never gave us a moment's anxiety as a lad. Good allrounder. Did well at his studies and at sport. The cream of English youth. I was grooming him to take over here. He wasn't very good with the men, he was the first to admit he found it difficult to talk to them on their level, but he tried. And they knew. They understood that it was only shyness on his part. He'd

162

have got over it. In time. Only time was the one thing he didn't have.' He banged the glass down on the desk. 'Oh, God! How many more of them will be lost in the mud and filth of battle over there before sanity prevails,' he said savagely, picking it up again and draining it.

Poppy waited. There was nothing she could say.

He got to his feet, suddenly a very old man. 'I think I shall go home. You can break the news to Soames and Templeton, they'll tell the workforce.' He leaned on the desk. 'God knows what will happen to this place, not that I care much now Alec won't be here to take it over. Not much point . . .' He knuckled his mouth again.

She laid a hand on his arm. 'You've still got Josh,' she reminded him gently.

He waved his hand dismissively. 'Oh, aye, but Josh's not interested. All he cares about is flying his bloody aeroplanes.' There was bitterness in his tone.

'He's still your son.'

'Oh, aye. He's still my son. But how long for, if this bloody war carries on?' he said mournfully. 'There won't be any mothers' sons left.'

She fetched his walking stick from the stand in the corner and propped it against the desk. He always made a point of walking from Kenton Hall to his office every day, saying the walk did him good, but today he didn't look as if he could manage it.

'Do you think it might be better if I sent for your chauffeur to bring the car, sir?' she asked.

'No. I'd rather walk. I don't want people fussing round me.' He brushed her to one side, picked up his walking stick and stumbled out, a broken man.

Poppy went back and told Albert, but he had already guessed from Sir Frederick's manner that the telegram had brought bad news.

'It's a sad business,' he said, shaking his head.

'Someone will have to tell the men,' Poppy said. 'It's only right that they should know.'

'Aye.' Albert thought for a moment. 'George Templeton's the man to do that. I'll tell him and he can pass t'news on tomorrow. It'll keep till then.' He looked up and gave her the ghost of a smile. 'Might as well get off home, lass. There'll be no more work done in this office today.'

Poppy put the cover on her typewriter and tidied her desk, glad to do as Albert suggested and go home.

It was hard to fit back into the rarefied atmosphere of Dale House, where the biggest catastrophe was the fact that Meg had mislaid her thimble.

'It was a silver one, too,' Kate said. She stared at Meg sternly over the top of her pince-nez. 'It was very careless of you, Meg.'

'I'm sure I shall find it soon,' Meg said, plucking ineffectually at the heap of material at her side. 'And I've got this bone one that I can wear. It was Mama's.' She held up her finger to show Poppy.

'Very nice,' Poppy said absently, passing her hand over her face as she sank into a chair by the table.

'What's the matter, lass?' Kate said, frowning at her. 'Are you ill?'

Poppy bit her lip. 'No, I'm not ill,' she said, shaking her head. 'But I've had rather a shock. Sir F—. My employer,' she automatically corrected herself. 'My employer has lost his son.'

Meg beamed. 'And I've lost my thimble. That makes two of us that have lost things. There'll be a third. Things always go in threes.'

'Oh, do be quiet, Meg. You don't know what you're talking about,' Kate said impatiently.

'I do. I do know what I'm taking about. I've lost my thimble. It was a silver one, too . . .' She muttered on and on about her thimble until Poppy was ready to scream.

Kate turned back to Poppy. 'Oh, don't take any notice of her. It's not been one of her good days.'

Suddenly, Meg began to shout. 'No, it hasn't been one of my good days. I've lost my bloody thimble. And it's your fault. I think you've hidden it! You're always hiding my things and saying I've lost them.' Then before anyone could speak she got up, scattering pieces of material in all directions, and rushed from the room. Seconds later the third movement of Beethoven's Moonlight Sonata came thundering from the drawing room.

'Tch. Tch. What an outburst,' Kate said, shocked. 'And such *language*! Where on earth could she have learned it! It's enough to make poor dear Papa turn in his grave.' She was quiet for a minute, then she turned to Poppy and said distractedly, 'Now, what was it you were saying, dear?'

Poppy shook her head. Her aunts simply didn't live in the real world and it was no use trying to make them. 'Nothing that would interest you, Aunt. Just something that happened at work.'

Kate shrugged. 'Oh, that. Well, if you will insist on going out to earn your living ...'

Poppy was in no mood to hear Kate expound on the follies of ladies going out to work. She pushed her chair back and stood up. 'I think I'll go up to my room, if you don't mind. I'm rather tired.'

Kate raised her eyebrows. 'But what about your dinner, dear? Mrs Rivers ...'

'I'll take something up on a tray.' She wouldn't. She wasn't hungry. But it would only provoke Kate's cloying concern to say so. Wearily, she climbed the stairs to her room, noticing with only half her mind that the music from the drawing room had ceased.

She went up the dimly lit stairs, her feet making no sound on the turkey carpet. As she reached the top a figure emerged from the shadows, her white hair falling out of its pins and tears streaming down her face.

It was Meg.

Chapter Sixteen

Meg put her hand out to Poppy. 'I'm sorry. I didn't mean to make you jump, dear,' she said quietly, her voice in total contrast both to her appearance and to her previous outburst. 'I just wanted to say how sorry I am about that man losing his son. You did mean he'd died, didn't you?'

Poppy nodded, too surprised to speak.

'Ah, I thought so. Was he very young?'

'Er, in his early twenties I believe.'

'I guess he must have been a soldier, then. Is that right?' Meg raised questioning eyebrows over startlingly blue eyes. Poppy was momentarily surprised that she had never before noticed quite how blue they were, and realised that it was probably because Meg's head was rarely raised.

She nodded again. 'Yes. He was killed in France.' She could still hardly believe that she was having this rational conversation with her Aunt Meg, the 'funny one' the one who it was hinted 'was not quite all there', the same person who had had such a crazy outburst over a lost thimble less than half an hour ago.

Meg was quiet for a moment, then she said thoughtfully, 'Killed on the Somme, no doubt.' She began to shake her head. 'Oh, this war is a dreadful business. Terrible. Such a waste of young lives ...' She closed her eyes. 'All that mud ...' She opened them briefly and glanced at Poppy. 'It rains all the time out there, you know.' She closed them again. 'And the noise of the guns must be terrible. Terrible.' Suddenly, her eyes flew open and she stared at Poppy, her blue gaze piercing. 'I read about the war, you know. Mrs Rivers lets me see the newspapers almost every day, so I know exactly what's going on.' She made a disparaging gesture. 'Kate doesn't follow the news. She says it's of no interest to people like us. She doesn't know I read the papers, she thinks I don't know what's going on, but I do.' She smiled a little inward smile. 'Kate thinks I don't know a lot of things, but it's Kate that doesn't always know.' Suddenly, bird-like, she put her head on one side. 'Would you like a cup of tea?'

Totally bewildered by yet another switch in Meg's mood, Poppy nodded. 'Oh, yes, I would, please.'

'I'll ask Mrs Rivers to bring it up to you. I'd bring it myself but if I don't go back to the parlour soon Kate will come looking for me rattling the pill box.' She shuddered. 'I hate taking the damn things but they're supposed to do me good so I have to.'

Poppy watched open-mouthed as Meg went down the stairs. She had just seen a side of her aunt she hadn't even known existed. Meg was usually so quiet and meek and muddled in her thinking it had been quite a surprise – a shock, even – to see her behaving in such a forthright and rational manner.

She went into her room and lay down on her bed. She felt utterly drained. The events of the afternoon coupled with the unpredictable behaviour of her two aunts made her wonder if she was in the middle of a bad dream and she would shortly wake up. It was either that or the whole world was going insane.

'Here you are, love. A nice cup of tea and some scrambled egg on toast.' Mrs Rivers elbowed her way through the door and put the tray down on the table beside the bed. 'Miss Meg just came and told me you'd had some bad news and all you wanted was a cup of tea, but you must eat summat so don't you go telling me you don't want it.'

167

Poppy opened her eyes, realising she must have dozed off briefly. 'Oh, you are a dear, Mrs Rivers.' She swung her legs over the side of the bed, more relieved than she could say at the old lady's down-to-earth normality.

Mrs Rivers looked at her, her head on one side. 'Ee, you do look a bit peaky. Want to tell me about it while you eat your tea, love?'

Poppy gave her a crooked smile. 'Is this just a ruse to make sure I don't leave any?' she asked.

Mrs Rivers sat down on a chair just inside the door and folded her hands over her ample stomach. 'Could be. Now come on, get it down you before it goes cold.'

Poppy began to eat, surprised to find that she was hungry. As she ate she told Mrs Rivers the sad news. 'I feel so sorry for Sir Frederick,' she said, placing her knife and fork carefully together on the plate when she had finished. 'He looked so old, so lonely, when he left the office. It must be dreadful to lose a son like that.'

'Aye,' Mrs Rivers nodded. 'Me and Rivers have never been blessed with family but Rivers's nephew has been like a son to us and we worry about him. It's a crying shame, all these millions of young lives being lost. Such a wicked waste.' She frowned. 'Hasn't Sir Frederick another son?'

'Yes. A younger son, Josh. He's a captain in the Flying Corps.'

'I expect they'll give him compatriot leave to come and see his father,' Mrs Rivers said sagely. 'They usually do.'

Poppy smiled at the malapropism, careful not to let Mrs Rivers see. 'Yes, I'm sure they will. But to tell you the truth I'm not sure how well Josh and his father get on together. As far as I can make out Josh has been a bit of a disappointment to Sir Frederick because he's never been particularly interested in the business. I suppose he thought that since it was Alec, being the eldest, who was being groomed to take over everything when the time came, he could pursue his real interest, which is flying.'

Mrs Rivers got to her feet. 'Well, no doubt they'll work

something out. Sir Frederick's not that old. It'll be a good many more years before he'll be wanting to give up. Men like him die with their boots on.' She moved to pick up the tray.

'I'll carry that down for you,' Poppy said. 'I ought to go and talk to the aunts for an hour, I suppose. They never cease to amaze me. Especially Aunt Meg. Does she read the newspaper every day? She seems to know far more of what goes on in the world than Aunt Kate.'

'Yes. She's a deep one, is Meg,' Mrs Rivers said, holding the door open for Poppy to pass through. 'Daft as a barm cake most of the time, yet she's mad keen to get her hands on the newspaper whenever she can. Mind you, I'm never sure how much she takes in of what she reads.'

'More than we realise, I shouldn't wonder,' Poppy said over her shoulder.

She carried the tray downstairs to the kitchen, then went along to the parlour. The aunts were sitting in their usual places, Kate in the armchair reading Dickens beside the fireplace, where a faded paper screen hid the empty grate, Meg busily stitching on the sofa by the window, surrounded by a rainbow of patchwork pieces.

They both looked up as Poppy walked in and Meg smiled her somewhat vacant smile. 'I lost my thimble, but I've found it again. It was under the cushion,' she said complacently. 'Did you have a nice day at work, Poppy?'

Somewhat taken aback Poppy managed to smile back. Who, or perhaps more accurately, *where* was the real Meg Russell? And what, if anything, was she hiding?

A black cloud hung over Kentons during the following days. The men and their wives were all stunned to hear of Mr Alec's tragic death. It brought the war close to home in a way that even the lengthening casualty lists in the newspapers could not. Because this time it was Mr Alec who had died. Mr Alec, Sir Frederick's son whom they all knew, some from when he was only a little lad. Mr Alec who was being groomed to take over when – God forbid – Sir Frederick had to give up. It was beyond belief. Even those men who had privately doubted Alec's ability to step into his father's shoes now bemoaned the loss of a potentially brilliant master.

The wives, too, grieved for the loss of a young man in the prime of life. Mary Smithers, who had felt her husband Harry's position was safe since Mr Alec had promised to keep an eye out for him, now realised with a shock that death in the trenches was no respecter of persons. Her talisman gone, she grew thin with worry.

George Templeton, although outwardly expressing his sorrow, was in his element. Whilst Sir Frederick was at home, grieving for his son and heir, it fell to him to keep things going. He strutted about, his beady eye searching for the slightest slackness, his competent finger on every aspect of the work in hand. Had he behaved in a less arrogant and bombastic manner he would have gained the respect of every man who worked there; as it was they all hated him for the way he continually criticised and complained, throwing his weight about and giving nobody credit for work well done.

If George was aware of this he gave no sign. As far as he was concerned there was only one fly in the Kentons ointment and that was Poppy Barlow. Since his thwarted attack on her he had kept out of her way as much as possible, clutching hatred and shame to his breast in equal measures. On the few occasions when they were forced to come into contact they had managed to maintain an icy armed truce. But now there were matters to be discussed practically every day.

George Templeton coped with this by being even more overbearingly businesslike and critical. In return, Poppy was distantly polite.

Albert couldn't resist a sly chuckle after one particularly icy encounter between them.

'Ee, you'll freeze his eyeballs one of these days, lass, that's for sure,' he wheezed.

Poppy raised her eyebrows. 'I'm never rude to him, Albert. I hear what he has to say and I tell him whatever I think he needs to know,' she said, feigning surprise.

'Aye, and not a word more,' he said with a smile. 'You don't give him an inch, do you?'

'No, and I'm not likely to. I don't like the arrogant way he behaves with the men. The sooner Sir Frederick comes back the better, as far as I'm concerned.' She was sorting through the post as she spoke. 'Oh, I should have given him these forms. Bother, I'll have to take them down to him. That means he'll make some sarcastic remark about incompetent secretaries. One of these days I shall hit him. I know I shall.'

'I hope I'm there to see it. That'll tek him down a peg or two,' Albert said with a laugh. 'Don't worry, lass. I'll tek 'em. I need to see Jack Earnshaw so I can do both at the same time.' He got up from his desk and took the papers.

'Thanks, Albert.'

'Well, we can't run t'risk of t'manager being beaten up, can we?' He grinned at her.

'All I can say is, I hope Sir Frederick will soon be back,' Poppy replied. 'For everybody's sake.'

'He'll not stay away long, I'm sure. They say work is the best cure.' He went off down the steps and Poppy continued dealing with the post.

A few minutes later the office door opened again. 'Goodness, you haven't been long, Albert,' she said, without looking up.

'Actually, I'm not Albert and in fact, I've only just arrived,' a voice said, half-apologetically.

Poppy's head shot up as she recognised Josh Kenton's voice. 'Oh, Mr Josh. I do beg your pardon. I thought it was Albert . . .' Her voice trailed off and she felt herself blushing as she looked into Josh Kenton's dark blue eyes.

He gave an apologetic smile. 'I'm sorry if I startled you, Miss Barlow. I thought it might be a good idea to come and see what's going on here before I go back. Do you mind if I sit down and talk to you for a few minutes?'

'No. No, of course not,' she said, surprised.

'Thanks.' He pulled a chair up and sat down, crossing one leg over the other. She noticed that he was wearing a finely tailored tweed suit with a cream shirt and a carefully knotted striped tie. His jacket hung open. He wasn't as obviously handsome as his dead brother but he had a pleasant, open face, tanned from hours in the sun.

'How are things, here at Kentons?' he asked, picking an imaginary speck of cotton off his trousers. 'Everything running smoothly?'

'Yes, I think so,' she said, a slight frown creasing her brow. 'But I'm hardly the best person to ask. Mr Templeton is running things at the moment. But no doubt you knew that.'

'Mm, I had heard. Not the most popular of managers, I believe.' He looked up and smiled at her.

She shrugged but said nothing.

'Oh, you don't need to defend him, Miss Barlow. I've been talking to the men. Mind you, I think I probably learned more from what they didn't say than from what they did.'

'That was very astute of you,' she said. 'And believe me, I wasn't defending George Templeton. I can't stand the man. But unfortunately at the moment I'm having to work fairly closely with him.' She was quiet for a minute. Then she said, 'How is Sir Frederick?'

He shook his head sadly. 'My brother's death has hit him hard,' he said. 'Well, it's hit us all, naturally enough, but the guv'nor has taken it particularly badly. To tell you the truth he hasn't left his room since he heard the news. I've been home four days and I've hardly seen him. I have to go back the day after tomorrow so I thought perhaps if I came here and saw how things were going I could report back to him, try and generate a bit of interest ...' He shrugged. 'This place has always been his life, to the exclusion of almost everything else, even his family. But now ...' He spread his hands in a helpless gesture.

'Your brother's death was a blow to everybody,' she said carefully. 'Even though we know these things are happening all the time it doesn't make it any easier when it comes so close to home. I think I can understand a little of how your father feels.' She broke off, biting her lip as she remembered the horror of her own father's death.

He shot her a look. 'And you? What about you?' he asked abruptly.

'Me?' Suddenly, she was on her guard. How much did he know? Had Alec confided in him? Did he know about the letter Alec had written to her? And hers in reply? No, he couldn't have ... unless Alec's personal effects had been returned... Oh, God. It was not something she could ask about ... 'Like everybody else, I was very shocked. And sorry,' she said carefully. 'He was so ...' She didn't know how to go on.

'I've been to see Claire,' he said. 'She's in quite a state.'

Poppy nodded sympathetically. 'I can imagine. She must be heartbroken.'

His mouth twisted. 'I don't know about that. To tell you the truth, I rather felt she was overdoing the part of the grieving bride bereaved on the eve of her wedding, so to speak.'

'That's not very kind,' Poppy said quietly.

'No. I suppose it isn't. But somehow I couldn't help sensing a hint of relief that she didn't have to go through with this marriage after all.' He ran his fingers through his hair. 'Oh, I know she was going into it of her own free will, she was as hungry for money as Alec was for power, with love coming a bad third, but I do wonder if she was having second thoughts and hadn't the courage to tell him.' He broke off. Then he shrugged. 'After all, if she'd *really* cared for Alec she wouldn't be dramatically going round cancelling all the arrangements herself, she'd be hiding away with her grief and letting someone else do it. Either that or she suspected he wasn't being entirely faithful to her.' He had been staring at the floor as he spoke. Now he looked up. 'That's what I think, anyway. What do you think?'

'Er, I hadn't really thought about it at all.' Poppy said uncomfortably. 'Different people deal with grief in different ways. Some people find it easier to keep busy. That's what I . . .'

'You find that the best thing?' he interrupted.

'That's how I coped when my father died.'

He waved his hand. 'That's different.'

'Is it? Maybe.' She thought for a moment. 'It was still a terrible shock because my father and I were very close.' Her voice dropped. 'You see, he committed suicide.'

'Oh. I'm sorry. I'd no idea.' His eyes were suddenly full of concern.

'It's not something I speak about often.'

He got to his feet. 'You live alone now?' he asked.

She hesitated. 'I have a room,' she said. It was true.

He studied her, his head on one side. 'You must be lonely sometimes,' he remarked.

'No, not at all. I live . . .' she began but he held up his hand.

'I'm sorry, Miss Barlow. I don't wish to pry. It's not my business. Forgive me.'

'I was only going to say that I live with relatives,' she continued, for some reason anxious that he shouldn't regard her as some lonely spinster living out her life in a dingy little rented room.

He smiled, and his smile lit up his face and crinkled the corners of his eyes. 'Good. I'm glad you're not lonely, Miss Barlow,' he said. He went to the door, then came back, digging in his jacket pocket for a pencil. He found a scrap of paper and scribbled something on it. 'That's my address.' He straightened up. 'If you need to get in touch with me for any reason this will find me.' He flicked it with his finger. 'It's just that I worry about the guv'nor a bit. I've never seen him quite so flattened, not even when Ma died. Not that they were very close, as I remember,' he

174

added thoughtfully. He looked up and smiled at her again. 'But he's a tough old codger. He'll pull himself together in a week or two, no doubt. It's early days yet.'

After he had gone Poppy picked up the scrap of paper and put it in the drawer of her desk. She didn't expect to need it.

Chapter Seventeen

The weeks went by and autumn slipped into winter in a last blaze of colour, the memory of which only seemed to emphasise the drab, grey, foggy days of November. Some mornings, if the weather was too foggy or wet for her bicycle Poppy wrapped herself in her warm winter coat and a fur hat and walked to work. She didn't really mind this, it gave her plenty of time to think and she was always content with her own company.

At work there was a great deal of concern over Sir Frederick. Since the day the fateful telegram had arrived, well over a month ago, telling him of the death of his favourite son he had not been near the place. Even George Templeton, although more than happy in his role of total responsibility, was becoming anxious at his absence.

'T'fact is, folk want to see t'organ grinder, not t'monkey, so to speak, when they're puttin' in orders,' he confided quietly to Albert, which Poppy, overhearing, thought a very apt description of the hated manager.

'Have you been up to t'house again?' Albert asked.

'Aye, but his man, Briggs, says his orders are still not to let anybody in. Briggs says the master just sits by the window looking out.'

'Mebbe if I went . . .' Albert said uncertainly.

'Why should he see you when he won't see me?' George said rudely. 'You're only his clerk.'

'I know that. But I've been here sin' I were fourteen. That must count for summat,' Albert replied with a lift of his chin. 'I'll call on my way home from work.'

'But you live in the other direction. Fat chance you've got of ever living in Twentywell Lane!' George was derisive.

'I've got my bike. It'll not tek me long,' Albert said, ignoring the jibe although Poppy could see he was having difficulty in keeping his temper. 'I'll just go and ask after him. I know Briggs. He'll likely let me in to see Sir Frederick, then I can tell him he's needed back here.' He could be quietly stubborn when he chose.

Poppy remained silent. She hoped against hope that Albert would be successful in persuading Sir Frederick back to work, for it was not simply business matters that needed his attention.

Some of the wives had begun to complain about George Templeton's manner towards them. At first they refused to be specific, saying with some embarrassment and not a little nudging and head-shaking that it wouldn't be right, since Poppy was still unmarried.

Poppy watched them for a moment, then gave a grim laugh. 'If you're saying what I think you're saying you've no need to worry. He's already tried his tricks on with me,' she said.

They were all sitting round the scrubbed table in Maud Benson's neat kitchen. Since it had become too cold for Poppy to sit on the wall to eat her sandwiches, Maud had suggested that she should spend her lunch hour in her warm kitchen. Poppy had been happy to accept, because otherwise it would have meant staying in the office with Albert and although she had grown fond of him, he did rather dwell on his ailments, both real and imaginary.

Once she had started eating her lunch with Maud it had seemed only natural that the other wives should drop in for their usual chat, and so it became a habit for them all to sit round the table drinking tea while the smaller children played and squabbled on the hearthrug.

Now all eyes were turned on Poppy. She shrugged without embarrassment. 'He only tried it once,' she said. 'I dealt with him in the way my father had told me was most effective. I hit him where it hurt most.' She took a bite of Mrs Rivers's excellent fruit cake. 'He's never tried it again.'

Lily Ferris hooted with laughter. 'By, you're quite a lass, even though there's not two penn'oth of you,' she said admiringly.

But Florrie Braithwaite wasn't laughing. 'That manager's a randy sod,' she said. 'I worry about my Milly. She's only thirteen and doesn't know about these things. I don't know how to warn her wi'out spoiling her innocence.'

'Oh, surely he'd never touch her! He'd never dare,' Daisy Frampton said, shocked. 'Any road, she's allus with the other children, specially the little ones. She's good with them, I've watched her. She's a lovely lass, your Milly.'

'Aye. He'd not harm her, I'm sure,' Maud said.

Florrie pinched her lips. 'Well, it'll not be for much longer, any road. She'll be going into service soon. She's a place up at Endcliffe Hall. She'll be going there after Christmas.'

'She'll need to keep her wits about her if she's going there,' Lily said knowingly. 'The sons ...'

'My sister works there as housemaid,' Florrie said quickly. 'She'll keep an eye on Milly, specially sin' she got her the place.'

Charity Jones had been sitting quietly, saying nothing. Her baby was due almost any day and she was wearing a voluminous shawl to conceal her pregnancy, even though she was among her women friends.

Suddenly, she frowned. 'Mr Templeton spoke to me once,' she said, going back to the previous conversation. 'I thought he was quite nice because he offered to carry my shopping for me. Then when we got to my door he wanted to come in. He said summat like, "a slice off a cut loaf is never missed." I didn't know what he meant at the time but I didn't like the way he was looking at me so I told him Mord would be home in a minute and shut the door in his face. It was rather rude of me, I'm afraid.'

'It was sensible of you, lass,' Lily said. 'That man thinks he's God's gift to women. If only he knew what we really think of him, strutting around, preening his moustache, oily so-and-so.'

'Mrs Templeton doesn't think he's God's gift to her,' Mary Smithers said sadly. 'He still knocks her about summat cruel.'

'Well, she's his wife. Husbands are allowed to knock their wives about,' Lily said. 'Specially when the drink's in. My Ted used to hit me when we were younger. He's not got the energy now. Not for that nor for owt else neither.' She gave a sly wink at Daisy.

'My Mord never lays a finger on me,' Charity said earnestly. 'He's ever so good to me. Allus brings me tea in bed of a morning.'

'Your Mord is one in a million. You want to tek care of him,' Maud said. 'Not that I've anything to complain of. My Jake's allus been good to me, even when he was study-ing hard.' She couldn't keep the pride out of her voice at those last words.

Poppy finished her tea and stood up. 'I must get back to work. Mr Templeton will be shouting for his letters and I've not finished them yet.'

She shrugged on her coat and made her way back across the yard. It was over six weeks now since the news of Alec's death and there was still no sign of Sir Frederick. It showed in many ways that he was not there. The yard was becoming cluttered with bits of rusting iron, split sacks and discarded clinker – things that Sir Frederick never allowed, saying a cluttered yard was a danger to the workforce. Grass was growing in the corners, too, giving the whole place a run-down and dilapidated air.

She climbed the steps to the office, wishing that

something would happen to shake Sir Frederick out of his depression.

George Templeton and Albert were in the office, obviously thinking along the same lines.

'I dunno what we're going to do,' Albert was saying. 'We shall have the auditors here next month. I wonder if he realises that.'

'According to Briggs, his man, he doesn't even know nor care what day of the week it is. Doesn't the man realise he's got a business here that has to be run? God sakes, I've kept things going all this time but I can't do every bloody thing,' George Templeton said, pacing up and down.

'You'll have to go and see him again,' Albert said.

George stopped pacing and shot round. 'Me? Why me? I've already been three times and he won't bloody see me!' He banged his fist on the filing cabinet. 'And it's no good you offering to go. He wouldn't see you when you went before.'

'I know,' Albert sighed. 'But summat's got to be done.'

'Well, somehow we've got to get him to sign these cheques or there'll be no more steel coming in, for a start.' George waved a wad of papers. 'And there's all these papers as well. T'place'd be in ruins if it weren't for me but there's a limit to what I can do.'

'Would you like me to go?' Poppy asked quietly.

'You!' George swung round to look at her and his lip curled derisively. 'What good do you think you could do? If he won't see his manager it's a sure thing he'll not see a bloody typist.'

'It's worth a try, George,' Albert said. 'Sir Frederick thinks a lot of Poppy. He might see her.'

'And he might not!' George said scornfully. He threw the papers down on the desk. 'But I don't care who bloody goes as long as I get these things signed.' He picked up his hat and marched out of the office and down the steps.

'Don't tek your coat off, lass,' Albert said with a smile. 'I'll put this lot in an envelope and you'd best be on your way.' He assembled the papers. 'And don't forget to smile at him, Poppy,' he added as she finished adjusting her hat. 'You've got a smile that'd charm a bird off a tree.'

Poppy was thoughtful as she went out of the yard. She felt so sorry for Sir Frederick. The loss of his son had hit him hard and she felt she would like to take him something – anything – to show her concern. Suddenly, a picture of her own father came into her mind. The greatest treat for him was a cigar. Perhaps Sir Frederick liked cigars, too. On impulse she caught a tram into the city and found the tobacconist that she knew supplied him with his pipe tobacco. The tobacconist was very helpful, he knew exactly what pleased Sir Frederick, with the result that she left the shop with two very expensive cigars and precious little money left in her handbag. Then she caught the tram back.

Briggs answered the door when she rang the bell.

'I've come to bring this gift for Sir Frederick. I hope these might help to cheer him up a little,' she said, handing him the neatly wrapped cigars.

Briggs looked uncertainly at the parcel in his hand. 'I don't know, miss,' he said. 'The master's not seeing anybody at the moment . . .'

'Then perhaps you'll be good enough to give them to him.' Poppy gave him her most winning smile. 'Just tell him Poppy sent them,' she said, and turned to leave.

'Just a minute, miss,' Briggs said, completely disarmed. 'Could you wait while I tell the master? He might want to send a message. If you've got a minute, that is?'

'Yes. I can wait.' Poppy stepped inside.

Briggs was not gone many minutes. When he came back he was looking surprised. 'The master says you're to go in,' he said. 'He must be feeling better. You're his first visitor. It's that door on the right.'

'Thank you, Briggs.' Poppy smiled at him again and walked across the hall and into the room where Sir Frederick was sitting.

He was in a wheelchair, staring out of the window.

'Good afternoon, Sir Frederick,' Poppy said, walking round to where he could see her.

He didn't look up. 'Hullo, lass,' he said, his voice little more than a sigh. 'How are you?'

'I'm well, thank you, Sir Frederick.'

He waved his hand, still not looking at her. 'Well, now you're here you might as well sit down.'

'Thank you.' She sat down on a chair near the window where she could study the old man, for old man he had become. His figure seemed to have shrunk and his face was gaunt and parchment-coloured.

'It was kind of you to bring me the cigars,' he said after a while, his voice flat.

'I wanted to bring you something. I miss you, Sir Frederick. We all miss you,' she said. 'The heart has gone out of Kentons.'

'The heart has gone out of Freddie Kenton,' he replied. Suddenly he glared at her. 'What's the use? What's the use of me working my fingers to the bone building a successful business when there's nobody to hand it on to? Tell me that.'

'You do have another son, Sir Frederick,' she said gently.

'He's got his head in the clouds. He'll never make a businessman. No, Kentons is finished as far as I'm concerned, now that Alec is dead.' Tears ran unchecked down his face.

'Then there are upwards of twenty men who will be out of work and homeless,' Poppy said, keeping her voice low. 'Do you want them and their families to starve?'

He shot her a look of resentment. 'What's that to me?'

'It's everything to you, Sir Frederick. You've always been a man who cared about your men and their families. Your conscience would never rest if you deprived those men of their living.'

He wagged his head from side to side. 'It's no use. I can't be bothered with it all. Templeton can see to things. He's no fool.'

'There are some things he can't do,' Poppy said, her voice still quiet. 'I've got cheques and papers in my handbag that need your signature. Will you sign them for me?'

He sat staring out of the window for such a long time that Poppy thought he was never going to answer and she should just get up and leave. Then, suddenly, he muttered, 'Get me over to my desk and give me the damn papers.'

With difficulty she pushed the wheelchair over the thick carpet to the desk and gave him the papers to sign. He signed everything she handed him without even looking. 'There you are. Now leave me in peace,' he growled.

'May I come and see you again, Sir Frederick?' she asked, pushing him back to his place near the window.

'Yes. But I don't want to see any of the others. They'll want to talk shop and I'm not interested.' He gave a deep sigh. 'I can't be bothered with it. I just want to sit here and . . .' He stared down at his hands. 'What have I got left to live for now my boy is gone? Tell me that.'

'Your other boy? Josh?' she said, saddened and a little annoyed that he should seem to have so little regard for such a fine man.

'Ah, Josh. He was always different. He's never cared for the things that interest me. Not like Alec . . . Alec was always ready for a round of golf or a game of chess. But all Josh thought of was aeroplanes and flying.' He put his head in his hands and began to weep.

Sadly, Poppy left him.

She took the documents back to the office and placed them on Albert's desk without a word. Then she went home, too distressed to stay at work.

When she arrived Kate was sitting by the meagre fire doing her accounts. She looked up as Poppy entered.

'You're home early, Poppy. What's wrong? Are you ill?'

Poppy slumped down on a chair by the table and rested her head on her hands. 'No, Aunt Kate, I'm not ill,' she said, her voice little more than a sigh. She sat up and looked round. 'Where's Aunt Meg?'

183

'She's gone to bed with one of her heads,' Kate said absently.

'I'll go up and see her then.' Poppy began to get to her feet.

'No. Leave her. She's only just gone up.'

Obediently, Poppy slumped back onto the chair.

Kate frowned. 'What is the matter with you, child? Are you sure you're not ill? You look as miserable as sin. It's not like you.'

'I've been to see Sir Frederick,' Poppy said without thinking. 'He's a broken man since his son was killed. It's dreadfully sad.'

Kate closed the ledger in front of her with a bang, making Poppy start. 'I've told you before,' she said sharply, 'I will not have that man's name mentioned in this house.'

'Well, you asked me what was wrong so I've told you,' Poppy said, a trifle irritably. She shook her head. 'Anyway, I'm sure you wouldn't say that if you were to see him. The poor man just sits in his chair looking out of the window and weeping. He seems to have lost all interest in life since his son was killed.'

Kate pursed her lips. 'Then it's no more than his due.'

'Oh, Aunt Kate, how can you say that! It's very unkind,' Poppy said, shocked.

'I can say it because he caused this family more sorrow and heartache than you can ever know.' Kate's face was like granite. 'Well, now it's his turn, so don't expect me to grieve.'

'Ah, yes, of course. I'm sorry.' Poppy hung her head. 'I should have remembered you were once engaged to him. He jilted you. You're bound to be bitter.'

'It was not just me!' Kate said, rearing up. 'Think of Papa! The shame of it all! You've no idea what he went through, poor Papa. It was dreadful. The humiliation ... the shame ...'

'But it was all such a long time ago,' Poppy said,

perplexed. 'There's no point in raking over the past. Not after all these years. Can't you let bygones be bygones, Aunt Kate?'

'No. And I never shall!' Kate gathered up her ledgers and stood staring down at Poppy. 'I don't wish to hear that man's name spoken in this house ever again, Poppy, do you hear me? Not ever again.' She went over to the desk where the ledgers were kept and put them away, slamming the drawer shut and locking it. 'And if you had any thought for my feelings you would leave that place. Of all the places where you could have found employment ... not that you needed to in the first place, I said that, right at the outset ... ladies don't take paid work ...' She almost threw the bunch of keys into another drawer and slammed that shut.

Poppy left her to seethe, Kate's muttering voice fading as she went upstairs to see if there was anything Meg wanted.

To her surprise her aunt was sitting up in bed wrapped in a large woollen shawl, drinking tea. Her face lit up when she saw Poppy.

'Oh, how nice. Come and sit on the bed, dear. How are you? You look a little tired. Pour yourself a cup of tea.' She pointed to the tray on the bedside table.

'How is your headache, Aunt Meg?' Poppy asked as she poured the tea.

Meg gave a little giggle. 'Oh, I'm all right. To tell you the truth I didn't have a headache at all. I was just cold. But I knew it was no use asking Kate to put more coal on the fire so I came to bed where I knew it would be nice and warm and Mrs Rivers brought me some tea and the newspaper.' She smiled at Poppy. 'Kate never puts enough coal on the fire. I expect you've noticed.'

Poppy smiled back. 'Aunt Kate doesn't seem to feel the cold.'

Meg hunched her shoulders conspiratorially. 'Don't tell anyone I told you, but I believe she wears a pair of Papa's trousers under her skirt.' She gave another delighted giggle.

'Oh, Aunt Meg, you're making that up,' Poppy said, unsure whether to believe her.

Meg put her head on one side. 'Am I? Yes, perhaps I am.' She frowned. 'No, I don't think I am making it up. I think it's true.' She looked up at Poppy, her deep blue eyes wide. 'Kate smokes in her room. I'm not making that up. I know it's true because I've seen her cigarettes. They're long, thin and brown and she keeps them in her bedside drawer. One day she'll set her bed alight, I shouldn't wonder, and the house will burn down.' Meg hugged herself and rocked to and fro. 'Just think of that. This dreadful old house burning down. Wouldn't that be a lark!'

'No, it wouldn't be a lark,' Poppy said sternly. 'We could all be burned in our beds. You mustn't say such things, Aunt Meg.'

Meg's face immediately crumpled. 'I'm sorry, Poppy. I didn't mean to be bad,' she said, for all the world like a naughty child. She slid down under the covers. 'I think I shall go to sleep now.'

Poppy pulled the covers away. 'It isn't time for sleeping. It's nearly time for supper. I think you should get up and come downstairs, Aunt Meg.'

Obediently, Meg got out of bed and put on her slippers. 'Very well, Poppy,' she said. 'I'll come down now. I'm tired of being in bed. Kate sent me to bed, you know. I don't know why, I hadn't done anything wrong.'

'No, Aunt Kate didn't ...' Poppy began, then stopped, shaking her head. For what was the use?

She followed Meg out of the room.

Chapter Eighteen

That night, Poppy couldn't sleep. Always in front of her eyes was the pathetic figure in the wheelchair by the window at Kenton Hall. A pale shadow of the vigorous, handsome man who held the reins of the Kentons Scythe and Edge Tool Works in firm, capable hands, who knew the name of every man there, always mindful of their families' welfare, yet who still found the time and energy to play eighteen holes with the golf clubs kept at the ready in the corner of his office.

The life had gone out of him like the air out of a pricked balloon. It was a tragedy; almost as big a tragedy as the loss of his favourite son, which had caused it.

And that, Poppy considered, was a tragedy in itself, the fact that Alec had so obviously been Sir Frederick's favourite son. As far as she was concerned Josh was by far the nicer of the two brothers. She remembered his easy manner, his laughing eyes, his face, not quite as handsome as his brother's but with far more character and appeal. He had good hands, too: strong and broad, with well-kept nails. But hands that could be gentle ... She pulled her thoughts up sharply. Josh had never looked on her as anything but his father's secretary. Nor was he ever likely to, she told herself sternly.

Not like his brother.

She sighed. Whatever had possessed Alec to write to her

as he had? She was sure she had never given him any reason to think she returned his infatuation for her. Because that was undoubtedly what it had been. Infatuation fanned by the appalling conditions he was living in. She sighed again. It could have been an awful mess. As it was, her letter had come back, mud-stained and dog-eared, marked 'Return to Sender', and she had burned it, thanking God nobody needed to know it had ever been written. That, at least, was a relief. Claire had been able to play her part as the bereaved bride-to-be without ever suspecting how close she had come to being jilted. And for a mere secretary, too. Not that it would ever have come to that, of course. Not if Alec had received her reply.

A reply that might have been quite different if it had been written to his brother, she realised with an honesty reserved for the small hours.

She turned over and thumped her pillow in an effort to calm her mind. Then suddenly another thought struck her and she was immediately wide awake again.

She must write to Josh. Oh, not a personal letter, of course, but before he went back last time he had given her an address in case he was needed. Well, if ever he was needed it was now, seeing the state Sir Frederick was in. Surely Josh, of all people, would be able to rouse his father out of his lethargy.

Having finally decided what she must do, Poppy began to compose the letter in her mind. Before long she fell asleep.

The next morning, with the idea still fresh in her thoughts, she went down to breakfast still turning over how she would word the letter, not too alarmist, not too familiar . . .

'You're very quiet, Poppy dear. And you haven't eaten your toast,' Kate said, peering at her from her position nearest to the meagre fire. 'Aren't you well?'

Poppy looked up. 'I beg your pardon? Oh, yes, thank you, Aunt. I'm perfectly well. I was just thinking.' Absent-mindedly, she began to spread butter on her toast.

'Not too thickly, dear. It's extravagant,' Kate said, her eagle eye missing nothing.

'Oh, I'm sorry. I wasn't thinking what I was doing.' Poppy scraped most of the butter off and reached for the marmalade, ignoring her aunt's disapproving look.

'What were you thinking about, Poppy?' Meg asked eagerly, wriggling hopefully on her chair. She was wrapped in layers of shawl against the cold.

'Me? Oh, nothing. Just a letter I've got to write.' Poppy bit into her toast.

'Oh.' Meg's face fell. 'I never get letters,' she said, wagging her head miserably. 'Nobody ever writes to me. I expect everybody thinks I'm dead.'

'Oh, don't be so ridiculous, Meg,' Kate snapped. 'You don't receive letters because you never write any.'

'I haven't got anybody to write to.' Meg's expression was still woebegone.

'Well, then. Eat your breakfast. And don't forget your pill. Didn't you say you were going to stitch some of your quilt pieces together today?'

'Oh, I'm fed up with pills and I'm fed up with bloody patchwork quilts!' Meg threw her napkin down on the table.

'Language, Meg! Please!' Kate said, shocked.

'Well, I am. *Bloody* well fed up!' Meg glared at Kate. Then without another word she got up from the table and rushed from the room.

Kate looked after her, scowling angrily. 'I've never heard such an outburst. I can't think where she can have heard such words. It's not like Meg at all.'

Poppy had a very good idea. She was paying for a lad to come and help Rivers with the garden and he had a choice turn of phrase when things didn't go right. But she felt it prudent not to mention this to Kate so she said nothing.

Suddenly, sounds of a Chopin polonaise began to thunder from the piano in the drawing room.

Kate raised her eyebrows and gave a theatrical sigh. 'Oh,

dear. I thought as much. It looks as if it's going to be one of those days,' she said resignedly. She leaned over to Meg's place. 'Did she take her pill?'

'I don't know. I didn't see.'

'It's not on the table. She must have taken it. Unless it's on the floor.' Kate lifted the tablecloth, frowning. 'No. I can't see it. She must have taken it. Or thrown it away. The mood she's in she could easily have done that.' She went to the cupboard beside the fire. 'I'll give her another one, just to make sure.'

'Should you do that, Aunt Kate?' Poppy asked anxiously.

Kate smiled. It was a funny, secret kind of smile that sent shivers down Poppy's spine. 'Oh, yes. On a bad day I give her three or four. They're only to calm her down, you know. They won't do her any harm, the doctor told me.'

'Well, if the doctor says it's all right I suppose it must be,' Poppy said, not convinced. She wiped her fingers on her napkin before folding it into its ring. 'Aunt Meg certainly plays the piano beautifully.'

'Hmph. On days like this she gets plenty of practice.' Kate's tone was caustic. She took a sip of her tea. 'She'll play for hours if I don't go in and stop her. It drives me mad. Sometimes I feel like locking that piano and throwing away the key.' She placed her cup very carefully back on its saucer. 'The trouble is,' she said very quietly, 'there's no telling what she might do if she hadn't got the piano to vent her temper on. That and the pills, of course.'

Poppy stared at her aunt. But before she could question her, the clock on the mantelpiece struck the half-hour. 'Oh, Lord, half past eight. And I wanted to be in early today. I must go. Excuse me, please, Aunt.'

'You're always rushing about, child. It's not ladylike.' Kate's voice followed her along the passage until it was drowned by the sound of the music thundering from the drawing room.

Walking to work, Poppy thought about what Kate had said. Her implication had been that Meg could be violent.

This was worrying if it was true, yet Poppy could hardly believe it could be. Meg was such a gentle little dumpling. Except when she was venting her feelings on the piano, of course. Then she was far from gentle. But all the same . . .

She hurried along. The wind was blowing a cold sleety rain into her face as she walked and she had to hold her hat on in the buffeting wind as she hastened into the yard and across the cobbles to the office, giving a smile and a quick wave to anyone she happened to see on her way.

The office door was still locked. Good. That meant that Albert wasn't in yet, so she could get the letter written to Josh without interruption. She unlocked the door and went in, hung up her coat and hat and quickly took the cover off her typewriter and wound paper in. Then she sat looking at it, wondering how on earth to begin. In the end, it was not until she heard Albert talking to George Templeton in the yard that she wrote hurriedly:

Dear Mr Josh,

You left me your address the last time you were home so that I could write to you if I felt it necessary.

I think you should know that your father is not at all well. Understandably, the death of your brother has affected him greatly, as I am sure it has affected you. But the worrying thing is, Sir Frederick appears to have lost interest in everything, including Kentons. I have been to see him – for some reason I am the only person he will allow to visit – and I was shocked and saddened to see such a once vigorous man simply sitting in a wheelchair and staring out of the window. Briggs says he eats very little and is becoming weaker.

I hesitate to worry you with this at a time when you must have many more things on your mind, but as you asked me to let you know if things were not going well I feel it would be remiss of me not to write. George Templeton and Albert Soames are running things at Kentons as best they can but it is very evident that Sir

191

*Frederick's hand is no longer on the tiller, so to speak –
in small ways as well as large. He is greatly missed. Yet
nothing seems to tempt him back. It is as if he has lost
the will to live and this concerns me more than anything.*

*I am more sorry than I can say to have to give you
such worrying news but I felt it only right that you should
know.*

Yours sincerely,
Poppy Barlow.

She didn't stop to read the letter through but quickly sealed
it in an envelope and stamped it. Then she put on her coat
and hat and hurried down the steps to the postbox.

George Templeton and Albert both turned when they saw
her.

'You're in a mighty hurry, Miss Barlow,' George said
with his habitual sneer.

'What's up, lass?' Albert asked, ignoring him.

'Nothing, Albert. Just a letter I forgot to send. I want it
to catch the morning post. I shan't be long.'

'I hope you've lit the oil stove,' he called, flapping his
arms across his chest. 'It's freezing cold standing here.'

'Then let's go up to the office,' George said amiably.

'No. You'll keep me gassing all morning and I've work
to do.' Albert left him and went up to the office.

When Poppy returned the oil stove was alight and Albert
was standing in front of it warming his hands.

'Ee, lass, you must be starved to death. Why didn't you
light t'stove?' he asked. 'It's like a morgue in here.'

'I didn't think ... Well, I was in a hurry.' She hung her
coat and hat up again and gave a shiver. 'Yes, you're right.
It is cold in here. I hadn't noticed.'

Albert looked at her, frowning. 'Is summat bothering
you, lass?' he asked.

She went over and stood beside him, holding her hands out
to the warmth of the stove. 'To tell you the truth, yes, Albert.
I don't know whether I've done the right thing, but I've

written to Mr Josh and told him about Sir Frederick. You see, he left me his address last time he was home and said if I thought it was necessary I could write to him. So I did. And now I'm wondering whether I should have bothered him.'

Albert laid a hand on her arm. 'I think you did right, lass. If it does no good it'll do no harm and if Mr Josh can get leave it'll buck his father up no end to see him. With any luck he might even be able to persuade Sir Frederick back to work.' He sighed. 'Heaven knows what'll happen here if he doesn't soon put in an appearance. George Templeton is getting above himself, chucking his weight about and riling the men, and the suppliers don't like dealing with him and he won't let me see them.' He shook his head. 'Things seem to be going from bad to worse.'

'I'll go and see Sir Frederick again on Saturday,' Poppy said.

'Why don't you go today? He'll see you when he'll not see anyone else and there's a document here he needs to look through. George says he can deal with it but I don't think we should do owt with it till t'mester's seen it.'

'Yes, all right. I'll go this afternoon, if I can get through what I've got to do here.'

Sir Frederick was sitting in the same position as when Poppy last saw him. He looked even thinner and more pallid than ever, wrapped in several layers of blanket. He was staring out at the winter landscape, his expression as bleak as the scene before him.

Poppy decided on a different approach.

She went over and turned his chair round so that it was facing into the room.

He looked at her in surprise.

'I've asked Briggs to bring some tea,' she said with a bright smile. 'I hope you don't mind, but it's very cold outside today and I could do with a cup.'

He turned his head away. 'You're very welcome, lass,' he said dully.

Briggs brought the tea tray and a chafing dish with muffins in it. Poppy poured the tea, talking all the while about the families at Kentons, dredging her mind for funny incidents that she could pass on. He listened without saying anything and when she handed him a buttered muffin he took it and ate it, apparently without noticing.

'But of course, they're all worried about you,' she finished, licking her fingers. 'They miss you. Even the children ask where you are.'

'Aye, they're a grand bunch of children,' he said on a sigh.

'Well, they'll not be there much longer. Not if the place has to close,' Poppy remarked, finishing her tea and leaning forward to replace her cup on the tray.

'I've told you I'll sign what's needed,' he said irritably. 'You've only to bring it to me.'

'It's not enough, Sir Frederick. You need to be there. The place can't run for much longer without you.'

He gave an almost imperceptible shrug. 'Then it'll close.'

'And you'll be happy for the families to be turned out onto the street?'

'They'll not be turned out. They can stay in the cottages. The men'll soon find work elsewhere. They're all good tradesmen.' He turned to look at her, his once bright eyes sunk deep into their sockets. 'I've no will to keep the place going now I've nobody to leave it to, lass. Josh'll never come back here, he's no interest in it, and I doubt there'll ever be grandchildren, so what's the point?'

She could find no answer to that.

It was a bleak Christmas. The war that was only going to last a few months showed no sign of ending and the casualty list grew ever longer. The cloud that still hung over Kentons took the heart out of any festivities.

The only bright spot was the birth of Charity's daughter on Christmas Eve.

A few days after Christmas Poppy went along to tell Sir Frederick the news in the hope of cheering him up.

'You remember Mordecai Jones, who works the big tilt hammer?' she asked him.

'Aye,' he said dully. 'What about him?'

'His wife has given birth to a daughter. They're calling her Rebecca.'

'That's nice.' He sat silently for several minutes. Then he said, the words almost wrung out of him, 'Josh's plane has been shot down.'

'Oh ...!' She put her hand up to her mouth. 'Oh, my dear Lord ... Is he ...?' She couldn't bring herself to ask the question.

'He's been brought back to England and he's in a military hospital in Colchester.' He stared out of the window. 'They don't say if he's badly injured, just that he's in hospital.'

'Oh, thank God he's still alive,' she breathed.

'Aye. But I expect he'll be back in the air again before long, silly young pup.' He turned the two cigars she had brought him over and over in his hands. 'He'll kill himself in the end, that's for sure. Then I'll have nobody. Nothing.' He gave a deep sigh. 'I should go and see him, I know I should. I've written ... But I've no strength ... no mind for the journey ... Any road, the doctor says it's out of the question.'

Poppy watched him for several minutes, biting her lip, wondering if she dare say what was in her mind. She would so dearly like to see Josh, to discover how badly he was hurt, to make sure he was going to be all right. And here was her excuse, if she dared ask. At last, plucking up her courage, she said, 'Would you like me to go and see Josh for you?'

From the scowl on his face she thought she had overstepped the mark. Then all at once his face cleared and he nodded. 'Aye, lass. I think I might. At least I could rely on you to tell me the truth.'

She managed to keep the relief out of her voice as she said in her best secretarial manner, 'Very well, Sir Frederick. I'll make arrangements to go next Saturday.'

'Why can't you go tomorrow?' he said, frowning at her.

'Because I shall be at work,' she said.

'Oh, take the day off. Go tomorrow.' He waved his arm, more animated than she had seen him for months.

'I can't possibly do that, Sir Frederick. I can't just drop everything and go. I need to make arrangements with Albert and I need to find out the train times.'

'Oh, don't keep putting obstacles in the way. Go the next day, then.' He sounded quite tetchy.

'Yes, all right. I'll go on Thursday.'

'Ask Briggs to give you some money. You can't go at your own expense.'

'Oh, I couldn't do that, Sir Frederick.'

'Oh, don't be so daft.' He raised his voice. 'BRIGGS!'

Briggs came running.

'Give this lass five pounds. She's going on an errand for me.'

Briggs raised his eyebrows. 'Five pounds, sir?' He obviously thought his master had taken leave of his senses.

'I'm sure I don't need that much,' Poppy ventured.

'Five pounds is what I said and five pounds is what I meant. No, on second thoughts make it ten. You'll not do the journey in a day so you'll need money for a decent hotel. Don't argue.'

Briggs raised his eyebrows conspiratorially at Poppy behind his master's back as he gave her two crisp five-pound notes. Neither of them had seen him so excited for a long time.

Poppy put the notes in her handbag. She had never had so much money in all her life and she was beginning to look forward to her journey.

But first she had to tell Aunt Kate where she was going.

At the mention of her employer, which was how she had learned to refer to Sir Frederick when Meg was in the room, Kate hustled her out into the hall.

'I've told you before not to mention him,' she whispered fiercely. 'You've no idea the kind of day I've had with her,' she jerked her head in the direction of the parlour. 'She's been on that piano nearly all day. It must be the cold weather.' She pulled the shapeless cardigan she had taken to wearing more closely round her, shivering as she did so. 'Now, what were you saying?'

'Sir Frederick has had news of his son. His plane has been shot down and he's in hospital in Colchester.'

Kate sniffed. 'That's no concern of ours.'

'I'm going to the hospital to see him the day after to-morrow.'

Kate's jaw dropped. 'By yourself?'

'Yes. Sir Frederick would like me to go.'

'I might have known it,' Kate said with a disapproving shrug. 'That man has no sense of responsibility at all. Never did have. They say a leopard never changes its spots. Well, you can't go. It's out of the question. I won't allow it.'

'Oh, Aunt Kate. This is the twentieth century,' Poppy said, exasperated. 'Women do all sorts of things they never used to do. I've told you that before.'

'I'm sure they don't travel unaccompanied on railway trains,' Kate said primly.

'Of course they do. I shall be perfectly all right.' It wouldn't do to let her aunt know that she had in fact never travelled quite so far alone.

Kate pinched her lips and said with obvious reluctance, 'Perhaps I'd better come with you.'

'No, indeed. I wouldn't want to put you to so much trouble, Aunt,' Poppy said, trying not to sound alarmed. To travel with an elderly, nervous maiden aunt was the last thing she wanted.

'What time will you be back?'

'I don't know. I shall probably have to stay overnight and get the train back in the morning.'

Kate's eyes widened. 'I've never heard of such a thing. A woman alone . . . I don't like it.'

'You don't have to like it, Aunt,' Poppy said, her patience becoming thin. 'I'm going, so there's an end of it. I'm touched by your concern but I'm perfectly capable of looking after myself.'

'I knew no good would come of your working for *that man*.' Defeated, Kate turned and went back into the parlour.

Chapter Nineteen

Although she went to bed early on Wednesday evening Poppy couldn't sleep. She was nervous, although she had her train ticket in her handbag and the times of all the connections firmly in her head as well as on paper so really she had nothing to worry about.

But that was not what was troubling her and deep down she knew it. She was nervous at the thought of meeting Josh Kenton.

She wished now that she had never taken matters into her own hands and written to him about his father. Supposing the letter had worried him to the extent that his concentration had slipped, causing him to be less vigilant ...? Supposing it was her fault his plane had been shot down? How could he ever forgive her? And now she was interfering again, offering to journey all the way to Colchester to visit him because his father was too ill to go himself.

An offer she had been glad to make, and not just for his father's sake, she admitted to herself.

But how would Josh view her visit? Would he see it as an intrusion? Indeed, would he even agree to see her? After all, why should he? As far as he was concerned she was only his father's secretary.

In spite of, or perhaps it was because of her misgivings, she dressed with extra care, wearing a smart blue costume trimmed with darker blue braid that she had paid far too much for in rebellion against Aunt Kate's parsimony, with a small fur toque and black shoes that would be comfortable to walk in. A warm grey cape against the bitter January weather completed her outfit.

'Ee, lass, you look as smart as paint,' Mrs Rivers said as she stood in the kitchen, ready to go, waiting for Rivers to bring the trap round. Mrs Rivers had insisted that she couldn't go on such a long journey without a good breakfast inside her, and Rivers had been equally adamant that he would drive her to the railway station to make sure she got safely on the train. They treated her almost as if she was their own daughter and certainly with more warmth than Aunt Kate, who was deliberately keeping out of the way.

Although she had started her journey before seven o'clock in the morning it was well into the afternoon before Poppy reached her destination. Arriving at St Pancras, she had crossed London to Liverpool Street only to find she had missed her connection by five minutes and had to wait an hour and a half for another one. But eventually she arrived in Colchester and after two tram rides and a longish walk she reached the military hospital, which was situated within the army barracks on the outskirts of the town.

Tired, and not a little apprehensive, she walked into the ward clutching the bag of fruit she had managed to buy between changing trams. It was a grim place, with wards and corridors alike painted up to waist height in dark green and above that in faded yellow. The ward Josh was in was filled to capacity with iron bedsteads, packed so closely together that there was hardly room to squeeze between them, with more beds placed head to foot down the middle. Every bed was occupied by a bandaged figure, some lying supine, some propped up with pillows. A few were actually out of bed, but sitting on the side because there was no room to put a chair. A strong smell of carbolic coupled with a rather unpleasant, slightly sickly sweet smell pervaded the whole hospital but was more pronounced here.

A nurse whisked past carrying a tray of medicines. 'Looking for someone?' she asked over her shoulder.

'Yes. Captain Kenton. Captain Josh Kenton.'

'Ah, one of our Flying Corps boys. Over there, look, in the far corner.' She nodded in the direction without slackening her step.

'Thank you.' Poppy made her way down the ward, blushing at the grins and complimentary remarks that followed her.

Josh was lying on top of his bed in a grey dressing gown, staring up at the ceiling. His head and one eye were heavily bandaged and his arm was in a sling. He looked very young, very vulnerable, and she felt a sudden rush of something she couldn't quite identify wash over her.

She leaned over until she was in his field of vision. 'Hullo,' she said, unsure of her welcome.

For a moment he looked startled. 'Poppy?' He struggled up onto his good elbow. 'What are you doing here?'

She thought she detected a note of sharpness in his voice.

'I've come to see you because your father was worried about you and he's not well enough to come himself,' she said honestly.

'That's a surprise,' he said, and she wasn't sure what he meant by that, the fact that she had come to visit or that his father was worried about him. He didn't look particularly happy to see her.

Dropping with tiredness she looked round for somewhere to put her bag of fruit. She wouldn't stay if she wasn't welcome. With any luck she could catch a train and be home before midnight.

He misinterpreted her gaze. 'Sit on the bed,' he said, moving his feet. 'It's not really allowed, but Sister can't complain because there's no room for a chair.' For the first time he managed a ghost of a smile.

She perched herself on the edge of the bed. 'I've brought you some fruit,' she said.

'Thank you.'

There was an awkward silence, which she spent gazing round at the other occupants of the ward whilst he stared at the brown paper bag of fruit. Then he said, still without looking at her, 'So you've come as my father's emissary. I'm surprised he didn't send what's-his-name, um, Templeton. Although on second thoughts perhaps he knows I can't stand the man.'

'He's much too busy.' She looked down at her hands. 'Anyway, I offered to come.'

'Did you, by Jove! That was very noble of you.'

'I wanted to see you because I felt guilty about that letter I wrote to you.' She flushed under the gaze he turned on her. 'I wanted to apologise. I realise now I should never have written it.'

'Why not?'

She didn't look up but she sensed his eyes were still on her. 'Because I should have realised you'd got quite enough to contend with, trying to stay alive, without having to worry about what was going on at home,' she said quietly. 'When I heard you'd been shot down I was afraid it might have been on your mind . . . afraid it might have caused your concentration to slip . . .' She shrugged. 'I don't know . . . I just felt . . .' Her voice tailed off uncomfortably.

He was quiet for several minutes. Then he said, 'The reason I was shot down was that the Boche was cleverer than I was. I didn't see him coming out of the sun. It was as simple as that. It had nothing to do with your letter, I can assure you.'

She should have been glad to hear that, but the way he appeared to dismiss the letter, as if it was totally unimportant to him, was like a slap in the face. This was awful. She should never have come.

He went on, 'Anyway, how is the guv'nor?'

'He's . . .' She hesitated. Suddenly Sir Frederick's troubles seemed insignificant compared with what she could see around her now. 'He's still in a very low state. He can't seem to get over Alec— your brother's death. He's simply lost interest in everything. Even the will to live.' She looked up for the first time. 'But I told you all this in my letter.'

'Um. So you did.' He was regarding her thoughtfully from one blue eye. 'How did you feel about my brother's death?'

She felt herself blush again. 'Me? I – I didn't really know him all that well, but naturally I was very sorry, like everyone else.'

He raised his eyebrows. 'Is that all?'

She looked at him, frowning. 'What do you mean? I feel very sorry for Claire, of course, having to cancel all the arrangements for the wedding.' She paused. 'I must say I was surprised that Sir Frederick took it quite so badly.'

He sighed. 'You shouldn't have been. Alec has always been his favourite, ever since we were boys.'

'I'm sure that's not true,' she said, although she knew it was. 'You probably thought that because it was Alec who was being groomed to take over the business.' She was quiet for a few minutes. Then she said, 'I suppose this is why your father has lost interest in it. He thinks there's no point in carrying on now that Alec is dead. He knows you wouldn't want to take it on.' She shook her head sadly. 'It's such a tragedy. All those people who have worked for him for years ... I can't understand it. He just doesn't seem to care about them any more.'

'It sounds as if you do, though.'

'Of course I do,' she said warmly. 'I work with them. I talk to their wives. They're lovely people.' Suddenly, she stopped and put her hand up to her mouth. 'I'm sorry. I shouldn't be running on like this. God knows, you've got enough to worry about. And I haven't even asked ...' She paused, uncertain how to phrase the next question because it was patently obvious he had a broken arm and an injury to his head and eye. She took a deep breath and settled for, 'How long do you expect to be here?'

He smiled, a rather grim smile, reading her thoughts.

'You mean what's the damage. Well, the short answer is, my left arm is shattered. They can't – or won't – say whether I shall regain complete use of it. And until they take the bandages off they won't know whether I'll still have any sight in my left eye. But what they can guarantee is a fairly unsightly scar round it and an end to my flying career.'

'Oh, Josh, I'm so sorry.' She spoke instinctively, unaware that she had used his Christian name. She longed to put her hand comfortingly on his but he seemed so cool, so remote, that she didn't like to.

'Yes. So am I,' he answered, turning his head away. He leaned back on his pillows and stared at the ceiling again. 'What time is your train?' he asked.

She took this as a sign he wanted her to go and she stood up. 'I can't get back tonight. I'll catch a train in the morning.'

'Where are you staying?'

'Somebody on the tram said the Red Lion was the best place.'

'Yes, I've heard it's good.' His voice was cool.

'Is there anything you want? Anything I can get you? If there is I could bring it in the morning.' It was only an excuse. She wanted to see him again in spite of the fact that he hadn't been very pleased to see her. Although the ward was crammed to capacity he looked somehow lonely.

He didn't answer for a minute. Then he said, 'What about your train?'

'I could catch a later one.' She was sounding too eager. She stood up. 'Still, if there's nothing you want . . .'

'I'd like some soap. The stuff they use here is pure carbolic. I can't stand the smell of it.' He didn't look at her as he spoke.

'Very well, I'll get you some that smells better.'

'I don't want highly scented stuff.'

'I'll see what I can find and bring it in the morning.'

'Thank you.'

She waited a moment but he didn't say anything else. 'Goodbye, then.'

'Goodbye.'

After she had gone he remained for a long time staring up at the iron girders that held up the ceiling. Life was so bloody unfair. It should have been he who had died, not Alec, then Poppy and Alec could have been married and lived happy ever after. He and Alec had discussed it at length in that little pub where they'd managed to meet on the edge of Amiens, when they'd both had a brief leave. Alec had told him he had written to Poppy. 'Life's too short for pretence,' he'd said. 'I know it'll cause ructions with Claire when I break it off but how can I marry her, loving Poppy as I do?'

Josh had listened to Alec but said very little. What was the use? Alec's mind was made up and he was quite convinced Poppy felt the same way. He hadn't seen Alec again so he didn't know if Poppy had replied. And Poppy had given nothing away today. She was too sensible for that. Whatever her feelings for Alec she would keep them to herself and allow Claire to preserve her role as the bereaved fiancée. His mouth twisted in a tight little smile. He could only admire her for that.

A nurse came by. 'Your visitor gone, dearie?'

'Yes, but she'll be back in the morning to bring me some soap.'

'Soap? What do you want soap for? There's plenty here.'

'I can't bear the smell of carbolic. She's bringing me some decent stuff.'

'All right dearie, I'll see that you get it.' The nurse was straightening his pillows as she spoke.

'Can't you let her bring it in? I know it won't be visiting time, but she's come a long way . . .'

The nurse winked. 'All right, dearie, I'll see she gets to see you for five minutes. Your young lady, is she?'

He smiled. I wish to God she was, he murmured under his breath.

*

The next morning Poppy was back at the hospital at ten o'clock.

'Ah, you're our RFC lad's lady friend, aren't you?' a young nurse said as she hurried up the steps. 'We're not supposed to allow visitors at this time of day but he said you'd come a long way. Is that your taxi ticking outside?'

'Yes, it is,' Poppy said.

'Well you'd better hurry, then, hadn't you?' She gave a wink and turned her back.

Poppy hurried to the ward. Josh was sitting up in bed watching for her. He smiled when he saw her. 'You remembered, then,' he said.

'Of course.' She handed him the bag of soap. 'I bought you some shaving soap as well.'

'Oh, that was thoughtful of you. Thanks.' He patted the bed with his good hand. 'What time does your train go?'

'Half past eleven.' She sat down.

His face fell. 'You can't stay long, then.'

'I don't think I'd be allowed to, anyway. I'm not supposed to be here. It's not proper visiting time.'

'No. I suppose not.'

'How long do you expect to be here?' she asked.

'I don't know. Probably about two weeks. Less if they need the bed.'

'Then what? Will they let you come home to convalesce?'

'You could call it that. I'd call it being thrown on the scrap heap.' His expression was bleak. 'I'll never fly again.'

'I know it must seem like the end of the world,' she said gently, 'but there are other things. It's not something you ever wanted to do, but I'm sure your father would be ...'

'I know what you're going to say and I'll think about it,' he said quickly. 'But first I've got to come to terms with other things. I don't know yet what the damage is to my eye. Or my arm.'

'No. Of course not. When do the bandages come off?'

'Next week.'

'I wish . . .' She almost said I wish I could be here with you, but changed it to 'I wish you luck.' For why should he want her by his side?

'Thanks.'

'You'll let us know how things go, won't you?'

'Yes. As soon as I know anything.'

She looked at her watch. 'I must go. I shall miss my train.' She made no attempt to get up.

'Yes. Thank you for coming back to see me.' He gave her a brief smile.

'I hope the soap will be all right.'

'I'm sure it will.'

'Is there anything else you'd like?'

Yes, I'd like to kiss you, he thought. But he said, 'No, I don't think so, thank you.'

'Then I'd better go.' She got to her feet and stood looking down at him, resisting with difficulty the urge to brush away the strand of hair that had fallen over his forehead.

'Is it very cold out there?' he asked. 'The windows are too high for me to see what the weather's like.'

She put her hand briefly over his. 'Yes, it's very cold. There was a frost last night.'

He turned his hand and gripped hers. 'Thank you for coming to see me.'

'You'll be home before long.' She smiled. 'It won't be so far to come to visit you at Kenton Hall.'

'I'll look forward to that.' He was still holding her hand.

'Yes. So shall I.' She looked at her watch again.

'Tell my father I'm looking forward to coming home.' He gave her a lopsided smile. 'It's partly true and it might cheer him up a bit.'

'Yes. I'm sure it will. I must go now.'

'Yes. Is it far to the tram?'

'I didn't come by tram. I've got a taxi ticking outside the door. He'll take me right to the station.' Another glance at her watch. 'I'll just about catch the train if I go now.'

'Thank you for coming.' Now, almost reluctantly it seemed, he released her hand.

'Goodbye.'

'Goodbye.'

She hurried down the ward and back to the taxi. She wished she could have stayed with him.

'Cor, she's a bit of all right,' the soldier in the next bed said when she had gone. 'You're a lucky bugger, ain't you, Birdie?' That was his nickname for all Flying Corps men.

Josh gave a mirthless laugh. 'Oh, aren't I just!' he said.

Chapter Twenty

Going home in the train Poppy went over and over her visits to Josh in the military hospital.

He really had seemed quite pleased to see her – but reason told her that he would have been pleased to see anyone from home, so that didn't mean much.

And he had asked her to go back again, which was why she had had to catch a later train and consequently again missed her connection – but only because he needed some soap, reason told her.

She stared out of the window and saw nothing in the darkness except the reflection of her own face. Why was life always so complicated? Why couldn't the letter she had received have come from Josh instead of Alec . . .?

It was eight o'clock before she arrived home, tired, hungry and cold, and she went straight to the warm, welcoming kitchen, where Mrs Rivers fussed around, making tea and scrambling eggs for her. When she had eaten her fill, rounded off with a slice of fruit cake, she got to her feet.

'Thank you, Mrs Rivers. You make the best fruit cake I have ever tasted,' she said.

Mrs Rivers was busy at the stove making cocoa. She half turned and gave a sly smile. 'That's my special recipe. I only mek it for me and you and Alf. I don't waste it on them up there.' She jerked her head in the direction of the parlour. She poured the cocoa into two cups on a tray and a large mug. She gave the mug to Alf, who was dozing in the chair by the stove.

'Would you like me to take the tray up to the parlour?' Poppy asked. 'I must go and see the aunts, they don't know I'm home yet.'

'Aye, they'll be thinking you're lost in Lunnon town,' Alf chuckled from the depths of his chair.

The two sisters were sitting in their usual places, Kate in her armchair by the fire, Meg surrounded by pieces of material on the settee under the window. It looked a cosy enough scene in the light from the oil lamp – Kate always insisted that gas was far too expensive for lighting – but the room struck chill and there were only a few dying embers in the fire. Both Kate and Meg were wrapped in voluminous shawls.

'You're very late, Poppy,' Kate said, looking over the top of her pince-nez without a trace of a smile.

'I've come a long way,' Poppy said briefly. She put Kate's cocoa on the table beside her chair.

Meg beamed at her. 'Did you enjoy meeting your friend in London, dear?'

So that was how Kate had explained her absence. 'Yes, thank you, Aunt Meg. Very much. Shall I put your cocoa on the stool, here?'

'Yes. Thank you, dear. Did you make it for us?' She looked decidedly vague.

'No. Mrs Rivers made it. I offered to bring it from the kitchen.'

'The kitchen? What were you doing there?' Kate asked, her voice sharp.

'Eating scrambled egg and drinking tea,' Poppy said cheerfully.

'Didn't you eat on the train?'

'No. I didn't. Well, I had a sandwich at Liverpool Street. But by the time I got home I was starving.'

Kate pursed her lips. 'I don't approve of the way you act

210

with the servants, Poppy. It's not appropriate. Papa was very strict about that kind of thing and I've tried to follow his example. You're far too familiar with Mrs Rivers. And as for eating in the kitchen ...' Her expression conveyed that it was only one step from eating at the pig's trough. She began to sip her cocoa delicately. When she had finished she handed her cup to Poppy to replace on the tray. 'Have you finished, Meg? Then it's time for bed, dear.'

'Very well, Kate.' Obediently, Meg replaced her cup beside that of her sister and gathered up her belongings. 'Goodnight, Kate. Goodnight, Poppy,' she said dutifully.

'I'm coming, too,' Poppy said, suppressing a yawn. 'I've had a long day.'

'Yes, you went quite early this morning, didn't you?' Meg said, her timing muddled.

'Aren't you going to sit by the fire for a few minutes before you go up, Poppy?' Kate asked, clearly anxious to talk once she could get her sister out of the way.

'No, I don't think so, Aunt Kate,' Poppy said, yawning again. 'I'm very tired. And cold.' She didn't feel at all inclined to indulge her aunt's curiosity.

'I could put another piece of coal on the fire,' Kate said in an uncharacteristic burst of generosity.

'I don't think that would help, Aunt. The fire's dead. And so am I, nearly. Dead on my feet. If I don't go to bed soon I shall drop. Goodnight, Aunt.'

'Very well,' Kate said huffily. 'Goodnight.'

Gratefully, Poppy escaped to bed, where she was even more grateful to find that her dear friend Mrs Rivers had already placed a hot brick.

Sir Frederick was waiting for Poppy when she called to see him after work the following Monday.

'Why didn't you come earlier?' he asked testily.

'Because after two days away I knew there were things I must attend to at work,' she replied. She was no longer afraid of him, regarding him as she might have done a rather irascible but well beloved old uncle.

'Oh, that.' He waved his hand dismissively. 'Well, how is the boy?' Then, in a louder voice, 'Briggs, bring in some tea.'

'It's right here, Sir Frederick,' Briggs said, coming in with a laden tray.

'Put it down, man. Put it down.' He turned back to Poppy. 'Well?' he barked impatiently.

She smiled. It was good to see him less apathetic.

He frowned as she told him about her visit to the hospital but he didn't interrupt. When she had finished he was silent for several minutes, staring down into the tea she had poured for him. Then he said, 'He can be nursed at home here. Nurse Cranfield is supposed to look after me but she spends half her time kicking her heels so it'll give her something to do and release a bed at the hospital for some other poor bugger. His arm, you say? How bad is it?'

'They don't yet know . . .'

'You mean they're not saying. Well, only time will tell how much use he'll get back in it. And the same with his eye.' He gave a sigh. 'It could have been worse, I suppose.'

'He'll never fly again.'

'Can't say that bothers me. If men had been meant to fly they'd have been given wings like birds. But I expect it bothers him, silly young pup.'

'Yes. I think it does.'

He gave her a brief smile. 'Well, thanks for going to see him, lass. I'm sure your pretty face'll have cheered him up more than my grizzled old countenance would have done.'

'I'm sure he would have been more pleased to see his father, Sir Frederick,' she said quietly.

'I've neither the will nor the strength to move out of this chair, lass,' he said, shaking his head. 'Not even for him.'

Albert Soames was suffering from his usual winter cough. He often had a day or two off each winter to 'pull himself round', as he put it. But this winter seemed even colder and wetter than usual, and with the habitual damp fog spreading its silent filth over the city, the cough grew steadily worse and Albert grew steadily thinner and weaker.

Poppy did what she could to lighten his burden at work, but it was difficult because he became easily offended and accused her of wanting to be rid of him, which was not like Albert at all.

There was nobody she could turn to for advice. Sir Frederick wasn't interested, and she didn't trust George Templeton. Jack Earnshaw and Jake Benson were both sympathetic: they could see the problem but there was no solution they could offer. She felt it would have been disloyal to Albert to talk to the wives of the men about what was purely a work matter.

But, inevitably, things came to a head the day Albert collapsed at his desk. A door was taken off its hinges to make a stretcher and two of the men carried him down the steps from the office to the waiting ambulance.

Two days later Albert was dead.

George Templeton attended the funeral with several of the men from the works. Poppy would have liked to go herself, but it was not the custom for women to attend the graveside, so she stayed in the office. There was more than enough to occupy her now that Albert was no longer there.

She raised her head from the receipts she was writing and stared out of the window at the rain, tapping her teeth with her pen. It was a miserable day for a funeral. She wondered if Sir Frederick would be there. Someone must surely have told him that his chief clerk was dead. She would have gone to tell him herself, but she had heard that Josh was home now and for some reason she was reluctant to visit. It was odd. She had quite happily travelled over two hundred miles to see Josh Kenton in hospital, yet she couldn't bring herself to visit him now that he was at home, not much over a mile away.

Late in the afternoon George Templeton came into the

213

office, shaking the rain off his bowler hat, still in his black funeral suit.

'Well, that's that. Soames is dead and buried. Now we shall have to see about reorganising this office,' he said briskly, rubbing his hands. 'We shall have to advertise ...'

'I really don't think it's our place to do that Mr Templeton,' she said coldly, 'even if it was necessary. Which it isn't. I'm quite capable of running this office.'

'You!' he sneered. 'I *don't* think so. I intend to have you out of this place that fast your feet won't touch the ground, missy. I'm not having a chit of a lass chucking her weight about in *my* office. I've had enough. I had to put up with you when Sir Frederick decided to hire you. And since he's been away Albert Soames has been sticking up for you, pretending he couldn't do wi'out you. Well, Albert's dead now and Sir Frederick's not here so as soon as I can find a man to do the job you'll be out, my lass.' He jerked his thumb at the door as he spoke.

She stood up, her face livid with anger. Her desk was littered with unpaid bills and invoices; time sheets on a spike waited to be dealt with and there was a pile of letters to be written.

'Perhaps you'd like me to go now? This minute?' she asked, picking up her handbag. 'Since my presence is so offensive to you?' She began to tick off on her fingers. 'No doubt you can work out the wages, finish the receipts for the accounts that have been paid, enter them in the book, pay the bills from the bought ledger, write to the iron foundry, the clay ...'

He held up his hand. 'I didn't say you'd got to go right now,' he muttered.

'Then you'd better be careful what you say. Because another word from you and I shall walk out of that door and leave you to get on with it. Which you won't find easy, especially as tomorrow's pay day.' She sat down again. 'You have no idea what Albert's methods were, nor the enormous amount of work that goes through this office. But I have.

214

And I know how to cope with it all. Albert taught me well. But remember this. When you find the paragon who'll run this office better than I do he'll have to submit to me teaching him our methods, just as Albert taught me. And no man is going to like being told what to do by a – what did you call me? – "a chit of a lass". At least, no man of the kind you're likely to employ.' She stared at him, her expression full of disgust. 'Now, will you get out of *my* office and let me get on with my work. Goodness knows, I've got plenty enough to do.' She pulled the receipt book towards her.

George, obviously taken aback, treated her to one of his oily smiles. 'Ee, lass, there's no need to get your dander up that road. I didn't mean to upset you. I spoke in the heat of the moment. Y'know, after the funeral, and that. We're all upset to think we'll never see old Albert again. Don't you want to know about his funeral? Good lot of folk were there, to see him off, like.'

'Not from you, thank you,' she said without lifting her head.

'Mr Josh were there,' he continued, as if she hadn't spoken. 'He'd come to represent his dad, no doubt. It seems he's been home for the past month. Looks as if he's been through the mill, poor lad. I reckon he was lucky to get out alive when his plane was shot down. Looked proper jiggered, he did, by the time the funeral was done.'

Poppy bit her lip. She was desperate to know exactly how Josh looked. Was his arm still in a sling? Were the bandages off his face? She wanted to ask about Sir Frederick, too, but she was determined not to question George Templeton and with only the merest hesitation she continued with her work.

He walked over and came and stood behind her without speaking.

She swivelled round, full of suspicion. After what had happened that evening when she had worked late she didn't trust George Templeton if she couldn't see him. 'What are you standing there for?'

215

'Just watching, lass. Just watching.'

'So that you'll know what to do when you've turned me out?'

'Ee, lass. Don't be like that. I were only . . .'

'I don't care what "you were only", George Templeton. I don't like you standing behind me like that and I'd be glad if you would get out and leave me to get on with my work in peace.'

He picked up his bowler hat and brushed it with his sleeve. 'I'll not have you speak to me like that, missy,' he warned with another change of mood, his voice ominously low.

'And I'll not have you prowling round my office like a cat on hot bricks. Now, get out before I call Jack Earnshaw to throw you out.'

'I'll go when I'm good and ready, miss. And not before.'

She didn't look up. 'Make sure you shut the door as you go out.'

A few minutes later, just long enough for him to feel he had made his point, he walked heavily over to the door. She sighed with relief as she heard him open it and slam it behind him. A few seconds later she heard it open again.

'I thought I told you to get out of my office and stay out,' she snapped, reaching over for the spike with the time sheets on.

'I beg your pardon? I've only just arrived.'

She shot round in amazement and then scrambled to her feet, blushing to the roots of her hair. 'Oh, I do apologise. I didn't realise . . . I thought George Templeton had come back.'

Josh Kenton stood just inside the door, leaning on the wall, his hat in his hand. She could see from the bulge under his overcoat and the empty sleeve that his arm was still in a sling, and he wore a black patch over one eye. Above the patch his forehead bore a livid scar that reached jaggedly up to his hairline, emphasising the pallor of his face.

She pulled a chair forward, her heart hammering strangely. 'Won't you sit down? You look as if you're all in.'

'Thanks.' He gave her a brief smile as he sat down. 'Yes, I am a bit fagged. It's my first time out since I got home. I've just come from Albert's funeral. I thought someone should represent the guv'nor, since he wasn't up to going himself. I always liked Albert, he was a good sort.'

'Yes, he was. One of the best.' Poppy turned away so that he shouldn't see the tears that welled in her eyes at the memory of the man she had come to consider as a friend.

'I went to the house after the funeral,' he went on. 'I told Mrs Soames she would be looked after. She's got four children, we mustn't let them go hungry now the breadwinner is dead.'

'I'm afraid there'll be more than Mrs Soames and her family going hungry if this place has to close,' she said sadly.

His head shot up. 'Surely there's no danger of that! Listen to the noise coming from the workshops.'

'Yes, I know. But it won't last much longer if things don't improve.' She shook her head. 'Well, you've seen how your father is. He's sorely missed. The place won't run much longer without him.'

He stared at her. 'I can't believe things can be that bad.' He got stiffly up from his chair and went over and opened the door to Sir Frederick's office. Poppy always kept it dusted, the blotter and inkstand placed neatly on the desk, pens and paper knife in the wooden holder, silver tobacco box beside it. 'Hasn't the guv'nor ever been near the place at all?' he asked, frowning.

'No. He's never been back since the telegram came telling him your brother had been killed. He's simply lost all interest in the place. I did tell you, if you remember.'

He nodded absently. 'But surely there are matters he has to deal with – cheques to sign, that sort of thing.' Clearly, coming face to face with the situation had shaken him, even though he had been warned what it was like.

'Anything that needs his attention has to be taken to him. Usually by me. For some reason he won't see anyone else.'

He turned. 'Yes, he said you used to visit him. He often speaks of you. Why haven't you been lately?'

She flushed. 'I heard you were home and I didn't want to intrude.' She gave a wry smile. 'I felt I had intruded into your family affairs quite enough.'

'What do you mean by that?' he asked, regarding her gravely.

'Well,' she shifted uncomfortably under his gaze, 'coming all that way to visit you in hospital. After all, it wasn't really my place, was it?'

His face cleared. 'I was very glad to see you,' he said with a smile. 'I didn't have many visitors. At least, not people I knew.' He didn't add that the memory of her face had stayed with him through many sleepless nights.

He turned back to his father's office and with a last look round closed the door. 'So who's in charge now?'

She gave a shrug. 'George Templeton, I suppose. But he's not very popular, either with the men or our customers.'

He came back and sat down again on the chair she had provided. 'I can see I shall have to have a talk with the guv'nor. Things can't go like this, can they?' He leaned his good hand on his stick.

She smiled at him. 'Oh, I wish you would, Mr Josh. Maybe he'll listen to you. He won't take any notice of anything I or anybody else says.'

'You should try smiling at him,' he remarked, so softly that she wasn't sure she had heard aright.

He got up to go, staggering slightly as he did so. Instinctively, she put out a hand to steady him.

'Thank you. I'm finding it a little difficult at the moment to maintain my balance. One really does need two eyes, you know,' he said lightly. 'But I expect I shall get used to only having one. In time.'

218

'Oh, I'm so sorry,' she said. 'Can't they . . .?'

'Save it? It doesn't look like it at the moment. But you never know. I keep hoping. At any rate, in a few weeks with any luck I should look a little less like a pirate chief.'

She smiled again. 'Oh, I don't know. You look quite dashing with that patch over your eye.'

'You think so?' He went over to the mirror she kept on top of the filing cabinet. 'Well, at least it partially covers the scar.' He turned away and picked up his walking stick. 'Bit of a wreck, really. Only one eye, limited use in one arm and a flying career totally up the spout.'

'But you're still alive, unlike your brother,' she said quietly.

He studied her for a long minute without speaking.

She flushed under his gaze. 'I'm sorry. That was a tactless thing to say.'

He nodded. 'True, nevertheless.' He walked over to the door and let himself out, closing it quietly behind him.

After he had gone she sat down at her desk and put her head in her hands. Why had she said that? Why had she made it sound almost accusing that he was alive whilst his brother had died? It wasn't what she had meant at all.

Chapter Twenty-One

Two weeks later, at half past nine on a rainy Monday morning, Josh Kenton walked into Poppy's office. The sling was gone from his arm but he still wore the black patch over his eye and he walked with a stick. He looked so pale and thin and somehow vulnerable that her heart went out to him.

'Good morning, Miss Barlow,' he said, giving her a slightly lopsided, faintly apologetic smile.

'Good morning, Captain Kenton.' She tried not to sound surprised. Then a sudden thought struck her. 'Is anything wrong? Sir Frederick . . . ?'

'No, no, no. He's fine. Well, as fine as he ever will be, I guess.' His mouth twisted. 'And it's *Mr* Kenton, if you don't mind. I've finished with the RFC. Or, rather, they've finished with me.' He gave her no chance to reply to this but walked over to his father's office. 'Will you come through, please.'

Poppy followed him. For a moment he stood just inside the door looking round at the banks of drawers and neatly stacked shelves and cupboards, then with a great sigh he hung up his hat and coat and sat down at his father's desk.

'God knows what I'm doing here, Poppy,' he said, putting both hands on the tooled leather surface, and she wondered if he was aware that he had used her Christian name. He went on, 'I'm completely out of my depth in this place. But I've come to realise that one of us has got to make some kind of effort to keep this business going and it's quite plain it's not going to be the guv'nor.' He glanced up at her as she stood by the desk, feeling as awkward as he seemed to be. 'Look, sit down. Please sit down. I need someone to talk to,' he gave a wry smile. 'Someone to tell me what I ought to be doing.'

She sat down on the edge of a chair. 'George Templeton is probably the best person for that,' she said carefully. 'He's been more or less running things for the past six months.'

He nodded. 'So I believe. Not a very popular character, I understand.'

She hesitated. 'He's good at his job but the men don't like the way he throws his weight around. He always did, to some extent, but he's worse now that Sir Frederick isn't here because he can more or less do as he likes.'

He nodded. 'Thank you for that. I'll get to him in a minute. But what about all this?' His glance swept the office.

She frowned. 'Well, I suppose the first thing you need is the authority to sign business papers and cheques,' she said carefully.

He waved his hand. 'Oh, that's all taken care of, never fear. Father couldn't wait to get his lawyer over to the house once I'd agreed to run things. He came over last week and sorted it all out before I had time to change my mind. The guv'nor's given me the authority to deal with everything.' He made a face. 'Quite a daunting prospect, I may say.'

'I'm sure you'll learn very quickly,' she said, trying to sound encouraging. 'But does that mean Sir Frederick is giving up altogether?'

''Fraid so. He wants me to take over completely.'

'Oh, dear. That's a pity.' She looked up quickly. 'I don't mean it's a pity you ... what I mean is, it's a pity he's giving up completely,' she said, floundering.

He gave a rather grim smile. 'I understand what you're trying to say and I couldn't agree more. I never expected it to fall to my lot to come here and run this place.' He flexed the hand of his wounded arm once or twice, staring at it as he did so. 'The fact is, since his breakdown – I don't know what else to call it – he's completely lost confidence in his ability to do anything at all, even to walk, let alone run a business the size of this one. The very thought of coming back here reduces him to a shaking jelly. It's not that he doesn't want to return, he's simply not capable of doing so. And he has terrible black moods. The doctor has advised that he should take up painting. He seems to enjoy that. But I must say his paintings are not at all to my taste. Some of them are quite weird.'

'So everything is falling on your shoulders,' Poppy said sympathetically.

He shrugged. 'That's life. I realise I've got to do something, since I'm never going to fly again.'

He paused, and Poppy realised that in those few words all his ambitions had been shattered.

He went on, 'I suppose taking this on is as good as anything else, at least it will stop me from brooding over what might have been. Mind you, it's about the last thing I ever thought of doing. Or wanted to do, to tell you the truth.' He glanced round the room, his gaze resting on the glass-fronted cupboard full of gleaming samples of the implements made at Kentons. 'This was to be Alec's career, not mine, that was made quite plain to me from a very early age. Of course, I knew this, after all, he was the eldest as well as being the guv'nor's blue-eyed boy.' His mouth twisted as he stared at the blotter in front of him and Poppy wondered just how deeply it hurt him to know this. After a few minutes he lifted his head and regarded her thoughtfully. 'So I made my own career, which has been, as you might say, shot down in flames, quite literally. But life has a habit of not turning out the way we'd have chosen, doesn't it?' he said quietly. 'You know that as well as anybody.'

She thought of her father, of the day she had found him hanging from the banister and she felt a sudden lump in her throat. 'That's very true,' she managed to say, her voice not much above a whisper.

His mood changed. 'Enough of that,' he said briskly. 'Let's get to business. If I'm to become involved in this shebang you'd better tell me what I ought to be doing next.' He gave another of his lopsided smiles. 'I shall need your guidance every step of the way, Miss Barlow, I'm warning you.'

She returned his smile. 'I think you're very brave, Mr Kenton, and I'll help you as much as I can.' She stood up. 'You could start by signing the letters I typed on Friday. I'll explain them to you as we go along. That will give you some idea of what goes on here. George Templeton has been signing them when I couldn't get to Sir Frederick but it isn't really his job. Although he likes to think it is,' she added as a note of warning.

'I see. Well, go and fetch them and we'll go through them together.' As he spoke he reached into his inside pocket and took out a fountain pen.

Poppy went back to her office humming under her breath. Josh Kenton was coming to take over from his father. He would be here, in the next office, every day. Suddenly, even though it was raining outside, the day seemed full of sunshine. She picked up the letters and went back, her step light.

The next hour went very quickly. Poppy sat opposite Josh whilst he questioned her about what he was signing. He was very perceptive and sometimes she had to think hard before she could give him an answer. She noticed that he made notes about everything she said on a pad at his side.

After the letters were signed and sealed she explained the various office procedures that she had inherited from Albert and the alterations and improvements she had made to them. Again, he listened carefully, now and again offering a suggestion or nodding with approval.

She was in the middle of explaining how the time sheets were worked out when he suddenly interrupted with a broad smile, 'This is a very dry place, Miss Barlow.'

She looked out of the window and then at Josh. 'Dry? It's pouring with rain.'

He was still smiling. 'What I mean is, doesn't your very efficient office run to a teapot? I'm dying for a cup of tea. All this brainwork is making me thirsty.'

'Oh, I beg your pardon.' She burst out laughing. 'Well, your father always keeps a bottle of whisky in that cupboard behind you,' she said.

It was his turn to laugh. 'Good heavens, no. Not that. I need to keep a clear head. A cup of tea would be far more acceptable, if that's possible.'

'As a matter of fact, we do have a teapot. And cups and saucers,' she said. 'If you don't mind waiting while I go down to the blacksmith's shop, Charlie will boil a kettle for me on the forge and I'll make some tea.' She looked at her watch. 'It's what I usually do about this time.'

His laughter faded. 'That's not very convenient, is it? Why haven't you got a gas ring in your office? You can't go running over to the forge every time you need to boil a kettle. Especially when it's raining, like today.'

She shrugged. 'It's what Albert always did, so it's what I do. Only I've replaced his tin mugs with china cups.'

'Good for you.' He gave her a boyish grin. 'I never drink whisky during the day, unlike my father. I drink tea and I shall depend on you to brew it, Miss Barlow, so I must make it as easy for you as I can. And that means not having to trip down to the forge to boil a kettle every time. We need a gas ring.' He scribbled Gas Ring on the long list at his side and underlined it.

'I'll be as quick as I can.' She left him looking through some ledgers and went down to the blacksmith's shop.

'So Mr Josh has come to tek over,' Charlie Braithwaite the blacksmith said as she waited, teapot in hand, for the kettle to boil.

She smiled at him. 'My word, news gets around fast in this place, doesn't it?' she replied without answering his question.

'Aye, it do. To tell t'truth, Mord Jones saw him come in and told the rest of us. It didn't tek us long to put two and two together.' He gave a satisfied nod. 'He'll be good, will Mr Josh. T'men all like him. He gets on wi' us better than Mr Alec ever did. Too toffee-nosed, was Mr Alec.' He took the kettle off the forge and poured the boiling water into the teapot. 'There y'are, love. Mind ye don't scald yerself as you go up them steps.' He said those words every day when she went down to brew the tea.

She went back up to her office, humming lightly to herself. But as she poured the tea her heart sank because she could hear George Templeton's droning voice coming from the next office. She could tell from his pontificating tone that he was regaling Josh with how well he was running things in Sir Frederick's absence. Reluctantly, she took down another cup and saucer and poured tea for him.

She left her own tea on her desk and took two cups into the other office.

'Ah, lovely. That didn't take you long.' Josh smiled up at her. 'Is there a cup for Mr Templeton?'

'This one is for Mr Templeton. I've left mine in my office,' she said briefly. 'I'll come back later and continue our discussion if you need me, Mr Kenton.'

'Aye, this lass is good at making tea, if nowt else,' George Templeton said expansively, picking up the second cup and taking a noisy slurp. 'Mind you, she gets plenty of practice. I don't know how many times a day she's over at that forge, wi' her little teapot.'

'Twice a day, Mr Templeton, as you well know. Once in the morning and once in the afternoon,' Poppy answered him. 'I have my tea break more or less at the same time as the men. The only difference is that they stop working while they eat their snap. I don't. I have mine at my desk.'

She turned to Josh. 'Will there be anything else, Mr Kenton?'

Josh looked from George Templeton to Poppy and back again, taking in the situation between them at a glance. 'Not for the moment, Miss Barlow,' he said. 'But don't go far. I shall need you again later.'

'That's summat I need to discuss wi' you, Mr Kenton,' George Templeton began before she could get to the door. 'Now that Albert's gone, God rest his soul, we need to look for another *man* to tek his place in t'office. It's nowt more than a shambles back there now he's not here.' He jerked his thumb in the direction of Poppy's office.

Poppy had her hand on the doorknob as he spoke. She froze for a second, then swung round. 'How dare you say that, Mr Templeton!' she said furiously. 'You know it's not true.'

He rounded on her. 'A woman's place is in the home, missy, not trying to do men's work. We need a man to run that office, not a bit of a lass who doesn't know A from a bull's foot about owt.'

'I worked in my father's office for several years and when I came here Albert taught me all he knew. Sir Frederick was more than happy with my work,' she said, her eyes flashing with temper. 'You just can't bear the thought that a woman might be able to . . .'

Josh held up his hand. 'All right, Miss Barlow. You've made your point,' he said without raising his voice. 'I'll deal with it.'

George Templeton turned and gave her a smug, self-satisfied sneer from his position opposite Josh. 'Aye. You run along and drink your tea,' he said, waving her away.

Seething with rage, Poppy went back to her office and sat down at her desk, resting her head on her hand. She hadn't meant to lose her temper. Goodness knows, Josh had quite enough to cope with on his first day without being dragged into the constant war between her and George Templeton. God, how she hated that man. She stared at the

226

closed door between the offices, knowing that at this very moment her fate was probably being decided. The manager had an oily, persuasive tongue. Would he be able to convince Josh that she was totally incompetent and that the Kentons works was no place for a woman? She felt sick with apprehension.

It seemed an age before George Templeton stalked out of Josh's office, leaving the door wide open, his expression set. But in fact it was less than half an hour.

Five minutes later Josh called, 'Can you spare a minute, Miss Barlow?'

She went in, her heart thudding painfully.

He was leaning back in his chair, his hands loosely clasped. He looked up as she walked in and nodded to her to take a seat.

'Not an easy man,' he said thoughtfully. 'He has very definite ideas about the way things should be run and he doesn't intend to give up his position of authority easily.' He was silent for a few minutes, then his face broke into a smile. 'But never fear, Miss Barlow, your position is quite safe. I made it quite clear to him that I would have no interference from him with regard to my office staff.' His smile broadened. 'So that's round one to me. Now, where were we?'

Cycling home, Poppy went over her day. She should be walking on air, she told herself. Josh Kenton had championed her against George Templeton, she had spent most of the day with him, helping him, guiding him in the ways of his father. He had been grateful for her help, she knew. Not only that, he had been impressed by her knowledge.

So why did she feel so flat?

The answer was not hard to find. It was in his own words, when he had told her that he would have no interference with regard to his office staff. His office staff. In those words he had made it quite plain how he regarded her. But what did she expect? How else did she imagine he would think of her? And why should she feel it mattered, anyway?

She put her bicycle away and let herself in the front door, wiping her feet on the doormat in the depressing dimness of the hall. Her grandfather's portrait glared down at her with an almost menacing air out of the gloom, and she hurried through to the parlour to get out of his gimlet gaze.

To her amazement it was Meg who was sitting in Kate's armchair by the fire, her little legs swinging because they were not quite long enough to reach the floor.

'Where's Aunt Kate?' Poppy asked, her eyes searching the room.

Meg hunched her shoulders in glee. 'Gone to bed. She's got a bad cold. Ring the bell for Mrs Rivers to bring your supper, dear, and then put some more coal on the fire.' She watched as Poppy knelt on the hearthrug and picked up the tongs. 'And put several lumps on, dear. It'll be all right, Kate's not here to see.'

Poppy made up a good fire, then sat back on her heels, enjoying the sudden warmth.

Meg held her hands out the blaze. 'Oh, this is nice, isn't it?' Like a small child, she gave her shoulders another gleeful hunch.

Mrs Rivers shuffled in with a plate of steak and kidney pie for Poppy and three muffins for Meg.

'Kate didn't want hers so I told Mrs Rivers I'd have it with mine when you had your supper,' Meg said happily. She drew a chair up to the table and began to spread a muffin thickly with butter. 'Well, what have you been doing at work today, dear? Kate says it's rude to ask you but I can't think why. I'm very interested in what you do at Coles. It's such a lovely department store. I used to go there a lot . . .' Her expression changed suddenly, becoming quite woebegone. '. . . when I was able,' she added sadly.

'I don't work . . .' Poppy began but Meg wasn't listening.

She carried on, her cheerful, almost garrulous mood returning. 'Could you get me some pale blue ribbon, Poppy? I seem to have run out. You do work in the haberdashery department, don't you? Where they sell ribbons?'

'No, I . . .'

'In that case, you could get me some green, as well. Very narrow, half an inch wide. No more.' As she spoke butter was dribbling down her chin. 'I need it for my patchwork, you understand. I like to put little ribbon bows here and there, it adds a pretty, dainty touch, don't you think? Kate says its over-fussy but I don't think so, do you?'

Poppy raised her voice. 'Aunt Meg, I don't work in the haberdashery department at Coles. In fact, I don't work at Coles. I work in an office at . . .'

'In an *office!*' Meg clapped her hands. 'Oh, how exciting. Have you got one of those typewriting things that you press the letters down and they print onto the paper?' As she spoke she was pressing her little fat fingers one by one onto the table, leaving little round grease marks.

'Yes, as a matter of fact I do use a typewriter,' Poppy said with a smile.

'Oh, how exciting.' Once again Meg clapped her hands. 'But of course, Coles would have up-to-date things, wouldn't they? They're such a big shop.' She shook her head sadly in another change of mood. 'I haven't been there for such a long time,' she said mournfully.

'Would you like me to take you there on Saturday, Aunt Meg?' Poppy asked. 'Then you can buy your own ribbons.'

Meg cringed and her eyes grew wide with fear. 'Oh, no. I couldn't go there. It's too far. And all those people. No, it wouldn't do. It wouldn't do at all.' She looked up at Poppy and said petulantly, 'Why can't you get my ribbons? You work there.'

'No, Aunt Meg. I don't work at Coles. I keep trying to tell you,' Poppy said, slightly exasperated. She had never been able to understand why Aunt Kate had insisted on such secrecy over the place where she worked. In any case, Meg was so muddled in her mind most of the time that she probably wouldn't know anything about Kentons, even if she was told. 'I work . . .'

Suddenly, the door was thrown open and Kate stood there, a thick shawl round her shoulders, her hair escaping from its pins and her pince-nez slightly crooked. 'I might have known,' she said imperiously. 'The minute my back is turned the fire is halfway up the chimney and the room is like an oven.' She came over to them, a scrap of lace handkerchief held to her nose, bringing with her the heavy scent of eucalyptus.

Meg looked up with a start, wiping her chin with her napkin. 'I thought you'd gone to bed, dear,' she said in a small, half-frightened voice.

'I went to lie on my bed for an hour, Meg. I told you that, but of course I could hardly have expected you to understand.' She turned to Poppy and gave a small, brave smile. 'You can see why I can never leave Meg for long, dear, can't you?' She bent over and tried to pull away some of the coals in the hope that they wouldn't burn. 'She has no idea what things cost. No idea at all. She thinks money grows on trees.'

'I hope you don't want any tea, Kate, because I've eaten your muffin,' Meg said triumphantly.

'That was very greedy of you,' Kate said sharply. 'Fortunately, I only want a cup of tea. Perhaps you would pour it for me, Poppy?' She sank down in her chair beside the fire and dabbed at her nose again. 'I have a very bad cold. I don't feel at all well.'

'Then perhaps you should go back to bed, Aunt Kate,' Poppy said gently. 'I'm here now. I can look after Aunt Meg, if that's what worries you.'

Kate looked at Poppy and then at Meg. 'No,' she said. 'I can't leave her. I need to be here. There's no telling . . .'

Meg stared at her sister, her eyes like bright black currants in her round pink face. Suddenly, she leaned forward and screwed up her eyes. 'You're afraid I'll tell her what you did, Kate, aren't you? You're afraid I'll tell her what happened!'

'Don't be so silly, Meg. I've no idea what you're talking about,' Kate said, but she was obviously flustered by her sister's words. 'And neither have you.' She peered at her. 'I think you'd better sit very quietly. When you begin to talk rubbish like that it often heralds one of your turns.'

'I'm not talking rubbish,' Meg said stubbornly. 'I'm perfectly all right. But if you keep saying things like that I shall tell Poppy all about me being locked in my room.'

'Oh, that,' Kate said, relaxing visibly. 'That was years ago, dear, when Papa was alive.' She turned to Poppy. 'Meg was rather a naughty lass when she was little and inclined to be rude to the vicar. So every time he called Papa had her locked in her room so that she shouldn't disgrace him.' She gave a small smile. 'Papa always forgave her in the end.'

'Yes. I was his favourite,' Meg said smugly. She put her head on one side. 'But he didn't know everything, did he Kate?'

'That's enough!' Kate snapped suddenly.

'I was only going to say . . .'

'I said, that's enough!' Kate got up from her chair and went to the cupboard beside the fire where Meg's pills were kept.

Meg saw where she was heading and got up quickly from her chair and hurried from the room. A moment later they heard the sound of crashing chords from the piano.

Kate sank back into her chair and dabbed at her nose. 'My sister is very unstable,' she said.

Poppy said nothing. What was it that Kate had been at such pains to prevent Meg from saying?

Chapter Twenty-Two

Poppy had little time or inclination to dwell on the problems and mysteries at Dale House over the next weeks because she was kept too busy at work helping Josh settle into his new role.

One of the first things he did was to tour the works, finding out how everything was done and by whom. When he got back he dictated copious notes for Poppy to type up for his future reference.

'Of course, I've met all the men and their families at the guv'nor's garden parties enough times, but I must say they look altogether different when they're not dressed up in their glad rags,' he told her, smiling ruefully. 'And the wives were never with their husbands so I've never managed to work out who's who. Now, can you sort it all out for me? There are often one or two women standing on their doorsteps when I arrive in the morning and it's not enough simply to doff my hat to them. I need to know who they are.'

Poppy smiled. 'A good many employers wouldn't even do that,' she remarked.

'Well, I think it's important to know them by name. Now, who is the big fair-haired woman at number six?' He consulted the notes she had typed. 'Is that Jack Earnshaw's wife? He works on the crucibles?'

'No. Jack Earnshaw is a widower. He lives at number

five and was married to Connie Templeton's sister. Now Connie cooks for him and does his laundry, that kind of thing.'

He raised questioning eyebrows. 'That's George Templeton's wife.'

'That's it. The big fair-haired woman is Daisy Frampton. She's a widow and she lives with her father, Sam Beckwith.'

'Ah, I know him. He works on the grindstone. He must be sixty if he's a day.'

'There's not a grinder to match him, though,' Poppy said, adding quickly, 'so your father says.'

'I can believe that.'

In this way they went through the entire workforce and by the end of the morning Josh knew about Mary Smithers at number two having been left penniless when her husband joined the army, how the other women had rallied round her and how his own father had managed to obtain her allowance from the authorities; he knew that Jake Benson at number four, a quiet man, had been to night school to educate himself and how proud Maud, his wife, was of his achievements. He knew, too, that the two boys who hung around waiting to run messages after school were Jake's sons.

And so it went on.

When they had finished he leaned back in his chair. 'I had a long chat with Ted Ferris, in the pot shop. His son is in the infantry in France and naturally enough he's worried sick over him. But what could I say? My experience was in the air, not on the ground, Thank God. Who did you say his wife was?'

'Lily. Number three. Quite stout. Always wears a white apron.'

'Ah, I know the one. They have a daughter, too, don't they?'

Poppy shook her head, smiling. 'No, that's Charlie Braithwaite the blacksmith. He and his wife live at number seven. Milly, their daughter, is thirteen. A pretty little lass.'

'Ah, yes. I've seen her.' He shuffled his notes together. 'Now, what about . . .'

'I think I ought to remind you you have an appointment with the manager of the steel works in half an hour, Mr Kenton,' she said.

He frowned. 'Am I going there, or is he coming here?'

'You're going to visit him.' He looked blank so she went on, 'To discuss the price of the blister steel, I believe. You thought George Templeton was paying over the odds for it.'

His face cleared. 'Ah, yes, I remember now.' He grinned at her. 'What would I do without you, Miss Barlow?'

'Find someone else, I suppose,' she replied, trying to keep her voice light.

'That would be impossible,' he said quietly, his gaze resting on her.

She bent her head and flicked over the pages of her note-book so he shouldn't see that his words had made her blush.

He stood up.

'Oh, before you go, will you sign the cheque for the men's wages, please? And there are three letters. They're all in my office.'

He followed her through and took out his pen and put his signature with a flourish on all the documents. Then he looked at her with his head on one side, smiling. 'May I go now?'

She smiled back at him and looked at her watch. 'I think you'd better, or you'll be late for your appointment. You'll find your car waiting, Mr Kenton.' She helped him on with his coat and handed him his hat.

He paused with his hand on the door handle. 'My father has never stopped singing your praises, Miss Barlow. I can quite understand why.' With that he strode off.

Poppy took the cover off her typewriter. Oh yes, she was a good secretary, her father had trained her well. But just at the moment Josh Kenton's compliment had a hollow ring.

He was back sooner than she expected, his face set. 'Could you come through, Miss Barlow,' he said crisply as he went through to his own office.

Puzzled, she followed him.

'Sit down.' He nodded briefly towards the notebook she had brought with her. 'You won't need that.'

She sat quietly, waiting while he threw his coat and hat at the hatstand and flung himself into his chair, pushing his fingers through his thick hair in a helpless gesture. 'I've got a real problem, Miss Barlow,' he said after a minute. 'Talk about being thrown in at the deep end. This is worse than being in a dogfight.' He gave her a faint smile. 'Well, almost.'

She raised her eyebrows but said nothing.

'As you know, I went to the steel works to complain about the increased price of the steel over the past six months.'

She nodded.

'They were very polite, very nice, asked after the guv'nor, etc. etc. Then they metaphorically patted me on the head and told me to go and look again at my books because their prices haven't increased at all in that time.'

'But we're definitely paying more,' Poppy said, surprised.

'I know that. I checked my facts carefully before I went.'

'So what does that mean?'

'It means that I was made to look like a greenhorn because somebody is falsifying the accounts in some way.'

'There's only one person who could be doing that,' Poppy said slowly.

He nodded. 'That's what I'd worked out. Our friend George Templeton.'

Poppy was quiet for a minute. Then she frowned. 'I don't quite see how, though. He does all the ordering but the invoices and receipts all come to me.' She chewed her lip. Then her face cleared. 'Oh, I can see how he might

235

have been able to do it. Since your father's illness the bills have mostly been paid in cash. Once a week I'd write out a cheque for him to sign that would cover all the wages plus any bills that had to be paid. It wouldn't be too difficult for George Templeton to keep two sets of invoice books, one for the steel company and the inflated one for me to pay. Then, as it was all in cash, all he would have to do is pocket the difference. I suppose that's one way he could have done it.' She frowned. 'But he must have realised he would be found out eventually.'

'No, he probably thought he was clever enough to get away with it.' He tapped his fingers on the desk. 'The point is, what do I do? We really can't afford to lose him, at least, not yet. Not until I've really got my feet under the table. So I can't sack him. But I can't let him get away with it.'

'Make him pay the money back, I should think. He must have it put away somewhere and if he hasn't it can be stopped out of his wages.' A smile spread across her face. 'I do the wages. I'd enjoy doing that.'

'Mm. Yes. Maybe that's the best thing.' He nodded slowly. 'I'll have to speak to him as soon as possible. But it won't be this afternoon. I've got a hospital appointment.' He stared out of the window. 'I have to go and see this eye specialist chappie. He's supposed to be very good.' He turned and smiled at her. 'But whatever the outcome, with any luck I should come back looking a little less like a pirate.' He pointed to the black patch he still wore over one eye.

She laughed. 'I shall miss that. It makes you look quite dashing.'

He held her gaze. 'Do you really think so?' He shrugged. 'Whether I'll have any sight left in the eye is another matter. They didn't hold out much hope at the other hospital. Anyway, we shall see.' He stood up. 'I'd better go.' His smile broadened. 'Thank you for your help, Miss Barlow.'

She looked surprised. 'I haven't done anything.'

'Oh, but you have.' He tried to shrug into his coat but his weak arm made it difficult and she had to help him. 'See? What would I do without you?' he said lightly.

She went back to her desk. For some reason his words hadn't cheered her at all.

At lunch time Poppy took her sandwiches over to eat in Maud Benson's warm kitchen, knowing that Maud would be quite offended if she didn't. As usual, all the wives had congregated there and today they were in a state of high excitement. They were all fussing round Mary Smithers, who was laughing and crying at the same time.

'It's all right, Miss Poppy,' Maud said, moving a pile of clean linen off a chair so that she could sit down. 'They haven't all gone barmy, it's that Mary's had news of her Harry.'

'Yes,' Mary could hardly contain herself. 'He's wounded. They're sending him home. But he's safe. Thank God. He'll not have to fight any more. Oh, I'm that relieved you can't imagine.'

'Is it bad?' Poppy managed to ask Maud without Mary hearing.

'Shot in the leg. He may lose it,' Maud whispered back. 'Bad enough but could be a lot worse.'

Poppy nodded. 'So you'll soon have him home, Mary,' she said in a louder voice.

'Aye. It can't be soon enough for me,' Mary said happily. She gave a short laugh. 'That'll put a stop to George Templeton's larks. He'll not be making a nuisance of himself when my Harry gets back, not like he does now.'

'What do you mean?' Charity asked innocently, looking up from feeding little Rebecca.

'He's allus sidling up behind me and pinching my bottom and asking me if I miss my Harry. When I say of course I do he offers to keep his place warm. I know exactly what he's getting at, the randy so-and-so, and I've given him the length of my tongue more than once. He's a perishing nuisance.'

'My Jake has trouble with that man,' Maud said. 'The trouble is, Mr Templeton is jealous because Jake is so much cleverer than he is and he tries to make out Jake's work isn't very good, or that he's slacking. I know it upsets Jake although he doesn't often complain.'

Once the wives began on the topic of George Templeton there was no stopping them. Knowing what she did about him, Poppy kept quiet. Her knowledge was not for their ears. As soon as she could she got up and left them still talking about him.

Back in her own office she carried on with her work and was surprised when Josh returned soon after four o'clock. The patch was gone from his eye, leaving a puckered scar round it that joined the livid one running up to his hairline.

'Not a pretty sight, Miss Barlow,' he remarked when she looked up. 'I think it was better with the patch, don't you?'

She put her head on one side. 'At least you no longer look like something out of *Treasure Island*,' she said, smiling. 'But the important thing is, can you see out of it?'

'Not much. They say it may improve a little. In time.' He seemed quite depressed.

'I'll make some tea,' she said, going over to the new gas ring in the corner. 'I'm sure you can do with a cup.'

'The Englishman's answer to every crisis,' he said. 'I'll be in my office.'

When the kettle had boiled she took the tea through. 'I've brought mine, too. I thought you might want to talk,' she said diffidently.

'No, I don't think so,' he said, staring out of the window.

She turned to go.

'No. Stay. I'm sorry. I don't think I know what I do want at the moment. I feel a complete wreck.'

'You don't look a wreck.' She put the tea down carefully

on the desk. 'A bit battle-scarred, but that's nothing to be ashamed of.'

'They say there's nothing more they can do,' he said gloomily. 'They say the skin round the area is too delicate to tamper with, unfortunately.'

'Never mind. It gives you a slightly raffish look,' she said with a smile, hoping to cheer him up.

'Never mind!' he repeated savagely. 'The trouble is, I *do* mind, Miss Barlow. I don't care for the idea of being a freak.'

'Oh, but that's ridiculous,' she exploded. 'I've never heard such nonsense in all my life.' Then, realising whom she was talking to, 'I'm sorry, Mr Kenton, I shouldn't have said that.' She paused but couldn't resist adding quietly, 'The important thing is, you're still alive.'

He turned to look at her. 'Unlike my brother, who had so much more to live for. Isn't that what you mean, Miss Barlow?' His tone was suddenly cold.

'No, Mr Kenton. That was not what I meant at all,' she said, surprised by his vehemence. 'I don't know why you should think it might be.'

'Because you and my brother ...'

She was immediately on her guard. 'I and your brother what?' she asked.

He shook his head and looked down at his hands, lying loosely in his lap. 'Nothing. Nothing at all. It doesn't matter.'

She watched him for several minutes, wondering once again whether it was possible that Alec might have confided in him about the letter he had sent her. But he remained where he was, saying nothing more.

She picked up her cup and saucer. 'I'll take this back to my office. I've quite a lot of work to get through before I go home,' she said.

He didn't look up.

That night she ate her supper in the kitchen with Mrs Rivers, where it was warm and comfortable. She felt miserable and flat and in no mood to sit in the chilly parlour with the aunts. When she had finished she decided to go to bed with her book.

Unfortunately, she had left it in the parlour so she had no choice but to go and fetch it.

'You're very late tonight, dear,' Kate said, looking up from yesterday's newspaper, which Rivers had bought and paid for.

'Yes, I was a bit late home.' Poppy yawned. 'And I've had a very busy day.'

'You've had your supper in the kitchen again, haven't you!' Kate reared up like an angry giraffe. 'You know perfectly well I won't have you eating with the servants, Poppy.' She gave an imperious shake of her head. 'I've told you before, many times, in this house we have Standards to uphold.' She always said the word as if it was spelt with a capital letter. She put her hand to her brow in what would have been a melodramatic gesture if she hadn't been so patently sincere. 'Dear Papa would turn in his grave, God rest His Soul, if he knew.'

The number of things that Kate considered would make the old man turn in his grave must mean he was going round like a spinning top, Poppy thought privately and irreverently, but she merely said, because she was weary of the argument, 'But it was so much less trouble, Aunt Kate. Mrs Rivers had it all ready for me on a plate over a saucepan and all she had to do was to pop it onto the table instead of carrying it through here. It saved her poor old feet.' And it's warmer in the kitchen, she added under her breath.

'I don't wish to discuss Mrs Rivers's nether regions, thank you, Poppy,' Kate said icily. 'But I shall be glad if in future you respect my wishes and take your evening meal in here, as you usually do, with my sister and me.' It was a measure of her anger that she referred to Meg as 'my sister'. She adjusted her pince-nez with an impatient gesture. 'I cannot bear to think what dear Papa would have said under the circumstances. A member of the family eating with the servants! It's quite insupportable.' She swung round and glared at Meg. 'I'm sure you agree, Margaret.'

Meg nodded meekly, afraid to do otherwise.

Poppy picked up her book. 'I think I'll go to bed and read,' she said.

This was not right, either. Kate couldn't see why she wanted to go to bed with her book, wasting candles, when she could share the oil lamp in the parlour.

'But I'm cold, Aunt Kate,' Poppy said desperately. 'I've had a very busy day at work . . .'

Before she could say more Kate held up her hand. 'Work! It's time you stopped that ridiculous charade and began to behave like a lady. I'm quite sure Dear Papa would never have countenanced a granddaughter of his earning her own living if he'd been alive. It simply isn't done, in our circle.'

Suddenly, Meg burst into tears. 'Oh, Kate, do stop. If you keep finding fault with everything Poppy does she'll leave us and then we'll have nobody, nobody at all.' She turned to Poppy, her face crumpled with crying. 'Don't take any notice of Kate, Poppy, she doesn't meant it, really she doesn't. It you want to take a candle and read in bed she won't mind, will you Kate?' She got to her feet and went to the shelf by the door where the candlesticks stood, ready to light them up to bed. 'Here you are, Poppy. Have mine. I don't mind going to bed in the dark, really I don't.' She thrust it into Poppy's hand, clumsy in her agitation.

Poppy put her arm round Meg. 'It's all right, Aunt Meg. Don't get upset. I won't leave you. I promise I won't leave you.'

Meg leaned against her, sobs still shaking her little plump body. 'I love you so much, Poppy. I think I'd die if you left us.' She sniffed and shot her sister a glance. 'Things are so much better now you're here.'

'Come and sit down, Meg, and don't be so silly,' Kate said

sharply. 'Of course Poppy won't leave us. She wouldn't be so stupid, not when she knows all this will be hers after we're gone.' She lifted her hands to indicate Dale House. 'In any case, where would she go?'

Poppy stood just inside the door saying nothing for several minutes. Then she said, her voice very low, 'It isn't the fact that I shall inherit Dale House that keeps me here, Aunt Kate, because I really don't care about that one way or the other. Neither do I stay because of the comfort of the place. In truth, I have never lived in such a cold, un-comfortable barn of a house.' She came and sat down, crossing her arms and leaning on the table, looking from one stern old face to the other, tear-stained rosy-cheeked one. 'No, I continue to stay because you're my father's sisters and I feel I have a duty to do what I can to look after you in deference to his memory, if nothing else.' She paused, then her face broke into a smile. 'But most of all, I stay here because I've grown to love you both, you funny, quaint, old-fashioned pair. And because I don't know what you'd do without me.'

A funny little sound came from Meg. She was crying again, but this time it was with tears of happiness. Even Kate's usually implacable expression had softened.

Poppy got to her feet again. 'Now I'm going to bed.' She held up her hand. 'No, Aunt Meg, I won't take your candle, thank you all the same. I just want to go to sleep. I really am very tired.' She went over and kissed them both and gave Meg an extra hug. 'Good night.'

As she went wearily up the stairs Poppy sighed. There was, of course, another reason why she didn't want to leave Dale House. It hadn't yet given up its secrets, secrets that she was quite sure she would one day uncover. If she was patient.

Chapter Twenty-Three

Predictably, Poppy slept badly. First there was the business of George Templeton to be dealt with, which would be tricky because he was certain to have some plausible tale and if that didn't work he was almost certain to try to put the blame on her, as the secretary. She felt reasonably certain that Josh would see through any of his ruses but supposing there was something she had overlooked? Something she had done wrong? After all, nobody was infallible. Then common sense prevailed as she realised that this was simply not the kind of mistake she could have made.

Having resolved that worry to her satisfaction, another niggling problem surfaced. Josh's strange mood. She frowned up into the darkness. Why had he acted so oddly when she had reminded him that even with the scarring round his eye the most important thing was that he was alive? Heaven's sake, it *was* the most important thing. The fact that his face was slightly battered was of little importance as far as she was concerned. Yet he seemed to have the idea that she was accusing him of living, as if she thought he should have died instead of his brother.

She went suddenly hot as she realised that there could only be one explanation for that. As she feared, Alec *had* confided in Josh before he died. He *had* told Josh about the letter he intended to write to her. Perhaps even shown it to him. That being the case, he had probably persuaded Josh – as he had mistakenly persuaded himself – that the feeling was mutual. So that was why Josh seemed to think she was blaming him for living whilst Alec had died.

She turned over and thumped her pillow. How in the world could she convey to him that nothing could be further from the truth? That she wasn't, and never had been, in love with Alec. But supposing she was mistaken and Alec had never confided in Josh at all? Then she would look a first-class idiot, even mentioning it. Oh, it was all a horrible mess. And anyway, why should she care what Josh Kenton thought? But she knew only too well the answer to that. She cared a very great deal.

It was the small hours before she slept.

The result of her restless night was that she overslept and was late for work the next day.

Fortunately, it was a bright, frosty morning, which helped to refresh her jaded senses as she pedalled along. When she arrived she propped her bike against the wall and hurried up the steps to the office, unpinning her hat as she went. With any luck she would be at her desk long enough before Josh arrived.

She needn't have worried. He didn't arrive until after twelve o'clock. Then he strode through her office to his own, saying over his shoulder, 'Would you come through, please, Miss Barlow. There's something I want to discuss with you. Urgently.'

She got up from her desk and hurried into his office, smoothing her hair as she went. What on earth could he want?

She soon found out.

He was already pacing up and down, throwing first his hat, then his overcoat, then his scarf onto the desk as he went. He turned as she entered. 'Ah, thank the Lord.' He threw himself down in his chair and put his head in his hands. 'Oh, God, the most terrible thing has happened.'

She stared at him. 'Not Sir Frederick?' she asked, shocked.

'No, no, not the guv'nor. He's all right.' He looked up at her and went on, 'I was in early this morning. I thought I'd take another look at those figures, just to make sure, before I started accusing Templeton. But I'd hardly set foot inside the yard when Mrs Templeton came out and called me over to her house.' He gave a deep sigh. 'She'd obviously been watching for me.'

'Mrs Templeton?' Poppy repeated stupidly.

'Yes. George Templeton's wife,' he said impatiently. 'She called me in to look at George.' He shook his head. 'God, he was a mess. It seems he was beaten up last night and left for dead on his own doorstep. She heard him whimpering in the middle of the night and somehow got him inside.'

Poppy put her hand to her mouth. 'Beaten up! But who on earth . . .? Will he . . .?'

He got up and began pacing up and down the room again. 'Oh, yes. He'll live,' he said, anticipating her words. 'But finding him like that must have been a dreadful shock for his wife. By the time I saw him she'd pulled herself together and cleaned him up as best she could but he still looked a mess. He's probably got a couple of broken ribs and he's pretty badly bruised all over. His face is a fearful sight, too, horribly cut and swollen, and he's lost a few teeth, but he'll survive.'

'But who could have done such a thing?'

'That's just it. She doesn't know and if he knows he's not saying. Not that he can talk much, since he's lost half his teeth and his mouth is twice its proper size. Of course, nobody's owned up to anything. All the men are at work as if nothing had happened. Maybe they don't even know that it has.' He shook his head. 'No, that can't be right. At least one of them must know something. It must be one of the workforce, nobody would come into the yard from outside to do it.'

'They might if they followed him home from the pub. If he'd got drunk and belligerent ... You know what he can be like.'

Josh thought for a minute. 'Mm. I suppose it's possible. But I don't think it's very likely. No, the best thing is to start from here. I feel sure it must have been one of our men because of the fact that he was left on his own doorstep. But how in hell am I going to find out? They'll all stick together, won't they?' He sat down again and waved his hand. 'Oh, sit down, for goodness sake.'

She sat down. 'Most of the men here have good reason to dislike the man,' she said thoughtfully. 'But I wouldn't have said any of them are violent – except when they've had a bit to drink – although that can be quite often, according to their wives.'

His face cleared. 'Ah, that's it. I knew there was something ... That's the difference, you see. This was a systematic beating. Not some drunken brawl.' He put his head in his hands again. 'God, this is the last thing I wanted. I've hardly been here long enough to get my feet under the table, let alone to know everything that's going on. How in the world am I going to deal with it?'

'Just a minute. Let me think.' She pressed her fingers to her temples. Then she looked up. 'Have you spoken to any of the men?'

'No, not yet. I wanted to talk to you first.'

She felt unaccountably flattered. 'Well, I think you should go and tell them what's happened and watch for their reactions. They may tell you exactly what happened – if they know. On the other hand ... Anyway, go and hear what they've all got to say. You'll probably be able to gather as much from what they don't say as what they do.'

'And what will you do?'

'Me?' She smiled. 'I'll have the kettle boiled ready to make you a cup of tea when you get back.'

He made a face. 'Do you think I'll need it?'

'I'll have it ready, anyway. Just in case.'

He was gone a long time. When he came back he was shaking his head.

'Apparently, nobody knew anything. Nobody had seen anything,' he said as he took the tea she offered. 'It was like coming up against a brick wall.' He sipped his tea. 'But what was most significant was that nobody was in the least surprised,' he added thoughtfully.

'So you think they were all in it together,' she said, picking up her own cup.

He shook his head. 'I didn't say that.'

'Several of them would have good reason to feel he'd got his just deserts.' She put her cup down again and began ticking off on her fingers. 'Jack Earnshaw is very fond of Connie Templeton. As you know, he was married to Connie's sister. He knows how badly George treats Connie and I'm sure he'd like to give him a taste of his own medicine. Then again, George keeps making rude suggestions to Mary Smithers. She can't do anything about it herself, but Ted Ferris is her next-door neighbour and he might, if only for the sake of her husband, who's away in the army. Well, Harry's about to be invalided out, I believe. Another one is Jake Benson. George Templeton is always making sarcastic remarks to and about him. He's always down on Jake and trying to make out his work isn't up to standard, things like that, because he knows Jake is far superior to him in intelligence. He's tried to get him sacked a couple of times, according to his wife, but Sir Frederick saw what was happening and made sure Jake was kept on.' She hesitated. 'But I wouldn't have said Jake was a violent man.' She began ticking her fingers again. 'Mord Jones is another one. He could well feel he has reason because Templeton once made lewd suggestions to Charity, which upset them both, but I don't think he would, somehow. Mord is a very peaceable man, his religion wouldn't allow violence. Then there's Sam Beckwith. He's too old, although he's wiry. But his daughter is well able to take care of herself, I would have thought, without any help from Sam.'

Josh shook his head. 'The damage that was done to George Templeton couldn't have been inflicted by a woman. I'd stake my life on that.'

'That only leaves Charlie Braithwaite,' Poppy said with a sigh.

'I'd hardly think Templeton would be daft enough to make advances to Charlie's wife,' he said with a grim smile. 'Have you seen his biceps?'

She smiled back. 'Well, he's a blacksmith, what do you expect? But he's a very gentle man, all the same. He's wonderful with injured birds and animals.'

Josh put his cup and saucer down. 'Well, we don't seem to have got very far with finding the culprit, do we?' he said with a sigh. 'But you've given me a very comprehensive rundown of my workers and their families and I'm grateful for that. I wouldn't have discovered that much in a month of Sundays. However, it doesn't seem to have solved our problem, does it? It looks to me as if it must have been a pub brawl.'

'Maybe you're right. Maybe that's just what it was.' She looked at her watch and got to her feet. 'It's time for my lunch now, if you don't mind, Mr Kenton. I usually go over and have it with Maud Benson and the other wives.' She picked up her bag and went to the door. 'I'll keep a careful ear out today. You never know, I might be able to discover something useful.'

'Like what?'

'I've no idea. At any rate, I'll be back in an hour.'

He stood up, looking worried. 'I'll go and have another look at George Templeton. See if he's recovered enough to talk about what happened.'

Maud had just taken a batch of bread out of the oven when Poppy arrived, and the kitchen was warm and the smell of the bread tantalising. It gave a feeling of normality to what had been a most abnormal morning as far as Poppy was concerned. She sat down at her usual place at the table and took out her sandwiches. The other wives drifted in one by one. Some of them couldn't manage to come every day and today Florrie Braithwaite was missing. Maud made a great play of giving the children crusts of new bread to chew on and then she made tea for Poppy and the others.

Poppy ate her sandwiches, saying little but listening carefully to the conversation going on round the table. It was the usual everyday gossip, yet she sensed a kind of wariness about all the women, almost as if each one was afraid of what the others might say.

'Where's Florrie today?' she asked briskly when there was a lull. It wasn't often Florrie missed, she loved a good gossip.

There was a definite silence, as if each was waiting for the others to speak. Then Daisy said quickly, 'She's at home. Is there another cup in the pot, Maud?' She pushed her cup over.

'Milly's poorly,' Maud added as she took it, 'so Florrie's stayed back to look after her.'

'Oh, I'm sorry to hear that. Nothing serious, I hope.'

'No. Nowt to worry over,' Maud said, busying herself with the teapot.

The conversation picked up again and it struck Poppy that perhaps she had imagined the previously strained atmosphere, and the women sitting round the table had no idea at all what had happened just across the yard. Josh had said that Mrs Templeton had dragged George inside in the middle of the night, so it was quite possible that they hadn't heard the news.

She waited a few more minutes until the children, full of new bread and jam, had been sent out to play, then dropped her bombshell, watching carefully for any reaction. 'Had you heard that George Templeton was beaten up last night?' she asked, keeping her voice level.

There was silence for a minute, then they all looked at each other. Maud licked her lips and remarked in a high voice, totally unlike her own, 'George Templeton? Beaten up? Oh, my goodness.'

'Fancy that,' Lily said, finding her voice.

'Well, I never,' Mary added.

'He had it coming to him,' Daisy said grimly, the only one of the group sounding normal.

Charity sat nursing her baby and said nothing.

'So you hadn't heard?' Poppy asked, raising her eyebrows.

They all chorused no, they hadn't heard a thing, and shook their heads vehemently. A little too vehemently, Poppy considered. She was pretty sure now that they knew about it. She noticed Charity had kept her head bowed and remained silent.

She finished the tea Maud had provided and put her cup down gently on its saucer. 'I suppose it could have been a pub brawl,' she said thoughtfully, trying to draw them out.

'Aye, that's what it must have been,' they all agreed, much too quickly.

She shook her head. 'I'm not so sure, though. And neither is Mr Kenton.'

Nobody spoke so she got up to go. If they weren't going to tell her anything she couldn't force it out of them.

She tried another approach. 'Of course, Mr Kenton is bound to find out the truth. Eventually,' she said thoughtfully. 'But this happening just at the moment makes things very hard for the poor man. He's only just taken over his father's business, as you all know. He didn't really want to but he knew that if he didn't the place would close, but you know that, too. The trouble is, he's got a lot to learn in a very short time and a lot of responsibility to shoulder. Added to that, he hasn't fully recovered from his war wounds.' She sighed. 'It really doesn't seem right that he should have this worry on top of everything else, so if you do hear anything I'm sure you'll let him know. Or me if you prefer and I'll pass it on. I know you're shy about talking to him.' She smiled at the faces round the table: they all looked so guilt-ridden that she was certain she had hit home. She decided on one more shot. 'Nobody likes

George Templeton, we all know that. In fact, I'm sure a good many people won't be sorry he's been given a beating.'

Lily bit her lip. 'Is he . . . will he live?' she asked.

Poppy nodded. 'Oh, yes, he'll live, there's no doubt about that. But he was pretty badly beaten up, from what Mr Kenton told me.' She looked at her watch. 'Goodness, I must go. I was due back in the office ten minutes ago.' She picked up her bag.

Charity cleared her throat and the others looked warningly at her so she made a great play of adjusting the baby's shawl.

Disappointed, because she was sure now that the women knew something, Poppy went to the door. She paused. 'Well, goodbye, thank you for the tea.'

She heard Charity murmur something but she couldn't make out what it was.

Then Maud called, 'Wait a minute, Miss Barlow.' She turned to the others. 'I think we should tell. Like Charity says, it's only right. For Mr Josh's sake.'

'But he might end up in prison . . .' Lily whispered.

'He didn't kill him.' Maud turned to Poppy. 'You did say he wasn't dead, didn't you? You did say he'd live?'

'Oh, yes, he'll live.' Poppy nodded, then, relieved, she sat down again and waited.

'Very well,' Lily began. She nodded at Daisy. 'You tell her, Dais. You live next door. You saw the lass.'

Daisy Frampton folded her fat arms and nodded her peroxide head. 'Ah, aye. We know who did it, all right. And I wonder he didn't kill the bugger. It were Charlie. Charlie Braithwaite.' Daisy was not one to mince words.

'But you couldn't blame him. Not after what he'd done,' Maud said quickly.

'Why not? What had he done? You must tell me,' Poppy said, leaning her elbows on the table and looking from one to the other urgently.

They were all silent for several moments, no-one willing

251

to speak. Then Mary said quietly, 'Charlie Braithwaite beat George Templeton up because he'd raped his thirteen-year-old daughter.'

Poppy drew her breath in sharply and her eyes widened. 'Oh, my dear Lord. Milly? That poor child.'

'Aye, Milly's a pretty lass and we all knew he'd got his eye on her,' Maud said. 'He used to give her sweets and suchlike, although time and time again Florrie warned her not to tek 'em. But she's only a lass, she's innocent. She didn't understand what he was after.'

'He took her behind the stables last night,' Lily said. 'Said he wanted to show her the new foal. But it wasn't any foal he wanted to show her,' she added grimly.

'Frightened the living daylights out of her, he did,' Mary said. 'She tried to get away but he's a strong man.' She shrugged. 'You can imagine the rest.'

'Oh, indeed I can,' Poppy said, remembering her own experiences with the man.

'So that's why Florrie's not here today,' Daisy said. 'She's kept Milly in bed.' She pursed her lips. 'Living next door, I saw the poor mite when he'd finished with her and she ran home. Her dress was all torn and bloody and she was terrified. It took her ma and me hours to calm her enough even to say what had happened. The man's a bloody animal.'

'So Charlie went for him,' Mary said.

'Aye, he did,' Daisy nodded. 'I wonder he didn't kill the filthy swine, too, the rage he was in.'

'I reckon he would have done if the other men hadn't seen what was going on and dragged him off,' Lily said. 'And not to blame him neither.'

'No, you couldn't blame him. Any man would have done the same if his daughter had been attacked like that,' the others agreed.

There was silence round the table for several minutes as they all waited for Poppy's reaction to their story. But Poppy was still trying to take in what they had told her. She had never expected anything like this and she was horrified.

At last Maud broke the silence. 'So now you know, Miss Barlow,' she said, worried because Poppy had said nothing. 'We all agreed we'd not say owt, for Charlie's sake. But after what you said about Mr Kenton, well, it didn't seem right not to.'

'But what'll happen to Charlie?' Lily said anxiously. 'He's a decent man, we all know that. He wouldn't hurt a fly, big man though he is. Will he lose his job?'

'I really can't say what will happen. It's for Mr Kenton to decide,' Poppy said, still shocked. 'But when I tell him the whole story, which of course I must, I'd be very surprised if Charlie was sacked. Mr Kenton is a very fair and understanding man, you know.'

They all nodded. 'Aye, he's a lovely man. Just like his pa.'

She sighed. 'Well, anyway, thank you for telling me. It's not a pretty story but I'll report it to Mr Kenton exactly as you've told me.'

The women watched as Poppy walked back to her office. 'I just hope to God we've done the right thing,' Mary breathed.

'Aye, my man'll kill me if owt goes wrong,' Lily said, looking anxious.

'We've just got to trust that Mr Kenton's a fair man,' Maud said.

'Aye,' the others nodded. 'That's all we can do.'

But they were all worried at having broken their husbands' vow of secrecy.

Chapter Twenty-Four

Poppy went back to her office and sat staring out of the window for a long time. What she had just heard was shocking beyond belief. Even knowing what she did about George Templeton's violent and lecherous ways, to defile a young lass like Milly was something she could hardly believe, even of him. Her thoughts turned to the girl. She was only thirteen. Too young to be anything but pleased and flattered when an older – and it had to be said, handsome – man paid her attention and offered her sweets. Her mother said she had told her not to accept sweets from him, tried to warn her ... but as Florrie had said, how do you warn an innocent girl about such things without frightening her half to death? In any case, who could have dreamt the man would go to such lengths? She was still sitting, looking blindly out of the window, when Josh Kenton walked in.

He frowned. 'What's wrong, Miss Barlow? You look as if you've seen a ghost.' He walked over to her. 'Heavens, you're as white as a sheet. Can I get you anything? A whisky?'

She shook her head. 'No thank you, Mr Kenton. I'll be all right. But I've had a bit of a shock.' She looked up at him. 'I've found out who beat George Templeton up.'

His frown deepened. 'You'd better come through to my office,' he said.

He stared down at his hands as Poppy sat opposite him and recounted what she had learned from the wives. She hesitated when it came to the attack on Milly, unwilling to say to her employer the word Mary Smithers had used.

'... he attacked ... he forced himself ...' she floundered.

His head shot up. 'Are you trying to tell me he raped the child?' he demanded, his voice harsh.

She nodded miserably.

'Then why in hell didn't you say so!' He passed his hand over his face. 'I'm sorry, Miss Barlow, I shouldn't have spoken to you like that. But my God! The man must be a maniac. I don't wonder the child's father half-killed him. I'd have done the same thing myself in his boots.' He got up and began to pace round the office.

'It was difficult to get them to talk. Nobody wanted to tell me anything because they were all afraid for Charlie,' she said, suddenly tired. 'Afraid he might lose his job.'

He swung round. 'What did you tell them?'

She spread her hands. 'What could I tell them? I said it would be up to you, but that you were a very fair and understanding man.'

He nodded. 'Thank you for that, Miss Barlow,' he said quietly.

She looked up at his words and found his eyes resting on her. 'Well, it's true,' she said, colouring slightly.

He gave her a ghost of a smile and resumed his pacing. 'I think the first thing I'd better do is to go and tell Charlie Braithwaite that his job is safe, don't you? He's probably worried sick.'

'Yes.' She hesitated. 'And what about George Templeton?'

'Oh, he'll have to go. He can't stay on here, not after what he's done. I'll give him forty-eight hours to get out. He should be sufficiently recovered by that time.' He shrugged. 'And if he isn't, then that's just too bad because I want him off my property.' He gave a wry smile. 'Then, of course, I'll have to find a new manager. As one problem is solved another one emerges. Life's never dull, is it, Miss Barlow?'

'You could think about Jake Benson,' she said slowly. 'He's a clever man and what he doesn't know about the workings of this place isn't worth knowing.'

He raised his eyebrows. 'Jake Benson? Hm. I hadn't thought of him, but you're right, he could be just the man.' He ran his fingers through his thick hair. 'You know, I can't thank you enough for your help, Miss Barlow. Goodness knows how long it would have taken me to sort this mess out without you.' He looked at her and the warmth in his eyes made her heart beat faster. 'I really don't know what I should do without you. You are the most . . .' he hesitated, then said quickly, 'thank you very much.' He turned away and began shuffling papers.

She got up from her chair, suddenly feeling strangely flat and disappointed. 'Will there be anything else, Mr Kenton?'

'No, no, thank you. That will be all, Miss Barlow,' he said without looking up.

When she had gone he threw the papers down, furious with himself. He had just very nearly told her that she was the most wonderful girl he had ever met. But that would never do. Because she was still grieving for Alec, his dashing, heroic brother, and would never look twice at an ugly battle-scarred wreck like him. He knew this, he had told himself so countless times since the day she had visited him in the military hospital. A day he had relived over and over during sleepless, pain-filled nights, dreaming of the happy ending that the cold light of day told him could never be. But that didn't stop him wanting to take her in his arms and kiss her until she was breathless. He cursed himself for a fool.

On the other side of the partition Poppy sat at her desk trying to work through a blur of tears as she remembered Josh Kenton's words. 'I really don't know what I should do without you. You are the most . . .' He hadn't said it, but she knew what had been in his mind, that she was the most efficient secretary he had ever known. It was a compliment. She should feel flattered. The trouble was, that was not at all how she wanted him to think of her.

The next morning Poppy made sure that she was at work well on time. Even so, Josh was there before her. He came out of his office just as she was taking off her coat and hat. He looked as if he hadn't slept much.

'Don't take your coat off, Miss Barlow,' he said. 'As if you haven't done enough for me already I've another favour to ask of you, if you wouldn't mind.'

'Of course, Mr Kenton.' She took her coat off its peg again and began to shrug it on.

'You've no idea what I'm going to ask you to do, yet,' he said with a laugh, coming up behind to help her.

'A good secretary doesn't ask questions, she simply carries out her orders,' she replied lightly, conscious of his hands on her shoulders.

He dropped them to his side. 'This isn't an order, it's a request. I'd like you to come over to George Templeton's house with me,' he explained. 'Over dinner last night I told my father what happened yesterday. He agreed with everything I—we had decided. But he suggested that it would be a good idea if I had a witness when I confronted Templeton and also someone to give comfort to Mrs Templeton. We both immediately thought of you. Do you mind, Miss Barlow?'

She went to the little mirror on the filing cabinet to pin on her hat. 'No, of course I don't mind, Mr Kenton, if you think I can be of some use.' Suddenly, she caught sight of his reflection in the mirror as he stood behind her, a little to the right. There was a such a look of longing in his eyes, such an unmistakeable look of love that the colour flooded into her face and she felt her heart thump madly in her breast.

But when she turned from the mirror the look was gone, replaced by a brisk businesslike expression, and she wondered if her imagination could have played a trick on her.

Yet she was sure this wasn't the case.

They walked together over to the Templetons' house and Josh knocked at the door. Mrs Templeton answered it and asked them in.

The house was pristine, from the highly polished linoleum to the shining leaves on the aspidistra in the window.

'If you've come to see George, he's not here,' she said, when they were both seated on the overstuffed horsehair sofa opposite her in the obviously little-used front parlour. 'He's gone.'

'Gone, Mrs Templeton? But where?' Josh asked, amazed.

She shrugged. 'I don't know and I don't care,' she answered flatly.

'But surely he can't have gone far. He could hardly move yesterday,' Josh persisted.

Connie shrugged again. 'That's as maybe. He looked a bit the worse for wear, I'll admit, but he could walk.' She lifted her head. 'He tried to make me go with him but I wouldn't. I told him I'd had enough of his disgusting ways. It was bad enough when he knocked me about, God knows, but to attack that poor little lass was the last straw. He ought to be locked up, if you ask me. Strung up, even, only hanging's too good for him.' Her voice was vicious. 'Any road, I said I'd have no more of it.' She gave a satisfied nod. 'So he packed his bag and went. And good riddance to him, I say.' She was quiet for a minute, then she said, 'I used to be very fond of him when we were first wed. We were very happy together. But we both wanted children and when they didn't appear he started to blame me, called me a barren cow. And worse. Always trying to put me down, he was, making out I wasn't any good at anything.' She

258

shrugged. 'It's like water dripping on a stone, being treated like that, it wears the love away. But when I didn't let him see how much his words hurt me he started hitting me so he could see it for himself.' She hugged herself. 'Well, he won't hit me any more, thank God.'

'But what will you do, Mrs Templeton?' Poppy asked, amazed in the change in the previously meek little woman. 'Where will you go?'

'Yes, I'm afraid you won't be able to stay in this house. But you do realise that, don't you?' Josh said, frowning anxiously.

A smile spread across her face, softening her features and making her almost pretty. 'Oh, you've no need to worry over me, Mr Kenton,' she said. 'I shall go across the yard and keep house for my brother-in-law. Jack's wanted me to go over there and live for long enough,' she nodded in the direction of the cottages, 'but I couldn't. Not while *he* was here. But now he's gone, thank God, so I can go with a clear conscience.' Her voice softened. 'Oh, you've no need to worry over me, Mr Kenton. My Jack will look after me. He's a lovely man.'

'I didn't expect to resolve that problem so easily,' Josh said on the way back to the office as he followed Poppy up the steps.

'Yes, but is it solved?' Poppy asked anxiously as she once again hung up her coat. 'Won't there be talk?'

He leaned against her desk. 'You know the women better than I do, Miss Barlow. What do you think?'

She thought for a minute, then she smiled and nodded. 'I think they'll all be glad she's out of that dreadful man's clutches. They've always felt sorry for her. And anyway, she's doing nothing wrong in moving in to keep house for her brother-in-law. A lot of men have housekeepers, don't they?'

His eyes twinkled. 'Indeed they do. And if it develops into something closer, well,' he shrugged, 'what goes on behind closed doors is nobody's business.'

'That's very liberal-minded of you, Mr Kenton,' she said, a little surprised.

He shook his head sadly. 'Miss Barlow, I saw enough heartache and bereavement to last me a lifetime when I was in the Flying Corps. Time wasted, lives ruined. I came to realise that life's too short to be too dogmatic over convention.' He walked over and looked out of the window. 'Take your own situation as a case in point,' he said quietly.

She frowned. 'What do you mean?'

He shrugged. 'Why, you and my brother Alec.' He turned and glanced at her briefly. 'It's all right, Miss Barlow, my brother confided in me. He even showed me . . .' He changed his mind and turned away from her again. 'If I may say so, I greatly admire the way you have behaved since his death,' he went on stiffly. 'Concealing your own feelings so that nothing could spoil Claire's memories of him, nor her part as the bereaved bride.'

She licked her lips. For some reason she felt as if someone had punched her in the stomach, making her feel slightly sick. 'Were you going to say that he even showed you the letter he had written to me?' she managed to say.

He swung round. 'I assure you I didn't want Alec to show it to me. I had no wish to read it but he insisted,' he said defensively. His mouth twisted. 'I think he was looking for my approval.'

'And did he get it?' she couldn't help asking.

'It was a very private matter between the two of you. It was not for me to approve or disapprove,' he replied, trying to sound off-hand.

She sat down at her desk and rested her head on her hand. 'You can have no idea, Mr Kenton, the anguish that letter caused me,' she said miserably. 'How do you reply to a letter like that? How do you write and tell a man who is risking death every day, who has poured his heart out to you, who was willing to face the scandal of jilting the woman he was to marry for your sake, that you don't return his affections? That you are not and never could be in love

260

with him?' She dashed away the tears that were running down her cheeks. 'Let me tell you it isn't easy.' She paused and blew her nose. After a few minutes she went on, 'I can only be thankful that he never received my reply, otherwise I should have had it on my conscience for the rest of my life that I had somehow contributed to his death. As it was I posted the letter the day after he was killed. It came back to me several weeks later.'

There was silence in the room for a little while after she had finished speaking. Then Josh said, his voice puzzled, 'But Alec was convinced you were as in love with him as he was with you.'

She shook her head. 'I can't think where he got the idea from. I never willingly gave him that impression.'

'But you wrote to him.' His voice was accusing.

'Yes. But only three or four times. And then only because he begged me to. I was going to say kept pestering me, but that would be unkind. I must confess I found the letters very difficult to write and I always made sure to sign myself as Miss Barlow, although he addressed me as Poppy and signed himself Alec. I didn't like it, Mr Kenton, I can tell you that, especially when the tone of his letters became more and more affectionate. But I didn't know how to stop without hurting his feelings. After all, he was risking his life every day at the front.'

'Poppy. An unusual name but it really suits you,' he said inconsequentially. Then he pulled his attention back to the subject in hand. 'You never wrote to me,' he said with a trace of bitterness.

She looked up, surprised. 'You never asked me to.'

'Would you have written if I'd asked?'

She smiled and nodded. 'Oh, yes. I'd have written to you.'

'And if I had signed myself as Josh how would you have replied?' He was watching her intently.

She looked down at the slightly soggy handkerchief she was holding. 'I'm not sure.'

'What do you mean?' His voice was rough.

She hesitated, then, 'I think I might have risked "love from Poppy",' she said softly.

It was the wrong thing to have said. He was silent for such a long time that she realised she had made a terrible mistake. Her face flamed and she said briskly, 'Well, if you'll excuse me I've an awful lot of work to get through today and I think I've wasted enough of your time. And mine.' She whisked the cover off her typewriter and scrabbled in the drawer for paper, carefully not looking at him.

'But would you have meant it?'

She looked up. 'I'm sorry? Would I have meant what?' she asked in her most professional voice.

He came round the desk and pulled her to her feet. 'Would you have meant, love from Poppy?' he asked, his hands sliding up her arms to her shoulders and staying there.

She risked a glance up at his face and saw doubt and hope mingled with that same look of love she had caught in the reflection of the mirror. She smiled and put her hand up to touch his face. 'Oh, yes, Josh, I would,' she said.

He caught her hand and pressed a kiss in its palm and closed her fingers over it. 'I've loved you for so long, Poppy, but I never thought I stood a chance against Alec,' he whispered.

She shook her head, still smiling. 'You were quite wrong, Josh. Alec never stood a chance against you,' she replied.

'I'm not exactly the catch of the season, am I? With a wonky eye and a funny arm?' He was looking down at her intently.

She frowned a little, then she smiled. 'I loved you before you were shot down, Josh. I loved you as you were then and I love you as you are now. It makes no difference to the way I feel about you.' She paused. 'Yes, it does. Because you've been so courageous in ignoring your own problems in order to pull this place round. I feel very proud of you,

262

as well as loving you the way I do.'

'Thank you for that, Poppy.' He put his finger under her chin and tipped her face up to his. He looked at her for a long moment then bent his head. 'You have no idea how often I've dreamed of doing this,' he murmured as his mouth came down on hers.

She closed her eyes and wound her arms round him, her fingers tangling with the springy curls at his neck as she felt herself melting inside at his touch, wishing the moment could go on for ever.

After a long time he lifted his head and smiled down into her eyes. 'But in my dreams it's always been somewhere a bit more romantic than this shabby little office,' he said unsteadily, 'and it's been by the light of a full moon, not in the middle of the morning. But all that will come later, I promise, my darling.' He kissed her again, then took both her hands in his. 'Come into my office. We must talk. My father will be delighted, I know. He'll want our engagement announced immediately. And what about your family? Will they be pleased? Do you realise I know hardly anything about you, Poppy, except that you're the most wonderful girl in the world and I love you to distraction? I don't even know where you live.' As he spoke he was dragging her into his office and sitting her down, as excited as a small boy.

Then he pulled her to her feet again. 'Oh, to hell with everything. Let's go home and tell the guv'nor. It'll buck him up no end. Then we'll go and see your people. Come along, darling, put your bib and tucker on and let's be off.' He smiled at her and kissed the tip of her nose. 'What's the matter, my dearest love? Aren't you happy?' He became suddenly serious. 'You do love me, don't you, Poppy? I haven't just imagined it all?'

She put her hand up and touched his face again, and managed to smile. 'No, Josh, darling, you haven't imagined it. I love you with all my heart.' But what she didn't – couldn't – tell him about was the chill that ran through her at the mention of her family. For how could she ever take Josh to Dale House where her two eccentric, not to say slightly mad, aunts lived? And worse, how could she tell them she hoped to marry the son of the man who had ruined Aunt Kate's life?

Chapter Twenty-Five

Poppy's head was in a whirl. She was as excited as Josh but she had to find some way of slowing him down to give herself time to think what to do about her aunts. It wouldn't be easy.

'We can't just rush off to your father in the middle of the morning, Josh, there are things to be done here,' she said, trying to sound businesslike.

'What things? There's nothing that can't wait, surely?' He was already shrugging into his overcoat.

She began to tick off her fingers. 'Well, you need to tell the men that George Templeton has gone. That's the first thing. And you need to talk to Jake – if you're going to promote him to manager, that is. And if you're not going to promote him you've got to decide what you are going to do.'

He gave a huge sigh and hung his coat up again. Then he came over and took her in his arms. 'Will you always keep my feet so firmly on the ground, Poppy?' he said with a groan as he began to kiss her again.

When he finally raised his head she leaned back in his arms and looked up at him, smiling. 'I shall try. But I must say you make it very difficult.'

'Good.' He bent his head to kiss her again but she put her finger to his lips.

'Seriously, Josh,' she said. 'I don't think we should say

anything about – us, not just yet.'

He sighed. 'Yes, darling, you're probably right. O.K. It'll be our secret for a few hours, at least.' Obediently, he went and sat down at his desk.

She burst out laughing. 'Not if you persist in calling me darling, it won't,' she said. She sat down opposite to him and put her elbows on the desk. 'Look, we must get back to reality. Someone ought to go and see the Braithwaite family,' she said briskly. 'You've already spoken to Charlie, haven't you?'

He nodded.

'Well, would you like me to go and see Florrie and Milly? That's hardly a job you'd relish.'

'Oh, I would. Please dar— Miss Barlow.' He inclined his head as he said the words and then began to laugh. 'This is ridiculous.'

'No it isn't, Mr Kenton,' she said with a wicked grin. 'If you don't behave I shall have to look for a new secretary for you.'

'I'll behave,' he said, immediately becoming serious. Then his face broke into a smile. 'But it's very difficult with you sitting there looking at me like that.'

'I'm sorry . . .'

'Don't be. I like it.' He stroked his chin. 'Perhaps I should have a word with Jake this afternoon.'

She flicked through the diary on the desk. 'You've an appointment with your bank manager this afternoon at two. After that you're free.'

'Righto, I'll see Jake after that.' Suddenly, he threw his hands in the air. 'Oh, how do you expect me to think about such mundane things?' He leaned forward. 'Let me take you out to lunch.'

'No, Josh,' she said firmly. 'I shall take my sandwiches over to Maud's house as I always do. And you can go home, as you always do.'

He shook his head. 'You're a hard woman, Poppy Barlow.'

She gave a theatrical sigh. 'I knew you'd change your mind about me when you got to know me better.'

He came round and pulled her to her feet. 'Then you were wrong. I shall love you for ever.' He began to smother her with kisses.

'We really should get some work done, Josh,' she murmured when he lifted his head long enough to allow her to speak. 'It's a good thing these windows are too high for anyone to see in or the whole works would know.'

He held her at arm's length. 'I'd like the whole world to know. I'd like to shout it from the roof tops,' he said, gathering her to him again. 'I'm just so happy ...'

She put her finger on her own lips and then to his. 'And so am I, Josh. But let's keep it to ourselves. Just for a bit,' she said softly. 'Our secret.'

'Whatever you say, my darling.' He released her with some reluctance and looked round. 'Now, where were we?'

'You were going home to lunch and I was going to Maud Benson's. I can hear the men are back at work after their break so it's time to go.' She helped him on with his coat and after a final kiss he left. She went over to the mirror in her office and combed her hair and checked that she didn't look too radiant with happiness and that her face didn't look too obviously recently kissed. Then she picked up her bag and went across to Maud's cottage.

The sun was shining as she crossed the yard, heralding an early spring, and Maud's door was open.

The women were all inside, sitting round the table while the children played outside on the step. Even Florrie was there. Milly, it appeared, had recovered sufficiently to help Connie Templeton move her things over to Jack Earnshaw's cottage.

'Connie came to see how Milly was and to tell us that George had gone and she was moving over to Jack's. Milly asked if she could help her move her things over,' Florrie said. 'I wasn't sure if it were the right thing but Milly was keen to go so I thought it might tek her mind off things.

And Connie seemed to think it might help Milly if she could see he was gone and not coming back.'

'Did you know Connie was moving in with Jack, Miss Barlow?' Daisy Frampton asked.

'Yes. I went over to see her with J— Mr Kenton this morning and she told us what she planned to do.' Poppy closed her eyes briefly. Was it only this morning? It seemed half a lifetime ago, so much had happened in the meantime. And she would have to be more careful with Josh's name in future. 'She told us George had taken himself off, too.'

'Aye. We'll not see him again at Kentons. Good riddance to bad rubbish, is what I say,' Florrie said. 'I just hope Connie'll find a bit of happiness and comfort with Jack now he's gone. Jack's wanted her over there for long enough.'

'Amen to that,' the others agreed.

'So you all think Connie is doing the right thing, then, in becoming Jack's housekeeper?' Poppy asked, accepting the tea Maud had poured her.

'Housekeeper?' Daisy cocked an eyebrow. 'Call it that if you like, but I'll be surprised if there's more than one set of sheets on that washing line come Monday. And good luck to 'em, that's what I say.'

'Oh aye. The pity of it is they couldn't get together years ago,' Maud said.

'Aye. It's been as plain as the nose on your face for years how Jack feels about her,' Daisy said. 'I've seen him rubbing salve into her bruises wi' tears running down his face, but there was nowt he could do about it.'

'Not while that animal was around,' Maud said. Her expression softened. 'Oh, she'll be all right now. Jack'll look after her.'

'It's a great pity they can't be wed,' Charity said, a worried frown creasing her brow.

'Well, they can't. Not while that devil still lives,' Maud said.

'But it's sinful ...'

Daisy turned to Charity and said quietly, 'Where do you

268

think the biggest sin lies, Charity, lass? Two people living together in love and respect but unwed, or two people living in cruelty and hatred but joined together in wedlock?' She shrugged her massive shoulders. 'I know what my answer to that is, without a second thought.'

Charity shook her head. 'I'm not sure . . .'

'Well, I am,' Maud said. And the others agreed.

Charity gave a nervous smile. 'I'll see what Mord has to say about it.'

There was a tentative knock at the door. When Maud opened it Connie stood there looking uncertain, with Milly by her side.

'Come on in, love. I've got tea ready mashed, you must be fair clemmed,' Maud said, taking hold of her arm and guiding her to a chair by the table with the others.

Connie sat down and looked at them all shyly. 'I wasn't sure I'd be welcome,' she said, 'but Milly said to come.' She smiled at Milly, hovering near the door. 'She's a grand lass, is your Milly, Mrs Braithwaite.'

'Not so much of the "Mrs Braithwaite", the name's Florrie,' Florrie said, openly pleased to hear her daughter praised.

'Are you all right now, love?' Lily Ferris asked, looking keenly at Milly.

Milly nodded but Poppy noticed the way she was nervously hugging herself. It would take a long time for the memory of her attack to fade.

'Milly was right to tell you to come,' Maud told Connie. 'You're one of us now you'll be living with . . .' she hastily corrected herself, 'at Jack's. You've had a rough time over these past years.' She saw the look of surprise on Connie's face, 'You surely to goodness didn't think we didn't know, lass!'

'Aye,' Lily added. 'But there was nowt we could do, him being works manager and you living in that house over there. A cut above us.'

Connie gave a sad smile. 'You've no idea how I longed

to come and talk to you, but George wouldn't let me. Said we had a position to uphold. He wouldn't even let me talk to Mary much when she came to clean.' She looked at Mary, her eyes brimming with tears. 'I expect you thought I was stuck up, but it wasn't that. I was afraid of what he'd do if I went against him.'

Mary put out her hand. 'Don't worry about it lass. I understood more than you ever knew.'

Poppy left the women chatting warmly. She was confident that Connie would fit very easily into their little community, welcomed and not judged. The wives, with the possible exception of Charity, were big-hearted enough to be glad that at last she and Jack, her sister's widower, would find happiness together.

It was after four o'clock before Josh came back to the office. She was busily typing when she felt his arms go round her and he nuzzled her neck.

'Oh, I've missed you,' he breathed in her ear.

She wriggled round in her chair but before she could speak he was kissing her.

'You'll have to stop doing this in working hours,' she murmured. 'We shall have the boss after us.'

'I am the boss,' he murmured back. 'And he says it's all right.'

Eventually, reluctantly, she managed to disentangle herself from him. 'We really must be more circumspect, darling,' she said, smiling up at him. 'Supposing someone came in?'

'Then they could be the first to congratulate us,' he answered, completely unabashed.

'No.' She spoke a shade too quickly. 'I mean, there's nothing to congratulate us on, yet.'

'What do you mean?' His face cleared. 'Oh, because you haven't had a formal proposal ...' He immediately dropped onto one knee.

She put her hand over his mouth and then pulled him back to his feet. 'No, Josh. Not now. Not here.'

He grinned down at her. 'Of course not. You're perfectly right. I must find a more romantic setting.'

'That won't be difficult,' she said with a laugh.

He laughed with her. Then he frowned. 'And I must do the right thing and ask your father first ... Oh, I'm sorry, darling, that was tactless of me.'

She shook her head, not trusting herself to speak. Her beloved father would have been so delighted in her happiness. Not like the aunts ...

'Then who ...?'

'That's something we have to talk about,' she said resignedly. 'But not just now, if you don't mind.'

He looked momentarily puzzled, then he kissed her again. 'Whatever you say, my love.'

Poppy pushed her bicycle up the hill on her way home wondering how she could tell the aunts about Josh without actually revealing his identity. It wouldn't be easy but as long as she didn't tell them his surname it might be all right. And she did so want to share her happiness with them. On the other hand, perhaps the best thing would be not to say anything at all yet about this wonderful thing that had happened to her, this marvellous knowledge that this lovely man loved her as much as she loved him. Because she couldn't bear it if Aunt Kate were to sniff her disapproval and make the kind of disparaging remarks she was wont to do. Better to say nothing.

She put her bicycle away and went in through the kitchen door. Mrs Rivers was preparing the tray with her meal on it. She looked up as Poppy entered.

'Ee, lass, you're looking all rosy-cheeked and cheerful. Had a good day, have you?'

'Yes, thank you, Mrs Rivers. I've had a lovely day. Mm, my dinner smells good.'

'I'll have it on the table for you by the time you've teken your coat off and washed your hands.'

Poppy hurried to the cloakroom to tidy herself up before

271

going to the parlour. She peered into the mirror. It was true, her eyes were shining, her cheeks were rosy and she looked bursting with happiness – as indeed she was. She tried to put on a suitably sober expression for the benefit of the aunts and went along to the parlour.

They were sitting in their usual places, Kate by the fire with a book, Meg on the settee under the window with her patchwork, an extra oil lamp at her elbow in reluctant deference to the fine work she did. The room had an air of genteel shabbiness: of old-fashioned, old-maid fussiness, with its lace doilies and antimacassars, the slightly moth-eaten stuffed birds under glass on the chiffonier, the china ornaments jostling for position on the whatnot in the corner and every other available surface in the over-furnished room. It looked cosy and cluttered, yet there was the habitual chill in the air because of the meagreness of the fire. Poppy knew she was seeing it afresh through Josh's eyes and she felt ashamed and guilty at one and the same time. Ashamed that her aunts persisted in living in such conditions and guilty at feeling such shame. But whatever her feelings, it didn't alter the fact that the carpet was threadbare, the curtains were torn and faded and the stuffing was beginning to escape from the arms of Kate's chair. Her previously euphoric mood flattened as she came back to reality.

Aunt Meg looked up and clapped her hands. 'I knew you were home as soon as Mrs Rivers brought your tray in,' she said happily 'I can always tell.' She put her head on one side. 'I'm fey, you know.'

'Don't be ridiculous, Meg. You're not fey, you're stating the obvious,' Kate snapped at her. She nodded towards the tray. 'Hurry up and eat it, Poppy. We don't want the place smelling of cabbage all evening.'

Poppy's spirits rose again. Josh wouldn't care about the way the aunts lived, it wasn't the aunts he loved. She could imagine laughing affectionately with him in the future over the two quaint old ladies and their idiosyncrasies. She smiled. Nothing, not even Aunt Kate's waspish tongue, could dampen her happiness tonight. 'I'll go and eat it in the kitchen if you like, Aunt,' she said wickedly, knowing what the answer would be.

'That won't be necessary. Just don't take too long about it.' Kate went back to her book.

'You're looking very pretty tonight, Poppy,' Aunt Meg said, looking up from her embroidery. 'And happy, too. Has something nice happened to you today?' She put her head on one side. 'It has. I know it has.' She wagged her finger at Poppy. 'As I said, I can always tell, you know. I'm fey.'

'Oh don't be so stupid Meg,' Kate said, looking at her over the top of her pince-nez. Then her gaze turned to Poppy and rested there. 'Well?' she asked, frowning.

'I can't talk and eat at the same time, Aunt,' Poppy said, playing for time.

'Hurry up, then,' Meg said, wriggling excitedly in her seat. 'I know you've got something to tell us. I just *know*.'

Poppy made her meal last as long as she dared, lingering over her apple pie and custard until it was quite cold. Then she took the tray back to the kitchen, still trying to decide just what to say and how to say it.

When she came back into the room Meg looked straight at her. 'I know what it is. You've met a young man,' she said triumphantly.

'Don't be so stupid, Margaret,' Kate said again and it was a measure of her annoyance that this time she used Meg's full name.

'I'm not being stupid. I'm right, aren't I, Poppy?' Meg lifted her chin.

Poppy nodded, unable to keep from smiling. 'Yes.'

Meg clapped her hands. 'I knew it. I knew it. I told you I was fey. Who is he? Do we know him?'

'Don't be silly, Margaret. We don't know any young men,' Kate reminded her sharply.

'Oh, no. We don't, do we?' Meg said, disappointed. Her

spirits lifted. 'But we shall when you bring him to see us. And you will invite him to tea, won't you? We should so like to meet him, wouldn't we, Kate?' She didn't wait for an answer, which was just as well, because none was forthcoming. 'What's his name, Poppy?'

'Josh.'

'And did you meet him at work?' Meg was excitedly doing all the talking while Kate sat glowering in her chair.

'Yes, I did.'

'And is he tall? And dark? And handsome?'

'He's tall and dark,' Poppy said, She smiled at the recollection of Josh's scarred face. 'I think he's *very* handsome.'

'Oh, how romantic.' Meg giggled. 'I expect he's the master's son. Is that right?'

Poppy nodded and saw Kate's hands immediately tighten on the arms of her chair and her jaw set rigidly. But before she could speak Meg was prattling on. 'Oh how lovely. To marry Mr Cole's son! You'll be able to have the pick of everything in the store. You'll be able to get me lots and lots of material and ribbon. Oh, won't that be wonderful, Kate?'

'Be quiet, Margaret!' Kate hissed. 'You've no idea what you're talking about. You're talking complete nonsense, just as you always do when one of your turns is coming on.' She got to her feet and caught Meg by the arm. 'You'd better go and lie down. In fact, you'd better go to bed.' She began to drag her to the door.

'But I don't want to go to bed. I want to hear about Poppy's young man. She might be bringing him to see us tonight and I don't want to miss him.' Meg began to cry, looking first to Kate and then to Poppy.

'He won't be coming here tonight. Nor any other night. You've made a mistake, Margaret. There's no young man, dear. You've imagined it.' Kate's voice was soothing now. 'I'll ask Mrs Rivers to warm some milk and you can take it with your pill.'

Meg frowned. 'But I've had my pill.' She looked bewildered. 'Haven't I?'

'No, dear. You haven't. You forgot to take it.' Kate was guiding her to the stairs now and she stood at the foot and watched while Meg dejectedly climbed them. 'Hasn't Poppy met a young man, then?' she was asking in a plaintive little voice. 'I was so sure . . .'

'You go to bed, dear. You'll feel better in the morning.'

Poppy came out into the hall. 'Would you like me to take Aunt Meg's milk to her?' she asked tentatively.

Kate swung round. 'Indeed no. You've done quite enough damage for one evening. Go back to the parlour. I want to speak to you.' She turned and stared up at the portrait of her father. 'All this would never have happened in dear Papa's day,' she said enigmatically. Then she hurried along to the kitchen.

Poppy went slowly back to the parlour and sat down at the table. The light from the oil lamps threw a deceptively warm glow over the room and a small fire still flickered bravely in the grate. Meg's embroidery silks were strewn over the settee where they had landed when Kate pulled her to her feet, and Kate's book was on the floor.

She gave a sigh of resignation. She had known she would have to face Aunt Kate's wrath at some time so she might as well get it over with tonight. But on one thing she was determined. Whatever Aunt Kate said she would not give up her chance of happiness with Josh Kenton. She clasped her hands together on the table and prepared to do battle.

Chapter Twenty-Six

It seemed an age before Kate came back into the room, an age in which Poppy sat pondering over the best way to placate her aunt.

When Kate finally returned she walked over to her chair without speaking, picked up the book that had fallen on the floor and replaced it carefully on the little table beside her chair. Then she scrupulously tidied Meg's embroidery silks and poked viciously at the dying embers of the fire before finally sitting down and turning to face Poppy.

'Am I to infer from the charade that has just taken place in this room that you have embarked on some kind of friendship with the son of your employer?' she asked coldly.

Poppy lifted her chin. 'That's right, Aunt Kate. I have fallen in love with Josh Kenton and he has fallen in love with me,' she said, her voice firm.

'Fallen in love!' Kate's tone was derisory. 'Then I suggest that you fall out of love as quickly as you fell into it. I won't have it. I will not have a niece of mine associating with the son of *that man*.' Each word was accompanied by a thump on the arm of her chair. She glared at Poppy. 'I take it he is the son of that man?'

'If by *that man* you're speaking about Sir Frederick Kenton, then the answer is, yes, he is.' Poppy answered. Her expression softened. 'Believe me, Aunt Kate, I do understand how you must feel. I know it can't be easy for you that I've fallen in love with the son of the man who jilted you all those years ago ...'

'You don't know the half of it,' Kate spat. 'You can have no possible idea what I went through.' Her eyes narrowed and she stared into the fire. 'No idea.'

Poppy went over to her and knelt on the hearthrug at her feet. 'But it was all so many years ago, Aunt,' she said gently. 'Can't you forgive and forget, after all this time?'

Kate looked down at her, her expression scathing. 'How can I forget what happened? And why should I forgive?' she said scornfully. 'He ruined our lives. Look at us, two dried-up sticks of humanity. And all because of *that man*.' There was pure venom in her tone.

Poppy sat back on her heels. 'I can't see what it all had to do with Aunt Meg,' she said with a shrug. 'I can't see why her life should have been ruined, just because you were jilted.'

'*Just* because! *Just* because!' Kate almost screamed the words at her. 'You young women of today have absolutely no idea what a broken engagement meant in those days. The stigma ... the shame ...' With an obvious effort she gained control and went on more quietly. 'It was also a terrible blow to poor Papa, of course, but he carried on in his usual dignified manner and encouraged me to do the same. When he became Master Cutler he even did me the honour of asking me to be his Mistress Cutler – a very important and prominent position to hold. I was not sure I could do it but he insisted.' She lifted her head proudly. 'And of course, he was right.' She smiled a little secret smile. 'Papa was always right but even he didn't know everything.'

'But it was all so long ago,' Poppy reminded her wearily.

Kate rounded on her. 'It seems like only yesterday to me.'

Poppy got to her feet. 'Well, Aunt, I'm very sorry about what happened to you in the past but I refuse to let it cast a shadow over my happiness with Josh. I love him and he loves me. Won't you let bygones be bygones and allow me to bring him here to meet you?'

Kate's mouth was a thin, hard line. 'Never!' she said through gritted teeth. 'And bear in mind the old saying, "Like father, like son". I'm warning you, if you persist in this infatuation you'll only be storing up trouble for yourself. If you take my advice you'll nip it in the bud before it goes any further. And as for bringing him here ...' she shuddered and then said through gritted teeth, 'While I live and breathe the son of *that man* shall never darken my door. And that's my very last word on the subject.' She got to her feet and swept past Poppy to the door, where she turned. 'I knew from the very beginning that no good would come of you going out to work like some common woman.' She opened the door and went through, her head held high. Then she came back and said, her voice little more than a hiss, 'And never, *never* mention any of this to Meg if you don't want her to end up in Lodge Moor, the hospital for the incurably insane.'

Poppy gaped. 'What do you mean? Why should it affect her?'

Kate sighed theatrically. 'You know very well that the least little upset affects the delicate balance of Meg's mind. She's ... unstable.' With that she left, closing the door behind her.

Poppy sat gazing into the last glowing cinders of the fire, going over Kate's words concerning Sir Frederick and his son. How on earth was she going to explain to Josh her aunt's vitriolic attitude to his family?

Poppy arrived at work the next morning feeling very confused. On the one hand the knowledge that Josh loved her gave her a warm glow, but at the same time she felt tired and rather jaded after a sleepless night spent worrying over Aunt Kate's attitude.

To her surprise, as she rode her bike into the yard she

saw that there was a Union Jack hanging from the upstairs window of one of the cottages and bits of brightly coloured material fluttered from every available windowsill and doorway of the others. She flushed. What were they celebrating? Had they found out that she and Josh ...? But found out what? There was nothing to celebrate. Nothing official. Yet. Puzzled, she carried on towards the office, trying to ignore the home-made bunting.

But Maud Benson had been watching for her.

'Miss Barlow, have you heard?' she called excitedly. 'Harry's coming home today. Mary's Harry. You know, he lost a leg in France and got invalided out.'

Poppy's face cleared. So that was what all the bunting was about. 'Ah. Yes. I remember now,' she said with a smile. 'So you're all celebrating.'

'Aye. But only in a quiet way. Poor lad's still not in very good shape so he'll likely want to be kept quiet. But we thought we'd like him to know how pleased we all are to have him back.'

'That's a lovely thought, Maud. And wonderful news for Mary.'

'Aye. She's right thrilled to think she's having her man back after all this time.' She hesitated, glancing over her shoulder. 'Do you think Mr Josh might pop in to see him when he gets back?' she said softly.

'Of course he will,' Poppy said warmly. 'But he'll want to give Harry time to settle in. What time is he expected?'

'Ten o'clock.'

Poppy nodded. 'I'll tell him.' She smiled broadly. 'Tell Mary I'm really delighted for her.'

'Oh, I will that.' Maud bustled back into her cottage. 'You'll be along later, won't you?' she said over her shoulder.

'Yes, I will.'

'I'll have the tea mashed ready.' The door closed behind her and Poppy continued up the steps to her office. She paused when she reached the top. Suddenly, the day seemed altogether brighter. It was warm in the spring sunshine and there was hardly a cloud in the sky. A tiny breeze was making ripples on the huge lake behind the building, the source of the water used to power the big tilt hammer, breaking up the sunlight that glinted on it into hundreds of dancing points of light. Everywhere seemed bathed in sunshine. Even the cobbles in the yard looked bright and there was a cheerful atmosphere in the workshops. Mordecai Jones was singing hymns in time to the thump of the tilt hammer, Charlie Braithwaite was whistling at his forge. The whole place was a hive of activity, the men calling cheerfully to each other as they went about their various tasks. And all this had come about since Josh's return only a few short months ago. What a contrast to the apathy that had reigned after Sir Frederick ceased to take an interest.

She unlocked the door and went in. Minutes later, Josh followed her.

'Oh. I've missed you, Miss Barlow,' he said, coming up behind her and nuzzling her neck.

She twisted round and kissed the tip of his nose. 'I've missed you, too, Mr Josh, but this is hardly the way for a secretary to behave with her boss,' she said wickedly.

'No, you're quite right. It must stop. In a minute.' He began to kiss her thoroughly.

He stopped abruptly and pulled away, straightening his tie, when there was a knock at the door. 'I'm in my office,' he whispered and hurried through.

She glanced briefly in the mirror on the filing cabinet, patting her hair before opening the door. Jake Benson stood there, twisting his cap in his hands. 'Mr Josh called out that he wanted to see me, miss,' he said diffidently. He rarely had cause to come up to the office.

Poppy smiled. 'Yes, that's right. Come in, Jake. Mr Josh is in his office.'

Jake stepped inside. 'Do you know what he wants me for, miss?' he asked, frowning nervously. 'Is owt wrong?'

She smiled again. 'Not as far as I know, Jake. Go on. Go through.'

She waited half an hour, getting on with her work, then she made a pot of tea and took it into Josh's office. Jake immediately scrambled to his feet. He was looking utterly bemused. 'I'll be off then,' he muttered.

'No, Jake. Don't get up. There are still things we have to discuss,' Josh said easily. 'Miss Barlow always brings tea in when I'm in discussion with my manager.' He raised his eyebrows. 'You will accept the job, I take it?'

'Oh, aye. Aye, indeed I will. Be privileged to, Mr Josh.' Jake swallowed. 'It's a bit of a shock, that's all. I never expected ... It's fair teken my breath away.'

'Then a cup of tea is what you need.' Josh smiled up at Poppy. 'Thank you, Miss Barlow. That will be all. For the moment.' The look he gave her as he said those last words sent her blushing from the room.

An hour later, after Jake had gone, still so bemused that he scarcely glanced at her as he passed through her office, Josh came in and perched on the edge of her desk.

'I've sent him home to tell his wife they'll be moving across the yard to the manager's house,' he said with a chuckle. 'He'll be good, Poppy. I've questioned him thoroughly and there's nothing he doesn't know about the way things work here. And even more important, he's popular with the men. Thank you darling, for recommending him to me.' He leaned forward and kissed her briefly, then he made a face. 'I don't know whether you'll regard this as a reward or a penance but we've been summoned to take tea with the guv'nor today at four, so you have the boss's permission to finish early tonight, Miss Barlow.'

'Thank you, kind sir,' she sketched a curtsy. 'Ah, there's one thing I haven't been able to tell you yet, later today you must find the time to visit Harry Smithers. You saw all the flags out?'

'Yes, I did. I wondered what they were for. I didn't think it could be for us,' he added with a wicked grin.

'No. They're for Harry. They're bringing him home today. I promised Maud Benson you would visit him when he's had time to settle in. It will mean a lot to him. And to Mary.'

He went over to the window and stood looking out, rubbing his chin. 'He's lost a leg, hasn't he?'

'That's right. He won't be working again for some time, I'm afraid.'

'No. But when I go to see him I want to be able to give him hope. Obviously he won't be able to do his old job. He was a pot-maker from what I recall, so there's no hope that he will ever be able to tread the clay again.' He sighed. 'I'll have to think of something he can do.'

Poppy came up behind him and put her arms round his waist. 'Maybe he can eventually work in the packing shed. But it'll be months before he's fit to do anything, so don't worry about it yet, Josh. One thing at a time.'

He turned and touched her face. 'You're good for me, Poppy Barlow. You keep my feet on the ground.'

When Poppy went over to Maud's cottage with her sandwiches the men had already been in for their midday meal and gone back to work. As she went in, Maud was busying herself with the teapot, Daisy and Lily were sitting at the table with Connie looking rather uncomfortable between them and Charity was fussing with little Rebecca on the hearthrug. There was an air of suppressed excitement in the room.

'So you'll be moving across the yard soon, then,' Daisy was saying.

'Aye. It looks like it.' Maud's voice held a mixture of pride and apprehension. She turned to Poppy. 'You've no doubt heard the news, Miss Barlow?'

Poppy nodded and smiled. 'Yes. I'm sure Jake will be a very good manager. And he's popular with the men. I'm very pleased for him. And you, Maud.'

Daisy turned to Connie. 'What's it like then?' She

nodded in the direction of Connie's old home. 'The house, I mean?'

Connie looked even more uncomfortable. 'It's a nice place,' she said. 'Nice big rooms. Nice bit of garden. Tap over the sink.'

'Better than these places,' Lily remarked, looking round Maud's small kitchen. 'One tap between three out in the back yard.'

'Well, you'd expect the manager's house to be bigger, wouldn't you?' Lily said. 'It's only right.'

'But it's not so friendly, standing all alone across the other side of the yard.' Connie blurted out. 'You've no idea what it was like being stuck over there, specially being wed to the sort of man I was. He wouldn't let me have anything to do with the rest of you, said we were a cut above, jumped-up little runt that he was.' Her voice was bitter. She shook her head and went on, her voice not quite steady, 'I used to see you all standing in your doorways talking and I just wished I could come and join in, but I knew what he'd do to me if I tried.' She looked round the table at the women sitting there. 'I suppose you all thought I was a toffee-nosed bitch.' She looked down at her hands. 'If only you knew.'

Daisy put her big hand over Connie's. 'Well, that's all behind you now, lass. You're one of us now you're here looking after Jack, and we're glad to have you.'

Connie looked up, smiling through tears that threatened to spill over. 'Thank you for that. I wondered if you might ...' She flushed, not quite knowing how to go on.

'We just hope you and Jack will be happy, lass. God knows you both deserve a bit of comfort,' Lily said. She turned to Maud. 'And you needn't think you'll be shut of us when you move across the yard, missus,' she said. 'We shall still expect our brew-up and gossip even if you have gone up in t'world.'

Maud had been looking a little anxious, now her face cleared. 'Thank the Lord for that. You all know my Jake would never try to stop you coming over, so it'll be just the same except we'll have a bit more room round the table.' She picked up the teapot. 'Just because Jake'll be manager doesn't mean we'll be any different. My Jake's got no airs and graces, clever lad though he is.' She poured out two extra cups of tea and put them on a tray. 'Pop along to Mary's with these, Lily. She'll not leave Harry, him only just getting home, but I wouldn't want her to feel left out. You can tell her the news and see if there's anything they're wanting.'

Lily was only gone a few minutes. She came back smiling. 'They're sitting there holding hands like a couple of lovebirds,' she said. 'Harry looks about ninety and as thin as a rake but he'll soon shape up now he's home. He looked happy enough, any road. And they both said to congratulate your Jake.'

'That's good. Thank God Harry's home safe, even if he was careless enough to leave a leg in France,' Daisy said, raising her cup. 'Here's to 'em.'

'Amen to that,' the others said, solemnly raising theirs.

'And to you and Jake.' Daisy lifted her cup again.

'Aye. To Maud and Jake.'

Poppy raised her thick white cup with the others. They were a close-knit, friendly, loving community. Jake's promotion would make a little but not too much difference because there was not an ounce of jealousy between them. She wondered idly who would fill number four when Jake and Maud had moved to their new home.

There would be no shortage of contenders for it.

Chapter Twenty-Seven

At ten to four Poppy put the cover on her typewriter and closed the ledgers she had been working on. Then she combed her hair and refastened the tortoiseshell slide at the nape of her neck and powdered her nose. When Josh came through from his office she was just putting on her hat, a jaunty little felt with a feather that swept round the brim, perching it carefully over one eye.

'Very fetching,' he said admiringly.

She turned away from the mirror. 'I'd have put on my best costume if I'd known we were going to tea with Sir Frederick,' she said with a frown, smoothing her grey work skirt and jacket.

'You look wonderful just as you are,' he said. 'Come on now, Hilton is waiting with the car.'

'Can't we walk? It's not all that far and it's such a lovely day,' she asked, biting her lip.

He raised one eyebrow. 'Trying to put off the evil hour?' he teased. 'Surely you're not nervous? The guv'nor isn't such an ogre, you know. And it isn't as if you didn't know him. Heavens, you were his secretary for – how long? Nearly a year.'

'I know that,' she said a little sharply.

He frowned, immediately concerned. 'Then what is it that's bothering you, my love? There's something you're not happy about, I can see that.' He took her arm. 'All right, we'll walk as you suggest, then you can tell me all about it as we go.' He dismissed Hilton and they set out for Kenton Hall.

They walked for some distance in silence as he waited for her to tell him what was troubling her. When she said nothing, he began to talk, trying to put her at her ease over what he could only imagine the problem might be.

'I suppose you think it's all right for me,' he mused as they walked. 'I won't have to go through the ordeal of facing your family.' He turned and smiled down at her. 'That is, unless you've got an old uncle tucked away in a cupboard somewhere, who'll come out brandishing a carving knife and shouting "over my dead body!" You haven't, have you?' He looked down at her in mock alarm. Then he grinned and squeezed her arm. 'No, of course you haven't.' He became serious again. 'Do you realise, Poppy, I know hardly anything about you, except that you're the most wonderful girl in the world? I do know that both your parents are dead and I've never heard you speak of any brothers and sisters, so I can only assume you haven't got any. I wouldn't even have known that you live in Whirlowdale Road if I hadn't been nosy enough to look your address up in your notes. It's a very nice area, isn't it? Big houses. Do you rent a room in one of them? Ah, no, I remember now. You once told me you lived with relatives. But they won't make a fuss, will they? Not when they ...' He looked at her and was shocked to see tears running down her cheeks. 'Poppy! Poppy, darling, what's the matter? What's wrong? What have I said?' He was tempted to take her in his arms then and there, in the middle of the busy street, but he refrained, sensing it would embarrass her.

She took out a handkerchief and blew her nose. 'You obviously know more about me than you realise, Josh. Only it's not a crazy old uncle I live with, it's two dotty old aunts,' she said miserably. 'Two dotty old ladies who live in an enormous house that's falling down round their ears because they won't spend any money on its upkeep.'

He turned her to face him. 'Well, that's not such a terrible thing, is it?' he asked, looking at her quizzically. 'At least you're not alone in the world. I'm sure I can manage two dotty old ladies.'

She shook her head. 'That's just the trouble. You won't have to manage them, Josh, because they flatly refuse to allow me to take you to meet them. At least, Aunt Kate does. Aunt Meg doesn't know about you. She's ...' She hesitated, then used Kate's word to describe her sister '... delicate and mustn't be upset.'

He raised his eyebrows. 'How intriguing.' He hugged her. 'I daresay they're afraid of losing their favourite niece.'

'Their only niece,' she corrected him.

'Well, there you are then.' He stopped as they walked up the drive to Kenton Hall and tipped her face up to his. 'Don't worry, my darling. We'll find a way.' He gave a wicked grin. 'I can always dress up as the butcher boy and charm them by offering them free sausages.'

She gave him a tremulous smile.

'That's better, Now, one thing at a time, Poppy, my love. Come on, let's go and beard my old lion in his den before we think about tackling your dotty old aunts. It's one of Pa's better days so he'll be pleased to see you.'

Sir Frederick was sitting in his wheelchair looking out of the window when they arrived. Briggs followed closely behind with the tea tray.

'You can pour, lass, like you always do when you come to see me.' He glared at her and said accusingly, 'You haven't been lately.'

'No. I didn't like to come after Josh – your son came home. I didn't want to intrude,' she replied. 'And when he took your place at work I had no reason to come.'

'Hmph. That's daft. You didn't need a reason. I've missed you. You're a bonny lass. You always brighten my day when you come to see me.' He gave her the nearest he could manage to a smile. 'Any road, you're here now, so come and sit beside me and tell me what you've been up to.' He nodded in Josh's direction. 'How's he shaping up?'

'You couldn't have left the business in better hands,' she said after a moment's thought.

'Whew! I wondered what you were going to say,' Josh said with a laugh.

Sir Frederick gave a satisfied nod. 'That's good enough for me. Now, pour the tea, lass, and help yourself to a muffin. It's true, I have missed you, you know. I've missed your pretty, smiling face. I always feel better after your visits. You remind me of somebody, I can't think who.' He wagged a finger at her. 'Don't leave it so long again.'

She smiled at him. 'I won't. I promise.'

The three of them spent a very pleasant half-hour over tea, and it wasn't until Briggs had been in and removed the tea tray that Sir Frederick turned to them and said in his blunt manner, 'So when do you intend to announce your engagement? I see no reason for any delay. What do your folks say, Poppy, my lass?'

Poppy swallowed. 'I haven't ... that is ...' She looked imploringly at Josh for help.

'Poppy lives with two elderly aunts. I think she feels she must break the news to them gently, Pa,' Josh said easily.

Sir Frederick chuckled. 'Yes, we old codgers have to be treated with care.' He frowned. 'I've forgotten. Where do you live, lass?'

'In Whirlowdale Road,' Poppy answered with some reluctance.

He raised his eyebrows. 'Do you, indeed! A very high-class area. And your name is Barlow.' He shook his head thoughtfully. 'No, I don't think I ever knew anybody of that name. Have your aunts lived in Sheffield long?'

'All their lives, as far as I know,' Poppy said wretchedly.

'And you say their name is Barlow?'

She shook her head and then said with a rush. 'No. *My*

name is Barlow. Their name is Russell. They are the daughters of the late Josiah Russell,' and then watched as Sir Frederick's face changed. It was as if a shutter had come down over his features, turning them to wood.

'I see,' he said, his voice coldly polite. 'And no doubt it was your aunts' idea that you should come to work at Kentons?'

'Indeed it was not,' she replied hotly. 'In fact, I didn't tell them for some time. When Aunt Kate discovered she was furious and insisted that I should leave. But I love my work and so I refused.'

'You should have taken her advice.' His voice was still cold. He turned his head away. 'I would rather you didn't visit my house again, Miss Barlow.' He glanced at Josh, who had been following the conversation, looking from one to the other in utter amazement. 'Will you ring for Briggs. I wish to go to my room. I shall speak to you later.'

As soon as Sir Frederick had been wheeled from the room Josh went over and sat beside her and put his arm round her. 'Oh, darling, I'm terribly sorry,' he said, holding her close. 'I can't imagine what got into the guv'nor to turn on you like that.'

'Oh, I can.' Poppy heaved a great sigh. 'It's a long story, Josh, and it all happened a very long time ago, but it looks as if your father is going to be as difficult as my aunts.' She laid her hand over his. 'I'm afraid it's not going to work, Josh,' she said sadly. 'They don't want us to be together.'

He turned his hand so that he could clasp hers. 'Then they'll just have to lump it. All of them. Because I'm not giving you up now I've found you.' His mouth was set in a thin, hard line. 'But why are they like this, Poppy? Why are they all being so bloody awkward?'

Poppy took a deep breath. 'I guess it's because your father and my Aunt Kate were once engaged to be married,' she said.

'The devil they were!' Josh was silent for several minutes. Then he frowned. 'But I can't see what that's got to do with us. Heaven's sake, it must have been all of thirty years ago so it's in the dim and distant past. Why did they break it off, do you know?'

Poppy shrugged. 'Not exactly. All I know is that it was broken off on the night of the engagement party and Sir Frederick married someone else – presumably your mother – soon afterwards.'

Josh rubbed his chin. 'Well, well, well. I suppose that means the guv'nor must have been a bit of a Lothario in his youth. I must say he never struck me as a particularly romantic figure. In fact, to tell you the truth he and Ma didn't hit it off all that well. They were always bickering, as I recall. Then again, Ma was often ill ...' He shook his head. 'I'll have to ask him about it.'

'If he's anything like Aunt Kate he won't tell you much. Mind you, I think as far as Kate was concerned her pride suffered as much as her heart. She seems to have been more concerned about the terrible shame it brought on the family. Particularly her father. He was Josiah Russell, the scissor manufacturer, although Aunt Kate was at pains to tell me that he himself never soiled his hands. There's a portrait of him hanging in the hall at Dale House. He has a cold, distant look about him.'

'You don't think you would have liked him if you'd known him?' Josh asked, to keep her talking.

She shook her head. 'I would probably have been frightened half to death by him.' She gave a slight smile. 'Aunt Kate obviously idolised him. I've never actually seen her genuflect as she passes his portrait but I would never be surprised if she did.'

Josh threw back his head and laughed. 'Oh, Poppy, darling, you're priceless. And your grandfather sounds an absolute ogre. And as for your aunts ... What about the other one?'

'Aunt Meg?' She frowned. 'Aunt Meg is a bit ... strange. Sometimes she talks in a perfectly rational way, sometimes she doesn't even know what day of the week it is. And she has terrible tantrums. When she gets into one of her rages she goes off into the drawing room and takes it out on the piano. She's a wonderful pianist. Apparently she has funny turns, too, although I've never seen her in one. She has to have pills to counteract them.' She smiled. 'But she's lovely, most of the time. A gentle little soul.'

'You don't think she would mind her niece taking up with Sir Frederick Kenton's son?'

Poppy smiled again. 'No, she would be delighted, I'm sure. She would probably insist on making one of her beautiful patchwork quilts for my bottom drawer. She's a very clever needlewoman.'

'You're very fond of Aunt Meg, aren't you?'

'I'm fond of them both. But Aunt Meg ... well, as I told you, she's delicate.'

He got to his feet and held out a hand to her. 'Come on. I'd better take you home. Your dotty old aunts will be wondering what's happened to you.'

She got to her feet. 'I can't ask you in,' she said in alarm.

'I know that, silly.' He kissed her. 'I haven't got a blue and white striped apron and a straw hat.'

'Nor a trade bike and a pound of sausages,' she whispered as she wound her arms round his neck. 'Anyway, I've left my bike at work.'

Josh was frantically busy over the next few weeks grooming Jake Benson for his new position. Jake was a conscientious man, anxious to learn every facet of the job, so Josh took him to visit the suppliers and customers. They all took to the new manager at Kentons, comparing him very favourably with George Templeton, whom most of them had neither liked nor trusted. Often the two men worked late, poring over books and papers.

Poppy got on with her own work but she was worried. She loved Josh. She knew he was the only man she would ever love, but the obstacles seemed insurmountable, not only on her side, but on his as well. Sir Frederick was as hostile as Aunt Kate. But why? What on earth could have gone so dreadfully wrong between them that it still rankled after all these years? Poppy knew that Aunt Kate wouldn't tell her anything more, so it was up to Josh to find out from his father. And until he did, there was little chance of their own relationship developing.

The problem nagged on at the back of her mind whatever she did, sleeping or waking, made worse by the fact that Josh was too busy to talk to her about it, so she didn't know how he was feeling.

On a more cheerful note, Poppy was pleased to see that Maud Benson was settling into her new home across the yard. The women from the cottages had helped her to move, bustling back and forth with furniture and bedding, delighted at their friend's good fortune and not a bit envious of her husband's promotion. It was not many days before the lunch-time tea parties resumed.

Poppy found she, too, was as welcome as ever and was given a tour of Maud's house and made to marvel at the size of the rooms, the slop stone in the corner of the kitchen with water on tap, and the privy down the garden that didn't have to be shared, before she could sit and eat her sandwiches.

'Jake says he'll get me a whatnot to put in the front room,' Maud said happily. 'I've allus wanted a whatnot and now I've got enough space for one without the boys knocking it over at every turn. Mind you, I don't know when I'll get it. Jake's that busy he's never here. Spends all this time with Mr Josh learning the ropes.'

'Is he liking his new job?' Daisy asked.

'Oh, yes. He's loving every minute of it,' Maud answered proudly. It's just that there's a lot to get used to.'

'And what do the boys think of their new home?' Lily asked, getting the cups down from the dresser.

'Oh, all they can think of is fishing in the stream at the bottom of the garden,' Maud said. 'Billy's fallen in twice.'

'That's boys for you,' Daisy said with a laugh.

'How is Harry?' Poppy asked when there was a lull in the conversation.

Lily shook her head. 'Mary says he gets a lot of pain from the foot that isn't there,' she said. 'That's a funny thing, isn't it? How can you get pain from something that isn't there? He must be imagining it.'

'No,' Connie said. 'I've heard that's quite a common thing when somebody's lost a limb.' She turned to Maud. 'Oh, I meant to tell you, that gas stove's inclined to pop, Maud. You need to stand back a bit when you put a match to it.'

'Thanks, love, I'll remember.'

'Mary says he gets dreadful nightmares,' Lily went on. 'And I know that's true enough because me and Ted have heard him through the wall in the middle of the night. Screams fit to curdle your blood, he does.'

'Poor Harry,' they all said.

'Poor Mary, too. And it doesn't make it any better that his children are all afraid of him. Well, they're only little. The youngest ones don't even remember him and none of them can understand what their dad's been through.' Lily smiled at Poppy. 'It cheers him up no end when Mr Josh goes to see him, though. Three times he's been now.'

'Has he?' Poppy said. She'd seen so little of Josh for over a week now that she hadn't realised. A sudden thought struck her. Had he been avoiding her? Had he discovered the secret behind the broken engagement and found, like his father and her aunt, that a liaison between the two families was totally unacceptable? A clutch of cold fear seemed to screw up her stomach and she pushed away her packet of half-eaten sandwiches.

Maud noticed. 'Are you feeling poorly, Miss Barlow?' she said anxiously. 'You've not eaten your snap.'

'I'm all right.' She smiled at Maud. 'Just not hungry today. But I'd like another cup of tea if there's one left in the pot.'

293

She let the conversation wash over her as she drank her tea, and as soon as she could she went back to her office.

Josh was there, alone for once. Immediately he took her in his arms. 'God, it seems ages since I was able to do this,' he murmured as he began to kiss her.

'I thought you'd discovered something about the past and had been avoiding me,' she said when he came up for air.

'Never,' he said, kissing her again. 'You know very well I've been tied up with Jake,' he said between kisses. 'I've sent him off to the steel works this afternoon on his own. It'll do him good and give me time ... Oh, hang it, put your coat on, I'm taking you somewhere where we can talk.'

'But I've got work to do,' she said, surprised.

'So have I. But it can wait. I want to take you for a spin in my new car,' he said gleefully.

'New car? I didn't know you'd got a new car.'

'I've only had it two days and I've been dying to show it to you but haven't had a chance.'

'Where is it?'

'At home. Look, let me borrow your bike and I'll go and fetch it. I didn't want to come to work in it in case it got scratched. Why don't you start walking up the road and I'll pick you up. You won't get far, I can tell you! She's a goer all right.' He was already holding her coat for her and grinning like a schoolboy. 'Come on, darling, we haven't got all day.'

As excited as he was, she struggled into her coat and rammed her hat on. It was all right. Josh still loved her. Nothing else mattered.

Chapter Twenty-Eight

Poppy hadn't walked far along the road before Josh pulled up proudly in his new car. It had a dark blue body and a black soft top and looked very smart.

Josh leaned over and opened the door for her to climb in. She stepped carefully onto the running board and then into the seat beside him.

'You'll have to hold your hat on, darling, it can be a bit breezy with the hood down,' he warned, grinning at her like a schoolboy. 'What do you think of her? A little beauty, isn't she?' He let in the clutch and drove off.

Poppy caught her hat just in time and pushed it back on her head. 'Should you drive quite so fast, Josh?' she asked nervously after a few minutes.

He threw back his head and laughed. 'Oh, darling, don't worry. You only think we're going fast because you're not used to going any quicker than you can pedal. We're only doing about twenty-five miles an hour! I used to travel much faster than that when I was flying.' Expertly, he swung the little car round the corner and up the hill towards Higger Tor, a local beauty spot.

'That was in the sky,' she pointed out, relieved that the car had slowed considerably to chug up the hill. She stole a glance at him and was glad to see that he could speak of his days in the Flying Corps without any visible sign of regret.

As they travelled he told her all about the car, but she

was far too busy holding on to her hat and enjoying the sensation of bowling along the road at high speed to pay much attention to words like engine capacity, elliptical suspension, and multi-plate clutch.

Eventually he parked the car near a gate and they got out and walked across a field and climbed the hillside to Higger Tor. Here great limestone boulders, left over from some prehistoric eruption and worn smooth by the winds of time, littered the area. Some were half hidden in the under-growth, others leaned massively and crazily against each other, while yet more were piled precariously like toy bricks discarded by some monumental giant.

Josh found a flat stone in the lee of the wind and pulled her down beside him, hardly noticing the grandeur of the scenery.

'I've neglected you. I'm sorry, my darling,' he said, putting an arm round her and holding her tight. 'But just lately life's been a bit hectic ...'

'It's all right, Josh. I understand how busy you've been,' she said, capturing his free hand and leaning her head on his shoulder. She sighed. 'Everything seems to have happened at once, doesn't it. That awful business with George Templeton, Jake having to be groomed to take his place, Harry Smithers coming home and in the middle of it all ...'

'Us,' he interrupted, giving her an extra squeeze. 'The most important and wonderful thing of all.' He bent his head and kissed her.

'I can still hardly believe it,' she whispered against his cheek.

'Me neither. But it's true, isn't it? Tell me I'm not dreaming, Poppy.'

'If you're dreaming I'm in the dream, too, so let's never wake up.' Suddenly, a gust of wind took her hat.

'Never mind it,' he said, loosening her hair from its slide. He took her face in both hands. 'You're beautiful, Poppy. Quite beautiful,' he said quietly. He traced the line of her jaw with his thumb. 'I'll never understand how a girl like you could come to love an old wreck like me.'

She put her hands over his. 'Don't talk like that, Josh,' she said sharply. 'I love you for what you are, not what you look like.' She smiled. 'It's funny, when I first saw you I thought, "He's not so strikingly handsome as his brother but he's got a kind face, a face it would be easy to fall in love with." So I did.' She fingered the scar round his eye and said thoughtfully, 'It gives you a rakish look, you know. The sort of look women find irresistible.'

He smiled into her eyes. 'Is that right, now?' he asked softly, easing her back against the mossy hillside and busying himself with her buttons.

Very much later Poppy captured her hair back into its slide while Josh searched for her hat. Then they walked down the hill, hand in hand, secure in their love for each other.

'I didn't know you were even thinking of buying a car,' she said as they reached it and he held the passenger door open for her.

'I wasn't. The guv'nor decided it would be a useful thing for me to have.' He laughed. 'Naturally, I didn't argue.'

Poppy made herself comfortable while he cranked the engine and got in the driver's side. 'Are you sure it wasn't meant as a bribe?' she asked thoughtfully.

He frowned as he let in the clutch. 'What do you mean?'

'Your father has bought you a new car, now he'll expect you to play ball with him and give me up.'

'Oh, Poppy, don't be absurd.' He looked offended. 'Pa wouldn't be so devious. Anyway, he knows I won't give you up. I've told him that. And certainly not for a bloody car.' As if to give weight to that statement he crashed the gears.

She twisted round to look at him. 'Thank you for that, Josh,' she said with a smile. Then she became serious. 'But you agree that your father seems to be as much against us being together as my aunt, don't you?' she asked sadly. 'Hasn't he said as much?'

297

He shrugged uncomfortably. 'Well he did go on about it being all right to sow wild oats with little secretaries but it didn't mean marrying them, which I told him I found particularly offensive under the circumstances. Then I walked out.'

'So you still don't know what happened all those years ago.'

'No. And to tell you the truth I don't much care any more. If they refuse to tell us what went wrong between them it means they think it's no concern of ours. And if it's no concern of ours then there's no reason for it to ruin our lives. That's the way I see it. Of course, we'll have to go away ...'

'Josh, that's not possible,' she said firmly. 'You've got a business to run. You can't just walk away and leave it. People depend on you for their livelihood.'

'Pa could ...'

'Your father won't, Josh, and you know it. He's handed everything over to you. You can't let him down.'

He heaved a sigh. 'You're too bloody sensible by half, woman.' He drove a little way in silence, then he said, 'It doesn't stop you from leaving Dale House. If you were out of your aunt's clutches the guv'nor might see things differently.'

'No!' The vehemence in Poppy's voice made Josh start. 'No, I couldn't do that, Josh. I couldn't leave the aunts like that. They took me in and gave me a home when I had nowhere else to go so I can't just walk out on them. Anyway, they need me too much.'

'But darling, if we're going to be married – and I hope ... more than that, I assume that's what you want as much as I do – you're going to have to leave them, eventually,' Josh said, trying to sound reasonable.

'I know. I know that, Josh. But that would be different.' She bit her lip, frowning. 'The thing is, I couldn't bear to leave them under a cloud, so to speak. I need to be able to go back and keep an eye on them. They're so unworldly.'

She was silent for several minutes. Then she said, 'The truth is, they live on a shoestring. If I didn't pay the butcher's bill they'd have no meat. When I arrived, Mr and Mrs Rivers – he does the garden and she cooks and looks after them – hadn't been paid for months, so I've been giving them a little each week out of my wages.'

He was immediately concerned. 'Oh, my love. I'd no idea.' He pulled the car into the side of the road and stopped the engine. Then he sat back and ran his fingers through his hair. 'Heavens, I didn't realise your aunts were in financial difficulties. After all, Whirlowdale Road is a very well-to-do area. The houses are big ...'

'That's just it. It's not because they haven't any money. As far as I can make out they're not at all badly off, Josh.' She felt wretched, admitting all these things to him, but now she had begun she had no choice but to continue. She went on, 'At least they wouldn't be if Aunt Kate didn't persist in giving a good part of their income away every month.'

'What? Good grief! Why? Who does she give it to, for God's sake?'

She shrugged. 'To anybody and anything that will ensure that she gets her name in the newspapers, as daughter of the late benefactor, Josiah Russell.' She put on a fair impersonation of Aunt Kate's voice. 'Dear Papa's tradition of generosity must be upheld at all costs.' She resumed her own voice, 'Even if the house falls down, the servants aren't paid and the bills get left. It makes me absolutely furious but there's nothing I can do except be around to pick up the pieces.'

He wrapped her in his arms. 'Oh, my darling. I had no idea what a burden you carried.'

She struggled free. 'No, you've got it all wrong, Josh. It's not a burden. At least, I don't really consider it to be one, because I love them both dearly. But, don't you see? It means I couldn't just abandon them. Not now. Not until ...'

'Not until what?' he asked, looking at her intently.

She shook her head. 'I don't know,' she said on a sigh. 'I only know that while they live I must at least be in a position to keep an eye on them. To help them. If I left now it would be under a cloud and I would never be able to go back. I couldn't do that.'

He nodded. 'Yes, I understand.' He drummed his fingers on the steering wheel. 'If only we could find out *why* there is such animosity between the families we might be able to clear things up between them ... If only there was someone we could ask, someone who might have known them both.'

'If only,' Poppy said gloomily. Then 'Sam Beckwith!' they both said together.

'Of course. He's been with Kentons ever since I can remember,' Josh said. 'In face he once told me he came there as a boy, got married and was given one of the cottages and has been there ever since.' He nodded. 'I'll go and see him. See what he knows.'

'And I'll have another go at Mrs Rivers,' Poppy said. 'I know she wasn't at Dale House when whatever it was happened because I mentioned it to her once before, but there may be something she's forgotten.'

He picked up her hand and placed a kiss in its palm, closing her fingers over it. 'But whatever happens, Poppy, whatever anybody says, I'll never give you up. Remember that. We're together in this and somehow we've got to find a way round it.'

He dropped her off at the bottom of her road. She refused to let him take her to the door just in case either of the aunts was looking out of the window.

'Dale House. It's that house up there on the right, isn't it?' he asked before he drove off.

'That's the one. But you're not to call,' she said anxiously. 'Promise you won't call.'

'Oh, I won't. Don't worry. But I took your bike when I went to fetch the car. Remember?' He grinned. 'You'll find it leaning against the wall tomorrow morning.'

She frowned. 'There's no need. I can walk.'

'I know. But it'll give me the opportunity to examine the crumbling edifice you call home without being observed.' Without waiting for her to argue further he drove off, waving to her as he went.

Mrs Rivers decided it was time to spring-clean the parlour. The chimney sweep had been booked for six o'clock on the Saturday morning, so on Friday everything that was movable was taken out and washed or beaten half to death with the carpet beater, and everything that was left had to be swathed in dust sheets on Friday evening. The two sisters ignored what was going on round them till the last minute, then Meg began to fuss about, making a great performance of collecting up her silks and bits of material and her sewing basket, and taking them up to her room. In contrast, Kate remained in her armchair, reading, like a rock in the ocean, heedless of all the activity going on around her, until nine o'clock, when she demanded hot milk from a tired and harassed Mrs Rivers.

'I'll get it, Aunt,' Poppy said, pushing a strand of hair back under the dust cap she had put on in order to help. 'Poor Mrs Rivers is worn out.'

Kate lifted her chin. 'You know very well I dislike you doing the work of the servants, Poppy.' She inclined her head towards Mrs Rivers. 'If you please, Mrs Rivers.'

Mrs Rivers shuffled off towards the kitchen. Poppy flung down the dust sheet she had unfolded ready to cover Kate's chair – she was very tempted to throw it over Kate as well – and followed her.

'You sit in the armchair. I'll do it, Mrs R.,' she said. 'I'll heat some milk for you as well.'

'She'll not like it, lass,' Mrs Rivers said wearily.

'Then she'll have to lump it.' Poppy banged the saucepan down onto the stove. 'Sitting there like Lady Muck all

301

evening while we worked round her. She could at least have given us a hand.' She fetched mugs from the dresser. 'Never mind, I'll be up early tomorrow so that I can help you and Rivers to take down the curtains and roll up the carpet before the sweep arrives. Where is he, by the way?'

'Rivers? Oh, bless you, he's teken himself off to bed long since. We don't keep late hours. Not as a rule, any road.'

Poppy poured three mugs of milk and put one on a tray.

'Aren't you going to tek yours up to drink with her?' Mrs Rivers asked.

'No. I'm having it in comfort, down here with you. I shan't be a tick.' Poppy hurried to the parlour.

'I think I shall take it up to bed with me,' Kate said, staring round the cold, comfortless room.

'I should think that's a very good idea, Aunt,' Poppy said cheerfully. 'I wonder you didn't go to bed hours ago.'

Kate gave her a condescending smile. 'You'll learn one day, child, that it is never wise to leave servants alone with one's treasured possessions. They are not to be trusted.'

Poppy gritted her teeth. 'What a wicked thing to say, Aunt! You should be ashamed to even think such a thing of poor Mrs Rivers.' She went out, slamming the door behind her, and hurried back to the warmth of the kitchen.

Mrs Rivers was half asleep, her mug perched on the arm of her chair. Poppy felt a rush of affection for the old lady, who for years had worked her fingers to the bone for the ungrateful Russells.

She sat down at the table, her mug of milk cupped in her hands. 'I've got a secret to tell you, Mrs R.,' she said, her eyes dancing.

The old lady's eyes shot open. 'A secret?'

'Yes. I've got a young man.'

A warm smile spread across Mrs Rivers's tired, lined face. 'Ee, love, I'm that pleased. Who is he? Do we know him?'

'His name is Josh Kenton.'

302

The smile broadened. 'The Gaffer's son?'

Poppy smiled back. 'I suppose you might say the Gaffer himself, since Sir Frederick doesn't come to work any more.'

'Ee, well, lass, you've done all right for yourself, haven't you?' Mrs Rivers said, delighted.

Poppy blushed. 'I wouldn't care if he was a crossing sweeper, Mrs Rivers. He's a lovely man.'

'Aye, I believe you, lass. You're not one to have your head turned by wealth. What do them up there say?' She jerked her head in the direction of the parlour.

'They're not happy. At least, Aunt Kate isn't. Aunt Meg's delighted but she's muddled. As usual.'

'Why isn't she happy about it?'

'Because of that business all those years ago. Can you remember anything about Aunt Kate's engagement to Sir Frederick, Mrs Rivers?'

Mrs Rivers shook her head. 'As I told you before, it were long enough before my time here, lass,' she said, shaking her head.

'I know. But didn't the other servants talk about it at all?' Poppy put her mug down. 'You see, both Aunt Kate and Sir Frederick are making things difficult for us. Oh, I know their engagement was broken off but that was ages ago, before either Josh or I were born. Surely, after all these years ...' She shook her head. 'I just don't understand ... I wondered if you might be able to think ...' She shrugged. 'Just a thought.'

Mrs Rivers finished her milk and smacked her lips. 'That were good.' She put down her mug. 'I only know what I've told you before, love,' she said, shaking her head. 'The engagement got broken off and the young man married someone else. I expect that was the cause of it, he'd met someone he liked better.'

Poppy nodded. 'That's what it sounds like. But you would have thought they could have forgiven and forgotten after all this time.'

303

'Aye, you would.' Mrs Rivers frowned. 'I don't know whether it was about that time that Miss Meg was ill. If it was, mebbe Miss Kate wouldn't leave her and the young man wouldn't wait ... found somebody else, and that was that.'

'I suppose that could account for the way Aunt Kate treats Aunt Meg.' Poppy nodded slowly. 'The way she doses her up with all those pills. I'm sure they're not necessary.'

'Well, she does have these funny turns.'

'Have you ever seen her in one?'

'Well, no. But I've heard the way she bangs away on that piano. That can't be natural.'

Poppy carried the mugs over to the sink and rinsed them. 'I just wish I could find out what happened. After all this time it couldn't hurt to talk about it.'

'Ah, but that means it's had years to fester,' Mrs Rivers said sagely. 'If the lid pops off there could be an explosion. Best to let sleeping dogs lie, in my opinion.'

'It doesn't help Josh and me though, does it?' Poppy said sadly.

Chapter Twenty-Nine

On Saturday Poppy had a frantically busy day helping Mrs Rivers. After the chimney sweep had left they swept walls, washed paint, beat carpets and polished furniture.

Aunt Kate took no part in this. To begin with, she demanded breakfast in bed. Poppy took this to her; it was the first time she had been into Kate's bedroom and she was surprised at the stark bareness of it. Not for Kate the frilly doilies and fussy ornaments that Meg so loved: there was a single bed, a large ugly wardrobe, a chest of drawers and a bedside table on which stood a candlestick and an ashtray. A plain wooden chair stood under the window and a dark blue rug did service as a hearthrug and a bedside rug, but was not really adequate for either. There was nothing else, not even a picture on the wall, in spite of the fact that it was a large room. Poppy noticed that her footsteps echoed as she walked across the floorboards.

'Thank you,' Kate said. She was fully dressed and her bed was made. 'I shall stay here until the parlour is fit for me to use again.'

'I'm afraid that won't be until this afternoon, Aunt,' Poppy warned.

'Then I shall take my lunch here.'

In contrast, Meg came downstairs and flitted about – if a dumpy little woman could be said to flit – trying desperately to help and only succeeding in getting in the way.

Finally, Poppy suggested that it would be nice to have some music as they worked if Aunt Meg would be kind enough to play for them. Meg was delighted – nobody asked her to play the piano as a rule – and before long the strains of a Chopin mazurka and then a Brahms waltz came wafting through from the drawing room. Poppy stopped polishing to listen. Aunt Meg was very talented – it was a pity her sister didn't seem to appreciate this.

It was late afternoon before the room was back to normal and Kate made her entrance downstairs.

Meg was still going round, touching things, admiring the sheen on the furniture, moving an ornament a fraction, straightening a picture. 'It all looks very nice now, doesn't it, Kate?' she said excitedly. 'And it smells lovely, too. I love the smell of polish.'

Kate said nothing. She went straight to the cupboard by the side of the fire.

'Oh, no!' Meg protested, her happy expression crumbling into dismay.

'Oh, yes,' Kate said firmly. 'You haven't had your pill today. I know you haven't. You never remember to take if I don't think of it. A glass of water, if you please, Poppy.'

'And you're never likely to forget,' Poppy heard Meg say miserably as she did as her aunt commanded.

When Poppy returned Kate was pulling out drawers and peering into cupboards. 'I hope nothing has been disturbed,' she said. 'I hope nobody has been poking about in my things.'

'We've been far too busy getting the place back to normal to concern ourselves with what you keep in your cupboards and drawers,' Poppy said, holding onto her temper with difficulty. 'That's something you can do, Aunt. You can clear out all the rubbish. I'm sure there's plenty that could be disposed of.'

Kate shot her a glance. 'How do you know that if you haven't been prying?'

'Oh, Aunt Kate, don't be so suspicious!' Poppy snapped.

'Anyone would think you had some dark secret to hide.'

'I keep everything in order. I know where everything is,' Kate said haughtily.

'Well, then, you'll be able to see at a glance that nothing has been disturbed,' Poppy said, putting an end to the conversation. 'I'll go and make a cup of tea.' Really, sometimes Aunt Kate was enough to try the patience of a saint.

But Poppy had little time to worry about her aunt's idiosyncrasies, being far too concerned with her own affairs. Both she and Josh had quickly realised that they were trapped in a situation not of their making but out of which there seemed to be no escape. Sir Frederick continued to refuse to entertain Poppy, in spite of his former regard for her, and Poppy dared not even mention Josh's name to Aunt Kate. Aunt Meg, blissfully unaware of the tension, occasionally asked innocently when Poppy would be bringing Mr Cole's son to meet them. It would have been almost funny if it were not so infuriating.

'Have you managed to see Sam Beckwith yet, Josh?' Poppy asked when he had finished dictating letters one morning, about a fortnight after their visit to Higger Tor.

'Yes, I was going to tell you. I saw him last night after work.' He turned his mouth down. 'Not very helpful, I'm afraid.'

'Oh, dear. What did he say?'

Josh smiled. 'Well, he talked a lot – you know what Sam is for a gossip – but it was quite a long time before he actually said anything.'

She leaned forward. 'Go on.'

'He remembered, of course. It was something of a nine days' wonder at the time apparently. He said that after the announcement of the engagement was called off, Pa – Freddie, as he used to call him then – went about with a face like a wet week for a bit, then upped and married a lass from Rotherham. My mother, of course.'

Poppy digested this, then she frowned. 'So the lass from

307

Rotherham couldn't have been the cause of the broken engagement.'

'Doesn't seem like it.' Josh was quiet for several minutes. Then he said, 'Old Josiah Russell was a bit of a tartar to his daughters, from what Sam said. According to Sam "The Old Man", as he called him, ruled them with a rod of iron. Perhaps *he* was the one who broke things up.'

Poppy nodded slowly. 'That might well be the case. Kate told me that she used to practically run the household after her mother died. In fact, she was very proud of this. If that was the case Josiah wouldn't want to lose his unpaid house-keeper, would he?' She shook her head, puzzled. 'But I really can't see, if Josiah was the cause of the break-up, why it should still cause such acrimony between my aunt and your father. Not after all these years.'

'No, darling. Neither can I.' Josh came round the desk and pulled her to her feet. 'But let's not worry about it right now.' He bent his head to kiss her.

'Not in office hours, Josh, please,' she murmured, her actions belying her words as she wound her arms round his neck and responded with enthusiasm.

As usual, Poppy took her lunchtime sandwiches over to the manager's house. Maud and Jake had settled happily into their new home and Jake was coping well with his new job. All the wives had been friends for such a long time that there were no tensions over Maud's new status as manager's wife, and she continued to welcome them into her kitchen as she had always done. Over the years it had become something of a club, providing tea and a gossip, a break from the day-to-day chores. Now Connie Templeton had become a part of it too, after her years of lonely isol-ation, and once she had overcome her initial shyness and awkwardness it was obvious she looked forward to the daily meeting as much as any of them.

They were all sitting round the table when Poppy arrived.

'Come in, love. You're a bit late today. Tea's already mashed,' Maud said, pouring milk into the cup placed ready for her.

'Mr Josh came to see me dad last night,' Daisy said, moving up to make room for Poppy. 'He's a nice young man, isn't he. And he's teken to his dad's business like a duck to water. Sir Frederick must be proud of him.' She took a noisy slurp of her tea.

'Aye. He's looked after my Jake, an' all, with him being new to the manager's job,' Maud agreed. 'Spent no end of time showing him the ropes, he has.'

'He's a real gentleman,' Florrie said. 'He must have been to see Harry Smithers five or six times and Mary says it does Harry more good than anything when he calls. Mr Josh is even talking of finding him a job in the packing department when he's fit. Mary says that's given Harry a real boost.'

Lily Ferris gave Poppy a wink. 'You want to snap him up, lass, sounds like he's worth having. Time you were wed, any road, pretty lass like you.'

Poppy lifted her cup to hid her blushes. 'I'm quite happy with things as they are at the moment, Lily,' she said ambiguously.

'Well, you want to think on before it's too late, and somebody else has got his feet under their table,' Lily warned.

'Oh, give over teasing the lass, Lil,' Maud said, joining in the laughter her words had caused.

Poppy looked round. 'Where's Charity?' she asked, anxious to change the subject. 'I haven't seen her lately. Is she ill?'

'No, I don't think so,' Maud said, looking rather uncomfortable.

'I think she's afraid little Rebecca might do some damage in Maud's new house,' Lily said, a bit too loudly.

'Oh, I'm sure that's not ...' Maud began, then changed her mind. 'I told her it was all right,' she finished lamely.

Poppy finished her sandwiches and folded up the napkin they had been wrapped in. Then she got to her feet. 'I must be going. I've a lot of work to get through before I leave tonight,' she said. 'Thanks for the tea, Maud.'

'That's all right, love. It's good to see you.' Maud came to the door with her. 'I wish you'd drop in at Charity's,' she whispered. 'Maybe you can make her see sense.'

Perplexed, Poppy went straight across the yard and knocked at Charity's door.

The girl was busily kneading dough at the table, whilst Rebecca played with her rag doll on the step. She wiped her floury hands on a large, spotlessly white apron when she saw Poppy.

'Ee, come in, Miss Barlow. Can I pour you a cup of tea? I've not long mashed.' A broad smile wreathed her face.

'No, thank you, Charity. I've just had a cup with the others. I missed you. We all did.'

'Oh.' The smile faded and Charity's face seemed to close up.

Poppy stepped inside the house. 'To tell you the truth that's why I've called. To see what's wrong. Why don't you join them any more? Is it because Maud's husband is the manager now?'

Charity was still twisting her hands in her apron. 'Yes. Well, no. Well, partly, I suppose,' she said, looking everywhere but at Poppy. 'After all, Mrs Benson has a position to keep up. We shouldn't treat her as if she was still like us, should we?'

'I don't see why not, Charity, since Maud herself has managed to bridge the gap so well. She's never tried to put on airs and graces, she welcomes her old friends just as she always did. I don't think you're being very fair to her. Or kind. I believe she would be quite hurt to know you regarded her in that light,' Poppy said firmly.

Charity flushed. 'It's not just that, Miss Barlow,' she admitted.

'Then what is it?' Poppy asked with a frown.

For a moment Charity hesitated, biting her lip. Then she said with a rush, 'It's Mrs Templeton. They call her Connie now, of course. She's living with Mr Earnshaw at number five. But you knew that, didn't you?'

'I knew she had decided to keep house for her brother-in-law. Yes.'

'Not just to keep house. The others ...' Charity jerked her head in the direction of the manager's house, 'they say she's *living* with him. You know what I mean, *living* with him.' Each time she said the word *living* she nodded meaningfully. She lifted her chin and said sanctimoniously, 'My Mord says it's not right that I should have anything to do with a woman who's living in sin with a man.'

Poppy sat down on the nearest chair. So that was the problem. 'Are you sure what you're saying is true, Charity?' she asked gently after a moment's thought.

'What do you mean?' Charity looked blank.

'I mean, how do you know Connie Templeton is living in sin with Jack Earnshaw?'

'Because the others said ...'

'And how do they know? Has Connie told them?'

'Well, no. Not as I know of. But everyone knows how fond Jack is of her,' Charity said uncomfortably.

'That doesn't mean they're living in sin, does it? In fact, it could mean quite the opposite of what you're suggesting. It could mean that he simply wants to look after her and protect her. After all, she's had a pretty rough time of it up to now, hasn't she?'

Charity nodded thoughtfully.

Poppy went on. 'So what it amount to is that the wives have put two and two together and made half a dozen and decided that if – and I stress *if* – Jack has taken her into his bed then good luck to them both, Jack's been on his own for a long time now and Connie deserves a little happiness in her life. And what you've done is to listen to their idle gossip and taken it to heart, condemning both Jack and Connie. That's not very Christian, is it?'

311

Charity hunched her shoulders.

'Well, I don't know what it says in the bible about listening to gossip but I think there's something about he who is without sin casting the first stone,' Poppy said, mentally thanking Aunt Kate for the quote. She smiled at Charity. 'I think you're being a bit silly, you know. You're depriving yourself of the company of several good women because of what you *think* Connie might be doing. But you've absolutely no proof, have you?'

Charity shook her head. 'Only what the others said.'

'That's not proof. That's wishful thinking on their part,' Poppy said with a smile.

Charity was quiet for several minutes. 'I have missed the company,' she admitted.

'They've missed you, too,' Poppy told her. 'Why don't you come across tomorrow?'

'I'd quite like to,' Charity said uncertainly. 'If Mord says it's all right, I really would.' She paused. 'I suppose really, I'm the one who's sinned, listening to gossip and believing it without any proof.'

'Well, I'm sure that's easily remedied. In future, just take what you hear round Maud's table with a pinch of salt and live up to your name. Show a little Christian charity.' Poppy got up from her chair. 'Come over tomorrow. I know the wives will be pleased to see you again. They've missed you.'

She left her then and went back to her office, feeling suddenly tired and drained from the effort of soothing Charity's conscience. In truth, she was fairly sure that by this time Jack would have taken Connie to his bed and she couldn't find it in her heart to do other than wish them the happiness they deserved. But she knew it wouldn't be prudent to admit as much to Charity.

Back in the office she opened all the windows to let in a little air, leaning on the windowsill and looking out over the busy, noisy yard below. Mord Jones was sitting on his swinging seat flattening steel under the huge tilt hammer,

312

the reverberations from it sending shudders right through the yard, Charlie Braithwaite was sweating at his forge and even from this distance she could see the white-hot glow from the crucibles. If she was feeling stifled they must be feeling it even more, she thought sympathetically. No wonder some of them drank too much. She looked up at the sky. It seemed to hang over the city like a heavy, oppressive blanket. What was needed was a good storm to clear the air.

It came. But not until the middle of the night.

Poppy woke from a deep sleep to a roar that at first she couldn't recognise. She sat up in bed, terrified for a moment that the house was collapsing round her ears, then sanity prevailed as she realised that what she could hear was rain: rain such as she had never in her life experienced before. Rain that hurled itself at the windows and drummed on the roof; rain that even drowned the sound of the thunder that crashed and rolled round the heavens as the lightning streaked and danced crazily across the sky.

Suddenly, she heard a scream and then there was banging at her door.

'Let me in. Let me in.' It was Aunt Meg's frantic voice.

Poppy got out of bed and dragged on her dressing gown. Outside the door Meg was cowering on the floor, a whimpering jelly.

'I can't bear thunderstorms,' she sobbed, her teeth chattering as she huddled there in her faded pink dressing gown, a little mob cap perched crookedly on her white curls. 'I can't go to Kate, she says I'm stupid but I can't help it. Can I come in with you, Poppy?'

Poppy helped her to her feet. 'We'll do better than that, dear. I'll take you downstairs and we'll have some cocoa,' she said as if talking to a child. 'Would you like that?'

'Yes. Yes, I would.' Meg clutched her. 'But don't leave me. I'm so frightened.'

'No, I won't leave you. We'll go down to the kitchen together. Come along.'

Poppy kept her arm round the terrified little woman as they made their way down the stairs and along to the kitchen. Every few steps a flash of lightning lit up the hall with a streak of blue light, eerily illuminating old Josiah in his heavy frame, accompanied by the inevitable crash of thunder. And all the time the rain was beating relentlessly down. Poppy could never remember a storm like it.

In the kitchen she lit the oil lamp and riddled the dying embers of the fire into life again, talking all the while to comfort poor frightened Meg. Then she made the cocoa and they sat down at the table to drink it. With the combination of the warm, milky drink and the sounds of the storm receding the colour gradually returned to Meg's face and she began to relax a little. As she relaxed she began to talk.

'I expect you think I'm silly. I know Kate does, but I can't help it. I've always been terrified of thunderstorms.' She took a sip of her drink. 'Kate's always been the strong one, of course, but I was Papa's favourite. Kate didn't like that. She was always trying to get me into trouble so that Papa would like her best.' She stirred her cocoa before drinking some more. Poppy said nothing. If talking was helping to take her mind off the storm she was prepared to let Meg ramble on. 'Kate was always jealous of me. Always wanted what I'd got. She used to take my dolls, even though she didn't really like dolls.' She smiled up at Poppy, a sad little smile. 'But I shouldn't say these things, should I. Kate's been very good to me. She looks after me. She says I would be dead if it wasn't for her. That's why I have to take my pills, although ...'

Suddenly, the door crashed open and Kate stood there in a grey check dressing gown, her hair hanging in a long iron-coloured pigtail over one shoulder, holding a candlestick.

'What are you doing sitting in the kitchen, wasting oil and coal in the middle of the night?' she demanded.

'I was frightened,' Meg said nervously. 'You know I don't like thunderstorms, Kate. Poppy made us some cocoa.'

'It was a very bad storm, Aunt Kate,' Poppy said. 'To tell you the truth I felt a little nervous myself. I was glad of Aunt Meg's company.'

'Well, it's over now so you can both go back to bed. And don't let me find either of you in the kitchen again. Kitchens are for servants.' She stood aside for Meg to pass.

Meg stopped when she reached her. 'Why are you wearing Papa's dressing gown, Kate?' she asked, fingering the cord.

'I'm not. Don't be absurd. This is my dressing gown,' Kate said, clearly annoyed.

'It's Papa's. Look, there's the spot where he burnt it with his cigar.' Meg pointed to a small brown hole.

Kate looked and when she realised that further denial was useless said, 'Yes. Well, mine wore out and it would have been wasteful to buy another when this one was hanging in the wardrobe.'

'Mama's hangs there, too,' Meg said. 'It's a pretty blue one. Why didn't you take that?' She smiled, a secret little smile. 'But it wouldn't have been the same, would it, Kate?' She lifted her head and marched past her sister.

'Oh, go on up to bed. The storm has affected your mind,' Kate said irritably. 'Don't forget to put out the lamp,' she said over her shoulder to Poppy as she hustled Meg along the passage to the hall and up the stairs.

Poppy followed. Old Josiah was in darkness now, yet his shadow was always there and she could feel his eyes watching her as she went up the stairs. She shivered, annoyed with herself for being so fanciful.

315

Chapter Thirty

Poppy woke early and went over and flung open the curtains. It was a beautiful morning. Everywhere looked fresh and green, the sun seemed to be shining extra brightly to make up for last night's storm, bathing everything in a warm, hazy light, heralding a hot day. Even the raindrops that still clung to the trees and bushes sparkled like diamonds in the sunshine.

She turned back into the room and was suddenly shocked to notice a large damp patch on the ceiling. She sat down on the bed and stared up at it. Obviously, the roof had leaked into the attic above her room and the rain had seeped through the floor onto her ceiling. Her heart sank as she envisaged the battle that would ensue with Aunt Kate over getting it mended. She pursed her lips. Well, Aunt Kate would just have to pay up. A leak like this couldn't be ignored, it would have to be repaired immediately. For once Aunt Kate's charity must begin at home.

Resolutely, she put on her oldest clothes to go up and find out the extent of the damage before confronting her aunt.

She went down the passage from her room, glancing into the bedrooms along the way to make sure there was no rain damage in them, and up the back stairs to the attics. At the top of the stairs the Rivers's bedroom door stood open, the bed neatly made and the room immaculate. No rain through the roof there. The other attics appeared dry, too. Apparently it was just the one situated above her room that had leaked. Predictably, it was the one that was locked. And there was no key. She looked at her watch. A quarter to eight. Too early to disturb Aunt Kate. She frowned. Then she remembered that the key to the drawer where Aunt Kate kept her account books was on quite a large bunch. Perhaps one of those would fit. She hurried downstairs to the parlour, hunting through drawers until she found them, then went back upstairs. At the third try she found a key to more or less fit and with a bit of jiggling in the keyhole it opened the door.

The room was absolutely crammed with rubbish: old packing cases, suitcases, cardboard boxes full of junk, an old rocking horse, a doll's pram, a chest of drawers that had once been painted bright blue, rolls of lino, folded-up carpets, a washstand in the corner, complete with ewer and bowl so ingrained with dust that it was difficult to see the pattern, and a wardrobe with the door missing. She heaved a sigh and blew out her cheeks. Oh, why couldn't the roof have leaked over one of the empty rooms! She glanced up at the ceiling. The plaster still held but it was sagging badly and there was still a steady drip of water onto the floor between the sodden rocking horse and the saturated cardboard boxes stacked near. She looked round in despair, then noticed a pile of old curtains and blankets inside the wardrobe. Those blankets would at least soak up some of the wet.

She began to clamber over the boxes and chests to get to the wardrobe, very conscious that if she fell and hurt herself nobody would hear her call. Scraping her leg on the corner of a tea chest on the way, she reached her goal and began to drag out the curtains to get to the blankets. There were some quite respectable-looking velvet curtains, and some in a rich brocade, many of them appearing to be in better condition than the ones that hung at the windows downstairs. She made a mental note to come up and look at them more carefully when this crisis was over. But at the moment, balanced as she was on an old chair with a broken back, it was the blankets she was interested in to mop up the worst of the water. Naturally, because she was in a hurry, they were at the bottom. She tugged and pulled to get at a particularly thick one, making the wardrobe, which she discovered too late had one foot missing, rock precariously. This dislodged a heap of boxes piled on top of it and they fell down round her ears in a cloud of filthy dust.

'Oh, sod it!' Her father's favourite expletive escaped as Poppy fell off the chair, coughing and spluttering, knocked sideways by a leather hat box that had landed at her feet. She brushed her hair out of her eyes and kicked at the box furiously, causing the lid to come off.

'That was your fault!' she said crossly, getting to her feet and looking inside it.

Then she sat down on the chair and stared, her mouth dropping open in horrified shock. She peered more closely, certain she must be mistaken. But there was no mistake. What she was looking at in the hat box was the carefully wrapped mummified remains of a newborn baby.

She stared round the cluttered attic, swallowing painfully, her brain racing. Maids' rooms. It was quite obvious what had happened. One of the maids must have become pregnant – but by whom? The gardener? The son of the house? No, surely not. That would have been her own father. No that wasn't possible. The master of the house, then? Old Josiah? The father Aunt Kate had been so devoted to? These things were known to happen. She recalled Josiah's cold eyes. She couldn't imagine ... Yet he was a man, like other men. She shuddered at the thought.

She got shakily to her feet, the leaking roof forgotten, and picked up the hat box. Now she knew of its existence she couldn't leave it here. Something would have to be done about it. She replaced the lid and wiped the dust off it with her sleeve, then carried it carefully down the back stairs to her bedroom.

But before she reached her bedroom door she met Aunt Kate coming up the main staircase.

'You're very late for breakfast, Poppy. I was just coming to see if you were ill,' she said, her voice full of annoyance. 'Do you know what the time is? It's past nine o'clock.' She peered at Poppy in the dim light. 'Goodness me, you're covered in dust. Where have you been?' Suddenly, she realised what Poppy was holding and her voice rose to a near shriek. 'What have you got there?' Before the girl could answer, Kate took her by the arm and with a strength she didn't look capable of, almost threw her into her bedroom and, following her, closed the door and leaned heavily against it.

Poppy sat down on her bed, still clutching the hat box. She realised her teeth were chattering. 'Do you know what's in this box, Aunt Kate?' she managed to stutter.

'Of course I do,' Kate said impatiently. 'Who do you think put it there?'

Poppy gaped at her, her senses reeling. 'You! It's your baby?' she said, her voice coming out as little more than a squeak.

'No, certainly not. I would never have ...' She pursed her lips and shuddered in disgust.

'You helped one of the maids?' Poppy still couldn't believe what was happening.

Kate began to pace about the room. 'Don't be stupid. I wouldn't have lifted a finger for one of the maids.'

Poppy swallowed. 'Then whose baby is ... was it?' She realised she was still clutching the hat box and now she put it carefully down beside her on the bed.

Kate glanced at it briefly. 'Why, Meg's, of course,' she said.

'Aunt Meg's! Aunt Meg had a baby!' Poppy's mouth fell open in astonishment.

'Oh, for goodness sake pull yourself together and stop

319

gaping like a fish,' Kate snapped, still pacing up and down the room. 'You'd never have found it if you hadn't gone poking your nose in where it wasn't wanted. Why did you go up there?'

Poppy pointed to the ceiling. She was beyond speaking.

Kate barely glanced at it. 'Oh, that. I suppose a few roof tiles have come off, that's all.'

Poppy took a deep breath. 'I think you owe me an explanation, Aunt Kate,' she said, trying to keep the wobble out of her voice.

Kate stopped her pacing and looked at her. Then she nodded. 'Yes. I suppose I do.' She frowned at Poppy's ashen face. 'But I think you'd better have a cup of tea first. You're looking a bit peaky.'

'It's hardly surprising, under the circumstances,' Poppy said weakly.

'No, of course it isn't,' Kate said briskly. 'Wait here. I'll go and fetch you some breakfast. I'll tell Meg you're not feeling well.'

'And that won't be a lie,' Poppy said, passing a grubby hand across her forehead.

'Well, go and wash your face and put some respectable clothes on while I'm gone. It'll make you feel better,' Kate suggested, not unkindly.

In a daze Poppy did as her aunt suggested, her mind reeling with questions about what Kate had said and amazement at her matter-of-fact acceptance of the bizarre situation. She had just finished brushing the dust out of her hair when Kate returned with a pot of tea, two cups and a pile of buttered toast.

'Oh, I couldn't eat a thing,' Poppy protested, sitting down on her bed and fastening her slide.

'Nonsense.' Kate poured the tea and handed her a plate with a slice of toast on it. Poppy took it, still in something of a daze.

Kate sat down in the armchair beside the empty fireplace and munched toast for a few minutes while Poppy gratefully sipped her tea. 'Now where to begin,' she said thoughtfully.

'At the beginning, I should think,' Poppy said, absent-mindedly taking a bite of toast and discovering that in spite of everything she was very hungry.

Kate sniffed. 'Well, of course, it all began with Freddie Kenton. He and I were to be married. But I've already told you that.'

Poppy nodded. 'Yes. That was why you were so against me going to work at Kentons.'

'And with good reason,' Kate said curtly. 'You see, what I hadn't known was that all the time Freddie was supposed to be courting me he was secretly meeting my sister Meg behind my back.'

'Oh, Aunt Kate! How awful for you,' Poppy said, shocked.

Kate shrugged. 'Meg was much prettier than me, I knew that, but Papa seemed to think Freddie would be a good match for me – I suppose he thought I wouldn't get many chances to catch a husband. To tell you the truth, I didn't particularly want to get married at all, I was quite happy running the household and looking after Papa, and I certainly had no wish to go through the business of having children, but it was what Papa thought best so naturally I agreed.'

'So what happened?' Without taking her eyes off Kate's face Poppy drained her teacup and held it out for more.

Kate poured more tea before she answered. 'There was a party – indeed, it was at the party that my engagement to Freddie was to be announced. It was to be a surprise climax to the evening. I remember thinking before the party began that Meg seemed rather over-excited, she looked extremely pretty, her face was flushed and yet she seemed rather nervous for some reason, I couldn't think why. After all, I was the one who should have been excited, it was to be my surprise announcement.'

'Well, weren't you?' Poppy asked.

Kate thought for a minute. 'No, not particularly. You

see, it was not really my choice. In truth, it wasn't my idea to get married at all. I was doing what Papa wanted. Oh, Freddie was a very presentable young man and I would have done my best to make him a good wife, I'm sure.' She wiped buttery fingers on her napkin. 'I quite liked him, I suppose.' She paused and dabbed at her mouth. 'Well, I went outside for a breath of fresh air ...'

'By yourself?'

'Of course I went by myself.' Kate looked surprised. 'To tell you the truth I'd missed Meg and I wondered if she was up to something, I'd no idea what, but she was full of pranks and tricks and I didn't want her to do anything stupid that would spoil things for Papa. I didn't find her, but I found her valise hidden under a bush just inside the side entrance. Obviously she was intending to run away. I couldn't think why.'

'So what did you do?'

'I took the bag back into the house and immediately told Papa. When Meg realised her plan had been thwarted she made the most frightful scene. Papa bundled her into his study and locked the door and I found Freddie in the library trying to listen to what was going on through the keyhole. It was then that he told me that he and Meg had planned to elope to Gretna Green that very night because he couldn't face going through the charade of becoming engaged to me when he and Meg were so much in love. He said he was sorry, he didn't want to hurt me, but he had always known that I didn't really love him, which was true enough.' With great deliberation she poured herself more tea, a small, self-satisfied smile on her face. 'While he was telling me all this Papa was giving Meg the thrashing of her life, which nearly drove Freddie wild, I can tell you. Then Meg was hustled upstairs and locked in her room and Freddie Kenton was sent away without being allowed to speak to her. We never saw him again.'

'But what about the party?'

'It went ahead as planned, but of course no engagement

was announced. Meg's absence was said to be due to a bad headache and Freddie was hardly missed at all.' She preened slightly. 'Papa told me afterwards he was proud of the way I had behaved throughout the evening, when I must have been so broken-hearted.' She drank some tea. 'I wasn't. Not really. More relieved than anything, I suppose, because it meant that I could stay at home and look after Papa as I had always done.' She treated Poppy to her tight little smile.

'But what about Aunt Meg?'

'Ah, yes. Meg.' She shook her head. 'She was quite ill. I really think she must have been very fond of the young man because she took it very badly. She wouldn't, or couldn't eat, and was constantly sick.' She glanced up at the ceiling. 'Oh yes, we shall have to get something done about that roof,' she mused. She put her cup into its saucer with a clatter. 'It wasn't until she started putting on weight that I began to suspect what was wrong with her.' She turned bright, hard eyes on Poppy. 'She, of course, had no idea. She had no idea where babies came from nor how they began.' She gave a distasteful shudder. 'I had to prise out of her what she had been up to. "We proved our love for each other in the summer house," was how she put it. Then, of course, I knew for certain.'

'Poor Aunt Meg,' Poppy breathed.

'Poor Aunt Meg!' Kate's eyebrows nearly disappeared into her hair. 'The stupid little idiot was overjoyed. Thought she would be able to marry Freddie after all and everything would be all right. I soon disabused her of *that* fairy tale!' She became more animated. 'But I knew the most important thing was not to upset Papa, it would have been a disaster for him to know that one of his unmarried daughters was to have a child. Clearly, the responsibility rested on my shoulders and I had to think what best to do.' She leaned back complacently. 'In the end it proved quite easy. I simply kept her in her room and never let her out of it. I told everybody she was very ill and that I would nurse her myself. Which I did.'

'So that was what her illness was,' Poppy said as awareness dawned.

'Yes. That's what her illness was. The night the child was born I was alone with her but I knew what to do because I'd read it all up in nursing books. It wasn't a difficult birth – at least she didn't make a lot of fuss. Fortunately, the child was stillborn, which was a great relief.'

Poppy licked her lips, which were suddenly very dry. 'And if it hadn't been?'

'What? Stillborn? I would have smothered it, of course. After all the trouble I'd taken what else could I have done?' Kate sounded surprised she had even asked. She continued, 'Then I put it in the hat box and smuggled it up to the attic.'

'Why didn't you bury it?' Poppy whispered.

'It was winter. The ground was frosty. Then, as time went on, it didn't seem important. After a while I forgot it was there.'

'Aunt Kate, that was a wicked thing to do.' Poppy still couldn't manage to speak above a whisper.

Kate reared up in her seat. 'Wicked! Wicked! How dare you say I was wicked! I think I handled the whole business extremely well. Nobody except Meg knew what was happening, not even the servants. And most important, I kept Papa in ignorance of the whole sordid affair. He couldn't bear illness so it wasn't difficult to keep him out of Meg's sickroom.' She gave a little secret smile. 'Although sometimes I felt almost tempted to take him in and show him what a little slut his beautiful Meg had turned out to be.'

'I wonder you didn't delight in doing that,' Poppy said caustically.

She shook her head. 'I thought about it. But he might have turned on me. I couldn't have borne that. In any case, I never liked to see dear Papa upset. I always wanted him to be happy. It was my life's aim to make him happy.' She nodded contentedly. 'I believe I succeeded.'

'But what about Meg? After ... after the baby ...'

'She was very upset. I called the doctor in. Oh, not our usual doctor, of course, but one from the other side of the city. I said she had had a nervous breakdown so he gave me some pills for her.' Again the secret little smile. This time it sent a shiver down Poppy's spine. 'I've been giving them to her ever since.'

'But it was nearly thirty years ago that all this happened. She can't still be under that doctor.' Poppy exploded.

'No. He told me where I could get the pills made up. The chemist delivers them. It's quite easy.'

'It's wicked. She doesn't need them. I'm sure she doesn't need them.'

Kate shrugged. 'You haven't seen her in one of her real tantrums. She could do herself harm, or get taken off to Lodge Moor. In any case, she couldn't do without them now.'

'I don't believe it.' Poppy was silent for a while, digesting the horror of all she had heard. Suddenly, Kate spoke again.

'What have you done with it?'

'Done with what?' Poppy said, startled.

'The hat box.'

'I put it under the bed. I couldn't bear ...'

Kate smiled. 'That's all right, dear. I'll take it.' She got up from her chair and pulled the hat box from under the bed.

Poppy licked her lips. 'What are you going to do with it? Are you going to take it to the police?'

'Why on earth should I do that?' Kate looked astonished. 'No. Don't worry about it, Poppy. It's my responsibility and I shall deal with it as I think fit.'

'But ...'

Kate had reached the door, the hat box in her hands. she turned. 'There are no "buts", Poppy. I have told you I shall deal with the matter. Let that be an end of it. I would advise you to forget the conversation we have had here this morning. Put it right out of your mind. Naturally, I would never have told you if I hadn't been forced to.' She smiled, her tight little smile. 'Now, I suggest you take the breakfast tray down to Mrs Rivers. You're obviously feeling more yourself.'

Poppy dragged her hand across her brow. 'I'm late. I must get ready for work.'

'Work! You're thinking of going back to that place! Not after all I've told you!' Kate quivered with indignation.

'But you told me to forget it, Aunt Kate,' Poppy said, spreading her hands. 'What better way than to carry on as normal?'

Not that anything would ever be 'normal' again. But she needed to get out of the house, to clear her thoughts, to come to terms with the morning's revelations. For one thing, she wasn't sure she was ready to face Aunt Meg yet in the light of her new knowledge. It was almost impossible to imagine the vague, fussy, dumpy little woman sitting with her patchwork as a young passionate girl, bearing the child of her lover.

More than anything she needed to talk to Josh. She needed his support; she needed to share the awful discovery of the contents of the hat box with him. Because the dead child had belonged to his father too, and its fate must not be left in Aunt Kate's hands.

Chapter Thirty-One

Poppy arrived at work nearly two hours late. She hung up her coat and hat and went through to Josh's office. Fortunately, he was there and alone.

'I'm sorry I'm late, Josh . . .' she began.

He looked up and immediately came round and took her in his arms. 'Poppy, darling, whatever's wrong? You look terrible. Are you ill? You shouldn't have come in . . .'

She leaned against him, so relieved at the comfort of his arms round her that she burst into tears.

He held her quietly, stroking her hair and whispering that it was all right, everything was all right, while his mind raced, trying to imagine what could possibly have upset his darling girl so much.

When she was calm enough for him to release her he sat her down and went over to his father's cabinet and poured her a glass of brandy.

'Now drink this, darling. Then you can tell me what's wrong,' he said gently, pulling up a chair beside her so that he could hold the glass because her hands were shaking too much to take it.

Gradually, between sips of brandy that brought a little colour back into her cheeks and further bursts of tears, she told him the whole dreadful story, every last detail, sparing nothing. When she had finished she was calmer.

She scrubbed at her face with a sodden handkerchief.

'I'm sorry to burden you with all this, Josh,' she said, her face beginning to crumple again. 'But it's all so awful. That poor little baby ... poor Aunt Meg ...'

Gently, he mopped her face with his own white handkerchief, then gave it to her. 'It's my burden too, Poppy,' he said quietly. 'It was my father's baby, remember.' He kissed her gently. 'We're in this together, darling.' He smiled ruefully. 'At least we can now understand why your Aunt Kate was so horrified at you coming here to work.'

She nodded. 'I'm surprised she didn't turn me out of the house when I refused to give up my job.'

'She must be very fond of you, Poppy.'

They were both quiet for some time, then Josh said thoughtfully, 'I wonder if the guv'nor knew Meg was carrying his baby.'

Poppy shook her head. 'He couldn't have done. Meg didn't know herself until after he'd been sent away. It was Kate who realised what was wrong with her and told her she was pregnant.'

'And they never saw each other again.'

'That's right. It's all so sad, Josh. I feel so sorry for Aunt Meg.'

He frowned. 'What about Kate?'

'Kate? Oh, Kate didn't care a bit about her engagement to Freddie being broken. After all, she had only agreed to it because it suited her father. No, her one aim was to protect her "dear papa" from her sister's sordid predicament. She was proud – you could almost say triumphant – about the way she handled the situation without him ever suspecting anything.'

'But didn't he ever visit Meg in her room? After all, she was supposed to be his favourite daughter.'

Poppy shook her head. 'Apparently not. Kate said he couldn't bear illness so he never went near.'

'Strange man.'

She turned to him anxiously. 'What do you think we should do, Josh? About the baby, I mean. Aunt Kate said she would "deal with it" – and the way she said it sent shivers down my spine. Heaven knows what she has in mind. Do you think we should go to the police?'

He thought for several minutes, then he shook his head. 'No, I'm sure that's not necessary. Far better to say nothing and give the child a quiet Christian burial. I'm sure we can find a vicar somewhere who would carry it out. I'll make some enquiries, shall I?'

She leaned her head on his shoulder. 'Oh, thank you, Josh, I feel so much better now I've talked to you.'

He smiled grimly. 'And I shall feel better when I've told my father.'

'Heavens, yes. I'd forgotten ... Oh, Josh, I wonder what he'll say? I hope he won't forbid ...'

He turned and took her face in both his hands. 'My father is in no position to forbid me to do anything, Poppy. And there is nothing he can say that could alter my mind about you. Now, let's not talk about it any more. Come along, tidy yourself up, I'm taking you out to lunch. Then we'll go up to Higger Tor. We need to blow some of the cobwebs of the past away. Kentons can look after itself for one afternoon.'

Lunch was not an unqualified success even though they went to one of the best hotels in Sheffield. Neither of them had much appetite, Poppy because she couldn't get the scene in the attic and the subsequent revelations from Aunt Kate out of her mind, Josh because he still had to face his father with the story. But a long walk over the hills helped them both to regain a sense of some kind of normality and by the time Josh left her at the end of her road – they both agreed it was not the right time to introduce him at Dale House – Poppy felt she could face her aunts.

In the event the biggest shock was that everything was so absolutely normal. Meg was sitting in her usual place with her silks and materials spread round her and Kate was in her armchair reading. She looked up as Poppy walked in.

'When will you be going to the library again, Poppy?'

she asked. 'I've nearly finished this book and I find I had already read the other one you brought me.'

'Library? Oh, I could go tomorrow, I suppose,' Poppy said, quite taken aback.

'Good.' Kate leaned over and tugged the bell pull. 'Mrs Rivers will bring your supper. It's toad-in-the-hole. It's what we had for lunch, isn't it, Meg?'

'Yes. It was quite delicious. I had two helpings.' Meg smiled proudly at Poppy.

Poppy smiled back weakly. She was still trying to come to terms with the fact that this virginal-looking woman had actually had a love affair and given birth to a child.

Mrs Rivers brought her meal and Poppy managed to eat most of it and the evening dragged on. At half past eight she pleaded a bad headache and went to bed. Half an hour later Meg came in with a glass of water.

'I didn't think you looked at all well, Poppy, so I've brought you one of my pills. Don't tell Kate. She's funny about that sort of thing. But it might help you to sleep.' She handed Poppy a round pill, smiling at her. 'It might make you feel a bit strange at first,' she warned, 'but you'll have lovely dreams.'

Poppy drank some of the water and pretended to take the pill, hiding it under the sheet, but Meg went off happily thinking she had done something to help her beloved niece.

For a long time Poppy lay awake, staring up into the darkness and going over the day's events. It seemed like years since the morning's revelations and the thing that was beginning to worry her most was the effect they would have on her and Josh. Now she knew the whole story she understood why her aunts would never accept him, and she was sure Sir Frederick would never allow her into his house again. Yet Josh couldn't leave his father, bound to him as he was by the business, and the aunts were too dependent on her for her to forsake them. She could see no way round the dilemma except to leave Kentons and never see Josh again.

That was a solution too awful even to contemplate.

It was a long time before she slept.

The next morning she got up and dressed, still feeling depressed. She tried to tell herself that whatever happened today couldn't possibly be worse than yesterday's events, and she put on a cherry red dress instead of the grey skirt and white blouse she usually wore to the office in an effort to lift her spirits.

'Are you not going to work today, Poppy?' Aunt Meg said when she saw the dress at breakfast. 'Is your head not any better?'

'Yes, I am going to work and my head is almost better,' Poppy answered. 'I felt I needed cheering up a bit, that's all.'

'Oh, are you sad? Well, you look quite charming, dear,' Meg said with a smile, reaching for a second piece of toast and the marmalade.

'Where is Aunt Kate?' Poppy asked. 'Is she not well?' If so, it was hardly surprising.

Meg looked blank. 'Oh, I don't know. I haven't seen her.' She looked into her empty cup and at Kate's unused plate and frowned. 'She hasn't had her breakfast, has she?' She pushed her cup over to Poppy. 'Never mind, you can pour.' She smiled happily.

Poppy picked up the teapot. 'I really think I should go and see if she's ill, don't you?'

'After breakfast. Eat your breakfast first.' Meg jiggled her shoulders. 'It's nice, just the two of us. We can eat as much toast as we like.'

Poppy poured the tea. 'I'll just take her a cup. Even if she isn't well she'll enjoy a cup of tea, I'm sure.'

'Oh, very well.' Meg helped herself to a third piece of toast.

Poppy took the tea upstairs. She could quite understand that the events of the previous day had taken their toll on Kate. She knocked on the door but there was no reply, so she knocked again and pushed it open. The bed was rumpled, just as Kate had got out of it, her clothes laid neatly on the chair. Her dressing gown was gone.

Puzzled, Poppy went along to the bathroom but it was empty. She looked in all the bedrooms and then went downstairs and checked all the rooms, but there was no sign of Kate anywhere.

She went back to the parlour and told Meg, who seemed quite unconcerned.

'But where can she be?' Poppy asked, exasperated. 'I can't find her anywhere in the house but she must be here somewhere because she's still in her dressing gown.'

'Have you tried the kitchen?' Meg asked, reaching for more toast. 'Oh, pour me another cup of tea before you go. Ah, no, don't bother, I'll pour it myself. Kate doesn't let me, she says I'll scald myself, but I'm quite capable when she's not looking. It's her. She makes me nervous.'

Poppy didn't wait. She went to the kitchen, where Mrs Rivers was preparing vegetables. Kate wasn't there.

'Have you tried t'attics?' Mrs Rivers said.

'No. But she never goes ... Yes, of course! Thank you, Mrs Rivers.' Poppy hurried up the back stairs and looked in all the attics. The junk room was still unlocked and that was where she expected to find her, but it was just as she'd left it yesterday and Kate wasn't there. Mystified, she went back down again.

'I've told Rivers. He's looking in t'stables and sheds,' Mrs Rivers said anxiously when Poppy returned. 'It's not like Miss Kate, is it? And her not even properly dressed.'

Rivers came clumping in without taking off his hat. 'Her's nowhere about,' he stated. 'I'll have a look in t'garden.'

'She'll not be there. She was in her dressing gown,' Mrs Rivers said sharply.

'Well, if she's nowhere else she must be in t'garden somewhere,' Rivers said reasonably. 'Any road, I'll go and look.'

'You're wasting your time,' his wife called after him.

'No, he's right. There's nowhere else she can be,' Poppy said. 'I'll go and look, too.' She hurried out of the back door and into the garden. It was large and not well kept, except for the kitchen garden right at the top. The grass between the trees and bushes needed cutting and the flower beds needed weeding, but Rivers concentrated on his vegetables. He had no time for what he called 'fancy gardening'. Poppy held up her skirts as she went through the damp grass towards the little arbour, hidden behind a large viburnum bush. Perhaps that was where she would find Kate, sitting quietly on the seat there. But in her dressing gown? Never.

She reached the arbour. The seat was empty. But Kate was there, lying not far from a patch of newly dug earth, the shovel still in her hand. She was dead.

Poppy sat down on the seat, staring at her aunt. Her dressing gown had ridden up, revealing a pair of very white, very skinny legs that ended in muddy carpet slippers. Her hair had come out of its plait and lay over her parchment-coloured face like a grey caul. Her expression was one of set determination.

It was quite obvious what had happened. Kate had 'dealt with' the hat box by coming out into the garden at the dead of night to bury it. The exertion had simply been too much for her. Probably her heart had given out, but only the doctor could decide that.

Slowly, Poppy went back into the house.

The morning went by in a daze. Rivers and the gardening boy carried Kate's body into the house and up to her bedroom to await the doctor, while Poppy broke the news to Meg that her sister was dead. She said nothing about the hat box. That would come later.

'What a silly thing to do, walk about in the garden in her dressing gown,' was Meg's first reaction. 'She could catch her death . . . Oh!' She put her hand to her mouth.

After that she was silent for a long time, sitting with her hands in her lap, staring out of the window. Poppy sat with her, waiting to comfort her when the tears started.

They never came. After nearly an hour Meg turned her head and smiled at Poppy.

'I can do as I like, now,' she said softly. 'I won't have to answer to Kate for every move I make. I can go out or stay at home, just as I choose. I can eat what I like and drink what I like without being told it's bad for me. I can stay in bed till noon or get up at the crack of dawn.' She raised both hands above her head. 'I'm free!' She let her hands fall back into her lap. 'And I shan't take any more of those bloody pills she forces on me.' She got up and went over to the cupboard by the fireplace. 'Where are they? I'll put them in the fire. Right now.'

'No. You mustn't do that, Aunt Meg,' Poppy said, restraining her. 'We must ask the doctor. It might harm you to stop them suddenly. After all ...'

'Oh, I've never taken as many as Kate thought I did,' Meg said gleefully. 'I used to hide them.' She smiled at Poppy. 'Just as you hid the one I gave you the other night. You thought I didn't know, didn't you?' She gave a delighted laugh. Then she sighed. 'Yes, I expect you're right about not stopping the pills suddenly. It's been such a long time since I've felt properly ...' she hesitated, '... real. I'm sure it's those damn pills. I haven't taken one this morning, you know.'

The doorbell rang. 'Oh, that will be the doctor,' Poppy said. 'I'll ask him to see you when he's finished ... upstairs.'

Josh kept looking at the clock on the office wall. Poppy was very late again. Not that he watched the clock on her behalf, but he had so much to tell her that he could hardly contain himself until she arrived.

He had been so worried, mostly about their future together. Although he hadn't said as much to Poppy, he could never see the two families being reconciled, not with such a past hanging over them, yet both he and Poppy were bound to their respective relatives whether they liked it or not. There seemed no way round it.

It had been difficult enough broaching the subject to the guv'nor. How do you tell your own father, for God's sake, that the girl he planned to elope with nearly thirty years ago had borne his child?

In the event it had been surprisingly easy.

Waiting for Poppy to arrive, he went over the scene again in his mind.

'I'm in love with her, Pa,' he had said. 'I know you don't approve, but nothing you can say or do can alter it.'

His father had shifted uncomfortably in his wheelchair. 'It's not that I don't approve, lad,' he said. 'She's a fine lass and I like her. But there are problems. Things you couldn't possibly know about ...'

'Like the fact that you were engaged to her Aunt Kate?' Josh said carefully.

'You knew about that?' his father said, surprised.

'Oh yes. Aunt Kate told Poppy.' He waited a minute, then added quietly, 'But it wasn't until today that I learned that you planned to elope with Kate's sister.'

Sir Frederick's head shot round. 'Who told you that?'

'Poppy. Kate told her. This morning.' Josh paused. 'You must have loved Meg very much, Pa.'

His father looked down at his hands as they rested on the rug over his knees. 'Aye. I did. I still think about her, although I never saw her again after that night.' He gave the ghost of a smile. 'My God, all hell was let loose that night, yet the rest of the guests never knew a thing about it. I thought the old man was going to have an apoplectic fit. I would have carried Meg off anyway, but that bitch of a sister locked her in her room and I couldn't get to her.'

'It wasn't long afterwards that you married my mother, was it?'

He hunched his shoulders. 'I don't want to be disrespectful to your mother's memory, lad. She was a good wife to me and a good mother to my sons, but I married her

335

because I needed sons to carry on the business. She gave me two, bless her, and I was grateful for that but I didn't love her. Not as I loved Meg.' He sighed. 'I guess as I still love Meg, although she must have changed a good deal over the years.' He turned to look at Josh. 'Tell me, did she ever marry?'

Josh shook his head. 'Neither of them ever married.' He took a deep breath. 'But Meg bore you a child.'

'Oh, my God!' Sir Frederick buried his face in his hands. 'My poor lass. My poor, lovely lass.' He rocked back and forth in his grief.

Josh laid a restraining hand on his father. 'Nobody knew, Pa. Kate looked after her and nobody knew.'

'And the baby?'

'Died at birth.'

His father digested this in silence, an expression of such pain and sadness on his face that Josh's heart went out to him. 'Would you like to see Meg again, Pa?' he asked gently after a long time. He couldn't think how he could possibly arrange it but seeing the agony on his father's face he knew he would do his damnedest to try, even if it meant tying Kate up to keep her out of the way.

Sir Frederick nodded slowly. 'I think I'd like that, lad. If it was possible.'

Josh patted his father's hand. 'I'll see what I can do, Pa,' he said, more optimistically than he felt.

Suddenly, he roused himself out of his reverie and realised he was sitting at his desk in the office. He glanced at the clock again. It was nearly midday. What could have happened to Poppy? Had the events of yesterday been too much for her and made her ill?

He got up from his chair so suddenly that it toppled over, and reached for his hat. Damn the consequences, he was going to Dale House to find out.

Chapter Thirty-Two

Poppy left Meg sitting on the settee and went along to the hall to open the door. But Mrs Rivers had got there before her and it was Josh, not the doctor, who stood on the doormat.

As soon as he saw her he strode over and took both her hands in his. 'I'm sorry, Poppy, but I couldn't wait. You didn't come to work and after what happened yesterday, I had to come and see what was wrong.' His eyes searched her face. 'What is it, darling? What's happened now?'

Before Poppy could speak there was a little cry from behind her. They both turned and saw Meg standing there, an expression of absolute joy on her face.

She came forward, her hands outstretched, and ignoring Poppy went straight to Josh.

'Oh, Freddie,' she said, holding out her arms. 'You've come back for me! I always knew you would.'

Josh caught her as she slipped to the floor in a dead faint. It was an opportune moment for the doctor to arrive.

He pronounced that Kate's death was due to sudden heart failure, probably caused by being out in the chill night air. He didn't ask what she had been doing in the garden in the small hours – after all, a good many elderly women were prone to insomnia and night-time perambulations. In any case, he was more interested in Meg and her pills and promised to get them analysed. In the meantime he suggested that the right thing to do would be to reduce her dose gradually until she could do without them altogether.

After he had gone the three of them, Poppy, Josh and Meg – who had taken quite a lot of convincing that Josh was not Freddie himself but Freddie's son – sat in the parlour drinking tea and trying to come to terms with the morning's events.

'Do you know what Kate was doing out in the garden this morning, Aunt Meg?' Poppy said carefully. She had already discussed the matter with Josh whilst the doctor was examining Meg and they had agreed that she must be told, although they were both apprehensive as to what her reaction would be.

'No, But she was always an oddity, wasn't she?' Meg said with a shrug. She was enjoying the thought of freedom from Kate too much to bother about trivial matters like that. She turned to Poppy. 'I don't think I shall stay here in this house, Poppy. I think I shall sell it and move to a smaller one.' She giggled. 'But I shall leave Papa's portrait to haunt the place as it's always done. I certainly don't want to take *that* with me.'

Poppy went and sat beside her and took her hand. 'Aunt Meg. Listen to me. Kate went into the garden in the middle of the night to bury something,' she said gently.

Obediently, Meg gave her her attention. 'What a funny thing to do. What was it? Why couldn't Rivers have done it in the morning?'

'Because it was a baby. A little baby that was born nearly thirty years ago.'

Meg's eyes widened and then filled with tears. 'Not *my* little baby?' she whispered, shaking her head.

Poppy nodded, 'Yes, that's right. It was your little baby.'

Tears were now running unchecked down Meg's face. 'Kate told me she was dead when she was born, but I wanted to hold her. Just once. But Kate wouldn't let me. Kate wouldn't let me hold my own little baby. I never

338

forgave her for that.' She turned to Poppy. 'But then you came and I began to think of you as my little girl grown up. My little girl might have looked a bit like you, mightn't she? After all, you're my brother's daughter. But I never told anyone. Especially, I never told Kate, she would have said I was being silly. She was always telling me I was silly.' A smile spread across her face. 'But now,' she nodded towards Josh, 'it's as if my little girl and Freddie's little lad are going to be together. Isn't that nice.' She smiled through her tears at first one and then the other.

Josh came and sat on the other side of Meg. 'Would you like to see Freddie again, Aunt Meg?'

She looked down at her hands. 'Oh, I don't know,' she said, flustered at the thought. 'He might not like me any more. He'll think I'm old. And fat. And ugly.'

'How could he think that?' Poppy said, surprised. 'I've never known anyone with such a sweet face and as for being old ...'

'I'm getting on towards fifty,' Meg said ruefully.

'Well, my father is no spring chicken. In fact, he's in a wheelchair,' Josh told her, although privately he was of the opinion that if anything would get his father out of it and walking again it would be the sight of his old sweetheart.

'Then if he's agreeable, I think I might like to see him again. Just for old times' sake,' Meg said softly.

A week later, Kate was laid to rest in a grave beside the father she had adored, with the figure of the tiny baby she had hidden away all those years ago in her arms. Surprisingly, this had been Meg's idea, but it was not until after the funeral that she gave her reason.

'I want her to remember for all eternity that she wouldn't let me hold my little baby,' she said, without a shred of remorse. 'I want her to know I've never forgiven her for that. It's a burden she'll always carry.'

'Oh, Aunt Meg,' Poppy said, holding her close.

Meg struggled free. Already with the reduction in pills

her mind was becoming clearer. 'But you don't understand, dear. You don't know what it was like, living with Kate. She hated me. She was always jealous because she thought I was Papa's favourite.' She frowned. 'I don't think I was. Not really. I don't think he liked either of us much, to tell the truth. But she was always trying to curry favour with him, always trying to make herself indispensable. I think it got on his nerves so much he wanted to get her married and out of the way.' Her expression softened. 'The only trouble was, he chose the wrong man for her. As soon as Freddie and I met ...' she spread her hands. 'That was that. We fell in love.' She took a deep breath and continued. 'And if it hadn't been for her interference ...' She began to cry. 'I'm not crying for my sister,' she insisted between sobs. 'I'm crying for what might have been if she hadn't betrayed me to Papa.'

'But that's all in the past,' Poppy said, putting an arm round her. 'Think of the future, dear. We've been invited to tea with Sir Frederick next week, remember.'

A year later, when the period of mourning had been observed (somewhat impatiently, it must be admitted), Poppy and Josh were married.

It was intended to be a quiet wedding. In the absence of a male relative, Poppy had asked the manager at Kentons, Jake Benson, to give her away, a task he had been honoured to fulfil. They were followed up the aisle by a selection of small bridesmaids and pageboys, all children of the workers at Kentons Scythe and Edge Tools Company, their proud parents, clad in their Sunday best, looking on. Harry Smithers was there, complete with an artificial leg that was still giving him some trouble, with Mary at his side, heavily and unashamedly pregnant. Jack Earnshaw was there too, with Connie Templeton. News had recently come through that George Templeton had been killed in a pub brawl so they were soon to be married, much to the relief of Charity Jones. She was carrying her baby son while Mordecai watched anxiously over their daughter Rebecca, the smallest of the bridesmaids.

The Rivers were there, of course, sitting right beside Aunt Meg since she had no living relatives of her own; Rivers in his Sunday suit – hardly worn since his own wedding some forty years ago but still a good fit – and new squeaky boots; Mrs Rivers in her best black bombazine and a hat with daisies round the brim.

As the bride, dressed in a beautiful dress of cream lace made by Aunt Meg, approached her bridegroom, Sir Frederick, looking rather pale but very distinguished in his morning suit, got stiffly to his feet with the rest of the congregation, supported only by a heavy walking stick. Several times as the bride and groom made their vows he stole a glance across the aisle to Meg, who, looking quite lovely in lavender silk with a wide straw hat, surreptitiously wiped away a tear.

After the ceremony Josh and Poppy emerged into the late summer sunshine looking radiantly happy, with Sir Frederick and Aunt Meg arm in arm not far behind.

Poppy and Josh climbed into the carriage that was to take them to Kenton Hall, where a lavish wedding reception waited, amid showers of rice and good wishes. Looking back and waving to the crowd, they could see Sir Frederick and Aunt Meg still standing arm in arm.

'Do you think it will be their turn next?' Josh whispered with a wicked grin.

Poppy turned to kiss her new husband. 'Oh, I do hope so, Josh. They deserve to be together after all those wasted years.'

After her niece's marriage Meg Russell, together with both the faithful Rivers, moved into a much smaller house. But to her consternation, Dale House took quite a long time to sell. Sir Frederick Kenton said it was of no importance because he rather hoped Meg might do him the honour of marrying him and moving with him into the house he had bought in the Fulbrook Road, leaving Kenton Hall, as well as the business, to Josh and Poppy.

The agent tentatively suggested the removal of the portrait of the rather stern gentleman that overshadowed the hall, and after that a sale was made very quickly.